SWP.

This book should be returned to any branch of the
Lancashire County Library on or before the date shown

LOST CITY RADIO

Also by Daniel Alarcón

War By Candlelight

LOST CITY RADIO

A NOVEL

DANIEL ALARCÓN

FOURTH ESTATE · London

First published in Great Britain in 2007 by
Fourth Estate
An imprint of HarperCollins*Publishers*
77–85 Fulham Palace Road
London W6 8JB
www.4thestate.co.uk

Originally published in USA in 2007 by HarperCollins

A catalogue record for this book is
available from the British Library

ISBN-13 978-0-00-720051-1

Designed by Joy O'Meara
Printed in Great Britain by Clays Ltd, St Ives plc

This book is proudly printed on paper which contains wood
from well managed forests, certified in accordance with
the rules of the Forest Stewardship Council.
For more information about FSC,
please visit www.fsc-uk.org

Mixed Sources
Product group from well-managed
forests and other controlled sources
www.fsc.org Cert no. SW-COC-1806
FSC © 1996 Forest Stewardship Council

Q.E.P.D.
Javier Antonio Alarcón Guzmán
1948–1989

It is the people who are executed and the people who make up the firing squad; the people are both vague randomness and precise law. There are no tricks, nor can there be.

—CARLOS MONSIVÁIS

PART ONE

ONE

T HEY TOOK Norma off the air that Tuesday morning because a boy was dropped off at the station. He was quiet and thin and had a note. The receptionists let him through. A meeting was called.

The conference room was full of light and had an expansive view of the city, looking east toward the mountains. When Norma walked in, Elmer was seated at the head of the table, rubbing his face as if he'd been woken from a restless, unsatisfying sleep. He nodded as she sat, then yawned and fiddled with the top of a pill bottle he'd taken from his pocket. "Go for some water," he groaned to his assistant. "And empty these ashtrays, Len. Jesus."

The boy sat across from Elmer, in a stiff wooden chair, staring down at his feet. He was slender and fragile, and his eyes were too small for his face. His head had been shaved—to kill lice, Norma supposed. There were the faint beginnings of a mustache above his lips. His shirt was threadbare, and his unhemmed pants were knotted around his waist with a shoestring.

Norma sat closest to him, her back to the door, facing the white city.

Len reappeared with a pitcher of water. It was choked with bubbles, tinged gray. Elmer poured himself a glass and swallowed two pills. He coughed into his hand. "Let's get right to it," Elmer said when Len had sat. "We're sorry to interrupt the news, Norma, but we wanted you to meet Victor."

"Tell her how old you are, boy," Len said.

"I'm eleven," the child said, his voice barely audible. "And a half."

Len cleared his throat, glanced at Elmer, as if for permission to speak. With a nod from his boss, he began. "That's a terrific age," Len said. "Now, you came looking for Norma, isn't that right?"

"Yes," Victor said.

"Do you know him?"

Norma didn't.

"He says he came from the jungle," Len continued. "We thought you'd want to meet him. For the show."

"Great," she said. "Thank you."

Elmer stood and walked to the window. He was a silhouette against the hazy brightness. Norma knew that panorama: the city below, stretching to the horizon and still farther. With your forehead to the glass, you could see down to the street, to that broad avenue choked with traffic and people, with buses and moto-taxis and vegetable carts. Or life on the city's rooftops: clothes hanging on a line next to rusting chicken coops, old men playing cards on a milk crate, dogs barking angrily, teeth bared at the heavy sea air. She'd even seen a man once, sitting on his yellow hard hat, sobbing.

If Elmer saw anything now, he didn't seem interested. He turned back to them. "Not just from the jungle, Norma. From 1797."

Norma sat up straight. "What are you telling me, Elmer?"

It was one of the rumors they knew to be true: mass graves, anonymous villagers, murdered and tossed into ditches. They'd never reported it, of course. No one had. They hadn't spoken of this in years. She felt something heavy in her chest.

"It's probably nothing," Elmer said. "Let's show her the note."

From his pocket, Victor produced a piece of paper, presumably the same one he had shown the receptionist. He passed it to Elmer, who put on his reading glasses and cleared his throat. He read aloud:

Dear Miss Norma:

This child is named Victor. He is from Village 1797 in the eastern jungle. We, the residents of 1797, have pooled our monies together and sent him to the city. We want a better life for Victor. There is no future for him here. Please help us. Attached find our list of lost people. Perhaps one of these individuals will be able to care for the boy. We listen to Lost City Radio every week. We love your show.

Your biggest fans,
Village 1797

"Norma," Elmer said, "I'm sorry. We wanted to tell you ourselves. He'd be great for the show, but we wanted to warn you first."

"I'm fine." She rubbed her eyes and took a deep breath. "I'm fine."

Norma hated the numbers. Before, every town had a name; an unwieldy, millenarian name inherited from God-knows-which extinct people, names with hard consonants that sounded like stone grinding against stone. But everything was being modernized, even the recondite corners of the nation. This was all postconflict, a new government policy. They said people were forgetting the old systems. Norma wondered. "Do you know what they used to call your village?" she asked the boy.

Victor shook his head.

Norma closed her eyes for a second. He'd probably been taught to say that. When the war ended, the government confiscated the old maps. They were taken off the shelves at the National Library, turned in by private citizens, cut out of school textbooks, and burned. Norma had covered it for the radio, had mingled with the excited crowd that gathered at Newtown Plaza to watch. Once, Victor's village had a name, but it was lost now. Her husband, Rey, had vanished near there, just before the Illegitimate Legion was defeated. This was at the end of the insurrection, ten years before. She was still waiting for him.

"Are you all right, Miss Norma?" the boy asked in a small, reedy voice.

She opened her eyes.

"What a polite young man," Len said. He leaned forward, rested his elbows on the table, and patted the boy on his bald head.

Norma waited for a moment, counting to ten. She picked up the paper and read it again. The script was steady and deliberate. She pictured it: a town council gathering to decide whose penmanship was best. How folkloric. On the back was a list of names. "Our Missing," it said, the end of the *g* curling upward in an optimistic flourish. She couldn't bear to read them. Each was a cipher, soulless, faceless, sometime humans, a harvest of names to be read on the air. She passed the note back to Elmer. The idea of it made her inexplicably sleepy.

"Do you know these people?" Elmer asked the boy.

"No," Victor said. "A few."

"Who brought you to the station?"

"My teacher. His name is Manau."

"Where is he?" asked Len.

"He left me."

"Why did they send you?"

"I don't know."

"Your mother?" Norma asked.

"She's dead."

Norma apologized; Len took copious notes.

"Father?" said Elmer.

The boy shrugged. "I'd like some water, please."

Elmer poured the boy a glass, and Victor drank greedily, trickles of water running down the sides of his mouth. When he finished, he wiped his lips on the sleeve of his shirt.

"There's more," Elmer said, smiling. "Have some more."

But Victor shook his head and looked out the window. Norma followed his gaze. It was a colorless, late-winter day in the city, the soft outline of the mountains disappearing behind the fog. There was nothing to see.

"What do you want me to do?" Norma asked.

Elmer pursed his lips. He motioned for Len to take the boy. Victor rose and left the room without protest. Elmer didn't speak again until he and Norma were alone. He scratched his head, then held up the pill bottle. "These are for stress, you know. My doctor says I spend too much time here."

"You do."

"You do too," he said.

"What's on your mind, Elmer?"

"The show isn't doing well." He paused, choosing his words carefully. "Am I right to say that?"

"Two reunions in six weeks. People don't want to be found this time of year. We always pick up in spring."

Elmer frowned and put his pills away. "This boy, Norma: he's good. Did you hear him? He has a nice, helpless voice."

"He hardly said a word."

"Now wait a second, hear me out. This is what I'm thinking: a big show on Sunday. I know 1797 is touchy with you, and I respect that, I do. That's why I wanted to introduce you to him myself. He doesn't know anything about the war. He's too young. So spend the week with him, Norma. It won't be so bad."

"What about his people?"

"What about them? They'll show up. Or we'll get a few actors and he won't know the difference."

"You're joking."

Elmer put his hand on her shoulder. His eyes were small and black. "You know me, Norma: I'm mostly joking. I'm not a radio man anymore, you forget that. I'm a businessman. If we don't find anyone, we'll send him home, bus ticket's on us. Or we'll give him to the nuns. Point is, he'll give the show a pick-me-up. And we need this, Norma."

"What about the teacher?"

"What about him? The prick. He should be in jail for abandoning a child. We can call him out Sunday too."

She looked at her hands; they were pale and wrinkled in a way that she never could have imagined. This is what growing old was, after all.

"What?" Elmer asked.

"I'm tired. That's all. The idea of getting some guy lynched for abandonment . . . It's not why I get up in the morning."

Elmer grinned. "And why do you get up, dear?"

When she didn't answer, Elmer put his hand on her shoulder. "That's life, Norma."

"Fine," she said after a while.

"Good. Can he stay with you?"

"You want me to babysit?"

"Well."

"Give me the week off."

"A day."

"Three."

Elmer shook his head and smiled. "Two, and we'll talk." He was already standing. "You do great things for this radio station, Norma. Great things. And we appreciate it. The people love you." He knocked on the door, and a moment later, Len came back in with the boy. Elmer beamed and rubbed the boy's head. Len sat the boy down. "Here he is, here's my champ," Elmer said. "Well, son. You'll be staying with Norma for a while. She's very nice and you have nothing to worry about."

The boy looked a bit frightened. Norma smiled, and then Elmer and Len were gone and she was alone with the boy. The note was there on the table. She put it in her pocket. Victor stared off into the wide, alabaster sky.

H E R V O I C E was her greatest asset, her career and her fate. Elmer called it gold that stank of empathy. Before he disappeared, Rey claimed he fell in love again every time she said good morning. You should have been a singer, he said, though she couldn't even carry a tune. Norma had worked in radio all her life, beginning as a reporter, graduating to newsreader, redeeming the tragedies it fell on her to announce. She was a natural: she knew when to let her voice waver, when to linger on a word, what texts to tear through and read as if the words themselves were on fire. The worst news she read softly, without urgency, as if it were poetry. The day Victor arrived, there was a suicide bomber in Palestine, an oil spill off the coast of Spain, and a new champion in American baseball. Nothing extraordinary and nothing that affected the country. Reading foreign news was a kind of pretending, Norma thought, this listing of everyday things only confirming how peripheral we are: a nation at the edge of the world, a make-believe country outside history. For local news, she relied on the station's policy, which was also the government's policy: to read good news with indifference and make bad news sound hopeful. No one was more skilled than Norma; in her vocal caresses, unemployment figures read like bittersweet laments, declarations of war like love letters. News of mudslides became awestruck meditations on the mysteries of nature, and the twenty or fifty or one hundred dead disappeared in the telling of it. This was her life on weekdays: morning readings of foreign and local disasters—buses plunging off the mountain highways, shootouts echoing in the slums by the river, and, in the faraway distance, the rest of the world. Saturdays off, and Sunday evenings, back at the station for her signature show, Lost City Radio, a program for missing people.

The idea was simple. How many refugees had come to the city? How many of them had lost touch with their families? Hundreds of thousands? Millions? The station saw it as a way to profit from the unrest; in the show's ten years on the air, Norma had come to see it as a way to look for her husband. A conflict of interest, Elmer said, but he put her on anyway. Hers was the most trusted and well-loved voice in the country, a phenomenon she herself couldn't explain. Every Sunday night, for an hour, since the last year of the war, Norma took calls from people who imagined she had special powers, that she was mantic and all-seeing, able to pluck the lost, estranged, and missing from the moldering city. Strangers addressed her by her first name and pleaded to be heard. My brother, they'd say, left the village years ago to look for work in the city. His name is . . . He lives in a district called . . . He wrote us letters and then the war began. Norma would cut them off if they seemed determined to speak of the war. It was always preferable to avoid unpleasant topics. So instead she asked questions about the scent of their mother's cooking, or the sound of the wind keening through the valley. The river, the color of the sky. With her prodding, the callers revisited village life and all that had been left behind, inviting their lost people to remember with them: Are you there, brother? And Norma listened, and then repeated the names in her mellifluous voice, and the board would light up with calls, lonely red lights, people longing to be found. Of course, some were impostors, and these were the saddest of all.

Lost City Radio had become the most popular show in the country. Three, sometimes four times a month, there were grand reunions, and these were documented and celebrated with great fanfare. The emotions were authentic: the reunited families traveling from their cramped homes at the edges of the city, arriving at the station with squawking chickens and bulging bags of rice—gifts for Miss Norma. In the parking lot of the station, they'd dance and drink and sing into the early hours of the morning. Norma greeted them all as they lined up to thank her. They were humble people. Tears would well up in their eyes when they met her—not when they saw her, but when she spoke: that voice. The photographers took pictures, and Elmer saw to it the best images were slapped on billboards, pure and happy images hovering above the serrated city skyline, families, now whole again, wearing resplendent smiles. Norma herself never appeared in the photos; Elmer felt it was best to cultivate the mystery.

It was the only national radio station left since the war ended. After the IL was defeated, the journalists were imprisoned. Many of her colleagues wound up in prison, or worse. They were taken to the Moon, some were disappeared, and their names, like her husband's, were forbidden. Each morning, Norma read fictitious, government-approved news; each afternoon, she submitted the next day's proposed headlines for approval by the censor. These represented, in the scheme of things, very small humiliations. The world can't be changed, and so Norma held out for Sunday. It could happen any week, or at least she used to imagine it could: Rey himself could call. I wandered into the jungle, he might say, and I've lost my woman, the love of my life, her name is Norma ... If he was alive, he was in hiding. He had been accused of terrible things in the months after the war: a list of collaborators was published and read on the air; their names and aliases, along with a shorthand of alleged crimes. Rey had been called an assassin and an intellectual. A provocateur, the man who invented tire-burning. More than three hours' worth of names, and it was decreed that after this public accounting they could not be mentioned again. The IL was defeated and disgraced; the country was now in the process of forgetting the war ever happened at all.

At the end of the first day, Norma gathered her things and the boy, and they left for her apartment on the far side of the city, an hour away by bus. Victor seemed bewildered by it all. She imagined herself in his situation, in this strange and unhappy city of noise and dirt, and chose to interpret his silence as strength. All afternoon, the boy had slept on the sofa in the broadcast booth, waking every few hours to stare morosely at her. Besides asking for water, he'd hardly spoken at all. Once, as she read the news, she winked at him, but this had elicited no response. Now she held his hand as they rode, and thought of the jungle: Rey's jungle. She had only seen it in photographs. It seemed to be the kind of geography that could inspire terror and joy in equal parts. The IL had been strong in Victor's part of the country. They had camps hidden beneath the heavy canopy of the forest, and had organized communities of Indians in revolt against the government. They stored weapons and explosives that might still be there, buried in the loamy earth.

The bus rolled through the streets, in fitful half-block spans. The city sang chromatic and atonal: honks and whistles and the low rumbling of a thousand engines. The man seated next to them slept, his head lolling about, his briefcase tight against his chest. A heavyset boy a little older than Victor stood, his face frozen in a scowl, brazenly counting money, daring anyone to take it. It was the same every day, but Norma felt suddenly that she should have taken a cab or a crosstown train, that the spectacle might be overwhelming for a boy from a jungle hamlet. And it was. Victor, she noticed, was trying to slip his little hand out of hers. She gripped it tighter and looked down at him sternly. "Careful," she said.

He glared and pulled his hand free, waving his liberated fingers in front of his face. The bus jerked to a stop, and he dashed off, through the door and into the street.

Norma could do nothing but follow.

It was the purple-hued end of the day. The boy was off and scampering down the sidewalk, in and out of the shadows. His footsteps went *tap tap* on the concrete, and Norma was alone in a part of the city she didn't know, on a street quieter than most. The buildings were low and thick, so stoutly built they seemed ready to sink under their own weight, their stucco walls painted in mottled pastels. Victor's spindly legs carried him down the block. There was no way she could catch him.

But she should have known by now how the city works. She was born here and raised here, and still its gestures bordered on the perverse, even more so after the war. Now it was something else entirely, something stranger. A white-haired man approached from a nearby doorway. He wore a thin, gray jacket over a yellowed undershirt. "Madam," he said, "is that your boy?"

Victor was a tiny moving shadow bouncing in the orange lights of the streetlamps. She nodded.

"Pardon me," the man said. He raised two fingers to his mouth and blew, piercing the low noise of the street with a sharp whistle. A head shot out of each window, and a moment later, a man or woman was standing at the door of each building. The man whistled again. He smiled benevolently at Norma, his warm face touched with red. They waited.

"Are you new to the neighborhood?"

"I don't live here," Norma said. She was wary of being recognized. "I'm sorry for the trouble."

"It's no trouble."

They waited for a moment longer, and soon a matronly woman in a pale blue housedress was walking up the block, Victor in tow. The man spoke to himself as she approached—here you are, there we go—as if he were coaching her. She held the boy's hand firmly, and he was hardly struggling at all. With a smile, she led the boy to Norma. "Madam," she said, bowing, "your son."

"Thank you," Norma said.

A bus gurgled by, imposing silence on them. The three adults smiled at each other; poor Victor stood stiff, a prisoner ready for marching. Night was falling, a cool breeze whispering through the street. The man offered Norma his jacket, but she declined. The woman in the housedress turned to Norma. "Shall we help you beat him?" she asked graciously, straightening the folds of her dress.

The government counseled solid beatings of children, in the name of regaining that discipline lost in a decade of war. The station ran public-service announcements on the subject. Norma herself had recorded the voice-overs, but she'd never actually hit a child, having no children of her own. It shouldn't have surprised her, but it did. "Oh, no," Norma stammered. "I wouldn't dare ask for help."

"It's no problem," the white-haired man said. "We look out for each other here."

They watched Norma expectantly. Victor, too, with steely eyes. They were such helpful people. "Maybe just a slap," Norma said.

"That's right!" The man leaned over the boy. "It's how we learn, isn't that right, son?"

Victor nodded blankly. Norma was struck again by how strange the city must seem to him. The truth is, everything had changed. She didn't even recognize it anymore. She'd heard of places in the countryside where life continued as it always had; of villages in the mountains, in the jungle, where the war had passed by, unperceived. But not here. Parts of the city had been abandoned, the IL had detonated buildings, the army had torched entire neighborhoods in search of subversives. The Great Blackouts, the Battle of Tamoé: wounds severe enough to be named. 1797 had not been spared, either. She could see that in Victor's eyes. We are in a new stage, the president had announced, a stage of militarized calm. A rebuilding stage. An unruly child should be punished. The woman held Victor by his shoulders. But how do you do it? Victor was a skeletal thing, a nothing child, easily broken. He didn't blink; he stared.

Norma raised her right arm up above her head, stalled for a moment. She brushed her hair back. She knew what she should do: let gravity guide her, imitate all the mothers she'd seen in the streets, in the markets, on public transport. Her duty. She closed her eyes for a moment, long enough to imagine it: Victor's head flopping to one side like a doll's, a red handprint blooming on his cheek. He wouldn't make a sound.

"I'm sorry," Norma said. "I can't."

"Of course you can."

"No. I'm sorry. He's not mine."

The woman nodded, but she hadn't understood. She smothered Victor in an embrace. "Your mother spoils you, boy," the woman said.

"She's not my mother."

Norma's fingers had gone numb. She looked at the boy and felt terrible. "He's not mine," she repeated.

The woman in the housedress rubbed the child's bald head. Without looking up at Norma, she said, "You sound so familiar."

Above, the streetlamp flickered on. It was night now. Norma shrugged. "I get that a lot. We should be going. Thank you for everything."

"She's from the radio," said Victor, folding his arms across his chest. "Lost City."

The white-haired man looked up, startled. "God is merciful."

Norma watched the glow of recognition pass across their faces. She pulled Victor toward her, took his hand in hers. "Don't talk nonsense, child," she scolded.

But it was too late. "Miss Norma?" The woman stepped closer to her, as if by looking at her she could tell. "Is that you? Say something, please; let me hear you!"

At her side, the man's smile was bright and orange beneath the streetlamp. "It's her," he said, and whistled a third time, while Norma muttered protests.

The streets filled with people.

BEFORE THE war began, those of Norma's generation still spoke of violence with awe and reverence: cleansing violence, purifying violence, violence that would spawn virtue. It was all anyone could talk about, and those who did not or could not accept violence as a necessity weren't taken seriously. It was embedded in the language young people used in those days. It was the language that her husband, Rey, fell in love with.

He also fell in love with Norma. She was studying journalism; he was finishing his thesis in ethnobotany. The university then was falling apart, strained well past capacity, underresourced and overcrowded. The buildings were crumbling, the classes choked with students. Professors were shouted down in midlecture, and graffitied walls announced the coming war. The president warned ominously of occupying the grounds, using force to punish the dissidents. In his famous Independence Day speech just before Norma met Rey, the president stepped on the dais in the main plaza and condemned "that illegitimate legion of rabble-rousers that provoke chaos and disrupt the general order!" He pounded his fist in the air, as if beating an imaginary enemy, and was met with thunderous applause. The president announced new measures to combat subversion, and the teeming crowd surged with approval.

The following day, the newspapers published the entire text of his speech, along with panoramic photographs of the plaza from the air, a weltering sea of flesh beneath the summer sun. It was impressive: the masses overwhelming the confines of the plaza, overrunning the fountain, pushing up against the steps of the cathedral. Of course, the president had rigged his reelection, but from the looks of it, he needn't have bothered with fraud. Men hung from street lamps, clutching banners, tambourines, and drums. Round-faced children smiled for the cameras, waving tiny flags they had made in school with crayons and newsprint and plastic straws. This was almost a year before the war began, when the government seemed invincible. The crowd, it was later revealed, had been paid for their services, for their enthusiasm. They'd been bused in, had accepted donations of rice and flour for a day's work cheering the speech. Many of them came from distant villages and didn't even speak the language. They cheered on cue like good workers, collected their payment, and went home.

Rey and Norma met through mutual friends at a dance that same week. Rey was handsome in a broken kind of way: the kind of young man who had looked old his entire life. His nose bent subtly to the left, and his eyes hid in the recessed shadows beneath his brow. Still, he had a strong jaw and an incongruously silly, dimpled smile and, for this, Norma liked him. He smoked incessantly, a habit he would later give up, but that first night it seemed integral to who he was. A group of them sat together, talking about the city and the government and the university and the future. They spoke of the crowds that had filled the plaza: the people, always myopic, always easy to fool. Indians, Rey said, imagine! They don't even know who the president is! It was all laughter and noise and the melting of ice cubes. They made fun of the president, who was weak and expendable and whose troubles were only beginning. The Illegitimate Legion! It was only a punch line then: how would these enemies be any different from those who had come before? Hadn't the war been just around the corner for fifteen years? It was impossible to take seriously, so they drank more and joked more, and spoke most obliquely about sex. Norma felt deliciously lost in the music, in the rising heat. She leaned in closer to the new stranger. He didn't pull away. She drank furiously. His foot tapped the rhythm, and she realized she'd been speaking for a while and had heard nothing for longer. Conversation was impossible. Their table emptied in pairs, their friends slipping onto the dance floor, until it was only the two of them. It was nearly midnight before Rey finally asked her to dance. They were in an old building with high ceilings, the band playing loud and brash, energized by the cathedral-like acoustics. Brassy bursts of sound cut through the din of the dancers and the drinkers. Rey took Norma by the arm and led her to the middle of the floor. He spun her and held her close, young in his movements, his old face adorned with a wry smile. During the third song, he pulled her in and whispered in her ear, "You don't know who I am, do you?"

The rhythm caught them and spread them apart again, the heat of his breath still tickling her ear. What did he mean? She felt his hand on her back, guiding her across the floor. The hall was filled with flashing colored lights, like a dream she'd had once or a film she'd seen. They moved. Rey was gliding through the crowd, in time with the song. *Bam!* A snare, a cymbal, a pulse within the music: the tight skin of the drum singing war! She was drunk, she realized, and her feet were moving without her. He led and she followed, and when the music brought them back together, she took her chance to tell him she knew only that his name was Rey.

He laughed. He raised his hand up Norma's back and pulled her closer, so close her lips almost touched his. She could breathe him. Then he spun her away, twirled her like a plaything.

They danced for the rest of the night and hardly spoke at all.

When the party broke up, he offered to accompany Norma home. This was before downtown was abandoned; there were little bodegas still open, selling gum and toasted plantains, aspirin and cigarettes. Rey bought a candy bar, and they shared it as they waited for the bus. There were young people everywhere, on every corner, sharing smokes, raising their voices in cheerful arguments—that four a.m. logic, that drunken lucidity. Norma's curfew had come and gone. It was summer, and there was even a moon in the sky, or a sliver of one, and the couples that walked by clutched each other tightly, beautiful people all of them. It seemed the war would never come.

Norma and Rey cramped together in the back row of a crosstown bus, their legs pressed up against each other. Rey wrapped his left arm around her. She felt his thumb rubbing her shoulder. Norma had nowhere to put her hands, and so she dropped them on his thigh. Her index finger stroked the fabric of his jeans, and it amazed her, because she was not this type of girl. His black hair had been combed back earlier, but with all the dancing, it was starting to fall in his eyes. It was nearly dawn, and the bus rolled lazily along empty avenues. He played absentmindedly with the silver chain around his neck, then pulled a cigarette from behind his ear. There was a match stuck in the end. While he looked around for a place to strike it, she asked him what he had meant by such a strange question.

Rey smiled and pretended not to remember. His eyes closed, as if he were still hearing the loud crash of a cymbal or the blare of a trumpet. "Nothing," he said.

"I'll guess then."

He nodded. They were in the back, the window open to the night air. He bent forward and lit the match against the back of the seat, where two names had been scratched into the metal with a pocketknife: LAUTARO & MARIA, FOREVER. Rey slung his right arm out the window and blew smoke over his shoulder. He watched her.

"You must be *somebody's* son," Norma said. "And by somebody, I mean somebody famous. Why else would you ask me?"

"Somebody's son?" he asked, grinning. "Is that what you think?" He laughed. "How astute. Aren't we all somebody's children?"

"What's your last name?"

"You'll have to ask your friends."

"Why would you ask me that unless you were well known?"

He smiled coyly. "I don't aspire to fame."

"You're clearly not an athlete."

He took a puff from his cigarette, blue smoke trailing from his lips. "Is it obvious?" he asked, amused. He flexed his bicep and pretended to be impressed with himself.

Norma laughed. "Are you a politician?"

"I hate politicians," he said. "And, in any case, there's no such thing anymore: only sycophants and dissidents."

"A dissident then."

He grinned and made a show of shrugging his shoulders.

"If you were, why would you tell me?"

"Because I like you."

There was something so confident about him, so brash, it was almost distasteful—except it was intoxicating. She remembered this night: the dancing and the drinking, their easy and light conversation in the early morning hours, so enthralling they didn't even notice the bus ease to a stop, or the idling rumble of the motor, or the flashing lights. It was a roadblock, only a few stops from her house. She remembered apologizing to Rey for the hassle, after he had come all this way to drop her off. Rey frowned but said not to worry.

Then a soldier was aboard, holding a flashlight in one hand, his right arm resting on the barrel of his rifle. Rey took two quick puffs from the end of his cigarette and tossed it to the sidewalk. He exhaled into the bus. The soldier took his time, let his gun do the detective work, and each tired passenger handed over identification papers without argument. When the soldier got to them, Norma took a good look at him and realized he was young, just a kid. It emboldened her, or maybe she just wanted to impress Rey.

"You don't have to point that thing at me," Norma said, handing the soldier her ID. "I'm not going anywhere."

"Be quiet," said Rey.

The young soldier scowled. "Listen to your boyfriend." He patted his gun gently, as if it were an obedient child. "Where's yours, boyfriend?"

"I don't have identification, sir," Rey said.

"What?" the solider barked.

"I'm sorry. It's at home."

The soldier examined Norma's ID under the flashlight, then handed it back. "There's always a wise guy," he mumbled, turning to Rey, then leaned over them out the window and yelled for an officer. "You're coming with us," he said to Rey. "Sorry, girlfriend, looks like you're going home alone."

A quiet panic seized the bus. Every head turned to face them, though no one made eye contact. Only the driver pretended not to notice: he held the steering wheel tightly and looked straight ahead.

"I'll go," Rey said quietly. "We'll straighten this out. My ID is at home. It's no problem."

"Good," the soldier said. "We all hate problems."

"Where are you taking him?" Norma said.

"You want to come?" said the soldier.

"No, she doesn't," Rey answered for her.

They led him off the bus. Norma watched from the window as they put Rey in a green military truck.

There were only a few more stops to her house. Norma rode them in silence, the cool air in her face, aware that everyone was aware of her. She felt young and frivolous: she was a drunk girl coming home from a party when everyone else, it seemed, was shaking off sleep, on their way to work. They felt no pity for her. Fear perhaps, or anger. As she got off, she could feel the bus exhale, as if she were a bomb that might have exploded, and now they were finally safe.

It was at her front door, as she was digging in her pockets for her keys, that she found Rey's ID card. Or rather, it was his picture. The name belonged to someone else.

T W O

O F C O U R S E , he'd heard Norma's voice before. In 1797, the
owner of the village's canteen had a good radio, with an antenna long enough to get a signal from the coast, and so, each Sunday, the
women and the children and the remaining men crowded in to listen.
It was what they did instead of church. They gathered an hour before to
eat and drink and gossip. Potatoes, mushy overripe fruit, and thin silver
fish salted in broth. Loud voices, the beginnings of a song. They brought
portraits of their missing, simple drawings that an itinerant artist had
done years before. They hung these on the walls, rows of creased and
smudged faces Victor didn't recognize, whose mute presence made the
village seem even smaller. Then, at eight o'clock, there was a hush, and
static, and that unmistakable voice through the tinny speakers: Norma, to
listen and heal them; Norma, mother to them all.

They were waiting to hear the names of those who had left. Boys,
some only a few years older than Victor, wandered away, leaving 1797

emptier and smaller each year. They grew up and became men elsewhere.
A few returned, after being gone for years, to choose a wife and take her
away, or to tend their father's plot of earth. But most never reappeared. It
was all the women spoke of: where had their husbands gone? Their sons?
Sad mothers still lamented the days of forced conscriptions, when their
boys had been rounded up in the plaza and given rustic wood carvings
in the shapes of machine guns. The children fell on their stomachs and
slithered across the dirt; the mothers watched them, terrified: oh, how
they played.

Victor had heard all the stories. Even when he was a boy of six, with
the war long over, his mother sent him to hide in the trees whenever an
army truck belched its way into the village. He watched from the forest: angry sergeants picking carefully between the plumpest chickens,
ordinary soldiers carrying rucksacks bulging with fruit. Did the soldiers
notice the village had no young people? When the truck left, Victor and
all the other boys emerged from the jungle to be received by their mothers with kisses and tears. Everyone knew the children who left on green
trucks never came back.

Some left for work, especially since the war ended and there was no
more need for fighters. Mostly to the capital, or to labor on the highways
being built up and down the coast, or over the spine of the mountains to
the sierra. There was always work in contraband along the eastern border, and the fisheries in the north hired anyone willing to work seven days
a week. Some, it was said, made it to the beaches, cultivating dreams of
foreign women, making a living selling trinkets to tourists. These were
the rumors anyway, but really no one knew for certain. There was no
resentment toward the lost, only sadness at being left behind. Those who
remained placed their hopes on the radio. The village had entrusted a
few letters to passing travelers, but nothing had ever come of it. So, they
waited for Sunday and the next and the next. Those evenings impressed
upon Victor the danger of remembering. His mother, he assumed, was
listening for news of that phantom, his father. Victor prayed: that she'll
forget me when my time comes. He planned to set out for the city one
day too; he'd known it since he was a little boy. Happiness, he'd decided,
was a kind of amnesia.

This is how it happened: Victor went off to school one morning and returned to a house filled with mourners. His mother had drowned, they said. They repeated the words, various women in tones of concern and affection, but none of it made any sense. What would they do with him? The women around him grieved loudly, they wailed and sang dirges in an old language he couldn't understand. No one explained a thing. No one had to. His favorite place in the village was an empty field at the edge of the jungle, a sometime park, sometime trash dump full of flowering wild plants and lizards with golden eyes, a field alive with the cawing of invisible birds—they can bury me there, Victor thought, they can bury me now because it's all the same to me. He could feel his fingers tingling. He had the strangest sensation of sinking, a curtain falling, his life going black. The women coddled him, fed him, sang, and prepared his things.

"Can I see her?" he asked.

They took him to the river's edge. It was swollen with the previous week's rain, and the water spun and quaked like a living thing. Victor could hear the adults whispering about him: Adela's boy is here, Adela's boy. He tried to ignore it. The village was there, and the men who wouldn't acknowledge Victor—the men who should have saved her—and his classmates, too, all eyes trained on a rock halfway between the shores, jutting above the water line, wrapped fiercely in white foam. His mother's body cut the current too, slumped, clutching the stone as if it were a life raft when, more likely, it had killed her. The men were trying to string up a safety line from the other bank. They seemed helpless. Above, the skies were clear and deep blue, betraying no trace of the last week's storms. Her body, Victor realized, wouldn't stay there forever: the men might reach her before the current carried her away, but, just as likely, they would not. She'd been fishing, one of the women said. She lost her footing in the eddies where blind silver fish gather to eat and be eaten, the village's staple food. She must have been distracted, because these things never happen. Then the river had carried her here.

Now the women were telling him things that made his head hurt. She's with your father now, they said, and Victor felt sick to his stomach imagining that dead and empty space. Victor had never known him. His mother told stories, but they were few and vague: your father was from the city; he was an educated man. Not much more, not even a name. But they were together now, the women said, and Victor blinked and wondered what that could mean. The river churned, and his dead mother clung to a rock, the moiling currents poised to take her away, downstream, toward further indignities. A boy approached him and then another, until Victor was surrounded by his friends. Together they waited for the disaster to end, and nothing was said. It was in their faces, in the shifting weight of their bodies: the tension, the despair, the relief that it was not their mother, dead, astride a rock in the river. One of the boys touched him, took him by the shoulder or squeezed his arm. Only a few moments more, Victor thought, and the river would undress her, strip her bare, exposing her skin, the muscles of her back. The men were rushing, but not fast enough. Elijah Manau was among them, Victor's teacher, his mother's lover. Victor had watched them walking through the village together, nearly every night since his best friend Nico left, never touching hands until they stepped into the forest. Manau worked alongside the men now, more frantic than the rest, more flushed and helpless. They were the two men of her life. Victor tried to catch Manau's eye, but couldn't.

She was dead anyway, he thought, why rush? For a moment, he hated these men, who moved as one to save her body but who had not saved her. They couldn't feel what he felt. Nico had left 1797 a few months before. Now his mother was gone, too, and the town might as well implode and sink into the earth. She clung to the rock. Nico's father worked clumsily, glancing up at the river, now back at his stumps and the knot he could not quite tie. He had the rope between his teeth. He'd lost his hands in the war.

"Good for nothing," Victor muttered to himself. "Useless cripple." It was the cruelest thought he'd ever had.

The line was nearly set, stretched taut across the river. Who would wade into the current to pull her free? The men had fashioned a raft to carry Victor's mother's body back to shore. They organized themselves, and there was Manau, barreling into the water, and the village watched breathless, and Victor knew before it happened that he wouldn't reach her in time. Manau was up to his chest in its turbid black waters when the river surged, and she let go. Victor never saw her face, only the back of her, his mother set free, her body bobbing and sinking beneath the surface, and then she was gone.

Victor had lied to Norma at the station. He knew why they'd sent him: there was no reason to stay. His mother had prepared it all. She'd wanted him to leave, they said, and it was her instructions that formed the essence of the note he carried to the station. The women of 1797 had sewn the note carefully into the pocket of his pants—there are thieves on the road, they warned him—along with a small sum of money, and a list of all the town's disappeared. Take it to Norma, they'd said, and he promised he would. He looked at the list, at the dozens of names filling two columns on both sides of a sheet of lined paper. Nico was there, the very last name, but the others he didn't recognize. One of them was his father, but Victor didn't know which one. There were so many, strangers mostly, young men who had gone and never returned. Did they suppose Victor could bring them back?

Just to have the names read would count for something. Victor's voice filling the crowded canteen would be enough. The old spinsters, the men who remained, his classmates—they would celebrate him, as if he had done something extraordinary: conquered a foreign land, crossed a frontier, or subdued a monster. He would read, that would be all; read the names and remind the radio listeners to pray for his mother, who had drowned and been carried by the river to the sea.

This was only three days ago. Since then, his life had acquired a velocity he could scarcely comprehend. Everything was out of order, the contents of his world spilled and artlessly rearranged. Here he was, watching the river boil and steal his mother. Here he was, planting a cross in the sweet-smelling field at the edge of town, a dark-clad throng of mourners behind him at a respectful distance. Here he was, having his head shaved—these were the protocols of mourning—and saying good-bye to his friends, one by one, trying not to cry.

Though his contract was for one more year, the town didn't have the heart to make Manau stay. He'd been in love. It was what everyone said, and Victor knew it was true. Manau would travel with Victor to the city. He'll help you, the women told him, and so they left 1797 at dawn, in the back of an old truck, mist still clinging to the hillsides, along a red-earth road cut through the jungle. A small crowd, a half-dozen women, some of his schoolmates, gathered to wish him luck. Victor carried a small, woven bag with a few belongings: a change of clothes, a photograph of the city his mother had saved from a magazine, a bag of seeds. On either side was the forest, a wall of green and black shadows. The truck bounced along the road, through deep ruts pooled with water, and left them in a village named 1793.

Here they waited, but no boat came. The morning grew hot and bright. There was a sign by the river, and a few young men waiting in its shadow. At noon, a small launch came, just a raft with a motor. He would take six, the captain said, but a dozen people pushed their way aboard. The vessel swayed and trembled. Victor sat on his bag and put his head between his knees. There was so much noise: the captain barking out prices, the passengers shouting back. A few people got off, cursing the captain: "Abuse!" a woman yelled. She had a baby in her arms. Then the engine came to life, and everyone pressed together tightly. Victor stayed low while the rest stood; he looked out between legs and baggage at the surface of the black river and the mass of vegetation that curled over the water's edge. The launch pushed upstream. Victor felt Manau rub his head, but he didn't look up.

The provincial capital was called 1791. It was an inelegant town of wooden houses clustered around a clapboard church. The bus, they were told, would come that evening or perhaps the next morning. No one could say for sure. "Where can we eat?" Manau asked, and the bespectacled man who sold tickets nodded in the direction of the market.

Victor and Manau wandered among the stalls where the old women were closing up and putting away their wares for the day. They shared a plate of cold noodles and soup. Manau ordered a beer and drank from the bottle. Patriotic songs played over the loudspeaker. "Your mother told me to take care of you," Manau said. The skin around his eyes was puffy and red.

Victor nodded but said nothing. It seemed for a moment that his teacher was trying to make a joke.

"But who's going to take care of me?" Manau asked, his voice cracking.

They successfully wasted the day, playing marbles in the plaza, visiting the church to light a candle for his mother. Manau read a newspaper he found beneath a bench. It was damp and yellowed, but only two weeks old. In the late afternoon, they slept a few hours with their backs against the town's only lamppost, then the bus appeared just before midnight, and 1791 came to life. Women rose to sell silver fish and cornmeal, cigarettes and clear liquor in plastic bags. Small, wiry men carried packages twice their size to and from the bus. The driver and his passengers ate hurriedly, plates of rice steaming in the nighttime chill. Young men smoked and spat, raised their hats at the girls selling tomato sandwiches. Dozens of people gravitated to the bus, were pulled into its orbit. It was loaded in the yellow-tinged darkness, by a group of boys Victor's age, who clambered atop the roof, tying packages to the rack in an impossible bundle. And then, as soon as it began, it was over: now they were leaving, the doors closing, the bus pulling away with a grunt of the motor. Victor had never seen so much movement. The district capital disappeared, spent by its burst of energy; the women went back to sleep, the men to drinking. In a few moments, the single streetlight had faded, and there was only the heat of the crowded bus and the complaint of the engine.

The road was bumpy, and Victor hardly slept, his head knocking against the window a dozen times in the night. Manau gave up his seat to an old man, sat stolidly on an overstuffed suitcase in the aisle, eventually sleeping with his head cradled in his hands. Victor was alone, and he'd never left the village before. Outside, there was only darkness, the blue-black sky indistinguishable from the earth. Just before morning, a thin line of red appeared at the horizon. He was in the mountains now. In the dim violet light, the ridges seemed like the ruddy spine of an alligator. Beside him, the old man slept, snoring fiercely, his head back and mouth agape, a stack of shiny plastic sheets in his lap. They looked like giant photographs. Victor had seen something like this in school. In a book. He thought he could recognize in them bones and the shape of a human chest. The old man's white hair was thin, his lips parched. Victor looked down again at the photographs: there were ribs! He touched his own, felt his skin slide over the bones. He felt his own chest, with the pictures before him like a map, this cloudy photo of a man's heart. They shone and had the color of science about them. He wanted to touch them, but the man's hands lay over them, even as he heaved and choked in his sleep. The sky was stained orange, now yellow, and the world outside was revealed, dusty and fawn, a scarcely living disappointment. Something dry and withered poked out from the pebbled earth. The bus moved slowly. Victor wanted to hold the photographs up to the light. When the man coughed himself awake, Victor tapped him.

"These?" the old man said, smiling. "I'm sick, child."

"I'm sorry."

"So is my wife," he said. "She's sorry. And my children too. And me."

The bus was waking now, but most of the curtains were still pulled to block out the rising sun. In the distance, the mountains seemed to be made of gold.

"Are you going to be okay?" Victor asked.

The old man frowned for a moment. "I'll show you." His fingers were thick and calloused. Pulling off the first of the sheets, he reached over Victor and placed it against the window. The morning light shone through the film. Victor saw a man's chest, his rib cage, his arms at his sides. Victor even saw his spine. The image cut off just above the jaw, a slab of white jutting unexpectedly into the frame.

Victor looked at the photograph and then at the old man. "Is it you?" he asked.

"Have you seen an X-ray before?"

Victor admitted he hadn't. He'd never heard the term before.

"Yes, it's me."

"What's wrong with you?"

The man sighed. He had a deep, red scar on his cheek, and he touched it carelessly. "My bones and my heart," he said in a singsong voice. "My lungs and my brain and my blood!"

"Everything?"

"Everything," he said brightly. "I am the complete man." He coughed and pulled another X-ray from the stack, placing it against the window. "These are my lungs," he said and clapped his chest. "My puny, weak lungs."

There were tiny holes in the tissue, like scattered coins.

"Diseased lungs," the man whispered. He said there was a hospital, in the sierra outside the city, for veterans. He said he'd had medals, but he sold them when the war ended, to pay for his medicines.

"My father died in the war," Victor said, and it was a fact he thought might be true, lost and dead being brothers.

"I'm sorry, child."

It was nothing to say that his father was dead because he'd never really known him. His mother being dead? That was a secret wound, something dark and hidden, not to be told. Victor coughed.

"Don't get too close to me, child. Not until I'm better. The air at the hospital is clean and dry. They'll fix me up."

They were silent for a while, and around them, the passengers shook off sleep, or held stubbornly to it. Manau hadn't looked up yet. The bus rumbled along. They were between ranges, on a rocky plain. There was nothing green, nothing at all that seemed to be alive. Tufts of pale, weedy grasses grew in the shadows at the base of the rocks. A stocky plant with needles. "A cactus," the old man said. To Victor, it looked as foreign, as strange as the moon or any distant planet. It was an ancient ocean, dry, disappeared. He imagined waves and currents and silver fish. He felt the note rubbing against his skin. His secret, his mission. Like the X-rays, the note was the picture of his insides. Next to him, the old man drifted in and out of sleep. Eventually, he coughed himself awake, and when he did, he winked at Victor. "I'm going to be fine," he whispered just before his eyes clamped shut, his head falling back against the seat.

The man woke for good when the bus started climbing. "Almost there now," he said. Then Victor took the note from his pocket, breaking the stitching with his long pinky nail. He didn't know why he did it exactly; he just wanted the old man to know.

The old man unfolded the paper and read slowly. He turned it over to the list of names. "Have mercy," he mumbled. "Are you traveling alone?"

Victor shook his head, and pointed at Manau. "My teacher is with me."

The old man seemed reassured. "Shall we wake him?"

"He's very tired."

But Manau was up already. He kneaded his stiff neck and offered the old man a handshake. "We're going to the radio," he said when the old man asked what plans they had. "We're going to see Miss Norma."

"Will you see her, do you think? Will you really see her?" The old man looked back and forth between them, his face suddenly animated.

Manau shrugged. "I don't know. I hope so."

"Have you been there before? To the city?"

"Yes. I was born there."

The old man sighed. "So you know the place. It's where the soul of this country is."

"In the city, they say it's out here."

"Who can tell?"

Victor couldn't follow. The old man turned and smiled. He asked for the list and pulled a pen from his pocket. He held the note against his thigh and wrote a single name in a bouncing, jagged script that shook along with the bus. "It's my son," he said to Victor and Manau. "You understand."

He got off in the next town. The hospital was there, a large, imposing building of brick and steel surrounded by an iron fence. Victor had never seen such a large construction. It looked like a factory he had seen in a picture once, dominating the minuscule town. "Home," the old man said. "You're not far now, child. Stay alert." Then he folded a few bills into Manau's palm. "Take care of him," he said. Manau promised he would. The old man gathered his X-rays and his bags, and shuffled down the aisle.

Not long after, the bus crested a pass, and shacks began to appear along the sides of the road. First one or two, then clusters of them. Then they were a steady presence as the bus descended to the coast. The road was better, and the bus seemed to be gliding now. Victor finally fell asleep and awoke to honks and shouting, the city's noise like a great engine: movement, a sputtering motor, the squalid borders of the capital, its sidewalks overflowing. The city had emerged all at once, the bus crept slowly through the crowded streets, and Victor peered out of his window. He wanted it all to be over. There was no sun, only a gray sky above, the color of the parchment he once did his school lessons on: at home with an oil lamp on the table, his mother frying fish, checking his penmanship and his spelling. That world was gone. The city moved like a forest moves: first sound, then sight, everything invisible and shadowed, a place full of walls. He felt glad to be on the bus, and he prayed it wouldn't stop. This can't be it, he thought. There were so many people and so much stone. There's another, better place ahead, but then the bus was slowing, and then it was pulling into a lot, vendors ready to pounce at the arriving passengers: women with baskets of cheese balanced atop their heads, men selling batteries and sodas and lottery tickets adorned with pictures of the Virgin. Everyone yelling. "Let's wait a moment," Victor said. "Please."

Manau nodded. The bus emptied, and still they stayed put. I'll make him move me, Victor thought. All he wanted was to sleep, to dream of places he had left behind, of his mother letting go, of rivers and people as transparent as ghosts.

The bus driver lumbered down the aisle and informed them they had arrived.

"We're aware," said Manau.

"You two got somewhere to go?" the driver said. He glared like an animal.

"We're getting off."

"Good," he said. It was clear he didn't believe them.

Then Manau's hands were on Victor's back, ushering him through the bus and out the door. What if he had said no? No, I'm not getting off. No, send me home. There's nothing for me here. My father is a phantom and my mother is floating on the river, halfway to the sea by now. Maybe it wouldn't have been different at all. Maybe—

They stood on the sidewalk for a moment. Manau was almost smiling. Of course he was: he was home. Victor had imagined approaching a city gentleman, a man in a top hat and severe black suit, and asking, "Which way to the radio, good sir?" He didn't have to. It was there ahead of them, an antenna piercing the sky.

N O W T H E street had filled, and he was surrounded by a hot and panting mass of strangers. Victor buried his face beneath Norma's arm, closed his eyes, and willed the moment to pass. The white-haired man had disappeared, and the woman, too, both absorbed by the rushing crowd. Victor breathed Norma's city smell, the scent of acrid smoke on her clothes, and felt her heart beating. Was she afraid too? Voices rose around him, urgent human sounds, the heat of shouted prayers, calling Norma, Norma, Norma! And so it was everywhere, he thought, this worship of her. Not just in my faraway village, but here too, in the central city, in the capital. He looked at the people, at the dark forest of men and women. There was no way out except through them. Norma was warm, but he could feel her body tense. He had brought all this on, this rush of needy pleas, of outstretched hands fingering tiny, faded photographs—all of this, by simply saying her name. A bearded man pressed closer, wailing toothlessly, his hands caressing an unseen figure as he repeated a name again and again. There was something pained in his eyes. He wore too-small rubber sandals, his toes pushing out beyond the soles, grazing the dirty pavement. He looked sicker than the man with the X-rays, closer to death. Victor could see their insides. The people were upon them, tangled and anxious; and suddenly they were moving, Norma holding him tightly, Victor unwilling to let go.

The white-haired man appeared and whistled again. He waved his arms frantically, and then, quite unexpectedly, there was silence. "Form a line," he ordered. The crowd thinned and spread and organized itself. Victor felt he was watching a choreographed dance. He looked up at Norma: she was pale and tense and afraid.

A moment later, a table and two chairs had been arranged for them. The line of people snaked down the block. A hundred eyes were upon them. It seemed they had no choice but to sit. The white-haired man apologized to Norma and Victor.

"What's going on?" Norma asked. "I can't."

"One name per person!" the white-haired man shouted. "No more! No cutting in line or you'll lose your ration card!"

He turned and smiled at Norma. "I'll begin, if you please, madam." He closed his eyes. "Sandra. Sandra Tovar."

Someone passed Norma a pen and a piece of paper. She looked at the page and back at the white-haired man, saying nothing.

"Aren't you going to write it down?"

Norma blinked.

"I'll do it," Victor said.

"Can you?" Norma lowered her voice. "Can you *write?*"

He nodded and took the pen. "Sandra Tovar," the white-haired man said again, and Victor wrote the name carefully. The man thanked them both and stepped to the side with a bow.

Victor took dictation. The line moved slowly: each person stood before Norma, patted Victor on the head, and uttered a single name. They lingered, each of them, until Victor had written the name out and Norma had checked it. She thanked them in a tired voice, offered her condolences. She promised to read the name on the air. A few names she had to spell for him, and for those moments, it seemed he was in school again, back home where nothing had changed. The chatter of the people became the sound of rain in the forest. And so it was all a nightmare; perhaps he had never left the village. He filled a page without thinking. He kept his head down, his eyes on the paper, on these names, on his own hand carefully tracing letters.

Then: "Adela."

He'd been at it for twenty minutes when he heard his mother's name. Victor looked up to see a thin, unshaven man holding a knit cap in his hands. Victor thought for a moment he must know the man, that the man must know him, that his two-day journey was over, that there was some sense in all this. Victor put the pen down. He noticed for the first time that it was night.

"Adela," the man said again in a low voice. He began spelling it.

"I know how to write it," Victor said. How could he not?

"What manners!" a woman in line said.

"Do you know her? Do you know my mother?"

The man frowned. "Who are you, boy?"

Victor felt suddenly light-headed. It wasn't his mother at all. It couldn't be: how many Adelas were there? He heard Norma ask if he was all right. Through nearly closed eyelids, he saw the man put on his knit cap and walk away quickly.

"Victor?"

He leaned over and threw up beneath the table. Then there was a commotion. "Don't hold up the line!" a voice called. "Move the child!"

Someone handed Victor a glass of water. They were surrounded again. How long had they been there? The white-haired man was yelling, but this time no one was listening. Norma had him in her arms. "We're going," she whispered to Victor. "We're going. Can you stand?"

He nodded. He was wobbly on his feet, but he managed.

The crowd parted, but they let their fingers graze over Norma as she passed—light, inoffensive touches, hopeful touches, as if she were an amulet or the image of a saint. Their hands washed over Victor as well. There was noise, shouting, an engine backfiring. The crowd swelled. It was impossible to tell how many people there were, or where they had come from. They towered over Victor and blotted out the sky. He wanted to tell Norma that he was sorry. He cowered. The people loved her, and he understood this. They called her name. They would never hurt her. He was safe.

Victor and Norma escaped the crowd through narrow alleys and crooked paths, the noise and the people fading with each step. The dirt beneath their feet was packed hard, cut by tiny streams of water drawn on the path like a system of veins. The farther they got from the crowd, the faster they went: soon they were running, Norma ahead, Victor doing his best to follow. His palm stuck to hers, his heart raced, and then they had emerged in a wide, desolate plaza graced with palm trees, lit by orange streetlamps. The buildings were ornate and self-important, but the fountain at its center was dry and gathering dust. An Indian woman sat on the curb, stooped over a coloring book, an infant asleep in her lap, and she didn't even look up at them. A lone soldier stood watch in front of one of the buildings, rocking back and forth on either foot, machine gun at his side.

Norma and Victor waited a few minutes, catching their breath, not speaking. A man tipped his hat as he pedaled his creaky bicycle across the plaza. It was night, Norma told him, and the city lived indoors at these hours. "It's all these years of curfew. We're accustomed to it now." It didn't look at all like the same place Victor had seen that morning. The people had vanished. After a while, a cab rolled by, tapping its horn lightly, and Norma stopped it with a wave of her arm. They rode silently across the city, Victor with his face pressed against the window, his heart still beating raggedly. He was sure he saw them in every shadow: the lost and the missing, huddled on corners and in doorways, asleep on benches. The cabbie drove and tried to chat with Norma, but she seemed to be in no mood to talk. She kept her lips pursed tightly, only nodding or responding when decorum demanded it. The driver didn't mind: he complained about his work, making a joke of it, his voice raspy and affected. "After a few hours," the cabbie said, "I lose feeling in my legs."

Norma sighed. "That sounds dangerous," she said.

Victor heard her alter her voice, draining it of its sweetness. The driver didn't know. He couldn't know.

It was dark when they arrived at home. Norma's apartment had a wide window that looked out onto a quiet street. She had said it was small, but to Victor it seemed palatial. "You'll sleep here," she said, and pointed to the couch. A neon sign cast a harsh blue light over the room. Norma explained that it was a pharmacy, that you could buy medicine there. She turned on a lamp, and the shadows dispersed. He could see she was tired. He expected to be reprimanded, but instead she slipped away into the kitchen and set some water to boil. Victor sat on the sofa, staring at his hands. He was afraid to look at the strange apartment.

Norma emerged with tea and a basket of bread. "Are you feeling better?"

He hadn't eaten all day, and the emptiness in his stomach stirred. She must have seen the hunger in his eyes. "Eat," Norma said. "A boy needs to eat."

The bread she served was strange: square, with a neat brown trim, its center a white the color of milk. Victor bit into a slice, and it dissolved in his mouth, coming apart like string. Still, he ate greedily, and it felt good. He strained to swallow mouthfuls of the stuff, but it expanded like bubble gum, rolling over his teeth and against his cheeks. He looked up. Norma, he realized, was smiling. He stopped chewing.

"It's okay," she said. "I was just watching."

Victor nodded. She wasn't old. She wasn't like the abandoned elderly that crept through town with their bent wooden canes, but she was older than his mother, and didn't have the copper glow his people had. She was pale, and her black hair fell straight in a ponytail down to the middle of her back. She gave the impression of not caring so much what she looked like. In 1797, Norma would have a hard time finding a husband. Victor ate and watched her. Her angular face contained a geometry he didn't recognize, like the bread she offered him, built of right angles. Maybe the softness of her voice clashed with her sharp features. He'd never seen anyone like her up close, not that he could remember. No one this color. After having listened to her for so many years, strangely, it had never occurred to him to put a face with that voice. He had never wondered what she looked like, not once. Did anybody? That lack of imagination struck Victor as strange: had he thought of her as some kind of spirit? As a voice without a body or a face or even a soul? More ghosts. He'd never thought of her as real.

"You must be tired," Norma said after a while.

Victor nodded.

"I've never been to the jungle," she said.

He chewed and nodded. "It's different," he offered.

"I imagine it is," Norma said. Could she see how tired he was? Did she know what he wanted to tell her? They were silent for a moment.

"You don't want to talk, do you?" Norma asked.

"No," Victor said, surprising himself. There was too much to tell.

THREE

I F N O R M A were honest, she might remember Rey's disappearance as what it was: a series of tiny flashes of light, a rising sense of danger, and then, in place of some plosive event, only this: a surreal, mystifying stillness. He leaves for a trip into the jungle—a trip like dozens he's taken before. Then there is the cold, hard fact of his silence. No news, no word, and Norma's life changing with each passing day, flattened beneath a crushing weight, bled of its color.

It had been ten years now.

The early days were torturous: a pain emanating outwards from each cell in her body, and the fact of his absence everywhere. She stopped strangers in the street, inspected the faces of people on buses and trains, their wrinkles, their smiles, the shapes of their tired eyes, even the shoes they wore. Each day her husband did not return, she felt herself losing her balance, the work of carrying on too much and too cruel. The ways she missed him were endless: his smell still pervaded their apartment, that mixture of sweat and cheap soap. She missed his dimpled cheeks, his kiss, and the affected way he read the newspaper, as if his sharp gaze could bore a hole in the text. He folded it into lengthwise thirds and was embarrassed to admit he indulged only in the sports section. She missed this, too: his body, his touch. His hands running up and down her back. Her own fingernails finding his spine, clawing, as if she could tear into him. She missed the face he made, always the same anguished expression, eyes flittering closed, deep concentration, and when he was behind her, she loved it, but she missed seeing him, seeing the blood rush to his face, the clouding of his features, the release. At night, she stayed awake and thought of him, too afraid to touch herself. Dread was everywhere. What if he never came back?

For ten years, he had existed in memory, in that netherworld between death and life—despicably, sadistically called *missing*—and she had lived with the specter of him, had carried on as normal, as if he were away on an extended vacation and not disappeared and likely dead. In the beginning, she had played detective, and in a sense, everything had been easier since she stopped. Not given up; simply stopped. In the first year of his absence, she had visited each of his colleagues at the university to ask for information. Where had he gone? It was a bent older gentleman who told her: he wasn't sure, but he'd heard the number 1797. What was he researching? Medicinal plants, said another, but this much she knew. Had they heard anything? And here they all shook their heads and looked away.

One professor told her Rey'd had a taste for psychoactives, jungle juju, he said, but this wasn't news, was it? Norma shook her head: of course not, of course not. It was a bright autumn day, and the war had been over for two months. The list of collaborators had been read on the radio a week before. The professor scratched his beard and looked distractedly out the window at a swatch of blue sky. His office and his person were in disarray. "Maybe he just lost it."

"I don't understand."

"It's just a thought. Took too much of something. Went native." He smoothed the wrinkles of his suit. "Maybe he'll snap out of it. Maybe he'll wander back."

Norma shook her head. It made no sense. "What about the list they read? What about the IL? Was Rey IL?"

Why did she ask? Did she even want to know? It was the same every time: a blank look, a stammered response, and then a pause as her husband's colleagues took the measure of her. Doors were closed discreetly, blinds drawn, telephones unplugged—all this at the mere mention of the IL. But the war was over, wasn't it?

This professor turned to face her. They had known each other socially—Christmas parties and birthdays, nothing more.

"Were you followed?" he asked.

It hadn't occurred to her. "Who would follow me?"

The professor sighed. "It doesn't matter," he said. "I knew your husband well. We were at the Moon together. He wasn't IL. He couldn't have been."

"What do you mean?"

"Everyone knows there was no such thing."

Norma was silent. She hardly breathed.

"It was a government invention, a fraud. Something the Americans cooked up to scare us."

"Oh," she managed.

"You'd do well to be careful when asking questions such as these." He paused and took a deep breath. "Someone might misinterpret."

Norma thanked him for his time, gathered her things and left quickly.

She scoured the papers for any news, but there was so much to tell about the end of the war. Who had time for a missing professor? There were battles to write about and lists of casualties to collect. The country seemed to be collapsing on itself: a shootout between decommissioned soldiers erupted in an underground bar in The Thousands. A man in Asylum Downs was run out of the neighborhood, his house set ablaze after his name had been listed among the collaborators. It was the war in its death throes, every day something new, the violence sputtering to its anarchic conclusion.

Still, the city was becoming accustomed to the idea of peace. She knew by now what his absence meant, but when the war ended, there was euphoria, a sudden and unexpected reason to smile. Norma had expected Rey to come home, sunburned and smiling, haggard perhaps, but alive, shaking his head and telling the tale of another close call searching for medicinal plants at the edge of a war zone. He was a scientist, first and foremost, an ethnobotanist committed to the preservation of disappearing plant species. This is what he told her, and for a time, she believed him. She had always wanted to believe him. When they were newlyweds, she had asked him: what about that night we met, the dancing, the ID? Where did they take you?

"They cured me," Rey told her. "They took me to the Moon and they fixed me right up. No more," he said. "I'm not interested in politics. I'm interested in living."

So he went into the jungle and returned with stories of insects the size of his hand, of dense, verdant valleys and their mysteries, of fluttering birds plumed in electric colors. And then he didn't return, and Norma waited. Then word filtered around the radio of a battle fought near the town of 1797 in the eastern jungle, of men captured and some killed. The rumors said many were buried and would soon be lost in the impossibly thick forest. They said it had been a slaughter, a victory celebration in the form of mass graves and anonymous dead—what does the end of a war mean if not that one side ran out of men willing to die? Peace was coming, now it was here. The battle near 1797 was ignored. And there were others: the war's coda, a string of killings in faraway places that were better left alone. In the city, there had been a battle as well, but now it was over; couldn't the people be forgiven if they noticed the sky for the first time in years, mistook its opaline glaze for sunlight, and began to forget?

There were two kinds of lists in those days, official and unofficial, and each contained different tallies of dead and missing, of exiled and imprisoned. With the right connections, Norma thought, she might be able to see those other lists, the real ones, that grim accounting of the war and its yield. But she never did. The next months passed in a haze, Norma going through the motions of living. She appeared at work, read the news without understanding or even attempting to understand what she was reading. She asked for a break from her Sunday-night show. Her many fans called in, expressing concern: was Norma all right? She had made the rounds at the university, been told in a variety of ways that the IL was not real, that her husband would be coming home, that it was only a matter of time, that he was on a drug binge in the forest, that the stress had finally gotten to him. Many refused to see her at all, citing their busy schedules or family obligations, but she sensed they were afraid of her. She didn't eat, spent a few nights a week at the station, afraid to go home and confront the empty apartment. When she returned to Lost City Radio, she was dispirited, her honey-voice weary, but the calls came anyway, by the dozens: with the fighting over, people were now asking, with sudden abandon, where their loved ones had wandered off to.

One day, when her condition could no longer be ignored, Elmer suggested they go to the prisons. Rey had been mistaken for an IL sympathizer, Elmer reasoned, which explained his name on the list that had been read on the air. He'd been found lost and wandering through the eastern jungle, and arrested. There, among the various half-dead in prison, she might find him, and, if he were there, strings could be pulled. Elmer was a friend then. He encouraged her. Papers were filed, permits granted, and the station, still currying favor with the newly victorious government, promised a positive report on conditions inside. The war had been over for a year.

Norma and Elmer drove to the prison in the station's four-by-four, through neighborhoods of haphazard construction, past homes with street numbers scrawled in chalk on the outside walls, past shanties topped with metal sheeting. They presented their papers at various roadblocks, some manned by uniformed soldiers, some by neighborhood thugs, and everything was solved with a few coins and a deferential smile. Children chased the truck as it sped by, waving through the billows of dust. They drove through communities whose essential feature was their color: a burnt, dry shade of yellowish gray, everything bathed in murky sunlight. These were the areas that Norma could just make out from the station on a clear day, where the mountains first appeared and city seemed to end—only it didn't. It never ended. More people arrived each day as the jungle and the sierra emptied of human life. The capital's new residents made homes here, in the inhospitable folds of the lower mountains, in the city's dry and teeming servants' quarters.

The prison was a sprawling complex, its watchtowers rising high above the surrounding neighborhood in a district known as Collectors. There were crowds of people by the visitors' door, women selling newspapers, sandwiches, and knickknacks to bribe the guards with: foreign coins, plastic key-chains, old comic books. Norma and Elmer waited in line with restless mothers, with anxious wives and girlfriends. They were all turned away.

Except Norma and Elmer, who passed through the first of a half-dozen locked doors: they stepped into a long corridor to another lock and another young man with a weapon. Each time, they were told to pull up their right sleeves, and the guard stamped their forearms. At the next gate, the guard would count the number of stamps, add his own, and wave them through. Eventually, they were ushered into a spare, windowless room with humming fluorescent light above. There were three metal folding chairs. They sat down to wait.

"Don't be nervous," Elmer said after a while. "It's not so bad. Look at your arm."

So she pulled back her sleeve once more and inspected the blurred purple markings. There was no state seal or a flag or code of any kind. She smiled. CITY'S BEST OFFICE SUPPLY, VETCHER BROTHERS CANNERY, A—1 WINDOW REPAIR, THE METROPOLE HOTEL, ELEGANCE WITHOUT COMPROMISE. This was her security clearance.

"I expected something more official," said Norma.

"That's because you haven't been here before."

Then a gruff man in a faded-olive uniform appeared and showed them to his office. He didn't shake hands, or even look at them, but the name tag on his uniform said ROSQUELLES. He sat down at his desk and announced that no one had informed him of their visit. "How do I even know who you are?" he asked.

They had decided it would be best for Elmer to speak, so as not to offend the official. With a nod to Norma, Elmer pulled some papers from his inside pocket. "We have letters."

But instead, Rosquelles stared at Norma, his gaze between menacing and dismissive. "Woman," he said, "why would you want to go in there?"

The office was dank and disordered, crammed with file cabinets that seemed ready to vomit their contents all over the floor. A cheaply framed photograph of a Swedish mountain scene hung askew. This was popular then, a way of idealizing life in the country's provinces: transforming the lost, war-ravaged hamlets into tidy Scandinavian villages with crystalline streams and quaint windmills, hills covered with bright swaths of green. Norma almost smiled. Our mountains are not like that.

She considered mentioning Rey, explaining that there had been some kind of mistake, but then she thought better of it. "We have approval, sir."

"That's not what I asked."

"I suppose I don't understand your question then."

Rosquelles sighed. "Inside we have the killers and the beasts and the assassins that we should have disposed of the moment we found them. These are the people you want to see?"

"I'm a journalist, sir."

"I hate journalists," Rosquelles said. "You make excuses for these killers."

"No one is making excuses for them anymore," Elmer said. "The war is over."

"It's not over in there," the official said.

"Yes, sir."

"How many prisoners are there?" Norma asked.

Rosquelles shrugged. "We quit counting years ago. It's a steady population now. No more growth. We don't take prisoners anymore."

"I see," said Norma.

"We kill them first."

"I see," she repeated.

He stood up. From a cabinet, Rosquelles removed a bottle of rubbing alcohol and a bag of cotton balls. He opened the bottle, soaked a cotton ball, and passed it to Norma. He pointed at her forearm. "You don't need those anymore. You're with me."

She hesitated.

"Take it," the official said. "You might as well clean it now. The kids outside will charge you fifty cents."

When they had finished, Rosquelles led the way with a jangling of keys, out of the office, along a dark corridor, then up a spiral staircase into a system of fenced-in raised causeways above the prison proper. They walked above the yard, along its perimeter: from this height, Norma could see the ocher mountains dotted with shanties, and below her, the prisoners standing in the dusty yard, staring back at her. A group of men were being led in stretching exercises by a fellow prisoner, others seemed to be debating among themselves. Some looked up in disgust, others with calm disinterest.

The sun was bright, and they squinted up at the visitors. There were whistles and catcalls at Norma; she was a woman, after all, in a community of caged men. Some followed her, swarming and clamoring in the yard below, kicking up clouds of yellow earth, laughing. "Baby," they called, and they said other things as well: about her pussy and the taste of it, about what they would do to her. Norma reached instinctively for Elmer's hand, and he gave it to her. She didn't feel safe. The causeway groaned with each step, and she imagined the entire structure collapsing, depositing her on the prison yard to be devoured. No one could save her, not with a knife or a gun or an army. Rosquelles ran his keys against the chain-link sides of the causeway. His graying hair was oily, and the back of his neck glistened. Periodically, he spat through the fence on the prisoners.

There were others, Rosquelles explained, locked in cells below the ground in lightless, stiflingly hot tombs. "These," he said, motioning over the yard, "these are the good ones."

"Can we see them?" Elmer asked. "The others?"

Rosquelles shook his head. The others were the ones who had shaken the country to its core. Out here were the soldiers, the triggermen. The leaders were below the ground, held incommunicado, only dimly aware that the war had ended, that they had lost. "Are you looking for someone in particular?"

"Yes," said Norma, at the exact moment that Elmer said, "No."

Rosquelles smiled. "Well, which is it?"

"My husband," Norma said. "There was a mistake."

A steady group of men had tracked the visitors' progress around the yard, but most had given up trying to elicit any response at all, had broken off. A few sat on their haunches, smoking and spitting. The sun glowed brightly, and Norma felt faint. She coiled her fingers around the chain-link fence, steadying herself.

A prisoner invited Norma to sit on his face.

"Animal!" Rosquelles shouted. He turned to Norma. "I'm sorry, madam. We don't make mistakes."

The prisoners responded with curses and laughter, and they called him by name. "Rosquelles!" they called. "Killer! Is that your girlfriend?"

He frowned. "You have fans," Rosquelles said. "This is no place for a woman. Are you well?"

Norma nodded. "May we see the lists?"

"There are no lists," he said.

They continued around the causeway above the yard. The men below were unshaven and dirty, shirtless and sunburned. The elevated metal corridor opened every fifty meters into a watchtower. Rosquelles greeted each guard the same way—"Friendlies behind!" Still, the young guards had fear in their eyes, and they kept their guns trained on Norma and Elmer until they had walked past.

Rosquelles led them to the observation tower, the highest one, two flights of stairs above the causeway. There were two soldiers inside and an imposing array of weapons trained on the prisoners below. Norma peered out: from this distance, the imprisoned men moved like ants, a dizzying and chaotic display. She studied them through binoculars: their faces, the lines of their jaws, their brows, and saw nothing and no one who could be her husband. He would recognize her, wouldn't he? And he would call out to her? But he wasn't there. She'd known it, of course, but hadn't allowed herself to think too much. What options were there? He'd been near the battle. There were prisoners and there were dead: wouldn't it be better to find him here, locked up among the warriors? Or was he a leader, entombed below?

No one had ever accused him of such a thing.

Maybe they saw her watching them. Maybe it was their way of mocking her interest. The buzzing crowd fell apart and regrouped in straight lines, row after row of thin, dark men. "Killers!" they chanted. They were fearless. Some smiled.

Norma turned away, stared into the mountains. Without the shanties, it could be a postcard.

Rosquelles shook his head. "They're going to sing."

Where before there was confusion, now there was order. Were these the same men who had chased them around the yard, the same feral pack of sun-scarred, hungry prisoners? A murmuring rose from below, a scratch of a melody, nothing more. There was a code at work, the men held their arms at their sides, statuesque and military. What could Rey be doing here, if he was? They were less than human, they puffed their chests and stood straight, and their faces were stern now. They were cogs of a machine. They sang.

"Is the IL real?" Norma asked. She could think of nothing else.

Rosquelles looked at her, disbelieving. He turned to Elmer. "Who is she?"

"I'm sorry," Norma said. "It's just that—"

"Why don't you ask them?" Rosquelles said, waving his hand at the prisoners below.

"What about the Moon? Are there still people there?"

"Woman, are you mad?"

Norma said nothing. She closed her eyes and listened as Elmer apologized on her behalf. Her Rey wandered the jungle and inhaled the soggy odors of the forest, he loved birds and verdure and the smell of wood smoke. He was not IL, because he told her he wasn't. He'd said those words, hadn't he? He wasn't IL, because the IL did not exist.

"Why are we here?" Norma whispered.

Elmer blinked his eyes. "You wanted to do this."

"Fire a warning shot," Rosquelles said to the guard.

The guard aimed at the ground in front of the prisoners and let off a few shots. Dust bloomed in tiny mushroom caps. The men kept singing. Norma looked over her shoulder at Elmer, and he shrugged when he met her gaze. The bullets kept coming at regular intervals, advancing toward the line of men. They sang, and Rosquelles cursed. There was something mechanical about them, something terrifyingly disciplined. The war planners hadn't counted on that mania. It had been the key to their success. The country's history was dotted with guerrilla episodes of varying intensities: here and there, a ragtag militia fired by an empty ideology or a provincial grievance, a lightly armed band led by a quixotic upper-crust dropout—it happened all the time, twice a generation, and ended the same way: the insurgents marched themselves to starvation, were felled by malarial fevers. They played at war on the fringes of the nation-state, then gave up as soon as the shooting began. The IL had been different. They didn't give up. They began the war and never planned for a truce. They wanted everything.

The guard fired a few more shots that pierced the ground in front of the singing prisoners. Norma watched the young soldier, beads of sweat gathering on his hairline, the heavy kick of the weapon pushing against his shoulder. The bullets advanced, and the men sang in unbroken harmony, about the war and the future, their paeans to outdated dreams. Some closed their eyes. It was prison opera, replete with bullets and dust and scorching light. The young soldier fired steadily around the men. They didn't flinch. "Sir," the soldier asked, "may I?"

Rosquelles shook his head. "I'm not allowed to hit them," he explained to the visitors.

Norma read disappointment on the young soldier's face. Elmer took notes, studying the scene. The sun had bleached everything of its color. She might fall at any moment.

The bullets whizzed by, the prisoners singing in sonorous swells. Rey sang, too, he'd always sung to her in a comically bad voice, with off-key trills, a theatrical falsetto. He sang because it made her laugh. Sometimes he sang in the crowded streets, in the park by the Metropole, unperturbed by the weary frowns of passersby. Another crazy, what can you do? I'm crazy, he'd tell her later, I sing because I'm crazy about you; Norma turning red, embarrassed, heat in her face. At home, too, songs of love, saccharine tunes from the era of the troubadours. She could hear the urgency now in the shots, the young soldier's longing to snipe one, just one, maybe wound him, a bullet to the shoulder, a slug in the meat of a prisoner's thigh. To watch a man fall—what joy! It's not possible Rey is dead. The singing forced Norma's eyes closed, she could feel the sun burning against her eyelids. A minor chord, a sad melody, an image: her Rey in his underwear, crouched at the foot of the bed, singing. Something romantic, something sappy. You are my sunshine ... or something even cheaper than that.

"He's not here," Norma whispered to Elmer.

The sun buried them in white light, and the shots continued steady, rhythmic. Melodies drifted skywards.

"Just one, sir?" the soldier said.

Rosquelles frowned wearily. He took Elmer's notepad from his hands. "I'm going to have to hold on to this," he said. "You understand."

Elmer said nothing. He reached for Norma's hand, and she let him hold it. She stepped closer to him.

"Show me the lists," Norma said to Rosquelles. "Please."

"What was the name? The one you're looking for."

She told him.

Rosquelles raised an eyebrow. "Never heard of him. Did he go by any other names?"

She bit her lip. "I don't know."

"How do you expect to find an answer if you don't ask the right questions?" Rosquelles sighed. "It was a big war, madam. A very big war with many, many players."

"Sir?" the soldier asked again.

The official nodded with a smile. "Oh, to be young and brainless again!"

Then there was a shot, and a man collapsed: third row, second from the back, so that most of the prisoners didn't see him fall. They sang, looking straight ahead. The downed man had been hit in the stomach. He slumped to his knees and tumbled forward, prostrate in the dust. His burnt-copper back arched, his arms buried beneath him. He was praying. Norma was too: her fingers curled tightly around the chain links, her nails digging into her palms. Rey wasn't coming back.

S H E   S L E P T   with the door open every night. At one time, when she was more hopeful, she had thought: if Rey were to come back tonight, he would see right away that I am sleeping alone. That had been the logic at first, but now it wouldn't be truthful to say that she expected anything of the sort. It was habit, pure and simple, of the kind whose origin was vaguely recalled but which existed nonetheless, a constant and unchanging fact of life. Her door was open.

But this night, the boy had come. He was there, resting on the couch. The apartment was small: from the living room, one could see through to the kitchen and into the bedroom. It wasn't exactly self-consciousness that Norma felt; it was an awareness, sudden and stark, of her solitude. It wasn't the boy. Victor said little. He was a tangle of emotions and wide-eyed observations buried beneath a rigid silence. She didn't know what he had seen, but it had rendered him nearly mute. He was small, thin-boned, and there was nothing at all imposing about him. She guessed he would be as content to sleep on the cool tiled floor of the kitchen as on the soft, pillowed couch. But he was there. She could have hidden his frail body in a cabinet under the sink, and still she would feel his presence. It wasn't him: it was his breath, his humanness, so close to her in the apartment. In the space that had been hers and Rey's, that had then been only hers. A sealed place, an impregnable store of memories where time had stopped for nearly a decade. Visitors? She could count them on her fingers. Without Rey, she had lived like this: spectacularly alone.

Victor slept on the couch, breathing softly in the humming blue light of the pharmacy. The blanket covered nearly all of him, except his feet, and these stuck out, his toes curling and straightening as he dreamed. The place was too small. They'd always meant to move to a bigger apartment when they had children, and they'd tried. She was thirty-two when Rey disappeared. They'd never stopped trying. On their last night together, they'd tried. The doctors had said there was nothing wrong with her, that he was in perfect shape, that these things took time. So time passed. When Norma and Rey were married, they'd daydreamed of a gaggle of children, a half dozen, each more beautiful than the last, each a more perfect representation of their love. His hazel eyes, his hair curling skywards. Her delicate hands, long, stately fingers. Her aquiline nose—not his that crooked slightly to the left—but Rey's skin tone, more suited to the sunny places where they would vacation once the war ended. They built variations of themselves, portraits of their unborn children, unique amalgams of their best features. My voice, Norma said, for speaking. No, Rey said, laughing: mine, for singing.

They made love regularly and hopefully, just as the doctor prescribed. And nothing. Passionately and desperately—still nothing. When he didn't return, Norma's period didn't come for ninety terrible days. She wrestled with the possibility of raising his child alone, almost allowing herself a glimmer of happiness—but it was only stress, her body as traumatized as her heart, shutting down, slowing very nearly to a standstill. She discovered in the mirror one day that she'd lost weight, that she was as spent, as ragged as the soldiers returning home from the countryside. All bone, gaunt and pale. She wasn't pregnant: she was dying.

Now the boy slept with his face buried in the cushions of the couch. Norma turned on the radio: softly, a melody, strings, a wistful voice. The boy did not stir. She edged the door closed, the blue light vanished. She was alone again, in darkness. She undressed.

FOUR

Y EARS AGO, a lifetime ago, it went this way: on a moonless night, Rey and a few friends tossed back shots of grain alcohol and then tested their aim against the front wall of the school, rocks against brick and glass. They were drunk and alive, just boys playing a prank. But that same night, something else happened: a small, homemade bomb exploded inside the mayor's office. This was the war's prehistory, its unnatural birthing, more than a decade before the fighting would begin in earnest. It occurred in a distant town, in a country as yet unaccustomed to such things. The blast awoke a restless, confused crowd. Fire tore at the roof, and windows were blown into the street in neat, glowing shards. The men lined up with pails of water, but it was no use. The water ran out, or their resolve did, and so they stopped. The sky was black, a soft breeze blowing. The building smoldered. It was a beautiful night for a fire.

Rey was only thirteen years old, but he would end up in jail that night, locked away for his own safety. Outside, a crowd would be calling for his head, gripped with the paranoia only a mob can feel. The jailer, his father's brother Trini, would be preaching calm. Inside, Rey's father, headmaster of the aggrieved school, would be red-faced and shouting, "What did you do, boy? What did you do?"

THE TOWN'S jail was two blocks off the plaza, sharing a quiet side street with the humble homes of maids and stonemasons. The exterior of the building was a pale blue, adorned with a rudimentary painting of the national seal, which, if examined up close (as Rey often did), was as blurry and inexact as the pixilated photographs that ran on the front pages of the town's only newspaper. An old Indian maxim—DON'T LIE, DON'T KILL, DON'T STEAL—was inscribed in severe black lettering above the doorjamb, perhaps giving the sleepy jail an import it didn't deserve. Rey liked the jail: he liked to sit with his uncle, whose job, it seemed, consisted of waiting for trouble to manifest itself. According to Trini, there wasn't enough of it. He complained bitterly about the quiet town, and liked to tell stories of his year in the capital. There was no way of knowing which were true and which were false. To hear Trini tell it, the city was peopled with thieves and louts and killers in equal parts. To hear Trini tell it, he'd been a one-man crime-fighting machine, justice patrolling the crooked streets, all grit and courage. The city! It was hard to imagine: a rotten, dying place, even then, crumbling and full of shadows. But what did it look like? Rey couldn't picture it: the boiling, black ocean, the jagged coastline, the heavy clouds, the millions draped in perpetual dusk. Here, there was bright sun and real mountain peaks capped with snow. There was an azure sky and a meandering river and a cobblestone plaza with a trickling fountain. Lovers held hands on park benches, flowers bloomed in all the municipal flower beds, and the aroma of fresh bread filled the streets in the mornings. Rey's hometown ended ten blocks from the plaza in any direction, giving way to dusty lanes and irrigated fields and small farmhouses with red-thatched roofs. Trini described a place Rey couldn't imagine: a city of glamorous decay, a place of neon and diamonds, of guns and money, a place at once glittering and dirty. Everything here bored Rey's uncle: the undulating countryside, the sharp teeth of the gray mountains, the scandalously blue sky. Most of all, the simple people, incapable of hatching plots against each other, or unwilling. Wholesome and therefore disappointing. "Why'd you come back, Uncle Trini?" Here Rey's beloved uncle always fell silent, as if under a spell.

"There was a woman," he'd say, and trail off. He'd fiddle with the keys to his kingdom, that empty cell. "There's always a woman."

Uncle Trini told stories and locked up the drunks that came in raving, the same ones who knew him by name, the ones who began all their confessions with the words: "I was minding my own business when . . ." It was part jail, part hostel for the hopeless drinkers, part psychiatric retreat for the colorful, if not criminal, elements of the town. And most nights, Rey rushed through his homework, walked the four blocks to the cramped little police station, and sat on the front step with his uncle. Together they waited for something to go wrong. The ordinary crimes of the countryside: purse-snatching was as common as the graceless theft of fruit from a market stall. Murders occurred twice each decade, usually the tragic finales to disputes over land, livestock, or women. The drunks. "Trini!" they'd protest when the sergeant brought them in, and Rey's uncle, impassive, would throw up his hands and unhook the keys from his belt loop. "Welcome back!" he'd say and smile despite himself. "Trini," the drunks would plead, but they knew it was no use, and Rey watched them hang their heads and stagger in, chastened. Later, after the sergeant left for the night, Trini would send Rey to the store for liquor, his nephew bounding through the empty streets to Mrs. Soria's all-night bodega, where you had to knock a certain way—*taptap tap tap tap*—before she would open the window and show her wizened face, squinting in the dim light: Who's there? It's me, madam. It's Rey. She'd hand him a bottle topped with a scrap of a plastic bag held tight by a rubber band, ah, the homemade stuff . . . Made in wooden vats and old bathtubs she kept in her courtyard, emitting odors her tenants grumbled about, the stuff that came out clear, stinking like poison, the stuff Trini drank, wincing, an involuntary spasm shutting his right eye. But Rey's uncle was a magnanimous drunk. He described the warm sensation in his chest, liquor's sweet embrace, described his mind under its influence as a tower built of loose, unmortared bricks, and he prattled on about the woman, the one who'd seduced him, whose ass was a most delicious thing, the one with blue eyes and a tiny scar on the side of her neck, which she covered with her curly, brown hair. She had ruined the city for him by getting pregnant.

She'd sent her brothers after him. "They beat me, boy," Trini said, still incredulous years later, "right in the middle of the street, in broad daylight. Me! A uniformed officer!" Rey listened, his uncle's words losing their borders to drink, syllables bleeding into each other. And the drunks gathered at the rusty bars of the cell to listen, to offer their condolences, their slurred and pithy advice: leave her, forget her, drink. Rey and Trini smiled. Trini's confessions, like those of his jailed charges, presupposed a circumstantial innocence, a helplessness, a purity of intent. He had a son—"I have a son," Trini shouted at the sky—somewhere in the city he'd been chased out of. After a few hours, Trini let his nephew take a shot—a small one—or pour a little in a plastic cup for the locked-up drunks, who had been stirred by the ammoniac smell of the stuff. Rey saw that the captives loved him in those moments. They took the drink with the reverence of the devout accepting Eucharist. He made them promise to be good. Rey made them swear. "Trini," they called out, "tell your nephew to quit torturing us." They drank, and the hours passed like this, until it was early morning. Rey's head spun, and he played with the radio until he got a scratchy signal, news from the capital or old Cuban songs or a show of weather predictions for Indian farmers. Eventually, everyone fell asleep, woozy, in their assigned places: the drunks on the cool floor of the cell, Rey and his uncle on the steps of the jail, the sky creeping toward orange, and day already breaking on the other side of the mountains.

And then, when he was thirteen, there was an explosion at the mayor's office, and, on the same night: the windows, the stones, the school. Rey and his friends had donned bandannas to cover their faces, nascent guerrilla tactics, like in the papers that came from the capital. Just that week, an arrest had been made, a man caught in a house full of weapons. He would spend a few years in prison, take advantage of an amnesty, and be released. Later, he would consolidate five disparate factions and form the IL, but no one knew that then. It had been big news in Rey's town, because the arrested man had spent part of his formative years there, before moving to the capital.

But really, who could worry about such things: wasn't there always someone trying to start a war in this country?

Under cover of night, Rey and his friends set out to prowl the streets. Stray dogs, here and there a bum resting in a doorway, the town asleep, the four boys raced down alleys. Rey and three friends—"Who? Which ones?" his father asked later on, but Rey wouldn't say. It didn't seem right to give them up. The town at the hour had seemed abandoned. It was easy to imagine that you owned it: every corner, every low-slung house, every park and park bench. The steps of the cathedral, the palm trees that listed gently west, the fields at the edge of town where the hungry mice scurried and stole grain. The whole of it—yours. It was easy to imagine you were the only ones in the streets, but you were wrong.

The school. There were no watchmen, only a wrought-iron fence held together with an ancient padlock. Easy to climb over. Later, "What did you do," his father asked him, "and why?" Rey's arms were bruised where the crowd had gotten hold of him, the tight clasping of hands and fists.

"I didn't do anything."

"Anything?"

Rey choked on a cough. Outside, the crowd clamored for justice. "I didn't do *that*," he clarified.

"Explain," his father commanded.

So he did: the boredom that had led to setting small fires in the field behind the clinic, the flames that had cast orange shadows over the gravelly earth, the smooth stones that had glowed in the firelight, and then, the target shining and obvious, calling them from the other side of town. The evening was clear and cool. It felt good to run with a pocketful of rocks. They stopped at Mrs. Soria's bodega—*taptap tap tap tap*—with coins they'd pooled together, and the liquor burned but they choked it down, closing their eyes as they swallowed, everything emerging jagged and blurry. "Why?" his father asked again, but Rey couldn't come to any conclusions about his own motives. He looked his father in the eye, a thirteen-year-old, still not sober three hours after his last swig, and felt something approximating pity, his father's black eyes like pools of oil, his father's graying hair, his face creased with disappointment, not a bad man, at least not at home. At school, he was a tyrant, of course, but in this sense, he was normal, no better or worse than any other headmaster. And Rey didn't hate school, at least not with the passion that his friends did.

"I don't know," Rey said. Is it possible to confess without acknowledging blame?

The fact was, he shouldn't have been caught at all. Rocks thrown at the school building on any other night? Harmless. A few windows shattered. What might have happened? Would anyone have thought to blame the son of the headmaster? There were dozens of poor kids from poor families, children with ashy knees and grim faces, who would have been blamed first. No one saw Rey. An elderly neighbor claimed to have spied four boys, but they were just shadows, laughing and carrying on. They could have been anybody. Then there was a flash of light and the boom: this changed everything. The explosion brought the army into town the next day. They came with guns, determined to find a culprit.

These things would come later, and still, that night, there was no reason to get caught. Rey and his friends raced to the plaza to see it. Curiosity, nothing more. His friends had disappeared into the crowd, hadn't they? Hadn't they drunk as well, weren't they in awe of the fire and as full of adrenaline? Why did you throw rocks at the school (in the end a meaningless crime, something that might have gone unnoticed on any other night), his father asked, but just as logically he could have said: Son, how did you turn the town against you? Why did you bring this all on yourself? On us?

Something important had happened. Rey knew it at once. The mayor's office was a small building, and when he arrived in the plaza, it seemed ready to collapse. Flame clung to the wooden roof beams. Glass had melted into yellow and red shapes, transfigured. Burning papers, burning chairs. Someone ran to tell the mayor. A plume of smoke curled into the sky, and there was heat. Everything had the air of urgency, of that long-wished-for, long-awaited trouble. And Rey was still drunk. He felt it in his breathing, in the strange glare of the fire. He felt shy and self-conscious. The fire crackled, and then the roof beam fell in a shower of embers. Smoke. The crowd gasped. Rey pulled his handkerchief up once again, resolved to find Trini, to share the excitement of this moment. His friends were gone, dispersed and disappeared, and Rey felt invisible at the peripheries of the crowd, but he was not. It took only a few moments for him to be spotted: ambling about unsteadily in the shadows of the plaza, wild-eyed, a dark bandanna covering his mouth and nose. As if terrorists dress this way! As if there were a uniform! But there he was, at the edge of the scene, looking very much the part.

Similar pictures had run that week on the front page of the newspaper—photographs of the arrested man in his youth—at a protest over school fees, and this was all it took.

"I'm innocent," he told his father later in the cell.

"You're stupid," his father said. "They think you tried to kill the mayor."

And in response, the town had nearly killed Rey, right there in the plaza. The tailor, who had made Rey his first suit, grabbed him by the arm and called out, "Here he is!" There was a struggle; the angry crowd surrounded him, his face still covered, and they yelled:

Arsonist!

Criminal!

Terrorist!

They didn't yet know who he was. The fire burned hot, and they puffed their chests out, a pack hungry for retribution. It was an instant, only an instant before his bandanna was removed, and then the crowd gasped again: the headmaster's son! A terrorist! They recognized his face, and he recognized theirs: the butcher with his heavy mustache; the mayor's secretary with her perpetually worried look; the stooped, old grounds-keeper, his leathery skin taut and gleaming. His town, the people who had raised him, aghast, betrayed. They surged at him, to eat him, Rey supposed; it was that kind of anger. He was an animal ready for slaughter. Just in time, Trini stepped out of the crowd, took his nephew away by the arm, led him ahead of the crowd, to the jail, the town parading behind the headmaster's captured son, certain they had found their terrorist.

YEARS LATER: the party where he met Norma, the evening he toyed with her. You don't know who I am, do you? They'd danced until the question had its own weight, until Rey himself was wondering who he was and why he had said it. Was he the boy who had stumbled into a crime, the boy who eventually fled the town for the city with his father and uncle? There was a drum and then a cymbal, a syncopated beat being broken and repaired. Who am I? What am I? Involved, he thought, I am involved. In what? Ah, he was asking himself too many questions. Dance, don't think. In things I can't talk about, not even to myself. Certainly not to her. A sympathizer? It sounded inessential and soft. Unimpressive. He watched her, her face in shadow, now in light. I am the vanguard, he told himself, and had to frown at the pomposity of the phrasing. Enough: the band played, and his feet moved, and he kept his eyes on her hips as they swayed. Can she see me? His hand was steady at her back. Music! Then they were on the bus, and then there was a roadblock, and in a moment of panic, he had given away all of his secrets, stuffed them in her pocket. She suspected nothing. He expected the worst.

He rode in the green truck that morning, forcing himself to think of his uncle Trini, of other, more hospitable jails. Trini would get him out of all this, would place a call to an old colleague. There were others in the truck, would they be as lucky? A bearded man in a wrinkled suit had the frazzled look of a man who had dressed quickly. Why would you wear a suit to jail? Rey wondered. A couple of young hardheads, stone-faced and bored. The younger one picked at his ear with his impossibly long pinky nail. The other practiced various poses of disinterest, staring into space as if his worst enemy were floating there, begging to be killed. A few ragtag students sat across from Rey, looking bewildered and drunk, undeniably scared. One of them had lost it, and he sobbed now into his hands. His ears had acquired an unearthly red color, as if they might start bleeding on their very own. No one comforted him. A soldier sat at the front end, rifle in his lap, rather unimpressed by the lot of them.

It was just before morning, the truck chortling through the vacant, predawn streets. Every pothole shook the old truck like a tremor, but even so, Rey managed to doze off. There was no curfew yet, but it was quiet at that hour. Rey had learned that night of the fire to mistrust quiet: somewhere, something was burning. Of course. Of course—because the army had come to his town the next day to ask questions. Because his friends hadn't come to his defense. Rey had assumed they'd come forward on their own, but they never did. They'd been afraid, or been told to keep quiet. Because Rey had spent that night asleep on the floor of the cell, wrapped in a blanket that left his feet exposed to the chill, his cheek on the dank floor of the jailhouse. He was a tall, lanky boy—a stupid boy, his father had said, but not a bad one.

When his anger had subsided, Rey's father said, "We'll have to leave, son."

The thought made Rey impossibly sad. "Where will we go?" he asked, but of course he knew the answer. The city, the city: it's where everyone went. They cried together, father and son, and then slept on the floor.

Like criminals. It was the only safe place in town for them. Trini let the drunks go so that father and son could have the cell to themselves.

The mayor, affable and corrupt, stood outside with a crowd behind him. Trini begged them all to go home, said that it would all be settled in the morning. And it was: the green army trucks pulled over the ridge, unloading a division of soldiers ready to speculate with guns about the origins of the fire. They poked around the ashes of the mayor's office and then through the home of the primary suspect, where even the soldiers remarked on his youth. The angry crowds hid in their homes, afraid to seem too interested, eager to let the authorities do their work. In Rey's home, the soldiers found a few books on unsavory topics, espousing points of view that had been deemed dangerous in the capital, though the decree had never made it to Rey's town.

They took Rey's father in for questioning. He was released a week later, with a few bruises and a broken rib. Hadn't Rey's father taught that arrested man, the one found in the city in a house full of weapons? And how is it that a young man from this town of upstanding citizens was transformed into a criminal? And who was responsible for such a tragedy? Everywhere there were rumors. The school board said it was a shame they had to let Rey's father go. They gave him two weeks to va-cate the house they had rented him, and planned a modest party, which none of the teachers attended. Rey went, dressed in his suit, prepared to say good-bye to his father's colleagues. He was seething. "They're afraid, son," Rey's father said. "Don't blame them."

Now Rey felt the jab of a rifle in his gut. "Wake up, lover boy." It was the soldier who had taken him off the bus. He was grinning.

Rey didn't have it in him to protest. His neck hurt, and his temples throbbed. Stepping out of the truck, Rey could see it was morning. They weren't in the city anymore, but in a completely empty place: a bleached, airless planet. The ground was brittle and flecked with glass, pockmarked with craters of all sizes that stretched ahead and all around him in the semidarkness. There were dunes and hills that he could just make out.

"Where are we?" Rey asked the soldier.

The soldier didn't respond.

"The Moon," said the bearded man in the wrinkled suit.

The prisoners were chained together in a group. "Walk straight ahead," one of the soldiers said, "exactly in the footsteps of the man in front of you."

The Moon is a minefield then, thought Rey. The man in the suit was chained in front of him, and he turned now, and smiled. He raised his chained hands and scratched his beard. "It's easy for me," he said. "I have small feet. It won't be so easy for you."

"I'll be okay," Rey said.

A shot rang out, not close by but somewhere in the distance. The procession paused for a second. There were the muffled, faraway sounds of people laughing.

"Have you been here before?" Rey asked the man in front of him.

The man bit his upper lip and nodded. "This is my second home."

They walked, enchained, toward the horizon.

FIVE

NORMA IS not a mother. Not in any sense, not remotely. In her apartment, there were two houseplants that could attest to this fact, houseplants whose dusty, dying leaves had bent hopefully and desperately toward light and were now in abject surrender, wilting and forgotten. She lived alone—not for herself, not selfishly, but alone. Her public life was the radio, where she was mother to an imaginary nation of missing people. Her private life was antiseptic and empty, a place for memory, music, and solitude. Norma, who was not a mother, couldn't comfort a child suffering from a toothache, or discipline one who had broken a piece of china. She couldn't brush tangled hair painlessly or sew a patch on the worn knee of a pair of pants. These things didn't come naturally to her. She had no pets: not a clumsy dog clawing at the door for her; not a tabby cat waiting to emerge languidly from behind a bed frame, to acknowledge her with yellow eyes and then slink away. There were no living things to make demands of her except her dying plants, not in her solitary apartment, not since Rey had vanished, no one who asked to be fed, or who needed to be washed, no one who awoke, sweating furiously and shouting, from adolescent nightmares.

There he was then, her first lesson: that morning, before dawn, Victor awoke with a scream.

It was torture to summon those kinds of emotions, the kind mothers routinely have: heart-swelling sentiments of selfless love. It was hard enough to pretend on the radio each Sunday. How could she do it now? Her impulse was to shut her door, to block out the sound—only the door was already closed. There was no escaping him: a human being, a child and his pain invading her space. She rubbed her bleary eyes and rose.

She found the boy still shaken, spent with the force of his yelling, heaving and panting, shirtless and thin, eyes red, looking every bit an animal liberated from a zoo. "Victor," she said. Norma felt she should touch him, but where? How? She put her hand on his head, and sat on the sofa—her sofa, hers and Rey's—and the boy melted into her. It was natural, instinct: he didn't hesitate at all. His hands clasped tightly around her. "It's all right," Norma said, "it was just a dream." It was a phrase she'd heard before, in a movie or on one of the radio soap operas.

He was breathing heavily, and the beating of his heart shook him from the inside. She could feel him trembling.

REY DISAPPEARED, and she didn't see him again for nearly a year. Norma took his ID card, with that strange, foreign-sounding name, and carried it with her. It felt dangerous to own it. She was curious. She should ask someone about it, she thought, one of their friends at the university, but just as quickly decided she couldn't. It would be some sort of betrayal. The man had secrets, and she suspected they were what made Rey's young face seem old. How dramatic it had all seemed, how exaggerated, the music and the lights and his absurd and self-important question. Then afterwards, once he had been taken away, the faces of the passengers on the bus, accusing her—rich girl, white girl, disturbing their morning commute with idiocies, putting all their lives in danger, teasing the soldier. It was somehow shameful, but what could she do now, he was gone, and Norma had only the memory of that night and a strange ID to remember him by. She was afraid to ask anyone if they had seen him or heard from him since the night of the party. She was afraid to tell anyone that he had been taken away, that she had seen it. In any case, she wasn't sure whom she should tell.

Norma kept quiet but found herself cultivating a fondness for Rey in his absence, even though she had only known him that one evening. Or perhaps that was why: it was as if she had seen him die—and what could be more intimate than that? What if hers was the last friendly face he saw? The last friendly touch? She thought of him at night, wondered when he might appear. She dreamed of marrying him, because it seemed the most romantic act possible. She thought of ways to inquire about him without raising attention: a note? A phone call? Every day the tension rose, and every day, at the university, she expected to find him there among the milling crowds, at the center of some circle of students, cigarette in hand, blithely holding forth about his brief imprisonment. What if she saw him? What if he asked for his ID? She daydreamed about this: I've been carrying it, she'd say. She would make sure to smile the way her mother had taught her, that way that her mother had sworn beguiles men without giving away too much. Her mother, the expert on men. Norma often came home from the university to find her alone, glassy-eyed, the radio serenading the empty house. "Your father is off carousing," she would slur. "He's abandoned me."

Norma would help her to the bedroom at the end of the hallway, undress her, and put her to bed, all the while repeating stories neither of them believed: "He's working late, mother. Don't be so suspicious, it'll make you old."

Other times, at the dinner table, Norma's father and mother spoke in curt monosyllables, and Norma played along. She did her best pantomime of pleasant family life until her eyes crossed and her thoughts slipped away from her, and there he was, Rey blowing smoke through the open window of the bus, smiling stupidly, unaware he was about to vanish. Pass the rice, her father would say, and it would take Norma a moment to place herself again. What's the matter with you? Nothing, Father. She would pass the plate with wobbly hands, her old man frowning and turning to her mother: You've spoiled this girl too much. And her mother would nod, meek in his presence, accepting blame for any and all errors, for the disappointing comportment of the girl on whose education they were wasting all that money. None of this had to be said; Norma knew it by heart, her father's cold logic, but preferred not to think of it, preferred to think of Rey, mysterious and brave, and not her home with its stillness and its tension and its secrets.

Later, when she and Rey were a couple, she told him that she'd thought of him while he was gone, before she even knew him, and wondered aloud why her mind had wandered in his direction. He grinned. "I'm irresistible," he said, as if stating a fact.

It was vanity, but she had to know: "Did you think of me?"

"Sure."

"Really?"

"It's an old story," he said.

They were near downtown, in a district called Idorú, outside a movie theater that only played Bollywood films, English-Bengali-Hindu monstrosities. It had been two years since the night they met, a year since Rey had reappeared. He was buying tickets, and now he led her inside. She reached for his hand. The theater played the same movie for two months or more, colorful epics that drew hordes of young girls for the choreographed dance routines, and swarms of teenage boys for the battles with ornate swords and sabers. "I can't understand Hindi," Norma whispered, but Rey explained there was no need for translation, that the stories were simple. And it was true: the villains were so recognizable they were met with whistles and boos every time they appeared on screen. The heroes were applauded boisterously, of course, and Rey joined in. He took her hands and clapped them together, and in the low darkness, she could see his smile. Norma was uncomfortable and hot, the theater was loud and smelled of sweat and liquor. On screen, the actors chattered incomprehensibly. "Why do you bring me to these places?" Norma whispered.

"Because they exist. Aren't you curious?"

The movie played continuously and the lights never came on. "All kinds of things happen here," Rey said, "and all kinds of people come." He was in the midst of educating Norma about her city. "You live too well," he'd told her importantly one day. "You don't know what this place is really like. I'll show you."

"That's cute, country boy. I was born here."

He'd insisted.

The theater, the dark guts of it, was something she'd never encountered. The people lit cigarettes and threw their butts at the screen, laughing, and the film was as impenetrable as the audiences' reaction to it: men sang, and women danced, exchanging glances heavy with longing. The audience cheered approvingly when a mustachioed rogue kidnapped a woman, and clapped again when the same man was killed. There were jeers whenever a kiss failed to materialize, and hoots at the svelte, doe-eyed lead, whose silken black hair shone with an otherworldly gilt. Arguments dissolved into song, and the audience came and went from the theater as if it were a waiting room, as if the film were an excuse and completely beside the point. The doors creaked open, washing the screen in pallid yellow light, and she found it hard to concentrate on anything in particular. Language was the least of it: a drunk strummed an out-of-tune guitar in the corner of the theater; in the darkness, a multitude of voices promised to kill him with it.

After an hour, Norma asked to go.

But Rey wasn't done. He walked her through the dense neighborhoods on the edges of downtown, past turn-of-the-century houses with peeling paint and glassless windows covered with thin, white sheets hooked on nails. Houses that looked like tombs, once-bright colors obscured by lay-ers of soot—finally, heads poking out, always a woman with fierce eyes, craning to see what was happening, what the noise was, who was com-ing up the street, who was leaving and with whom. Ornamented ladies, grim-faced men, loud packs of boys who wore their sneakers without laces, the tongues flapping out in some strange salute. Neighborhoods like these are networks of impulses, Rey said, human, electrical, biologi-cal, like the forest: in the summer, inexplicable carnivals of flesh; in the winter, blankets in the windows and darkened homes. It was winter that day. "They use candles," Rey said. "Like in the mountains."

If Norma had known the future, she might have said, "Like we all will, when the war comes to the city," but she couldn't know, so she didn't.

No one knew how bad it would get.

She clutched his hand and pressed close to him as they made their way down the crowded sidewalk. "What's the forest like?" she asked.

He considered her question, which she had asked more than once simply because she loved to hear him speak of it. "It goes on forever. It's endless invention, it's gaudy, it's gnarled trunks and rotting husks, sunlight peeking through the canopy, and bursts of rain hitting the roof of the forest like tapping on metal. And color, color, color."

"You don't sound like a scientist; you sound like a poet."

Rey smiled. "Can I be both?"

"But you'd rather be a poet."

"Who wouldn't?" he said.

They walked on, and Norma only wanted to talk about love. The sidewalks were dirty, and the gutters and the streets, and she was imagining the jungle as he described it: its vastness, its astonishing impurities, its beautiful people and their customs. She didn't want to see the city, not this part of it, not the ugly part. She was tired, and her feet ached, and on the other side of town, there were cafés and restaurants and parks where people wouldn't rob you. "Were you always like this?" she asked. "Don't you know how to treat a woman?"

"This is where we lived," Rey said, ignoring her, "when we first came to the city." He pointed at the second-floor window of a green house. "Don't you want to see it?"

"No," she said. "Not really."

His face fell into a sad smile. He was hurt.

"You look tired, honey," Norma said. "Let's go home." By home, she meant the room he rented near the university. She slept there some afternoons, into the early evening, then took a bus to her parents' house, crawled into her own bed, and stayed up thinking of him. Now Norma pulled close to Rey, stood on her tiptoes to kiss his temple. "Are you still having the nightmares?"

"Not so bad."

"When are you going to tell me," she said, "when are you going to tell me what they did to you?"

Now Rey frowned, then caught himself. "When we're married," he said.

NORMA HELD Victor until his breathing slowed. He looked at her with needy eyes, then shut them tight. "Are you okay?" Norma asked, but Victor didn't want to talk. He wanted to sleep again, he said, if he could. "Do you want me to stay here?" Norma asked, and the boy said he did. She lay beside him on the couch, he was thin, after all, and the two of them fit snugly. He buried his face in her side, and she let him be. After a while, Victor was asleep again. She'd wanted to ask him what he had dreamed, but somehow it seemed wrong. In a strange place among strange people, he had the right to private nightmares.

She rose again at daybreak. Without waking Victor, Norma made her way to the kitchen to brew some coffee. She turned on the radio, just low enough that she could hear the crackle and hum of the signal, the morning host's raspy voice reading the news. They would have to be at the station in a few hours, she and Victor, and God knows what would be waiting for them. Not for her, she was safe, for the boy. Elmer had promised a tearjerker. She looked back into the living room. The boy was still asleep. Even at this early hour, they were planning things for him, even as he slept. It's no wonder he was having nightmares; it must not be hard to sense your own helplessness. He must have known yesterday at the station, and later, when he darted off the bus. Poor boy, poor family, poor friends that had believed the lie of her affection and sent him here, sent him to her. How do you tell them it's a show? Lost City Radio is real, but not real. That honey-voice wasn't something she controlled, it simply was. The morning newsreader, her replacement, droned. He had no charisma. An emergency landing in Rome without casualties, a tropical depression threatening to erupt into a hurricane, the findings of a study about the causes of diabetes. She couldn't help but think of the ways her reading would have been different, better. Locally, there was nothing: potholes filled with great fanfare, ribbon-cutting ceremonies planned for newly painted buildings, a famous writer caught with a prostitute down by the docks. In Miamiville, an overnight fire had destroyed a house, leaving seventeen people homeless. Faulty wiring, the newscaster read. Then he cleared his throat, moving on—had she heard right? Norma was struck with the image of a smallish house in that district, expelling seventeen people from its flaming shell. Seventeen people? she thought. She sipped her coffee and counted them on her fingers: a father, a mother, four kids, a grandmother who spoke only the old language, an uncle, an aunt, four more kids, a cousin just visiting with his sometime girlfriend, a distant great-aunt's favorite nephew and his pregnant wife, and how many more? An entire village would be on the sidewalk now, on the streets, Norma thought. They would sleep in the park, all of them, or on the rocky beaches with whatever blankets they had salvaged, with whatever trinkets to remind them of the life they'd once had. It made Norma shudder. They'd shake off the ashes and stay together, they have to: once separated, a family can never be made whole again, not here. They'd disappear like trash scattered in the breeze.

Norma's own family wasn't like that, no extended lineages or childhood memories crowded with cousins. No one to disappear on her. Her recollections of family were oppressively small: just her and her parents. She could count their dislike for one another as a separate person, a monster that stalked them, or she could count them each twice: the people they were together—disfigured, unhappy, resentful—and those they might have been if they had not married each other. Or, if she were really intent on expanding the family tree, she could count her father's mistresses as well. There were a dozen of these well-dressed, dark-haired women Norma's mother hated and envied, and Norma simply hated. They came and went, changed names and faces, but Norma was aware of them always: their perfume, her father's guilty grin.

Only Rey had a smaller family: he was the only one left. His mother had died so young Rey scarcely remembered her at all, and Rey's father, he'd told her, died a few years after they moved to the city. No brothers or sisters. Rey had lived with his uncle Trini after that. But who knew really? He played tricks with the past; he always had. If he is alive, she thought, he might still be at it, even now. That cold, dreary day at the door of his first home in the capital, Rey had insisted they knock, just to see. Norma hadn't been so sure.

"Do you remember anybody from the block?" Norma asked. "Will they remember you?"

He shrugged. "I'll tell them I used to live here. It's no big deal." He seemed sure that it would be enough. "That, plus my smile, plus this beautiful young lady."

Norma blushed. The steps creaked as they climbed to the second-floor landing.

Rey made her knock. The door was old, made of wood that had swelled and shrunk and aged with decades of summer heat and humid winters. It was somehow illicit, her being there, on the wrong side of town, knocking on a stranger's door, visiting the museum of her lover's early life. She kissed Rey; she knocked again. On the other side, Norma could hear a slow shuffling of feet and the metallic click of a few locks. It seemed the door was about to open, but there was a pause. "Yes?" a voice called out. It was the airy, weak voice of an old man. "Who is it?"

There was silence. Rey grinned, but he didn't say anything. Norma elbowed him. "Come on," she whispered. Hadn't he dragged her up here?

"Who is it?" the old man repeated, confusion in his voice. Rey made a show of zipping his lips. Norma could feel herself turning red, aghast at the rudeness of it. She wanted to laugh. "Say something!" she hissed, but he cupped his hand to his ear as if she were calling him from far away.

She cleared her throat and was about to speak, but Rey covered her mouth with his hand.

"Father," he said. "It's me, Rey."

MIDMORNING FOUND Norma and Victor in the control room, wearing ancient headphones, listening to the sounds of actors straining to imitate the jungle accent. A string of them had come and gone. They had plied Victor with candy and pastries and toured him around the station as if he were royalty. Everything else seemed to have been quickly forgotten. Still, here they were, the red lights on the console rising and falling to the rhythms of the actors' voices, Len in the sound booth, furiously typing out his inimitably melodramatic scripts. Elmer surveyed the room the way a duke might observe his duchy. Behind the smudged glass, a sad-looking man read about leaving his village to work on the dam, only to have it destroyed in the war. He was an actor, of course. "Bombs!" he shouted. "The sound drowned—" He stopped and coughed into his hand. "Is this right?" he asked. "It doesn't sound right. Who wrote this?"

Norma cringed. They were on the fifth or sixth take. The actor had Shakespearean training, or so his résumé claimed. Each time he finished, he looked up hopefully at Len, who looked at Elmer, who shook his head. Next take. Norma took her headphones off and sighed. Elmer let the smoke filter from his open mouth. He looked bored. His brown suit was worn to a dull sheen at the knees and elbows. Victor seemed to be enjoying himself though, laughing and even correcting the actor when he mispronounced a word. Now, with her headphones off, Norma felt the true absurdity of it:

the actor dove into another take, looking down intently at his text, reading soundlessly behind the glass. Halfway through, Elmer was already shaking his head no. Len tapped the feckless actor on the shoulder. The man put his paper down, and left the sound booth, dejected. Victor laughed.

"The promo's on in thirty," called Elmer on the intercom after the actor had been shown out. Len clapped twice. Victor had been told not to touch anything, but he'd never seen a place like this, and obviously his own curiosity was strangling him. He interrupted a few takes by pushing the wrong button. He apologized, everyone except the actor laughed, and then a few minutes later, Norma caught Victor staring at another blinking light, as if daring himself to touch it.

"It's like a helicopter," he'd said over and over when they first showed him in. He'd seen them floating in the skies above the village, he said. Drug eradication programs, Norma supposed. He'd drawn a picture and asked his teacher what they were. "There's an Indian word for it, but I wanted to know the *real* word."

"What was the Indian word?"

Victor thought for a moment. "I can't remember," he said.

Now the boy played. She could see it in his eyes: the station was a chopper, this control room speeding around the nation, over valleys and rivers, along its coastline and over its deserts. She was dreaming with the boy, and it made her happy to see him distracted. He seemed suddenly young for his age—or was it only that yesterday he had seemed so old?

Len tuned in the station. A commercial for detergent faded out, the sounds of children playing. They all settled in to listen. There was a crackle as it began, then the plaintive sound of a violin emerging from a low, gravelly rumble. The voice-over began:

This Sunday on Lost City Radio … From the jungle comes a boy … To tell a story you won't believe … It will touch your heart … Bring you to tears … Bring you joy and hope … Hear the harrowing tale of his journey … By foot to the city … And the dreams that brought him here … Can Norma help him find his loved ones … ? This Sunday, on a very special Lost City Radio …

Here the violin gave way to nature sounds, birds chirping, water bubbling steadily over smooth stones, and then, the boy's trembling voice, saying simply: "My name is Victor."

Len clapped. Victor beamed.

"Bravo!" said Elmer. "Norma?"

"It's fine," she said. "There's nothing wrong with it."

"Are you kidding? He did it in one take! The boy's a natural."

Victor fiddled with a knob on the console, and a wave of sound streamed from the speakers, then disappeared. They all turned to the boy. "I didn't walk," he said.

"Of course you didn't walk." Elmer scratched his forehead and lit another cigarette.

Norma stood up and pushed her chair to a corner of the small control room. "It's not even possible, is it?"

"It sounds fine," said Len.

Elmer cleared his throat and sent the boy out with the promise of food just beyond the door. Victor rose without complaint. Len turned the volume down and followed the boy out. The door swung closed behind them.

"What's wrong, Norma?" Elmer asked once they were alone. There was a low buzz from the speakers, like the sound of a balloon deflating. Elmer ran his fingers through his hair. Norma didn't say anything right away. He loosed his tie and undid the top button of his shirt. "Talk," he said. "I'm listening."

"I'm tired." Norma slumped back into her chair. "I'm no good at this. He woke up crying this morning."

"Children cry, Norma. What can you do?"

"That's it exactly. I don't know." She bit her lip. Rey used to cry the same way, used to wake up in a sweat, a fever, a fit. Those nightmares.

"This show bothers you?" Elmer said. He pulled off his suit jacket and draped it over the console, burying the little red lights.

"He didn't walk, Elmer. And we can't send him back. We can't trick him."

"Norma, you know how this works."

"Promise me." She looked him in the eye. In spite of it all, he had a kind face, round and pudgy, an almost featureless softness to it. When he smiled, as he did now, his cheeks bulged, his eyes shrank to a squint. He'd aged, but they'd been friends. Once, on a day when her sadness had been so profound she could scarcely speak, Norma had even allowed him to kiss her. It was after the prison, when everything was lost. This was years ago and so far in the past she could barely remember it.

"I'll try," Elmer said.

"Thank you."

He stood up, fumbled through his pockets for a cigarette. "What will you do with him?" he asked. "Does he talk?"

"A bit," Norma said. "He seems nice enough."

"Careful he doesn't steal anything."

Norma smiled. "What is there to steal? You don't pay me enough."

"Complain to the government, not to me," said Elmer, cigarette dangling from his lips. "I can't do anything, Norma, you know that." He offered her a smoke, but she shook her head.

"Let me look for his people," she said. "I'll take the list and go."

Elmer looked up. "Why?"

"He ran off last night. Got off the bus and ran into a neighborhood down by The Cantonment. Can you imagine how scared he must be?"

"He didn't seem scared in here."

"Elmer, you're not even listening to me. He woke up screaming this morning."

They were quiet for a moment. Elmer scratched his head. "What did I promise you? A day off?"

"Two."

"Have you looked at the list?"

"No," she said. "Have you?"

"Haven't had time." He sighed. "We have nothing on these people, you know? Not even districts. Just names. I could guess that they're scattered somewhere in Newtown, but beyond that, who knows?"

The city was an unknowable thing, sprawling and impenetrably dense, but there were nearly sixty names on the list, and some of them must be alive.

"I'll have to run it by legal, of course. Vet all the names first," he said.

"Of course."

They were interrupted by a rap at the window. Victor had entered the recording booth through the side door. Len stood behind him. The boy waved. Elmer and Norma waved back.

Elmer pressed the intercom button. "How you doing there, kiddo?"

Victor grinned. Len gave a thumbs-up. His voice crackled back a few moments later. "He wants to know when we can leave."

Elmer smiled at Norma and hit the intercom. "Where does he want to go?"

The boy gave a soundless answer, and then Len was back on: "Everywhere. He says he wants to go everywhere."

"Isn't that something?" Elmer said to Norma.

"It's great." She could see the boy was happy. "It's wonderful."

"It's progress," Elmer said. "Go on, Norma. Do what you want. It's not what I had in mind."

"What did you have in mind?"

"I'm not sure exactly. I'm tired of seeing you sad. That's all. I thought this might be good for you. You've been in a rut."

"It's not like giving me a puppy, Elmer. He's a child."

"I know he is." Elmer leaned closer. "I thought it might shake you up a bit. I saw 1797 and I thought of you. What can I say?"

"Nothing. You can't say anything. You never can."

"What are you talking about?"

She stopped. "I don't know."

He threw up his hands. "Norma, can I tell you something?" He sighed. "When I say I care about you, it's because I do. That's all. Now, you want to look for his family, that's fine. Live your life."

"Thank you."

Then Elmer asked for the list. She had it, didn't she? While she searched her pockets for the scrap of paper, Elmer turned back to the intercom. "Bravo," he said. "You're a good boy."

In the recording room, Victor flexed his biceps.

IT WAS Rey's own fault if she had a hard time letting go. He was into disappearing acts. Before her very eyes, a gun-wielding soldier pulls him off a bus. He resurfaces a year later; "the Moon" is all he says when she asks where they took him. And then, at the door of a second-floor apartment in a squat, green building at the western edge of downtown, Rey resurrects his own father, whom he had perversely killed off, just like that. Why? These things stayed with her, formed into solid structures in her mind: My husband can venture into a war zone and return unharmed. He can, he has, he does, he will again. The dead come back to life. He exists outside death. A strange faith to have, certainly, but was it Norma's fault?

Rey's father opened the door and looked his son up and down. Norma stood at one side, feeling uneasy. "Is that you?" the old man whispered. "Is it?"

"It's me, Father," Rey said, and the old man seemed not to believe it, seemed not to trust his eyes at all. He reached out and touched Rey's face, the slightly crooked nose, the dimpled smile, the heavy brow. Rey pushed into his father's touch the way a housecat might. Norma turned away, suddenly embarrassed, focusing instead on the water-stained wall.

The apartment seemed hardly big enough for one. Everywhere there were stacks of papers rising from the floor, each crowned optimistically with a palm-sized stone to hold everything in place. There were dictionaries everywhere, on the desk, on the coffee table: French-Wolof, English-Russian, Spanish-Hebrew, Quechua-Catalan, German-Portuguese, Italian-Dutch. Norma and Rey sat on the sofa, its springs poking uncomfortably through the fabric, and waited for the old man to bring water. Norma listened to the complaints of the old pipes, a gurgling, groaning sound from deep within the walls. She turned to Rey. "You're a piece of shit," she said.

He smiled and nodded in agreement, but she wasn't joking. She couldn't grasp the callousness of it: to present his father as dead, then to spring him on her like this?

The old man's eyesight was failing, but he maneuvered expertly through the apartment. The tray hardly trembled in his hands, and he spilled no water. Rey cleared a spot on the coffee table and, after the old man had refused space on the couch and sat instead atop a pile of newspapers, they each took their mason jar of water and raised it in a toast. "To reunions," the old man said. They were quiet for a moment, sipping the turbid tap water. Then Rey's father coughed into his wrinkled hand. The room was dim and moldering. "Where have you been?" he said to his son. "Waiting for me to die?"

There was an odd silence between the three of them. Rey sat still, as if considering what his father had said. Norma blinked away a fly that had landed on her face.

"Well, don't let's start there," the old man said, laughing, and he waved away the question, as if scattering smoke or fog, as if it had meant nothing at all. His face was yellowed and tired, his few hairs combed straight back. His bald pate was severe and pale. "Are you well, son?"

Rey nodded.

"I get by," the old man said. "And thanks for asking. Do you see your uncle?"

"Now and again."

It was an interview, and Norma was superfluous. The old man had barely acknowledged her, and Rey hadn't introduced her. She sat, trying to be invisible, while father and son stared each other down, ping-ponged questions at one another: studies, health, money, distant family ties.

When they seemed to run out of topics, the old man pulled a pack of cigarettes from a drawer and offered them around. Rey took one, and then the two of them were smoking. They held their cigarettes the same way, between their second and third fingers. It looked odd. "You should quit, son," the old man said.

"I will. You should too."

The old man nodded. "So who is this pretty young lady?"

"This is Norma."

The moment called for a smile; Norma did her best. The old man nodded and tipped an imaginary hat. Then he placed his hands in his lap and said, "Child, you deserve better than my derelict son."

"Don't fill her head with ideas," Rey snapped.

"Has he told you?"

"Told me what?" Norma asked.

"That they took him to the Moon." The old man eyes were gleaming. He shifted on his pile of newspapers, gave her a wry smile. "My son is a wanted man," he said.

"That's why I don't visit you, Father," Rey said, shaking his head. "You talk crazy."

"But how long has it been since you saw each other?" Norma asked. As soon as the words were spoken, she regretted getting involved.

They both shrugged, together, as if on cue. "Not so long," Rey's father said. "A year. He lived here when he came back. Have you told her?" he asked again.

"Came back?"

"From the Moon," Rey said.

"I know they took him," Norma said. "I was there. It was two years ago."

"You were at the Moon? How romantic: you met my boy at the Moon?"

"No, sir."

"My son, the terrorist," the old man muttered. "It's what you get for talking loud in this country."

"But I was there when they took him," she said. Her most private memory: the bus, the vanishing. The long weeks of waiting, of falling in love with a stranger. "I——"

"We're getting married," Rey said, interrupting her. "Norma is my fiancée."

Norma shot Rey a fierce glance. He pinched her leg.

"Aha!" the old man exclaimed, putting his water down. He clapped and smiled like a child presented with a new toy. "I knew there was a reason you came!"

There was hardly any air in the apartment, and barely any light. The smoke had gathered in clouds at the ceiling. Married? The old man seemed genuinely delighted, watching intently as Rey pushed the table away from the dilapidated couch. He bent down on one knee. Norma looked at Rey, at the old man, puzzled, dismayed. Then Rey was speaking, and this was exactly as she hadn't pictured it: in a cramped apartment on the wrong side of town, in winter, in front of an old man risen from the dead. "Norma," he was saying, "will you be my wife?" It had been two years since they'd met, and the time had passed so quickly. Rey grinned wildly, the old man clapped, and the totality of it was too strange.

"Yes," she said, scanning back and forth between Rey and his father. It was the only answer that occurred to her. The walls looked as if they might cave in. Rey's father was up again. "Spirits," he called. "A drink!" Norma examined the simple silver ring Rey had just placed around her finger. "Is this just a show?" she asked. "For him?"

"It's for us," Rey said.

The old man came back with a bottle of clear liquor, emptied his water into a potted plant that stood wilting next to a stack of books, and beckoned Rey and Norma to do the same. He poured them both generous shots and again proposed a toast. "If only your mother was alive. Have you told Trini?" Rey's father said. He was talking fast, very nearly running out of breath. The old man was excited. "When will you have the ceremony?"

"We don't know, Father."

The old man squinted. "Will I be invited?"

"Of course!" Norma said.

"Of course," Rey added.

Things were happening that Norma didn't understand. The old man poured some liquor onto his handkerchief, and cleaned the lenses of his glasses with it. "Let me see that ring," he said. Norma held her left hand out, and the old man shook his head. "I see your career is not so lucrative, son."

"I should have been a poet like you," Rey said, and the old man laughed. They raised their glasses again, and everyone smiled.

"But child," the old man said, turning to Norma, suddenly serious. "If you're smart, you won't take this name of ours."

"What do you mean, sir?"

The old man and his yellow skin; the old man and the crooked teeth of his yellow smile. His lonely, wrinkled face. The room full of smoke. "This is no time to play dumb, child."

"Don't listen to him," Rey said. "My father's talking crazy."

In the control room, years later, Elmer scanning the list: "Norma," he said abruptly. "We have a problem."

"I love you, Norma," Rey said.

Those nightmares, Rey, where do they come from? What did they do to you?

"Our name is tainted, child." The old man bit his lip and looked down. "I did my part, and my son has done his. I promise you: you don't want it."

"And I love you, Rey."

The boy rapped on the window. He pressed his face to the glass and puffed his cheeks out. He was a beautiful boy.

"Norma, I'm sorry," Elmer repeated, "but we have a problem."

PART TWO

SIX

ELIJAH MANAU was a rosy-cheeked man from the capital, and had been living in 1797 for six months when the soldiers came. He was a timid man, and not without reason. To be exiled here to teach in this humid backwater was a testament to his consistent mediocrity. He had scored near the bottom on the regional placement exam, well below the cutoff for a job in the city at one of the better schools. The dispiriting results were announced on the radio a few nights after the test, in alphabetical order. It took several hours. His family was neither wealthy nor well connected, and so nothing could be done. He was thirty when he left home. He had never been to the jungle before. In fact, he had never left the city.

Manau carried with him the shame of an exposed man who had imagined his mediocrity to be a secret. It was dawning on him that he may have become the failure his father had always predicted he would be. The town, his new home, was perpetually soggy and heat-swollen. The rains came and brought little relief. He rented a room from a man named Zahir, who had lost both hands in the war. Zahir's son, Nico, was an unwilling student, seemed to distrust his teacher and housemate. Sometimes Manau helped them tend to their small plot, but in truth, he had no skill for it. The earth held no romance for him. Manau longed for concrete and everything else he had left behind. Nico's crippled father dug holes with his stumps, he carried heavy loads on his back, balancing rucksacks on his broad shoulders with help from his son. The man was a rock. At night, Manau listened to the mosquitoes thrumming in the humid air, to the distant cawing and various shrieks the jungle produced and, with his thin curtain drawn, he checked his naked body for the progress of the sores and rashes that were always afflicting him. It was his daily chore, an exercise in personal hygiene that had devolved into a strange kind of vanity. The pitiable condition of his person played a central role in his sexual fantasies. To be nursed back to health! To be massaged and anointed in fruit essences, in herbal potions! With a cloudy shaving mirror and the kerosene lamp, he examined himself—the carbuncular skin blossoming on his back and buttocks, beneath his armpits—and was satisfied that one day soon, he would look pathetic enough to stir something soft and generous in a woman's heart. In the city, it was assumed that the heat made jungle women freer, and the prospect of these unknown women, their bronzed and beautiful legs spread wide, had, in fact, been Manau's only consolation when he was informed of his teaching assignment.

Most mornings, after the rains, Manau arrived to the school early, to sweep the puddles away. The roof leaked, and there was nothing to be done about it. At the very least, he could be grateful for the raised wooden floor of the schoolhouse. Zahir said it would have to be replaced in a few years, but for now, it was fine: able to withstand, with a minimum of creaking, Manau's unhappy pacing. The government had seen fit to send fifteen primitive desks where his students sat diffidently, waiting to be entertained—twenty had been promised, but an official in 1791 kept five for himself, and no one complained, so neither did Manau. He taught cheerlessly every morning, and sent his students home for lunch a bit earlier each day. They were all primitives. Manau had hoped to be seen as a knowledgeable and cultured gentleman from the city, but instead they were amused by his ignorance of trees and plants, disappointed by his inability to distinguish between the calls of various birds. "I don't care about birds," he said one day, and to his surprise, the words came out angrily.

It wasn't that the children disliked him. Manau was inoffensively boring, taught listlessly, but he let them out early, on some days canceled class altogether, and no one seemed to mind. The day that the soldiers arrived in a pair of rusty, creaking green trucks, Manau was quick to call off school: there was an excitement in his students' faces that he couldn't compete with. He'd written some rules about fractions on the blackboard. He had never liked arithmetic. Outside, the engines rattled, and the soldiers set up tarps in the plaza. It was, he would later learn, the first time in more than a year that the soldiers had come. The presence of outsiders was electric and disconcerting. Eyes were wandering. Manau heard anxious fingernails scraping against the desks. It was no use. Go out into the streets, he ordered, learn about life! He smiled proudly as the schoolhouse emptied, as if, by dint of laziness, he had stumbled upon a new pedagogy, an educational masterstroke. His students left, all of them except Victor, whom he asked to stay.

In Manau's visions, it was Victor's mother, a widow, who would eventually take him in. She was older, he knew that, but with these jungle people, one could never tell. In his time in the village, Manau had learned a little of her past: she had fallen in love before with a stranger from the city, who had disappeared into the jungle at the end of the war. People said he was dead. So she was a free woman, and wasn't Manau also a stranger from the city? The possibilities were quite obvious. But what stirred Manau most was what he could see: she was a real woman, with substantial thighs and a pleasing weight to her. She wore her black hair tied with a red band, and her smallish mouth seemed always ready to break into a smile. She was doe-eyed, a hint of pink in her cheeks. Her name was Adela.

Now the classroom had cleared, and her boy stood before him, waiting. "Victor," he said. "Was your father a soldier?"

The boy looked baffled. In fact, Manau wasn't sure himself why he had asked it. Only recently had his isolation become so stark, so complete, that he had resolved to do something about it. He saw her every day in the village, carrying a tray of silver fish on her head. Her undersized boy sat in the first row, next to Zahir's son. Manau saw them; they were there—all he had to do was speak.

"No, sir," Victor said. "I don't think he was."

"Oh." Manau nodded. The boy was anxious to leave, swiveling his head every few moments toward the door. "Do you want to be a soldier?" Manau asked.

"I don't know, sir."

"It would break your mother's heart if you left."

"Do you know my mother, sir?" the boy asked very politely.

Manau suddenly felt the red skin beneath his clothes awaken in complaint. He steeled himself against the urge to itch. "I do," he said.

"Oh."

"But not well," Manau added. "Not well."

Insinuating a woman through her child, thought Manau, what a despicable and cowardly thing to do! He wanted to be done with it. From his bag, he produced a new lead pencil. He offered it to Victor, and the boy took it without hesitation. Manau meant to send the boy off, but Victor coughed into his hand and asked permission to speak. When Manau assented, the boy said, "Sir, how old were you when you left home?"

"What a strange question!"

"I'm sorry, sir."

Manau stood, and wondered what he might say. Was it a trip around the world at age twelve, a stowaway in the hold of a ship headed north? Could he lie and say he'd been to the other side of the continent, or farther—to Africa? Might he say, I have seen the grand cathedrals of Europe, the skyscrapers of New York, the temples of Asia? Of course, by leaving home, the boy meant something completely different. Seeing the world was incidental: if you were born in a place like 1797, leaving was what you did to begin your life.

"I'm from the city, boy. We don't have to leave."

Victor nodded, and Manau was aware that what he had said was terrible, cruel, and untrue. In the city, like here, the children dreamed of escape.

"I'm thirty years old and I've only just left my home," Manau said. "Why?"

The boy bit his lip, shot a glance toward the door and then back at his teacher. "It's Nico," he said. "He's always said he would leave with the soldiers. He says he doesn't care if his family starves without him."

Manau nodded. His landlord had often confessed that fear: "Without Nico's hands, we'll go hungry. What can I do with these stumps?"

"Why is it your business?"

"Somebody should do something," Victor said. "He's my friend."

"You're a good boy," Manau said. He thanked Victor, patted him on the shoulder, and told him not to worry. "I'll talk with his father." He led the boy to the door and watched him scamper off to join his friends. The teacher returned to his desk, straightened some papers, then erased the board with a wet rag. Outside, the boys hovered around the soldiers, entranced. Soon their mothers would come to shoo them away, to send them into the jungle to hide. But that fear was old-fashioned, and the children knew it. When he strolled by on his way, Manau saw in their eyes looks of excitement, looks no student had ever shown him.

LATER, WHEN his mother died and he left 1797, Victor would remember this day as the beginning of the village's dissolution. Nico spoke of leaving, and Victor worried. The two of them watched the soldiers, admired them from a distance and then up close, brought water and fruit when they were told to. After an hour, Nico asked one soldier where he was from. The young man looked barely eighteen. He gave a number and said it was in the mountains. Victor and Nico nodded in unison.

"How can you boys stand this heat?" the soldier said, scowling, his face flush. He sat slumped and sweating beneath the shade of the tarp.

"We can't," Nico said. "We hate it here."

The soldier laughed and called over a few of his friends. "They hate it here too," he said, and everyone agreed they were smart boys.

Victor didn't hate it. He watched his friend enumerate the town's shortcomings for the soldier and felt ashamed. There's no work, Nico said, but that wasn't exactly true: all anyone did was work. Nico said there was nothing to do, but Victor still considered climbing trees an activity. All Nico's complaints sounded cruel, uncharitable. In the afternoon, they would go swimming in the river—that's how we stand the heat, he wanted to say. And it's great. It's beautiful. The water is cool and murky, and at the bottom you can plunge your toes into the cold mud, feel it close around your feet, suctioning like it wants to drown you. The thought of it made him smile. You come out clean. But he didn't say any of this. Nico spoke with such confidence that to contradict him seemed almost dangerous. He listened in silence until the young soldier eyed him and said, "What about you, little man? What do you have to say?"

The soldier pointed with a thin, bony finger. Victor looked quickly over his own shoulder, and everyone laughed.

Just then, the mothers arrived and hurriedly dispersed their children. His own mother was there, and she glared at the soldier. "Shame," she said, and the soldier backed away, as if from a wild animal.

"I'm fine, Ma," Victor muttered, but it was no use. She wasn't listening. The mothers were taking turns shouting at the soldiers; the children hung their heads and listened. Victor's mother held his hand tightly; her voice rose above everyone else's. There she was, with an accusing finger drawing circles in the air, upbraiding the captain. "What do you want with our boys?" she said. "Can't you see they're all we have?"

The captain was a burly giant of a man with wide, round eyes and a mustache flecked with gray. As Victor's mother spoke, he nodded apologetically. "Madam," the captain said when she was finished. "My sincerest apologies. I will instruct my soldiers to avoid speaking with your boys."

"Thank you," Victor's mother said.

"Do you hear that, men?" the captain shouted.

A round of *yessirs* came from the enlisted men. They stood at attention out of respect for the women.

The apologies continued. As the captain spoke, he twirled his cap by the bill. "I'm afraid we have sullied relations with the people of this fine village," he said, shaking his head. "We are only here to help. It is our solemn mandate."

The women all nodded, but Victor knew the captain was only addressing his mother. He could see it in the man's eyes. She squeezed his hand, and Victor squeezed back.

"I assure you we want nothing with your boys, madam," the captain continued, his lips curling into a smile. "It's this town's women who are so beguiling."

• • •

THAT EVENING, the canteen was crowded with soldiers. They were stripped down to their undershirts, had taken off their boots and laid them in a pile by the door. The heat that day had been an animal thing: scalding, heavy. The entire village had given in to its weight, with the evening set aside for recovery. A breeze blew now and again through the open windows of the canteen. Inside, it smelled of feet and beer. The soldiers were drinking the place dry, singing along to the radio. The wooden floor was shiny and slick. Manau was feeling gloomy, sharing liter bottles with a few disaffected, unhappy men. They grumbled about the dwindling beer supply and the thirsty soldiers. There was only one glass, so they drank in circles. "Who do these brats think they are?" Manau heard a man complain. "They'll leave us with nothing."

It was a real concern among the regulars. Periodically, someone offered the soldiers a rueful smile and a toast, then mumbled curses under his breath.

Nico's father arrived, placed his stumps on the bar, and confirmed their worst fears. It would be ten days before the next truck came. "That's if the roads aren't washed out," Zahir added. He knew the delivery schedules well. Whenever the beer truck or any other truck came, he lent his broad back to the driver for loading and unloading. He had a special cart that clasped around his chest so that he could be useful even without his hands.

Manau nodded at his landlord, at the gathered men, and felt tolerated. Nothing builds community like complaining. He looked Zahir in the eye and knew there was something he should tell him. What if Nico were to leave? Victor had spoken of it as a child would: without nuance, certain of right and wrong. "He doesn't care if his family starves without him," Victor said of his friend, horrified. Manau didn't see it so clearly: what a place this is to grow into adulthood! No one would starve—even Zahir must know that! Of course, the boy wanted to leave. He was the oldest boy in the school by nearly two years. He had celebrated his fourteenth birthday a few months before, on a dismal, rainy day, surrounded by children who barely reached his shoulders. All the boys his age had gone off to the city. Let them, Manau thought. Let Nico go, too. It struck Manau as comic: the slow disappearance of the place, the boarded-up houses all along the streets off the muddy plaza. Padlocked, shuttered, rotting inside. Their owners don't visit, they don't send money. It won't be long now; soon they'll stop pretending, pack up en masse, and close the town for good. They'll say a prayer, turn their backs on this place, and let the jungle surround it, colonize it, disassemble it.

After the mothers came to scatter their children, a few parents had come to Manau to complain: How is it that you let them go? Why on this day? The mothers were desperate that their children stay, because mothers are the same everywhere. What if they leave us? Manau's mother had been worried for her child as well, had stayed up with him the night he listened nervously for his score on the radio. She had wept when it was announced; she knew what it meant. Where will they send you? she'd asked. Now here he was. Manau had felt for a while the unreality of his own actions. Nothing had the weight, the shape, or the color of real life: it was what allowed him to observe his naked, degraded body with amused detachment; to imagine, with eyes closed, Adela loving him on the creaking wooden slats of her raised hut near the river. It was what allowed him to glare now at the captain across the fetid, smoky canteen, without fear, certain that no matter what he might say or do, the town's demoralized men would back him up. He hummed along to the radio, felt the distant beating of his own heart, and smiled to himself.

Outside, Victor, Nico, and a few other boys stood on plastic crates, looking through the window at the canteen. Nico's sister, Joanna, was there, with a friend, teasing the boys. "Monkeys," the girls pronounced. "No minds of your own." The boys shrugged off the charge. Nico had been at it all day, stalking the soldiers around town, even following a few who went off into the jungle on a reconnaissance exercise. He returned, not a little disappointed, and told Victor that they hadn't fired their guns.

"Not even once," he said.

The canteen was bursting with noise and life. It was such an odd sight: these fifteen strangers, and in the background, a few of the regulars nearly hidden behind a curtain of smoke. Someone sang tunelessly, the melody soon eclipsed by whistles and laughter. Victor stood on his tiptoes to take it all in. Was that his teacher there, now turned away, now smirking toward the soldiers? The captain who had smiled at Victor's mother sat in the center of a circle of soldiers, their eyes glistening with reverence. He told war stories that contained no corpses, no dead: only long stretches of marching with guns at the ready. "Nothing to shoot at. Just walking. Enough to wear out two pairs of boots. Enough to rot your feet."

"You never found a battle?"

"The jungle is endless," he said. "We called our squadron leader Moses. We were the wandering tribe."

Victor strained to see. Nico, by contrast, could rest his elbows on the ledge. Still, Victor could hear all of it, and now he looked at his friend, unimpressed by these mundane accounts of the soldiering life. "*That's* what you want to do?" he asked. "Walk around?"

Nico shrugged. "What do you know about anything?" he said. "There's no war anyway."

"It sounds stupid."

"You sound stupid," Nico snapped. "At least they go places."

Victor punched him in the arm, and his friend tumbled off his crate. He hadn't meant to do it. The other boys stepped back, hushed.

Nico stood up. One of the younger boys started to wipe the dirt off his back, but Nico slapped his hand away. He was smiling. "An accident, huh?" Nico said.

"Yeah."

"You're good at those, aren't you?"

Victor didn't speak. He didn't breathe.

"Say you're sorry."

"I'm sorry," Victor muttered. He held his hand out, then felt Nico's open palms shove his chest. He fell back, his head bumping hard against the wall. He heard a gasp. He was sure that one of the girls screamed. It was dark, then light. Victor gasped for air. He blinked: Nico was over him, along with a dozen others. There were haloes of light around all these young, familiar faces.

"You can't tell anyone."

"He's fine."

"You killed him . . ."

Once, climbing trees over the river, Victor and Nico had seen a helicopter skirting the treetops downstream, bobbing unsteadily in the sky. A vision from a long-ago windy day. They had climbed the tree hurriedly, nearly falling twice, to get a better look at it. Transfixed by its motion, Victor wondered where it would land, where it was headed. He hadn't considered for a moment that the machine held people inside; to him, it was shiny and steel and alive of its own accord. It was male and female, a being unto itself. He saw its past and its future. It lived on a mountain top overlooking the city. It had blood inside and a beating heart. And then, just before it faded from view, the helicopter caught the sun's reflection: an explosion of silver light, like a star against the bright morning sky. The distant whirring trailed off, but for minutes after, Victor blinked and could still see the helicopter's glow etched in red, burning against the black insides of his eyelids.

It was only when he dived into the cool river that the last traces of the moment had passed.

Strange, Victor thought, that they were even friends.

Noise, shouting; his peers forming a wall around him. Nico crouched by his side. "I'm sorry, Vic," he said. "Are you okay?" Victor felt himself nod. One of the girls ran her fingers through his hair, and he felt he loved her.

AT THE bar, the men of the town listened with their backs to the soldiers. War stories. Manau noticed his landlord had dropped his head down into his chest, as if he were trying to see into the workings of his heart. It was his turn to drink, and he was taking his time. Another man was rubbing his back, and it was a long moment before Manau's landlord looked up. He was squinting. "I don't like this talk," he said. He lifted his glass between his two stumps, effortlessly, raised it to his lips, and drank. Not a drop was spilled. He passed the glass to Manau.

What elegance, Manau thought. He emptied the foam on the floor, nodded to his landlord. The soldiers were boisterous and happy, and Manau was sure he hated them. They would come and go, they would forget. He would stay. *We* will stay, Manau thought, and that pronoun crackled in his brain. In the local dialect, there were two kinds of *we*: *we* that included *you*, and another, which did not. Barely anyone spoke that language anymore—a few of the ancient women of the village, and no one else. But some of the old words had slipped into the national language, including these. *We* that includes *you* was one of Manau's favorite words. On this evening, as he watched his landlord raise a glass and lament the distant war, he felt something like kinship. It was the drink. It was the heat blurring everything into a gauzy half-light. The soldiers were unrepentant strangers, the captain a morbid comedian, but Manau belonged.

Victor's mother stepped into the canteen. She was met with cheers from the soldiers. The captain, his ruddy face beaming, proposed a toast—To the children! he shouted importantly. Manau watched Adela blush and then frown. Were they making fun of her? The idea scandalized him. She wore a simple blue skirt and a thin white T-shirt decorated with a sailboat. The shirt was old, the neck stretched wide enough to reveal her right shoulder. She was barefoot. When the toast had finished, the captain insisted she sit with them. "For only a moment, madam," he said. She demurred, instead walked up to Manau and asked if she could speak to him. In private.

It took his breath away. "Of course," he said too quickly. He almost added, "madam," then didn't. He wondered if it were bad taste. Did his breath smell of beer? Did he seem drunk? He offered her a smile and pushed these thoughts aside. Was there a trace of romance in her tightly pursed lips?

He followed her outside. The children didn't bother scattering. They stood crowded around the window, surely up to no good. Tonight, he thought, we are the carnival. We are the circus at the center of the world. Let the generator hum and the music play; the glasses clink and the bottles clang! God bless the coarse men and their churlish grins, the soldiers stupefied by drink—they are the children's heroes! Again, the word *we* passed ahead of him, a fluttering banner, and Manau made a decision to improve his posture starting the very next day. It was a beginning, a place to start. He would improve everything about himself. Become a better man and make his mother proud. He followed Adela into the darkness that began just a few meters beyond the canteen. She held him by the arm, as if he might get away. "Your son is a good student," he said as they walked. Was he slurring? "A real smart one."

"I see him reading all the time," she said. "Old books his father brought him."

They were a distance now from the canteen. It hadn't rained all day long, and the air was humid and full of insects. They walked slowly along the town's empty paths, almost to the end, where the forest began.

"You asked him, Mr. Manau? About my boy's father?"

"I did."

"Why?" she asked.

There was a strength to her he admired. When she passed through town, Manau always noticed her calves, her supple leg muscles. They made him feel weak. Her hand was wrapped loosely around his bicep, but he knew she had him. His body, no matter how disfigured or warped by the heat, would never be to her liking. An itchy patch of skin smoldered beneath her faint touch. He had the irresistible urge to be honest. It didn't come often.

"I'm lonely," he whispered, shutting his eyes.

He opened them a little later—a few seconds, a minute—and she was still there. Adela had softened a bit, or seemed to. It was hard to tell in the weak light. She touched his face. "Our teachers never last very long," she said. "It's not easy."

"It isn't," he insisted in a low voice.

The night seemed to be momentarily empty of all sound. It was her hand on his face, and only that. In an instant, it had passed. She withdrew her touch and, in the darkness, he followed her hand with his eyes. It dangled by her side, a glowing thing, and then she clasped it with the other and hid them both behind her back.

"I'm sorry," he said.

Adela shook her head. "Victor doesn't know the whole story. He was very young."

"I won't ask again," he promised.

"It's okay," she said. "You didn't know. I'll tell him. Soon."

"I should be going."

"Of course," she said.

He wanted to leave—he meant to—but instead found himself looking down at his feet, immobile, planted in the earth before her. He met her gaze. She was waiting for him.

"Yes?"

"It's a terrible thing to ask of you."

She shook her head, not understanding.

"It's my skin," he said. "I itch."

Her head turned almost imperceptibly. "Are you asking me to scratch you?"

He nodded—was she smiling?

"Where?" Adela asked.

They were hardly a hundred meters from the canteen, from the children and the soldiers and the war stories. It was a universe away. The night was pierced with stars. When she died, he would remember this, this touch: her fingers clawing his back, softly at first, then vigorously, as if she were digging in the earth for treasure.

THERE WERE dozens of children by the time he made it back, so Manau had to wade through them to get to the door of the canteen. It was as if they had become drunk just by being near the place. They were all his students. "Mr. Manau," they yelled. "No school tomorrow! No school!" He smiled and felt buoyant. Some of the children pulled at his pant legs. A soldier's head poked out from the window and nodded at him. Manau didn't spot Victor or Nico among them, and again, the idea flashed through his head that he should tell his handless landlord about the boy, but the thought lingered for just a moment, and then he was inside.

In fact, Victor was there, hidden among the children, leaning against the wall of the canteen. He was fine, he told himself, but there was a softness to everything, a pliability that he found startling. He felt that he could look at something and bend it—a tree, a rock, a cloud—and it worried him. Gingerly, he touched the knot on his head. There was no blood, only this heat within him. He felt faint. The canteen's walls quivered, the entire structure shaking with laughter.

Inside, everything had come unmoored. Drunkenness had exploded inside, and no one had been saved. The soldiers had spread about the room like ivy, a couple of them leaned over the open window, chatting with the children, blowing smoke above their heads; the men from the bar had joined the smaller group in an oblong orbit around the captain. When Manau entered, Nico's father raised a shout, and soon everyone was applauding the teacher. The scratching still warm on his back, the burning trails of Adela's fingers, and now this: he felt like weeping. Manau accepted the ovation with a raised hand, and took a seat between his landlord and the captain. A glass was poured, and he raised it to his lips, nodding first at the men gathered around him.

"Mr. Zahir was just telling us about his hands," the captain said as Manau drank. "Weren't you?"

Manau's landlord nodded and cleared his throat. He was hopelessly drunk, his gaze scattered and diffuse. "It wasn't far from here, you know." He motioned with a waving stump, and Manau saw the scarred flesh, dimpled and leathery, that closed around the place where his arms ended so abruptly.

The captain poured Zahir a glass. "Terrible," he said.

"I was accused of stealing from the communal plot. It's overgrown now, and no one tends to it, but it used to be at the edge of the town, just past the plaza. They did *tadek*."

Tadek, Manau thought, shaking his head. "Here? Who?"

"Why, the IL, my friend. Who else would commit such an atrocity?" the captain said. "Please, go on."

"It was Adela's boy that chose me," Zahir said. "He was only four years old. Let's go, they said. I went." He motioned for more beer, and one of the soldiers filled the glass and passed it to him. Zahir began the balancing act, but the glass slipped from between his wrists. He stopped. "But why speak of this?" he cried, turning to the captain.

"These soldiers don't remember, Don Zahir. They don't know. Even this teacher of yours, this learned man—even *he* doesn't remember."

"But I didn't live here then. I'm from the city."

"Of course."

"And in the city," Zahir said, "everything was fine?"

Manau met his landlord's gaze. His son would leave, if not now, soon. He would starve. His wife and his daughter, too. The town, with any luck, would disappear into the jungle. Manau shook his head. "No, you're right. In the city everything was—"

"Terrible," the captain said. He smiled. "Pardon me, good sir. But let it be said: everything was terrible."

Manau nodded. "I'm sorry, Zahir. I didn't mean to interrupt."

"That's all of it. They took my hands! And yet I am not a helpless man."

"Of course not, Don Zahir," murmured the captain.

"And do you know what I miss most?" Zahir asked in a low voice. He leaned in close.

"Playing guitar," one of the other men said. "Don Zahir, you could play beautifully!" He sang a *tra-la-la*, a rising melody, and lovingly stroked an invisible instrument.

"No, no, that's not it."

"The earth, fertile and damp, in your hands."

Zahir shook his head. "You talk like a bad poet!"

"What then?" Manau asked.

"I'll tell you." He threw an arm over Manau, another around the captain. "My fingers," Zahir whispered, "inside my wife."

"No!" the captain protested, overjoyed.

"Yes!"

"Don Zahir! What vulgarity!"

But he had the face of an oblate praying for grace. Manau sat in awe. He would have lent Zahir his own hands for a night of love, if such a thing were possible.

"She was so wet," Zahir said, "and so warm . . . Dear God!"

"To women!" the captain said.

"To women!" shouted the roomful of men.

And even outside, a few of the children saluted as well. The girls among them blushed and curtsied.

"I'm still a girl," said Joanna, smiling beatifically.

"Victor, are you okay?" Nico asked for the hundredth time. He was starting to worry.

Inside, Nico's father fell silent, and Manau felt a warmth descending from above, something narcotic. The glass was passed to him again. No one mentioned the beer truck or the impassable roads. They would drink it all. What is tomorrow? An idea, nothing more.

WHEN VICTOR was carried into the canteen a few minutes later, the men and the soldiers were still in ecstasies over Zahir's revelation. The radio played unaccompanied by a single voice, each man plunged into private ruminations of warm vaginas they had known. Years ago, decades ago, it didn't matter how long it had been; the smell and the sheen of imagined sex was everywhere in the room. They looked at their hands and fingers with hopeless devotion. Beer had been spilled in great quantities, the floor now wet enough to skate on.

All around Manau, men dreamed lustily. The captain and Zahir whispered conspiratorially about the pleasures of the flesh. A few of the soldiers had fallen asleep, splayed out on the floor, musty boots beneath their heads as pillows. Manau was done with memory's women; they were few anyway. He looked up to find Nico standing awkwardly in the doorway, with Adela's boy, limp and dazed, in his arms.

Victor was a frail and sickly child. It wasn't something that Manau had always recognized. He was a smiling, good-natured kid, and his mother kept him clean and neatly dressed. But now Manau was sure he had never seen such a fragile human being.

"I fell," Victor said, before Manau had a chance to ask. "Will someone call my mother?"

The child's voice was enough to blot out waking dreams. The captain snapped to attention, his face contorted in an exaggerated expression of worry. These army men love a crisis, Manau thought. But Zahir was up at once, took Victor from his son. The boy's thin arms slung around the older man's neck. "You'll be fine," Zahir said. With his right stump, he patted the boy's head.

"I pushed him," Nico said. "It was my fault."

But no one was listening. The captain was up. "We're taking the boy home," Zahir said.

"Will he be okay?" Nico asked.

"Yes," Manau said quickly. "He'll be fine."

"He won't die?"

"Of course not." Manau paused.

Nico nodded.

He wasn't a boy anymore. He could be reasoned with. The bar had emptied, and they were alone. "You can't leave," Manau said. "Not now. Victor told me everything. And I forbid it."

Manau let that final grand statement linger there. *I forbid it.* It had authority, weight. "Do you understand me?"

Nico nodded.

"Do you have anything to say?" Manau asked.

But he didn't. Or wouldn't. So Manau left him in the empty canteen and went off into the night to see about Adela's boy.

HIS HOME wouldn't be this crowded again until his mother died. Then he would once again be the center of attention, women and friends and strangers huddled around him, afraid to speak, afraid not to. But this night, the night before Nico left, a drunk army captain told him he was a tough boy, a true son of the homeland. This night, his best friend's handless father carried him through town, and his nervous, frightened teacher kept pace, scratching himself as discreetly as he could. A midnight procession beneath an infinity of stars, and the children followed, worried for their classmate. They sang songs, they saluted women. They'd tried to rouse him unsuccessfully by the canteen wall, before Nico had finally said, "Enough, I'll take him." In the end, it had for Victor that same movement and madness that his mother's death would have—except this was a celebration. He was the center of the world. A battalion of soldiers stood guard outside his door. Don Zahir dropped him in his bed. Victor heard his mother's voice, too concerned to scold him. Warm rags were placed on his forehead, and he dreamed of a helicopter made of silver light. The old women appeared by his bedside, uttering prayers in the old dialect.

Did he whisper in Don Zahir's ear, did he tell him Nico was leaving? He meant to. Later, he told himself he had. It was no use: in the morning, his best friend was gone.

SEVEN

S H E H A D held it in her hands, glanced over the names: not one had registered. How had she not seen it that first day? While Victor played in the control room, pressing buttons and turning knobs haphazardly, Len watching over him, Elmer took the list and pulled out a black felt-tip marker. Norma gasped. What was worse: realizing Rey's name was there, that she had somehow missed it, or seeing it disappear again?

"Wait. Let me see it." She reached for Elmer's hand. "Why do that?"

"It's not safe."

"Let me hold it."

He relented with a sigh and passed her the paper. "Did you know about this?" he asked.

Norma spread the list across her thigh, smoothing its wrinkles with the palms of her hands. "Of course not," she said, without looking up. "I never know." She ran her fingers over the letters of her husband's name. It was there, Rey's false name hidden among two dozen others. "Did you?"

He shook his head. "I'm sorry, Norma," Elmer said. "Either I destroy it or we go to the police. This list—they could be collaborators, sympathizers. Rey is still a wanted man."

Even if he's dead.

And so everything would be canceled, the list never read, no special program for Victor or the rest of them, the sons and daughters of 1797, with no one to tend to their memory. People disappear, they vanish. And with them, the history, so that new myths replace the old: the war never happened at all. It was just a dream. We are a modern nation, a civilized nation. But then, years later, a tiny echo of those missing. Do you ignore it?

"It's a mistake, it must be a mistake." She wanted to laugh, and she did—but it came out nervously, awkwardly, as if she were hiding something. Elmer frowned. "I'll keep it," Norma said. "I can do the show without his name."

"But I'll hold the list."

"Don't you trust me?"

Elmer sighed. "Everyone on this piece of paper could be guilty of something. I don't want to take that chance. It's my life too, you know. I'm responsible for this station."

"I'll get to the bottom of this."

Elmer shook his head, and he certainly had his reasons—good, solid reasons—but she wasn't listening. He spoke, he explained with his hands, his fists opening and closing. His face was soft and understanding—it didn't matter. Surely he invoked her own safety, their friendship, strained at times but real—she couldn't hear him. Hadn't he always cared for her? Hadn't he stayed by her side through all of this, and never betrayed her? There were other men—he said carefully—who could not truthfully make such claims.

But Norma wouldn't hear him. She stood and knocked on the window of the control room until she had the boy's attention. She gave him a big smile, and could feel the muscles of her face working. He was young. He smiled back.

Norma held the list up to the light. There was a single spot of black ink next to her husband's false name, where Elmer had touched the paper with the very tip of the marker.

"What are you doing?" Elmer asked.

The boy watched through the window. Norma folded the note into fourths. Without saying a word, she lifted her shirt and slipped the list into her underwear.

Elmer rubbed his chin. "Is this your idea of a joke?"

She pointed Victor to the door. On the other side of the window, Len shrugged. The boy disappeared through the door. He would wait for her. Norma turned to Elmer. "I'm sorry," she said, and left the control room without another word. He let me leave, she thought, the door closing behind her. "Norma," Elmer said, but that was all.

Victor was waiting for her in the station's dilapidated version of a green room. He sat on a couch of sunken cushions, poking his pinky finger into the torn upholstery.

"Lunch," Norma said in her sweetest voice. Her heart was pounding: she could feel it in her chest, in her throat. "Do you want lunch?"

Victor grinned. Boys his age were always hungry. Of course he wanted lunch. To the elevator then and through the lobby—give the receptionist a smile and a nod—now out into the streets. She took his hand.

They left the radio and made their way to Newtown Plaza, to the reconstructed heart of the city, twenty blocks or more from the station. At the station she'd left behind, Elmer was stewing. She felt sure of this, could almost see him, pacing the halls of the radio, considering his options. Maybe he would send someone after her. Maybe there would be police waiting at her apartment that night. Norma doubted it. Elmer had let her go, after all, with the list. She could feel it against her skin. She was safe for now. Norma and Victor passed restaurant after restaurant, and at each one, the boy slowed, lingering for a moment at its doorway. Chickens turning on spits in the windows, buxom waitresses handing menus to passersby, and Victor took each one, stuffing them into his pocket as Norma dragged him on. She wanted to be tolerant of his curiosity, but it was hard at a moment like this. There were soldiers on every other corner, so much a part of the scenery that they had become nearly invisible: the same boys with rifles that had tormented her once, that had dragged her Rey off a bus twenty years before. Pedestrians moved chaotically between the featureless, modern buildings, beneath a clouded sky that threatened to clear. Taxis honked, vendors shouted, police whistles squealed.

They found a place and sat in the back, far from the noise of the street, in a corner of mirrored walls and glowing tubes of neon light spelling out the names of local beers and sports teams. The waitress was pretty but with bad teeth, and had a jungle accent she seemed to be trying to mask. The food came quickly. Victor drank orange soda through a straw and ate greedily with his hands, content to do so in silence. Norma picked at the fries, sipped her water. Eleven: in a year, Victor would be a different person; in five, unrecognizable and nearly a man. He ate, smiling now and then with bits of chicken stuck between his teeth. He swished mouthfuls of orange soda, puffing out his lips and cheeks. She had the urge to rub her hand across his shaved head: it would be prickly, like sandpaper. Her mind skipped over moments of the previous ten years, and then the decade before that, images of Rey and his various names, his hidden histories, his evasions, his disappearances and disguises. The boy deserved to know.

"There was a name on the list." She breathed deeply and exhaled. Slowly. Norma took a pen from her purse and wrote the name on a napkin, in capital letters. She observed it. How long had it been since she'd written it out—this oddly spelled name from her past? A decade—or more? Since she wrote him love letters in the weeks after his disappearance, addressed to the name on the ID she'd found in her pocket—*that* long. She sighed. "Do you recognize it?"

Victor worked on a mouthful of chicken. Looking the name over carefully, he shook his head. "How do you say it?"

Norma smiled. She took a sip of Victor's soda. The bottle was cold and moist in her palm. She wiped its wetness on her forehead. The headache she'd had since the station subsided for just a moment. Her voice nearly broke.

Victor repeated it. "What was he like?"

The boy wanted to know what he was like. She'd never heard anyone say the name aloud; it made her smile.

Or rather, nearly cry. One of those smiles that hold back so much, a dishonest smile. Where to begin? In the mirrored walls, Norma could see the street and its furious movement, men and women caught in the city's fevered charade of reconstruction. It was worth asking: Had there ever been a war? Was it something we all imagined? Newtown Plaza was only a few blocks away, a monument to forgetting built atop the ruins of the past. *What was he like?* Thank God for mirrors, Norma thought, and for these people and those people rushing past, for the frantic work of survival, but none of them were Rey and none of them knew his name: he was a liar, a beautiful man who told beautiful lies. In the restaurant, there were neon lights and long-legged waitresses with breasts bursting from orange tube tops, women dressed like candy to be eaten, bedecked in the colors of boxes of laundry detergent. Clean, young vixens! This city would drive her mad, or her loneliness would, and still Victor watched her in the mirror, eyes darted about, a nation at feeding time, chicken was torn from the bone, devoured, a dozen young and old faces were adorned with greasy smiles. An insipid melody floated just below the hum of conversation, and Norma felt her head might explode.

"Are you all right?" the boy asked. His voice was soft.

Norma shook her head. "No."

"My mother was this way sometimes." He paused and leaned forward. "Like her head was coming loose."

That was it exactly. Her head had come loose. Norma drew a deep breath. It had come loose that first night she met Rey, had stayed that way for decades. How much longer would this swoon last? Victor wiped his mouth carefully with the same napkin she'd written on. Norma took it from him and spread it flat on the table. It was stained and greasy, the smudged ink barely legible. Unrecoverable. She could feel the blood coloring her cheeks.

Victor apologized, but she waved it away. "See," she said, "I don't know what he was like. I thought I did. He wasn't a stranger. We were together for so long. And we've been apart so long." She sighed. "Then he reappears sometimes. And today, it feels"—how did it feel?—"like a joke."

The boy looked confused. "A joke, Miss Norma?"

"No. You're right, not a joke exactly." She curled her bottom lip. "I don't know what to call it. I've been waiting for so long."

Victor was a child and a stranger, as much a foreigner as she would be in Arabia or the Ukraine—but she wanted him to understand. More than that, she felt that he *could*, if only he wanted to.

But what was he really thinking? She could only guess: about the chicken probably, its lingering taste on his lips, or the satisfying heaviness in the pit of his stomach. The glittering jukebox behind her, with its shiny buttons and compact discs and selection of songs he'd probably never heard? The buxom waitress and her bad teeth? It was as if Victor had suddenly gained a new tint to him, something that set him apart: he wasn't a boy any longer. His gaze could move in a hundred different directions, find a hundred distractions, but Norma could see only this: that he had brought a piece of paper from the jungle. And on that piece of paper, a name that proved he had communed with the dead.

"I haven't seen my husband in ten years," she said. Victor seemed to be listening, and that was enough for her. "I'm not stupid, Victor. He's not missing. He's on a list they keep in the palace: his name can't even be said out loud. Every night on the radio—can you understand this—I want to talk to him. But I don't. If I let myself say his name, it would be terrible."

"What would happen, Miss Norma?" the boy asked.

"At the very least, inconvenient questions. More likely, arrests, investigations, disappearances." She sighed. "It's worse than that: if I said his name again, it would be admitting I still thought he might hear me. I'm not sure I can take that."

"What if I said it?"

She cupped her hands over Victor's. "Can I tell you something?"

"Yes," Victor said. He pushed his plate away and reached for the soda, offered her the last of it. When she demurred, he drank it, sucking on the straw with a frown.

"I'm a bit afraid of you."

He raised his eyebrows for an instant, then let his eyes drift to the table. He wouldn't look up.

"It's okay," Norma said. "I expect you're probably afraid of me too. Aren't you?" She pressed his hands; they were still a boy's hands, his fingers thin and bony, the skin soft. "A little bit scared?" she asked.

The boy nodded.

"It's scary," she said, no longer to Victor or to herself, but to the space between them. "It is."

"I didn't come alone." Victor paused and took a breath. "I came with my teacher. He might know. His name is Manau."

"Tell me what happened."

The boy slipped his hands from beneath hers and scratched his head.

"He was my mother's friend. Her boyfriend. He was supposed to take care of me. But he didn't. He left me at the station."

"Just like that? What did he say?"

Victor took the empty glass and jabbed the straw at the ice melting at the bottom. He sucked, and there was a gurgling sound for a moment. Then he stopped. "Nothing. He said you would take care of me."

"I-I am," Norma stammered. "I will. But why did he say that? Why did he leave you?"

Victor shrugged. "He was sad. The old people said he loved my mother."

Norma sat back, suddenly amused. As if being in love excused everything. How much could be explained away that easily, how much of her past? This Manau: he had abandoned a boy in the middle of the city because he was heartbroken?

"It's like being dizzy," she said, sighing. "Trying to make sense of all this. It's like being very, very dizzy."

"He knows. I'm sure Manau knows. He can help."

"My husband is . . . was not a simple man," she said. "He plays tricks."

"That's not nice."

Norma rubbed her eyes: the lights, the boy, the note. "You're right. It isn't. I'm dizzy," she repeated. "That's all."

THE TABLE had been cleaned off, the bill paid, when Victor confessed he'd dreamed of his mother. She died in the river, he said. "I'm sorry, I'm sorry, you poor thing," Norma said, but that wasn't why he told her: maybe the river brought his mother here. The lunch hour had died down, the waitresses congregated by the neon-lit bar, chatting and sipping sodas.

"So what do you want to do?" Norma asked the boy.

"The ocean," he said. "I want to see it."

The city's beaches are desolate for most of the year, lonely expanses of windswept sand beneath crumbling bluffs. Vagabonds warm themselves around crudely built fires, and sometimes the waves drag a swollen body onto the shore. In winter, the city turns its back to the sea, the clouds drop low and heavy, flat and dim, a dirty cotton ceiling. What beach? What ocean? Every now and then, the wind changes and brings hints of it—a brackish smell rising through the city—but those days are rare. A highway runs along the coastline; the sounds of passing cars and crashing waves melting into a single, blurred noise. Some of the beaches farther north double as work areas, the careful labor of separating and burning trash carried out by a diligent army of thin, tough boys with matted hair. They poke through the heaps with sticks, gathering pig feed from the festering piles.

Victor, Norma thought, could be one of them. They were his age, his build, his color, their stunted brown bodies stepping expertly through the refuse. And if he were? If he had come from 1797 and not found the radio that first day, if he had wandered the streets hungry and dazed, if he had made a home in the alleys of Asylum Downs, or been picked up by police in the slums behind the Metropole, would that have been surprising? A boy like Victor could live and die in any of a dozen squalid shanties, in The Settlement or Miamiville, in Collectors or The Thousands or Tamoé, and no one would ever know. No mysteries or questions to be asked: another child of obscure origins come to scrape out a life in the nether regions of the city, his success or failure of no consequence to anyone other than himself.

They rode to the coast to look for her. Norma told him—or began to tell him—that it didn't work that way, that the river flowed across the continent in the other direction, that the ocean was infinite. But she stopped. This was for him to discover, and he would be cured of his dream when he saw it himself. Norma let him talk, he sputtered on about his village, about his mother, about Manau—"We'll find him!" he said, though the city was as large as the sea, and this Manau was only one man. She was happy to be in a taxi, with the windows down, the air rushing in, so loud she couldn't hear her own mind thrumming. She watched his lips move, hearing only scattered words, and held his hand to reassure him.

At the beach, Norma and Victor watched a small, stooped woman drag a sack behind her. She moved glacially, arthritically, along the ebbing and flowing line of surf, and together the three of them were the only ones there. They watched her for a moment: she sifted sand into her sack through a sieve, then inched forward and did it again. The wind scattered trash across the beach. An occasional strong gust lifted sand into the sky and out to sea. Though the sun was still hidden, it wasn't too cold.

Victor went to work, untying his laces, pulling off his socks with greedy resolve. He wiggled his toes, stuffed his socks into his sneakers, and put them all beneath a stone bench at the edge of the sand. He peeled off the sweater that Norma had lent him that morning—given him—an old wool thing that Rey had shrunk in the wash years before. Norma shouldn't have been amazed, but she was: to Victor, the sweater was simply something to wear against a chill. It meant nothing to him, did not signify anyone living or dead. Of course! He was free of her past, and why wouldn't he be?

Norma and Victor walked out onto the sand. She didn't reach for his hand, as she had in the taxi, though she had an urge to. Instead, she watched him as he bounded ahead, almost to the water's edge and back. He spun and waved his arms. She followed him toward the water and stopped just where the sand became moist and mushy. It had been years since she came to the beach, since she was a girl. Had she ever come in winter? It seemed possible that she never had. Norma took off her shoes, rolled up the cuffs of her pants, and stepped into the wet sand with one foot. She pressed firmly into the cool earth, and it felt good. She pulled her foot back to the dry sand, and crouched to admire her work: a perfect imprint of her foot. She made another, just ahead, and walked this way to where the waves spread out over the sand, a thin skin of advancing and retreating water. Then she retraced her steps, walking backwards. There it was: her disappearance. She had walked into the ocean and not come back.

As a girl, she'd spent an afternoon at this beach, carving massive foot-prints, giant paw-prints, around her father, while he slept with a straw hat slung low over his eyes. How old was she then? Eight? Nine? Norma smiled. Her mother, she recalled, wore a black bathing suit and hat with a dramatic, swooping brim. A bow, perhaps. She'd had the air of a movie star, thought herself much too elegant to swim, so she alternately read or smoked or stared off at the sea. Norma crawled in the hot, bright sand around her parents, carving a trail of strange footprints. She lost her-self in it: the curve and sharpness of the claws, the heft of the heel. She filled her plastic bucket with seawater, wetting the sand so it would stick. When her father finally woke, Norma showed him her work. She was serious and determined. The beast she had imagined as she worked was terrifying and vicious. "A strange animal came while you were sleeping, Daddy," she said. "He had fangs and claws."

He took the cigarette that Norma's mother offered him. He squinted at the footprints around him. "What did the animal do?"

"He ate you whole."

Her father looked at her, feigning worry. "Am I dead then?"

She told him he was, and he laughed.

A gust of wind blew sand in her face, and she realized Victor had been talking. His teacher had come with him all the way to the city. They'd left 1797 a few days before, been together all the way to the central bus station in the capital. Then Manau walked Victor to the radio station and left him there. Norma nodded: it was inexplicable, cruel. To abandon a boy in the city, to leave him to fend for himself? And just as inexplicably, Victor seemed to hold no grudges. Why did Manau leave?

"He was home," Victor said, as if it were that simple. Of course, Manau left me, Victor said. Of course: he was heartbroken.

Norma sat on the sand and stretched her legs in front of her. Victor ran off and returned a few minutes later, carrying an armload of driftwood and kelp and a tin can of mysterious origin, rust blooming at its edges. This forgiving boy, this Buddha—he was panting, out of breath, his face flush. "It's pretty," he said. "Isn't it?"

She smiled. It wasn't clear if he meant the ocean, the sand, or his collection of debris, but in any case, Norma felt it impossible to disagree with the boy about this or anything.

THE DIRTY sand, the lightless horizon—these details couldn't obscure the beauty of what lay before him: endless water. It moved, it was alive: its briny smell, its mottled surface of foam and breaking waves, an infinity of water and surf, rising, falling, breathing. The ocean simply could not disappoint.

Everything had been tinged with green, the bodies and hands and faces of everyone in 1797. His mother was there, too—he was sure of it—but beyond this, his dream had left him nothing: a bitter taste in his mouth, perhaps, but no image to be interpreted, no narrative to untangle. Back home, there was an old woman who interpreted dreams. She claimed to have lived with the Indians deep in the forest, claimed to know their language: *medicine*, she told Victor, and *tree* are the very same word. Victor had gone with his mother once to visit her, had waited outside, digging in the earth with a sharp stick. His mother paid the old woman with a bundle of dried tobacco and a half dozen silver fish.

"What was the dream about?" Victor had asked then.

"Your father," she'd said, but hadn't told him anything more.

Before they left this morning, Victor had asked permission to look through Norma's bookshelves. He'd never seen so many books. He didn't tell her he hoped to find a map of some sort and, on it, his village and its river. If he could trace its crooked and curving path to the sea, it might be possible. Which way did the river flow? These were things they had never learned. At home, tacked in the wood by the door, there was a map, yellowed with mold, its lines and colors fading. It was from before the war, with names, not numbers. His father's map. But Victor couldn't remember anything about it, except that when he asked his mother to point out their village, she had sighed.

"We're not on it, silly."

When he took the map down to show to his teacher, Manau looked at it and smiled. He pointed to the capital, traced the shoreline with his fingernail, then took his red pencil and scratched out the old name. To the left of the starred city, somewhere in the vast ocean, Manau printed the word ONE.

"What's it like?" Victor had asked.

"Beautiful," said Manau.

For homework that long-ago evening, Victor corrected his map, updating the names of the various cities with a mimeographed map Manau gave him, replacing each name with a number. The order of it became clear as he worked: less than three digits along the coast, below five thousand in the jungle, above that in the mountains. Odd numbers were usually near a river; evens near a mountain. Numbers ending in ones were reserved for regional capitals. The higher the last digit, the smaller the place.

At Norma's, he thumbed through books and found nothing. Books on the history of radio, picture books of jungle plants, dictionaries for languages he'd never heard of. She sat in the kitchen while he blew dust off heavy leather tomes, turned the frayed, dissolving pages of books that hadn't been opened in years. There were line drawings of birds and plants in notebooks of heavy parchment. Others had text so small that he could barely read them. Victor spent a moment with a graying book of faces, photos of young men and women in formal dress. Each page had a few faces crossed out, with a date beneath the picture. He looked for Norma, but when he couldn't find her, he put the book away. Closing his eyes, Victor saw it again and again: his mother at the rock, now steady against the current, now floating away, now diving into the foamy waters. Which way did the river flow? When he'd come to the city, had he moved closer or farther from her? Had he followed her to the sea?

All day, he thought of the ocean. He imagined the word ONE inscribed somewhere in the sea. When they rode to the beach and he saw the size of it, he didn't despair. It filled him with energy. He felt certain his mother was there. Now he sat beside Norma to gather his breath, and thought of his dream, and before him was so much water. Her eyes were on the surf, on the waves that broke at the horizon. He dropped his armload of stuff on the sand. "What do you have there?" she asked.

He showed her. "This," he said, "is a sword." He gripped the driftwood by its base and took a few swipes at the air in front of him. "See?"

She took it from him and, with florid strokes, carved her name in the air. "Dangerous. And this?"

The kelp reminded him of home, of the green moss that clung to the lower limbs of the trees. Was it possible to explain? How it formed curtains of green swaying in the wind, its lowest edges skimming the surface of the river? He tried. The color was just right: a deep, dark green, nearly black, soggy and waterlogged. "Can you picture it?" he asked.

She said she could.

They sat listening to the sea. It was neither cold nor warm. A bank of clouds had fissured, jagged bands of light breaking through. Victor asked, "Are you still dizzy?"

Norma scooted closer to him. "No," she said. "Are you?"

"What's going to happen to me?"

Norma smiled. "I don't know," she said. "You're a strong boy, aren't you? You may be stuck with me for a while."

He jabbed his driftwood sword in the air. For a moment, it was just the ocean and its rhythms. "Is that all right?" Norma asked, and something in her voice made Victor blush. He didn't answer right away.

"My mother loved you," he said. "Everyone in my village did."

Norma said nothing.

The stooped woman had made her away across the beach, dragging her sack behind her. Victor stood suddenly and walked over to her. She smiled and kept working, scooping the sand into the metal screen, letting the smaller grains fall through. Whatever remained, she dropped into her sack. "Auntie," Victor said, "can I help?"

"Nice boy," the woman said.

He took a handful of sand, and let it fall through his fingers, then offered her the pebbles stuck to his palm. She smiled and dropped them into her sieve. They didn't fall through. She thanked him and tossed them into her bag. She patted his head, and nodded at Norma. "Nice boy," the woman repeated, "helping an old woman like me."

"Won't you sit and rest with us a moment?" Norma asked.

The woman smiled, exposing a mouthful of pinkish-red gums. "Oh, you young people have time to sit and rest! Not me!"

"I'll gather rocks for you," Victor said.

She sat and handed Victor her sieve. He knelt down and scooped a handful of sand into it. He ran his tongue along his teeth and stared at the sand as it slipped through the wire netting of the sieve. When he was done, he brought it to the woman for inspection.

"Very good," she said. From an inside pocket, the woman unrolled a piece of bread. She tore off the crust and offered it to Norma and Victor, but both refused. She ate only the doughy, white inside of the bread, chewing slowly, methodically. A tiny radio hung around her neck by a shoestring. After finishing her bread, she took the single battery from her radio, rubbed it between her palms, then replaced it. The radio crackled to life, spitting out scratchy sound, static, voices.

Norma glanced at her watch. "One of the daytime shows, Auntie," she said. "Love advice or police reports."

"On Sunday," Victor announced, "I'll be on the radio."

The woman looked up. "How nice."

"I'll say your name. If you want me to."

She glanced at Victor. "That would be just fine."

Victor was on his knees again, sifting pebbles. The woman began explaining to Norma how she had stumbled upon this work, how her

husband had been in construction. She wanted to talk, she couldn't help
it. Victor listened as she told how her husband had fallen from a beam
and died, how she had approached his partner and begged him for something to do. She'd stayed home all her adult life. What could she do? This
is what she was offered. She sold the pebbles to a concrete mixer on
Avenue F.

"He cheated me," she said, her voice breaking. "My husband promised
me. He said he wouldn't leave."

"They do that," Norma said. "They say those things. They may even
mean them, Auntie."

Victor listened and emptied the sieve into her sack of pebbles, and
twice interrupted to ask her name. Both times, the woman ignored him
and stared at Norma. "Are you from Lost City, madam?"

Norma blushed and nodded.

Smiling, the woman took Norma's hand in hers and squeezed. "Why
weren't you on the radio this morning?"

"A day off, Auntie. That's all."

"You'll be back?" the woman asked. "Tomorrow?"

"Or the next day," Norma said.

A flock of sea gulls circled overhead. The clouds were thin and gauzy
now. "I'm so happy," the woman said after a while. "I'm so happy you're
real."

Norma held her hand and stroked the back of her neck. Victor sat
and placed his hand on the woman's back. She was dirty and smelled of
the sea. She had crumpled into Norma's embrace and didn't even notice
Victor.

"Auntie," Norma said, "is there anyone I can help you with?"

The old woman leaned back, nodding. "Oh, Norma," she whispered.
She pulled a piece of paper from her pocket. "I had a man type it for me,"
she said. "What does it say?"

Norma read two names aloud, and the woman nodded. "God is merciful," she said. "Tell them I work this beach. They're my children." Then
she gathered her things, and thanked them both. "But especially you, boy,"
she said. "Give Auntie a kiss."

She bent down and offered him her cheek. Victor kissed her obedi-
ently.

When she had walked a little ways, Victor grabbed his sword. Then he grabbed a handful of sand and dropped it into his pocket. He stared off into the ocean, scanning from right to left across the horizon. His mother, of course, wasn't there. But Norma was, walking just ahead of him to the highway, holding the old woman's list in her hand, tightly, so it wouldn't fly away.

EIGHT

WHEN HE was still a young professor, as the war was beginning in earnest, Rey revived his old pseudonym to publish an essay in one of the city's more partisan newspapers. The central committee had decided it was worth the risk: a calculated provocation. In spite of the paper's tiny circulation, the essay caused something of a controversy. In a series of articles, Rey described a ritual he had witnessed in the jungle. He named the ritual *tadek*, after the psychoactive plant used, though he claimed the natives of the village had more than a half-dozen discrete names for it, depending on the time of year it was employed, the day of the week, the crime it was designed to punish, et cetera. *Tadek*, as Rey described it, was a rudimentary form of justice, and it functioned this way: confronted by a theft, for example, the town elders chose a boy under the age of ten, stupefied him with a potent tea, and let the intoxicated child find the culprit. Rey had witnessed this himself: a boy stumbling drunkenly along the muddy paths of a village, into the marketplace, seizing upon the color of a man's shirt, the geometric patterns of a woman's dress, or a smell or sensation only the boy, in his altered state, could know. The child would attach himself to an adult, and this was enough. The elders would proclaim *tadek* over and lead the newly identified criminal away, to have his or her hands removed.

If Rey's article had been merely an anthropological description of a rarely used ritual, that might have been the end of it. This much was not controversial, as the jungle regions in those days were known primarily for being unknown, and the lay person could hardly be surprised by a violent pagan rite emerging from the dark forest. But Rey went further. *Tadek*, he argued, had been near extinction, but was now experiencing a renaissance of sorts. Furthermore, he refused to condemn it, did not call it barbarism or give any pejorative spin at all to his descriptions of its cruelty. *Tadek*, in Rey's view, was the antique precursor to the absolutely modern system of justice now being employed in the nation. Wartime justice, arbitrary justice, he contended, was valid both ethically (one could never know what crimes were lurking in the hearts and minds of men) and practically (swift, violent punishment, if random in nature, could bolster the cause of peace, frightening potential subversives before they took up arms). In measured prose, he applauded a few well-publicized cases of tortured union leaders and missing students as successful, contemporary versions of *tadek*, whereby the state assigned guilt based on outward signifiers (youth, occupation, social class) no more or less revealing than the geometric pattern of a woman's dress. The drunken child was perhaps extraneous in a modern context, but the essence was the same. *Tadek*'s presence in the jungle was not some vestigial expression of a dying tradition but a nuanced reinterpretation of contemporary justice as seen through the prism of folklore. The nation-state, in wartime, had finally succeeded in filtering down to the isolated masses: to condemn them now for re-creating our institutions in their own communities was nothing less than hypocrisy.

In the city, among the literate classes, there was shock and disgust. *Tadek* was discussed on the radio (there were nearly a dozen stations then), and to the surprise of many, some people, often calling from scratchy pay phones in the city's dustier districts, defended it. They didn't employ Rey's arguments—no one did—but invoked instead tradition, community, culture. They were happy to see it coming back. They told stories of village cripples, living symbols, who took their punishment without complaint. They were lessons for the children. Detractors called it retrograde and barbaric. A few case studies of *tadek* appeared in other local papers, alongside similarly disquieting dispatches from the interior: shootouts in formerly calm and altogether forgotten villages, policemen kidnapped from their posts in broad daylight, army patrols ambushed and relieved of their weapons on windy mountain passes.

The government had no choice but to shut down the partisan newspaper and a few others. A radio man who had done a series expanding on Rey's articles was jailed briefly, questioned, and released. A congressman who considered himself very progressive introduced a bill to outlaw the practice. The bill passed, of course, with senator after senator rising to the dais to express his indignation. The president himself denounced the practice of *tadek* when he signed the legislation, saying the very concept offended the dignity of a modern nation. He preached continued faith in progress, and, as he did in nearly every speech in those days, alluded vaguely to a discontented minority bent on disrupting the calm of a peaceful, loyal people. The war itself, so long in coming, had finally arrived, but received only these oblique official references for the first five years of its violent life.

When Rey published his articles, the war had been raging in the interior for nearly three years, but in the city, it had scarcely been felt at all. Everything in the capital was different when the war began, so clean and ordered—before The Settlement was settled, before the Plaza was razed and replaced with Newtown Plaza, back when The Cantonment was a cantonment and not a furiously expanding slum along the northern edge of the city. In this place—which no longer exists—it was an affront to imagine *tadek* could be real. It offended the city's sense of itself: as a capital, as an urban center in dialogue with the world. But it wasn't only that: the war itself was an insult to the literate classes, and so *tadek* was patriotically legislated out of existence, and with it the war—all nation's unpleasant realities excised from newspapers and magazines, deemed unmentionable on the radio.

Early on, Rey's editor at the newspaper went into hiding—this had been previously agreed upon—but before he did, he promised Rey no one would give him up. That name of his hadn't been in circulation in many years, and he had never really been a public figure outside of the small, insular world of campus politics. But still, the tension was real: for weeks after, Rey expected armed men to burst into his home, to kick open his door at dawn and take him back to jail, back to the Moon. No one will read it, they'd told him. But Rey slept nervously, tightly entwined with Norma, with a chemical certainty in his blood that each evening together would be their last. They had been married only a few months, and he hadn't even warned her.

Somehow, he had imagined he could take this step without her ever knowing. One afternoon, before the worst of it, he came home and found his wife in the kitchen of their one-bedroom apartment, standing by the stove, stirring a pot of rice. He kissed her on the back of her neck, and she shrank from him. The obscure newspaper that no one read was right there, on the kitchen table. "They're going to kill you," she said.

He'd had precisely the same thought when the project was proposed. He'd been assured it was safe. He composed himself before he answered her. "No one knows who I am."

Norma laughed. "You're serious? You can't really believe that."

But what else could he believe?

"Why would you write these things?"

Of course, he'd been asked to, and it had been approved. But he couldn't tell her that. Rey reached for her, and she pulled away. Rey had proposed, and they had married; four years had passed since the day they met, and still the questions had not come. Now, with the essays published, out in the world, Norma was going to ask what she was entitled to know. She was his wife, after all, and he her husband. These were the questions he had expected since the day he proposed to her in his father's apartment: "Who are you?"—in various permutations. Now they had come. "Ask me anything," he said, and she began, as any journalist would, at the beginning: "Why didn't you tell me your father was alive?"

"I thought I was going to die."

This much was true.

"And I was sure they would come back for me. I wanted to protect you. The less you knew about me, the better."

He had not lied—not yet. It still shocked him sometimes: that he hadn't died in a pit and never been heard from again. But here was the proof: he was in his own apartment, with his wife, who was preparing dinner for the two of them. Hundreds of men might be doing the same thing at that exact moment. Thousands. Who could say he was any different from them? Many of these men, he could suppose, did not expect to die that day. Rey sighed. The kitchen was dark and claustrophobic. He longed for a beautiful day, for thin, high clouds spread like muslin across the sky. For a breeze. Before the war came to the city's finer neighborhoods, there were parks of olive trees and lemon trees planted in rows, and flower beds bursting with flowers of alarming colors, shady places for napping on a spread blanket, places where couples might stroll, hand in hand, and discuss in whispers all manner of personal things. This, too, the war would bring to an end. The city would become unrecognizable. In only a few weeks, at the height of the *tadek* controversy, Rey would write his will, would go over it with a colleague from the university, a law professor, who would view the entire affair as a morbid paranoia. You'll live to be old, the law professor would say over and over again, laughing nervously, laughing all the more because Rey would not. Rey would leave Norma everything. When the radio man was jailed, Rey knew they would come for him, too. It was only a matter of time: he visited his father to promise him a grandson but didn't explain. He begged his wife for forgiveness. All this would come later, but now he approached Norma, felt her tense when he touched her. He turned her around, until she faced him, but she wouldn't look up. He took Norma's hand in his, and worked his thumb along her knuckles, weaving figure eights. He could hurt her, he realized, and it could happen easily. The thought frightened him.

"Are you IL?" she asked.

He thought for a moment he should say what they had taught him, what the bearded professor at the Moon had told him: that there was no such thing. That the IL was an invention of the government, designed to frighten and distract the people. He almost said it—and just then she batted an eye. "Tell me the truth," Norma said, "and I'll never ask you again."

She was his wife, and they were in their own home; the doors were locked and bolted, and they were safe. Rey felt his heart surge for this woman, for this illusion called life: tomorrow the longed-for sun might come out, and they could walk through that quiet city park. The worst of the war was so far off it was unimaginable.

And so Rey had pronounced himself cured, as if subversion were a disease of the body. "No, I'm not IL. Let me explain." At the Moon, he told his wife, they buried him in a pit and he stood there for seven days, unable even to bend his knees properly, unable to squat. The hole was covered with wooden boards, with tiny slats wide enough to see a sliver of the sky: just a sliver, but enough to pray on. What did you pray for, Rey? Clouds, he said. By day, when the sun blazed above, it was stifling and hot, like being baked alive, and he felt insects all over but couldn't decide if they were real. He convinced himself they weren't. If he jumped, he could almost reach the top, but after the first day, he couldn't jump. Rey spent hours trying to reach down to massage the cramped and leaden muscles of his calves. It was a delicate procedure that involved pulling his leg up toward his chest, until his knee hit the earthen walls of the hole he had come to think of as his, tilting to one side, and reaching down into the darkness. My hole wasn't wide enough, he told Norma. My tomb, he might have said. He dug at the sides with his fingernails, scraped at the bottom with his curled toes. Rey longed to knead his calves, but had to content himself with scratching a spot just below the knee. He scratched until it hurt, and then he scratched some more. On the fourth night, a couple of drunken soldiers took the cover off. Rey saw stars, the glittering firmament full of light, and he knew he was far from the city. The sky was beautiful, and for a moment, he believed in God. Then the soldiers unzipped their pants and urinated on him: a wordless, joyless transaction. He expected them to laugh, to joke, to find happiness in cruelty, but there was nothing, only the starlight and the marmoreal glow of his tormentors' faces. Rey slept standing. He could smell himself. The fifth day passed, and the sixth. He was unconscious when they pulled him out on the seventh and placed him in a cell with a half-dozen prisoners: the bearded man in the wrinkled suit and a few others, all of them shrunken, deformed, able simply to lie on the floor, unable to speak.

Rey promised Norma: he'd been cleansed of all political ambitions. "It's simple," he said with such fervor she might have believed him. Indeed, the essence of what he said was true: "I want to live. I want to grow old with you. I don't ever want to go back."

• • •

B u t i t began only six months after he'd returned from the Moon, a few
years before the *tadek* controversy, on a morning crosstown bus, the day
Rey spotted the man with the beard. He wore the same wrinkled suit, the
same look of amused indifference. Was it him? It was; it wasn't. Rey rubbed
his eyes. Here, among strangers, he usually did his best thinking: divaga-
tions of the mind, blurring and then effacing that which he did not care to
remember. The Moon, the Moon: it stayed with him, a song whose melody
he couldn't escape. His uncle Trini had found him a job in Tamoé, inspecting the settlements, working for the government agency that ratified land
takeovers. It was temporary, an invisible post in an invisible bureaucracy,
something to hold him over until he could muster the strength to return
to the university. He'd been there only three weeks, wandering among the
shanties, asking questions of mothers who eyed him suspiciously, as if he
were coming to take their homes away. He wrote names on his clipboard,
drew rudimentary maps of the squalid neighborhoods on graph paper the
office provided him. He lunched in silence at the open-air market, and
these were his days. He remembered the Moon, imagined it just behind every hill. The bus ride was an hour and a half each way, spent between sleep
and a kind of autohypnotism he'd perfected: watching his fellow passengers
until his eyes crossed, until they became shapes and colors and not people
at all. The city passed in the window, now and then a word calling him from
the newspaper someone might be reading, the war appearing in headlines,
still on an inside page, still a distant nightmare. He himself never read the
newspaper; he made a point not to.

Now the bus took a tight turn, the passengers swaying with it—dancers, all of them—and Rey caught another glimpse of the man: we were
chained together, Rey thought, and he shut his eyes tightly. The dreams
were evenly spaced now, not every night, but twice-weekly explosions of
filmic violence. He ground his teeth in his sleep, could feel the soreness
in his jaw each morning, the grit of enamel peppering his tongue. He
stayed with his father, slept on the sofa, and Trini came over every evening to see his shell-shocked nephew; together, they relived better days
over steaming cups of tea. "You need a woman," Trini said, and it was the
only thing Rey's father and uncle could agree on.

The man in the wrinkled suit was staring at him. Or perhaps Rey was staring. It was impossible to tell: one would have imagined that the city was a perfect place for anonymity, a place to disappear, a place so opaque it would do your forgetting for you. But here he was. Their eyes met. It's my second home, the man had said. Rey shuddered. It meant he was marked. A time bomb. More than anything, Rey wanted to get off at the very next stop: he was content to wait for the next bus on any strange, unknown corner of the city, anywhere far away from this man—I'll be late for work, he thought, it doesn't matter. Rey noticed he was sweating, his heart skipping along, frantic, while the man in the wrinkled suit—Rey could see him now, amid the somnolent, workaday crowd—the man seemed perfectly calm. He met Rey's gaze; he didn't flinch or turn away.

Rey rode the rest of the way with his eyes half-closed, pretending to sleep. When he awoke, the man was gone. It was a clear day in Tamoé, a day of bright sun that acted upon him as a drug might: Rey found himself knocking on the wrong doors, stumbling over his prepared speech—I represent the government; I am here to help you legitimize your claim on this land, on this house. Sweat beaded on his brow, stung his eyes. Doors were slammed in his face, women refused to speak with him without their husbands present. He left business cards and promised to return, but the day stretched on in an opiate haze, Rey trudging from one dusty street to the next. He represented the government—just as those soldiers had, the night they pissed on him beneath the stars. The generous embrace of power, Trini called it, with a smirk. "Don't worry, boy," his uncle had said. "If they blacklisted everyone they sent to the Moon, there'd be no one left to hire."

A couple of days passed before he saw the man in the wrinkled suit again: on the same morning bus ride through the city to Tamoé. This time, the man boarded a few stops after Rey and nodded at him—it was unmistakable! brazen!—before burying his face in a newspaper. The next day, it was the same thing. And the next. Rey called in sick on the fourth day, an unnecessary courtesy he felt compelled to provide: he was a minion in a swollen bureaucracy, and no one would have noticed. Still, he wrapped himself in a coat, stumbled outside, and called from the pay phone on the corner, shivering. He dutifully reported symptoms as vague as they were real: a slight sense of vertigo, a pain in his shoulder, a shallowness of breath. He said nothing of the fear or the nightmares of paralyzing intensity. What he needed, he decided as he spoke to an uninterested secretary, was some rest.

Rey returned to work the following day, and this time, the man in the wrinkled suit was waiting for him at the bus stop, seated on the bench with a newspaper folded under his arm, staring blankly at the passing traffic. Rey hadn't mentioned this apparition to anyone—not to his father or Trini. It felt like an assault. There was no one else at the bus stop. Rey glared at the man, and the man smiled back.

"Are you following me?" Rey asked.

"Won't you sit?" The man's tone was warm, avuncular. "We have things to discuss, you and I."

"I find that hard to believe," Rey said, but he sat anyway. "I'm not scared of you."

"Of course," the man said. He had gained some weight since Rey saw him last. Then again, one might assume they all had. At the Moon, a soldier came by twice a day and dropped pieces of bread into the hole, along with a plastic bag full of water. "Tamoé," the man said, "is the future of this stricken nation."

A bus came; a woman with a bag of vegetables stepped off. The bus driver held the door open, waiting for Rey, but the man in the wrinkled suit waved it away.

"In Tamoé, the foundation will be laid. Is being laid, I should say, at this very moment. Tell me, do you enjoy your work?"

What was there to like? It was a slum like any other. Rey coughed into his hand.

"We have people there," the man continued. He nodded slowly, the edges of his mouth creeping toward a smile. "I would like you to meet them." He reached into an inside pocket and pulled out an envelope. "I can't visit them with you. It wouldn't be safe."

Rey looked at the man and then around him at the busy avenue. From a distance, they were simply two men—strangers, acquaintances—chatting. Was anyone watching them? Listening? They could be speaking of the weather, or the weekend scores, or anything. The man placed the envelope on the bench between them. "Why me?" Rey asked.

"Because I know your name," the man said. "Not the one you were born with. The other one."

The name, the ID. For an instant, an image flashed before him: the woman he hadn't seen since the night his misfortunes began. Norma was her name. *Norma.* "I don't know what you're talking about," Rey said, but the words had a disappointing lack of weight to them: they sounded weak, tenuous.

"I see they succeeded in frightening you at the Moon. There are other things you can do for us. Quiet things. Clean things. You needn't be public anymore to be useful."

"I don't understand."

"Of course. There aren't many of us who really know you." The man eyed him and didn't blink. "Shall I say your other name? Shall I prove it?"

Rey felt suddenly that his youth was a decade in the past, that he had become, seemingly overnight, old and decrepit, a man with nothing to lose. He was dying. He shook his head. He hadn't seen Norma again, hadn't thought of her until that exact moment. Would he even recognize her? He had spent six months confined by the unsettling substance of his own dreams. Rey took the envelope without looking at it, slipped it into his inside coat pocket. It was thin and waxy. He knew instinctively the envelope was empty. It was a test.

The man smiled. "Avenue F–10. Lot 128. Ask for Marden."

They'll lock me up again, Rey thought, and this time no one will see me. This time they won't spare me. If he went to the police, what would he say? What would he have for them? An empty envelope and vague descriptions of a man with a thin beard and an ill-fitting suit. And where did you meet this man, the police would ask—oh, here it is, where I give myself away: when I was a prisoner, sir, at the Moon.

The man scratched his brow. "You have questions I can't answer," he said. "In the meantime, I'll ask you one: those soldiers. The ones who kept us company when we last met. Do you hate them?"

The bus was a half-block away. *Hate* was a word Rey never used. It meant nothing to him. The soldiers had pissed on him joylessly, with the detachment of scientists performing an experiment. When Rey was a boy, he and his friends captured beetles, placed them in plastic tins, and set them on fire, blissfully cruel: a group of boys, charmed by this collaborative act of malice. Why did this memory fill him with such nostalgia, and why were the soldiers so dispassionate in their cruelty? They had tortured him with the same conviction with which he wandered around Tamoé. That is to say, they had done so listlessly, by rote. How could he hate them? It was their job. If they had so much as snickered, Rey felt certain, he could. Loathe them. Absolutely. Without that, they seemed strangely innocent.

The bus jerked to a stop before them, and Rey made as if to rise, but the man in the wrinkled suit held him back. "You'll wait for the next one," he said. He got on the bus and didn't look back.

H E K E P T on to the envelope for two weeks. That first night, after Trini had come and gone, after his father had gone off to sleep, Rey held it up to the light and verified it was empty. There was a script letter *M* in the upper right-hand corner. The envelope was sealed, thin, and insubstantial.

Rey returned to Tamoé all that week, expecting each morning to see the man with the thin beard. He never did. He walked around the neighborhood as he always had, taking notes, drawing his crude maps, filling out forms with illiterate men who insisted on looking everything over before signing an *X* to the bottom of the page. He studiously avoided Avenue F–10, never crossing it on foot: if he was to work on the north side of F–10, he took the bus a few stops past and spent the entire day there. On other days, he confined himself to the south side, never nearing this new, artificial border.

It took him two weeks, but when Rey finally decided to see Marden, he did it right away. Later he would wonder why he went at all, and decide it was curiosity—a natural curiosity—and tell himself that a healthy interest in the unknown would always be useful. In his career as a scientist, and in his life, if he were allowed to live it. It was not the hate that the man in the wrinkled suit wanted him to feel: Rey felt proud of that somehow. Still, he was afraid. He dressed that day as he normally would, washed his face under the cold-water tap of his father's apartment, and folded the empty envelope into his front pocket. When he pulled the door shut behind him, Rey felt a heaviness in the act.

Avenue F–10 ran roughly east-west through Tamoé, a potholed four-lane road divided by a gravel median, dotted with the occasional withering

shrub. The avenue was lined with squat apartment houses, crowded repair shops, and a few restaurants of questionable cleanliness and limited
menus. If a place like Tamoé could be said to possess a center, F–10 was
it: one of two avenues with streetlights in the newly colonized district.
On his north-side days, Rey's bus ride home crossed the avenue: he
could sense its glow, its energy from blocks away. After dark, groups of
boys congregated beneath F–10's streetlights: laughing, alive, they squatted around these totems, bathing in the pale orange glow. Rey found it
perplexing: it seemed the youth of the district never left Tamoé; instead,
they came here, to this avenue, just to stand in the light.

That morning, Rey got off in the heart of F–10 and walked east.
Even by day, it was crowded with young people. Women sold tea from
wooden carts, emollients of pungent odors, syrups that promised to
cure any cough. Moto-taxis clustered on the corner, ferrying vendors to
the market a few blocks away. But ten blocks on, the avenue regained the
provincial air that defined the rest of the district. The asphalt disappeared
abruptly, and the four- and five-story apartment houses, Tamoé's most
solidly constructed buildings, were replaced by shanties, of the kind that
concerned Rey and his work most directly: ad hoc homes of considerable ingenuity, homes built of material scavenged from the city. Illegal,
ubiquitous, inevitable, the city would grow and grow and no one could
imagine it ever stopping. The avenue itself petered out at the base of a
crumbling, yellow hill, a dusty lane running headlong into a mound of
scree. Here, a shirtless child had planted a red flag in the pile of rock. A
half-dozen children ran around it, ignoring Rey, now and then clamber-
ing up, only to be repelled by a hail of stones. They played war. A thin,
black dog sat at a safe distance from the children, chewing nervously on
a piece of Styrofoam.

Lot 128 was set just off the dusty edge of the street, to the left of the
pile of rocks. It was a house like any other on the block, mud brick with
small, paneless windows on either side of the door, and lined with a knee-
high fence of woven reeds. Rey stepped over it. The number was painted
neatly in the center of the door. Rey resisted the urge to peek through the
windows. He knocked twice and waited.

"Marden," Rey said when the door opened. "I have a message for
Marden."

The man in the doorway was large and pale, wearing an undershirt and dark drawstring pants patched at the knees. He was older than fifty, perhaps much older. His hair was the color of a used cigarette filter, and his face, jowly and slack, had that same exhausted, yellow-gray pallor. If he was Marden, the name seemed to have no effect on him, or rather not precisely the effect Rey had been expecting: a look of recognition, even camaraderie. The man looked down the street suspiciously, then waved Rey in. He pointed to a chair in the center of the room, and squatted in front of a tiny gas burner resting on the dirt floor. With a bent fork, he tended to a single egg. It bobbed and sank in a pot of boiling water.

"Breakfast," the man said. He apologized for having nothing to offer his visitor, but he did so in a tone Rey could not mistake for warmth.

"I ate, thank you," Rey said. The man shrugged and tapped his egg.

The room was dark, the air full of dust and smoke and steam. Besides the chair, there was a twin bed and a radio on the nightstand. In the generally colorless room, there was one grand splash of reddish orange: a finely knit bedspread, fiery and bright and out of place.

The man must have caught him looking. "My mother made it," he said. "Years ago."

Old men have mothers, too. Subversives, too, even those who live Spartan lives. Rey tried to smile. The man turned off the burner and flipped the egg into a bowl. The water settled in the pot, steaming. He tapped some instant coffee into a cup, then filled it with the same water he'd used to boil the egg. He stirred with a fork and handed the cup to Rey. "When you finish," he said, "I'll have some."

Rey nodded and took the cup. Sugar? he almost asked, then thought better of it. He held the cup to his lips. It smelled like coffee, at least.

"This message?" the man said, without looking up. He sat with his legs crossed and peeled his egg carefully, gathering the tiny bits of eggshell in his lap. "Who gave it to you?"

"Are you Marden?"

The man glanced at Rey, then brushed off his fingers and took the egg into his mouth whole. He chewed for a minute or more, nodding. Rey drank his coffee, for lack of anything else to do. It burned his tongue. Then he sat forward, with his elbows on his knees and his chin resting in his palm. He watched the man eat. The loose skin of the man's cheeks puffed and stretched. He swallowed with an exaggerated expression of satisfaction and rubbed his belly. "I'm Marden," he said. "Where'd you get this message?"

Rey put down his coffee and joined the man on the floor. He pulled the envelope from his back pocket. "I don't know his name."

Marden looked the envelope over, squinted at the *M*, and broke into a grin. "Very nice," he said. He tore the envelope in half, then into quarters, then into eighths. He handed the bits and pieces back to Rey. "Where is he finding people these days?" he said, amused.

Rey held the scraps of the envelope in his cupped hands. "What do I do with this?" he asked.

Marden shrugged. "Smoke them. Bury them. Confetti at your wedding. It doesn't matter, kid."

"I don't understand."

"When he asks, tell him there were eight pieces. When we need you, the professor will find you. He'll tell you where to leave a message for me and you'll do it." Marden coughed dryly into his hand. "You work in Tamoé?"

Rey nodded.

"Avoid this part of the district. Wait for us. It could be months. It could be a year, or even two. No one knows."

"No one?"

"I don't. You don't. Not even the professor does. We do as we're told. You'll be a messenger. Your job is to wait."

Rey put the pieces of the envelope back into his pocket. His coffee had cooled a bit, enough for the bitter liquid to go down without too much trouble. He finished it and passed the cup to Marden. Was this all? Had he waited two weeks to have an empty envelope torn to pieces before him by a jowly, yellow-haired old man? It didn't seem right.

"Were you at the Moon?" Rey asked.

Marden frowned. "I've been there," he said after a moment. "You have as well?"

"Yes."

"Keep it to yourself." Marden sighed. "You won't be coming back here. We have people all over the district. Things are happening."

The meeting was over. There were no good-byes, no handshakes. The door opened, and the small room released him.

Outside, the children ran in frantic circles, raising a film of fine dust, a low, sandy fog over the street. He could feel it in his nostrils, he could taste it. The day was just beginning. The children paid him no attention. Rey walked away from the hill, down the avenue, absentmindedly scattering remains of the envelope along the way.

WHEN REY returned to the university that year, just before his twenty-fifth birthday, he still hadn't seen the man in the wrinkled suit, or been to the eastern end of F–10. He'd worked, documenting scores of Indian families and the exact addresses of their ramshackle homes. He interpreted hand gestures and forged signatures for people he thought might benefit. He learned a bit of the Indian dialect, enough to say "good day" and "thank you" and "you're welcome." A half year in Tamoé, and the dust became a part of him: in the evenings, his clothes shook off clouds of it, his skin felt heavy with it. He was going to be buried alive if he stayed much longer. Every Friday, he made his way to the central office of the district, a blandly decorated room with a single desk and a sun-faded flag, on the district's other lighted avenue. He turned in his paperwork, wondering only briefly what became of these maps and forms and records. Once settled, Rey knew, nothing would move these people. They didn't need his help for anything beyond peace of mind: only a cataclysm would clear the area. He thought now and then of the man in the wrinkled suit, but on these rare occasions, the entire episode was cloaked in absurdity. There was no war of subversion in the making: where were the soldiers? The young men of the district seemed content to spend their evenings leaning against lampposts, posturing for the girls that passed by. The man in the wrinkled suit had invoked the future of the nation when he spoke of Tamoé, but who was the mysterious contact in this vanguard district? A terse, phlegmatic man with an unhealthy pallor, peeling eggs, alone. Marden, with his faraway look and peripheral existence, hardly seemed capable of leaving his home—to say nothing of instigating a general revolt.

Rey arranged to work part-time and resumed his studies. Despite all the talk, the president's warnings, and the bellicose editorials, life at the university had not yet changed. There were no soldiers inside its gates. Students still gathered in the main courtyard and discussed the coming conflict as they had before, with that strange mix of awe and anxiety. It made Rey nervous to return: there were more than a few people who might remember one or another of the speeches he'd made, his brief and intoxicating turn at the university as an outspoken critic of the government. The prospect of meeting these people made his heart quicken. He'd been on committees that planned trips to the mountains. He'd met in dark rooms to plan protests. Most significant, he'd acquired another name, and with it came responsibilities. But then he had disappeared. His old friends would have questions: Where have you been? What did they do to you? Are you all right? Every so often, in the months of his recovery, Rey's father handed him a note that some concerned young man had brought by the apartment. They were always polite but insistent: that he contact them, because they were waiting. Rey never responded: what could he say? There were people at the university who had looked up to him. He hadn't seen anyone in nearly a year; he had fled to Tamoé. By now, they must consider him a traitor. They had surely interpreted his silence this way, and if they asked, he would have no answers.

Do you hate them? It tormented him, this question. At the university, Rey slipped into class just as the professor began lecturing, and left before the hour ended. He wore hooded sweatshirts even on sunny days, and walked quickly through campus, careful to keep his gaze fixed on the ground before him. All the things he would say to Norma years later were true. He was afraid of politics. He was afraid of dying. He was afraid of finding himself a broken man of fifty, living in a slum at the edge of the city, waiting for the arrival of obscure messages from the great brain of subversion. When Rey met her again, when he saw her and saw that she had seen him as well—he felt a shiver: even at a distance, she recalled for him, in all its immediacy, the terror of what he had done, of Marden and the man in the wrinkled suit and the blank horrors that still penetrated his dreams. He had risked too much. He had come so far from that night of dancing, that night of bombast and boasting. He'd only wanted to impress her. Because she was beautiful. Because she didn't seem to mind looking at him either. And now she was walking toward him. The IL had found him at a bus stop; why did he believe, even for a moment, that they would forget him now? That he could just walk away? It was a cold, cloudy day—the malaise of winter.

Norma smiled at him, and she looked like sunshine. She hadn't forgotten him, either. Rey panicked.

It was true. It was always true: you could believe one thing and its opposite simultaneously, be afraid and reckless all at once. You could write dangerous articles under an assumed name and believe yourself to be an impartial scholar. You could become a messenger for the IL and fall in love with a woman who believed you were not. You could pretend that the nation at war was a tragedy and not the work of your own hand. You could proclaim yourself a humanist and hate with steely resolve.

When, after the conflict, the displaced thousands returned to the site of the Battle of Tamoé, they found their homes burned, their avenues cratered, their hills littered with unexploded ordnance. Tanks had run through their streets, bulldozers had razed entire blocks of houses. Their beloved streetlights had fallen too, but in any case, there were few young people left to gather around them. The entire district would be rebuilt. Without a monument to the dead, without so much as a plaque to commemorate what had been there before. It was announced that the families who had their paperwork in order would be permitted to return, would be forgiven. If they could find their old plot, it was theirs, regardless of their role in the battle or their sympathies for the IL. An office was set up on a burned-out block of F–10 to process the petitions. A line gathered there each morning before dawn. For months, they came, heads bowed like penitents, carrying the forms Rey had written for them or the maps he had drawn, and it was all they owned in the world.

NINE

MANAU ARRIVED in the city and inhaled. Its odor was
enough: that potent mix of metal and smoke. He was home. Adela's boy held his hand, and Manau felt keenly the possibility of forgetting:
her taste, her body, her caresses. He shut his eyes.

The boy looked up at him: "What will we do?"

Manau squeezed his hand and pulled him along. He carried both
their bags over his shoulder. The street outside the bus station was full of
people, spilling off the sidewalks, scrambling between the cars. The boy
had said almost nothing the last hour of the bus ride. Even this simple
question—what will we do?—had to be viewed as progress. He gazed
at everything with wide, fearful eyes. The boy was not home: he was
in hell. And the city was a terrible place, to be sure, but the world was
made up of terrible places. Maybe Victor was too young to take solace in
that fact. And there were other facts: Adela was dead, and now they were
both alone. Manau tried, as he had for the previous four days, to clear his

mind, but still he was pursued by the urge to weep. Ten days before, he had made love to Adela on a mat of reeds. It had been a moonless night. Around them, above them, in the near distance of the forest, birds had made their bright and inscrutable music. A pang of desire shot through him at the memory: he and Adela had scratched one another and pushed, they had rolled clumsily off the mat and onto the ground. The moist earth had stuck to their bodies. Later, the rains came to clean them: a sky split by lightning, curtains of purple water crashing loudly over the trees.

In the city, the sky and its clouds glowed white. It was a year since he'd seen this shade of color above.

"Is it going to rain?" Victor asked. "Is that what you're looking at?"

Manau managed a smile. "I don't think so." He didn't say that they were in the coastal desert now, that as long as he stayed in the city, Victor would not see anything recognizable as rain. Always cloudy, this city, always humid. It's a trick, Manau wanted to say. "Are you hungry?" he asked instead, and the boy nodded.

An Indian woman squatted on the sidewalk, selling bread from a covered basket balanced on a crate. She puffed on the stub of a hand-rolled cigar and did not smile. Manau took two rolls of bread and paid her with a handful of coins. The woman held them in her palm for a second, then frowned. She took one between her molars and twisted it. The metal coin bent in her teeth.

"It's fake," she said, handing it back. "Don't give me this jungle money."

Her mountain accent was thick with masticated vowels. Jungle money? Manau mumbled an apology and fished a bill from his pocket. The boy watched the proceedings without comment. He had already eaten half of his roll. The woman scowled. "Pay first, then eat, boy." She held Manau's bill up, inspecting it. "Where do you come from?" she asked.

"From 1797," Manau said. He tried a joke: "The money's good, madam. I made it myself."

She released a mouthful of smoke. Not even a smile. "You people have ruined this place." She handed Manau his change and turned to serve another customer.

Manau felt his blood rising. The city was impregnated with the smell of ruin: it swirled in the sodden air and stuck to you, wherever you went. It followed me all the way to the jungle, Manau thought, and now he stood accused of bringing it home again. He looked at the woman, at the boy. In the neighborhood where he was raised, there was an Indian woman who shined shoes and sharpened knives. She walked the streets, chatting with the women who knew her, offering candy to the children. She lived beneath the bridge at the end of the street, and she always smiled and never complained, not even when the war got bad and half her customers moved away—that's how they were supposed to be: these mountain people, these desperate poor.

Manau spat on the sidewalk in front of the woman.

"Move on!" she hissed.

Then he had done it, not for himself but for the boy: with a swift kick, Manau upended the woman's basket of bread, knocking it off the crate. There was a shout. Bread spilled everywhere on the dirty sidewalk, rolled into the gutter. In an instant, the woman was up, her face hot, her fists clenched. She would have attacked and certainly hurt him—but there was no time: the passersby had turned on her, had swarmed her, they were stealing her bread. The woman scurried behind them, swatting at hands, but it was no use. Her bread disappeared into the hands of men in work clothes, and mothers in housedresses, and ratty street kids with matted hair. "Thieves!" the woman yelled, red to bursting, her face a livid, unnatural color. Something animal had been unleashed in her, and she waved her cigar in frantic, menacing loops. She attacked a man who had snatched a roll and, for a brief and shocking instant, it seemed she might bite him.

A day's worth of bread vanished in fifteen seconds.

It happened so fast that he couldn't be sure why he had done it, only that he did not regret it. Not at all. Manau tossed some change at the upturned basket, took Victor's hand, and backed away. He looked down the avenue. In the distance was the radio's spire, a woven metal phallus pointing skywards, adorned with blinking red lights. "Let's go," Manau said to the boy, and they went toward it, first walking, then racing, as if someone or something were chasing them.

It was only ten days before, as they drank palm wine and waited hopefully for a breeze, that Zahir had invited Manau to touch his stumps. "Be kind to an old man," he said, though Manau did not think of his landlord and friend as old. "I'm sad today."

"Are you sure?"

"Of course I'm sure. It's about time you did. You stare."

Manau blushed and began to protest, but Zahir interrupted him. "It's all right," he said. "Everyone does."

The sun had sunk behind the trees, and the sky dimmed toward a lacquered blue-black. It was the edge of night in the jungle: a nimbus of mosquitoes buzzed around the kerosene lantern. Manau sipped his wine from a gourd. Nico had been gone for months now, and no one had heard from him. That night and every night, Manau was careful not to mention Zahir's son. When the wine loosened his tongue, Manau felt he might confess, but then he was unsure what to say, and so said nothing. Nearly half a year had passed this way. A harvest had come and gone.

In a few hours, the night breezes would blow, Manau would excuse himself, and wander off to look for Adela, forgetting Nico and his unfortunate father for another day. If the moon was out, or even if it wasn't, he would invite her to swim.

Now Zahir was waiting, eyes shut tight, holding his arms out for inspection. Manau took another sip from his gourd and set it on the floor. He placed a hand over each stump, felt the rough skin against his palms. He held Zahir's right arm by the wrist, and went over the wound with his thumb. Where it had scarred, the flesh turned in on itself, like a sinkhole or a crevasse or the dry and jagged bed of a stream.

"It's been seven years," Zahir said, opening his eyes. "Seven years today."

Manau let go. He had come to think of his landlord's stumps as a cruel birth defect, a trial Zahir had always borne. Of course, this wasn't true. He knew it wasn't. Still, it was startling: seven years ago yesterday, Zahir could scratch his temple, light his own cigarette. He could love his wife with ten more possibilities. Manau looked down at his own hands, and they seemed like miracles. He cracked his knuckles; they gave off a satisfying pop. He wiggled his fingers, then caught Zahir watching him.

"I'm sorry."

"You get used to it. Really. Do you believe me?"

Manau made a point of looking Zahir in the eye. "Of course," he said.

The dark began just a few feet beyond the steps of Zahir's raised hut. The townspeople shuffled by, nearly invisible, now and then calling a greeting. Manau felt unable to speak. In a little more than a week, he would leave this village, and all the stories he'd heard here would seem burdensome and foreign, woeful tales foisted upon him: his crippled friend, the dozens of missing, the town and its never-ending battle against the encroaching forest. Flood, neglect, war. Manau would look at the boy—his fellow traveler—and be reminded of this day and others, when Zahir told him of 1797 and its history. He would feel disappointed in himself, that he had allowed it, that he had accepted these memories that were not his. At the time, it had seemed painless, even pleasant: the crepuscular light, the lulling haze of the wine, the stories that always ended badly. He had very nearly belonged. He might have made a home there, if Adela hadn't died.

Zahir said, "The IL came and asked for food. We told them the war was over. They accused us of lying. We told them there was no food to spare. They said someone must have stolen the food if there was none to give. There was a thief in town, they said. So they took the boy and did *tadek*."

He rubbed his face with the end of his arm. On feast days, after he drank, Zahir let his wife tie tassels to his arms. Red and white. Manau had seen him, had seen the whole process. When she reached his stumps, she slowed, massaging the rough skin there, gently, adoringly. Surely she missed his hands too, but the way she lavished attention on his stumps, you would never guess it. She tied thick blooms to them. Then, when the music began in earnest, Zahir danced to the drum and the flute, waving his arms like a bird.

"And Victor picked you?" Manau asked.

"Because he knew me, I suppose. He was Nico's friend, you understand. They were always good friends. He could have picked anyone. It's a miracle he didn't go to his mother."

Adela without her hands—Manau was seized with terror, imagining it.

"Victor doesn't remember it," Zahir said, "and that's for the best. What good would it do?"

None, thought Manau. But did Nico remember it? What good would that do? Or what evil had it already done? Manau fumbled for his glass. His wine was warm, but it went down easily. The breezes would begin soon.

"Do you want to know something else?" Zahir said. "I deserved it. The boy was right."

"No one deserves that."

"I did."

Manau waited for his friend to go on, but Zahir didn't. The silence lasted a minute or more, and Manau didn't ask for explanations. He didn't dare. They listened to the forest. When Zahir spoke again, it was in another tone of voice.

"But that was the second time the IL came," said Zahir. "The first time they came to shoot the priest."

"There was a priest?" Manau asked.

Then, a woman's voice from the darkness: "Oh, yes, there was a priest."

It was Adela. She had snuck up on them. She stepped into the orange lamp light, and Manau felt something warm in his chest: he wouldn't have to look for her later. She was right here; maybe she'd been looking for him.

"You found us," he said.

Her hair was braided loosely; a few strands fell just above her eyes. She very nearly glistened. Adela held her hand out, and Manau obliged with a kiss.

"Don Zahir," Adela said, with the slightest bow.

He received her with a nod.

Manau offered Adela his chair, but she sat at the top of the stair instead. She pulled her skirt above her knees. He noticed her bare feet, her ankles. "Is there wine?" she asked.

"For you, my dear, there is always wine," Zahir said, and Manau stood without waiting to be told. He went inside and came back with a gourd. He poured carefully. A full cup. She took a sip.

"Zahir," Adela said, "you were telling a story."

"The priest and his fate. These are old tales."

"Tell it," she said.

Zahir sighed. She was irresistible, and not just to Manau.

The beginning of the war: a sun-drunk group of fighters stumbled into town. They were young, Zahir said. They stank of youth, and for this reason, many people forgave them. Also, if truth be told, the victim was not a man universally liked. The priest had come from abroad some thirty years before and, at the time of his death, still clung stubbornly to his accent. He refused to learn any of the old language, and did not contribute to the upkeep of the communal plot. He looked down on the Indians who came to trade medicinal plants and wild birds for cornmeal and razor blades and bullets. They didn't know God, he said. And so the IL waved their weapons and bound his hands, and no one protested. The rebels kept their faces covered. They ordered the entire village, some hundred and twenty families in those days, to gather to watch the execution. The shooter was a young woman. She was very pale.

Zahir took a deep breath, then drank from his gourd. He asked for a cigarette. Manau lit one and held it to Zahir's lips while the old man smoked. Manau took a few puffs as well, held the cool smoke in his lungs: It was that last detail that seemed so strange to him: a woman! They were bad people, these IL, but he couldn't help being intrigued. This jungle wine did strange things to the brain: he had to touch Adela right then. He stretched his leg out; his right toe could just graze her elbow if he nearly slid off his chair. The night had come swiftly, and the breezes were beginning.

She turned to Manau and smiled. She swatted his foot away and pinched her nose.

When the cigarette had burned down, Zahir announced he had come to the interesting part of the story. "Isn't it so, Adela?" he asked.

"If I remember correctly, Don Zahir."

"Of course you do," said the cripple.

The IL gave the priest's home to the poorest family in the village, the Hawas, and they had no choice but to accept. A great show was made of carrying their few possessions to the priest's house. But when the IL left a few days later, Mr. Hawa moved his family back to their lean-to near the river. The village begged him to stay, but he wouldn't listen to reason. His wife was heartbroken. She insisted on bringing with her a large bronze crucifix, and would have brought the priest's iron stove as well, had her husband allowed it.

"We were all very afraid for him. We told him, if the IL comes back and finds you have refused their gift, they'll certainly kill all of you. But Hawa would not be convinced. He was a hunter. He spent most of his time on his canoe, deep in the forest, killing the animals he saw on the shores of the river: pythons, alligators, the spearfish you can only find three days' walk from here. He said he had seen these IL. They were jokers, he said. He wasn't afraid. I talked to him myself. What about the priest, I asked him. The priest had it coming, Hawa said."

"And what happened to Hawa?"

"He left, with his two sons, for the war. Years ago. His wife stayed. And then she left too." Zahir shrugged, as if to indicate the story was over.

"You've left out the best part, Don Zahir."

"Have I?"

Adela nodded. Manau could make out the sly contours of her smile. The evening's breezes had begun.

"What we did to the house."

Zahir grinned. "Well, yes. Of course. What else could we do? We burned it."

The empty house was a hazard. The IL were killers: what if they returned, and Hawa was away? They would kill someone else in the village just to make it right.

On a warm February evening, in honor of Independence Day, the priest's home was burned. They prepared it with axes and saws: disassembling the simple structure until it was just a pile of wood and paper and old, musty clothes. A bonfire. It burned cleanly, part of the last Independence Day that would be celebrated in 1797 until the end of the war. By the next year, the men had begun to leave, and then the boys, and the conflict could be ignored no longer. Manau knew the story. No one was sad to see them go, because they were expected to return.

Zahir never left, and that must have been its own challenge. Almost every man his age went. Manau had heard him say it before, part apology, part denial: "I liked it here; why should I have left?"

Now Zahir recalled playing his guitar while everyone sang, while the fire burned. He sang; he danced. It seemed impossible that he could have forgotten this part. "Was it a beautiful festival, Adela? He doesn't know, you must tell him!"

There was something not right with the story. Where did they bury the priest? Manau wondered. He pushed the question from his mind, and focused on the scene: the party, the breezy night, the townspeople when they were still optimistic. He reached for her again, and touched her. She pinched his foot this time. A breeze curled around them.

"It was very beautiful," Adela said.

MANAU WALKED Victor to the station. Adela's boy. *Adela*. He took him by the hand to the front desk, where a receptionist typed disinterestedly with two fingers. They stood before her, Victor just tall enough to peek over the edge. They waited. A half-minute passed before she made eye contact.

"Yes?" the receptionist asked finally.

"We need to see Norma," Manau said. He was tired, a kind of exhaustion he'd never felt before. "Norma," he said to the boy, "will take care of you."

The receptionist smiled. She had a round face and lipstick on her teeth, just a tiny red smudge of it, and Manau wondered if he should tell her. He didn't.

"I'm sorry, that's not possible," the receptionist said. She pointed upwards, to small speakers in the ceiling. "She's on the air."

Of course she was. That was her voice filling the room, reading the news so sweetly. He hadn't even noticed the sound before. It had registered in his mind as a lullaby.

"What is this about?" the receptionist asked.

"The boy," Manau said. "He has a list for Lost City Radio." He turned to Victor. "Show her. Show her the note."

Victor took it from his pocket and passed it to the receptionist. She read it quickly, running her index finger beneath the words as she did. Turning the page over, she glanced at the list of missing, and then instructed Manau and Victor to sit. To be patient. To wait. She handed the note back and picked up the phone. She spoke in a low voice. They dropped their bags and slumped into the cushions of the sofa, while Norma read the news without comment, even-toned. She was masterful. Manau could hardly concentrate on the words.

That night in the jungle, on Zahir's porch, when the breezes began, he excused himself and led Adela into the darkness, to love her. He carried with him the reed mat that Zahir's wife had woven for him. Manau bade Zahir a good evening, stepped down the raised porch onto the ground, still soft from the afternoon shower. Adela asked him to wait, and he did, around the corner, just beyond the reach of the light. The moon had not yet risen, and the black night made him impatient. There were murmurings from the top of the stairs. The jungle breathed, noises of all kinds, but there was nothing to see in the inky darkness. Manau was aware of people walking by him in twos and threes, scarcely perceptible, dim shadows. Whoever they were, they said his name politely as they passed by: Manau, Mr. Manau, professor. Could everyone see but him? He smiled brightly, hoping the passersby—his students? his neighbors?—might mistake his smile for recognition. He couldn't see a thing. It could have been the trees talking. Or any of a dozen ghosts that his pupils believed in. Nico was the latest phantom all the boys and girls claimed to see. Where? he asked. At the edge of the forest—where else? Manau, Manau, Manau. Have you seen Nico? they asked. No, I haven't. Unless dreams count. They do, mister! the children clamored. Of course, dreams count! The children, like everyone in the village, were always accompanied. Manau was alone. He didn't allow himself the luxury of believing in ghosts. Now he smiled in the darkness and waited. What were they discussing? It was this obliterating loneliness that Adela had begun to cure. Manau thought then that he didn't miss the city anymore and never would again. He thought then that he would die here in this jungle redoubt, of old age, having mastered the antique language of the forest, having learned which plants brought nourishment and which were poisonous. It occurred to him to light a match, to survey his kingdom, but it flared and blew out in the breeze: an instant of flittering orange light—and that was all. Enough to see his hands. Clouds had blotted out the sky. It was a lightless, moonless night. Still, he would take her to the river or to the field. Or both. And he would love her.

Then he heard her descending the stairs, heard the creak of the wood. He turned back, but he couldn't see her. The lamps had been extinguished, and the darkness was complete. Manau reached for her.

"Today is seven years since Zahir lost his hands," she said.

"I know. He told me."

"I had to pay my respects. Give him my apologies." She sighed. "It was my boy that did it."

Manau nodded, though he was sure she couldn't see him. They were walking, he thought, toward the field. He could feel the soggy earth beneath his feet. Her voice, he noticed, had nearly cracked. Was she crying?

"It was the IL, not Victor," Manau said to the darkness. He heard her sigh again. She must know I'm right, he thought. The boy is innocent. Except for her fingers between his, he might have been alone. "What does Zahir say?"

"He won't accept money. I offer it to him every year. He says he deserved it."

"He told me the same thing. What did he do?"

"I don't know."

They made their way to the field, walking through the town on instinct, muscle-memory: turn here, go straight, let the mud slather your feet, step over this log that has fallen across the path. Even Adela agreed it was the darkest night in years, and so the storm, when it appeared on the distant horizon, was welcome. Lightning shivered across the sky, and Manau turned in time to see her: Adela, made of silver.

"Don't cry," he said.

"He has nightmares. They're worse this year since Nico left."

Manau pulled her to him. In a week, she would be dead. "Does he remember?"

"Of course he does. Nico never let him forget it."

The storm began, a music all its own. They were silent for a spell.

"I gave him tea so he could sleep." Her voice was a whimper. "Poor boy, poor Zahir, poor Nico."

"Don't cry," he said again.

They waited for the rains to begin. Manau lay his mat down. She said no, that she should go back and check on her boy. He kissed her. She kissed him back. In the distance, there was more lightning. Then they were naked, and then they were being rained on. The sky heaved, and the wind blew. "I have to check on my boy," she whispered, but her body did not complain. Instead, she moved beneath him, with him, the rain falling faster now, until they had both arrived at the same place.

"I'M STEPPING out for some air," Manau said, and surely he meant it. Surely he did not mean to walk away and leave the boy there at the station, waiting for Norma alone. He might have suspected himself capable of such a thing, if he believed what his father had always said about him. But he didn't—not until that day. He was a weak man, which is different from being a bad man. Manau would walk home from the station, walk through this gray and noisy city, and console himself with this distinction. He'd managed to hide this from himself for a short time in the jungle. Now it was clear. Why had Adela counted on him? Why had the town?

When they were finished, when the rains had passed, Manau rolled up his mat, and invited her to swim.

"I don't know how," she said.

The clouds had cleared; the stars cut a bright swath across the night sky. They could see each other. She dressed, she covered her silver body. Manau remained naked. He carried his clothes in a bundle.

"I'll teach you."

"But it's bad luck to swim on a moonless night."

It was what she said as he dragged her in. "Superstition!" he exclaimed, and soon after she was laughing and must have forgotten it herself. He tickled her. The water was black and slick and calm. When the wind blew, raindrops fell from the trees, disturbing the surface of the slow-moving river. It would rain every night for the next week, and each night would be darker than the last. The river, when it took her, would be something altogether different. Unrecognizable. Violent.

She splashed; a bird chirruped. The silver fish swam invisibly about their ankles. Manau did not teach her anything that night. Nothing about swimming or the currents or the rain-swollen river.

"What's this?" Victor asked, looking up from his list.

"The money the man gave me for you. On the bus. So I don't forget."

"Where are you going?"

Manau said, "I'll be right here. I'm stepping out for some air."

The boy nodded. It wasn't a lie. Outside was the city with its leaden sky, and the street with its waves of sound. The boy didn't protest, nor did the receptionist with her lipstick-stained teeth.

Outside Manau breathed deeply, that city smell, and he was hit by a nostalgia that surprised him. The station sat on a busy boulevard of ashy green trees. Perhaps he'd been here before, perhaps not, but it was

all familiar. Across the street, a computer school had let out its morning classes. Dozens of students loitered in front of the entrance, gossip-
ing, making plans. They had about them that optimism all young people
have. Foolishness. A bus came and went, depositing a family of Indians at
the corner, and the students paid them no attention. Mother and father
looked about with dismay, at the size of the place, at the crowded sidewalk. Perhaps they were coming to the station as well, to see Norma, to
be found. The children cowered and disappeared into the folds of their
mother's dress.

Four lanes of traffic and a row of dying trees stood between them and
the station. They didn't cross, and Manau didn't cross to them. Maybe
they were waiting for someone. The crowd of students thinned. Some
returned to class, a few waited impatiently for a bus, others set off in
loud, happy packs down the avenue. It occurred to Manau that there
were more people in the building of the computer school than in the
entire village of 1797.

After some debate, the family of Indians trudged off down the boulevard. They clasped hands and walked slowly.

When he looked back through the window of the radio station lobby,
Victor was gone. Manau ran in. "The boy," he said to the receptionist.
He was breathless. It was no longer Norma's voice over the speaker, but
someone else's. "Where's the boy?"

The receptionist looked startled for a moment, then regained her
calm. "They called him in, sir. I'm sorry. The producer came to get him.
He's talking with Norma." She paused. "Are you all right? Would you like
to go?"

It hit him then, a live-wire shock. That last word. "Go?"

"Go in," she clarified.

"Oh." He felt numb. A smile adorned the receptionist's moon face.
"No. That's all right. I'll wait outside."

She nodded. He took the bag he'd left by the couch and stepped through
the doors again. The street was indifferent and loud. Buses passed, and
women on bicycles, and boys on skateboards. He recalled the size of the
city, and it awed him. The possibility existed that someone here might
be happy to see him. The jungle town he had known would soon sink
into the forest. Where was the boy? He was speaking with Norma. Even

now, she was solving his problems. Whatever she can do, he thought, is more than I can. He still heard the voices—Manau, Manau, Manau—and they came from everywhere. From cracks in the bricks that had built this place.

He realized suddenly he'd been holding his breath. He inhaled deeply. Then he walked down the avenue. It was so simple. A block passed by as if in a dream. And then another and another.

Each was easier than the last.

When they were done swimming, they gathered their things and walked back to the village. Their wet clothes clung to them, but the night was cool and dry. Everything was fine. He recalled it now as he walked through the city, how recently his world had been dismantled. The storm passed that night, but of course another was on its way. They found Adela's hut, and she lit a lantern so she could check on the boy. A forest of insects was sawing away at the night.

"Will you take care of him?" she asked. "If something happens to me."

"Nothing's going to happen to you."

"But if it does." She was serious. She whispered in his ear, "Say yes," and Manau did as he was told.

TEN

F OR N ORMA , the war began fourteen years earlier, the day she
was sent to cover a fire in Tamoé. She was just a copy editor at the
radio station then, and had never been on the air, her voice an undiscov-
ered treasure. She and Rey had been married for more than two years,
but she still thought of herself as a newlywed. He was due to return from
the jungle that afternoon. It was October, nearing the sixth anniversary
of the beginning of the war, though no one kept time that way in those
days.

Norma arrived on the scene to find the firemen watching as the house
burned. A few men with guns and masks stood in front of the fire. A polite
crowd had gathered around the house, arms crossed, blinking away the
acrid smoke. Norma could still make out the word TRAITOR painted in
black on the burning wall. The terrorists didn't move or make threats—
they didn't have to. The firemen were volunteers. They wouldn't take a
bullet for a fire. It was late afternoon at the edge of the city, and soon

it would be dark. There were no streetlights in this part of the district. Norma's eyes stung. The firemen had given up. One of them sat on his hard plastic helmet, smoking a cigarette. "Are you going to do anything?" Norma asked.

The man shook his head. His face was dotted with whitish stubble. "Are you?"

"I'm just a reporter."

"So report. Why don't you start with this: there's a man inside. He's tied to a wooden chair."

The fireman blew smoke from his nose in dragon bursts.

And for the duration of the war, more than the firefights in the Old Plaza, more than the barricaded streets of The Cantonment or even the apocalyptic Battle of Tamoé—this is what Norma remembered: this man inside, this stranger, tied to a chair. For the rest of that long night and into the early morning, as the news came from a dozen remote points in the city, news of an offensive, news of an attack, as the first of the Great Blackouts spread across the capital—Norma took it all in with the drugged indifference of a sleepwalker. Cruelty was something she couldn't process that day. On another day, perhaps, she might have done better. She looked the fireman in the eye, hoping to find a hint of untruth, but there was none. The people watched the flames dispassionately. The fire crackled, the house fell in on itself, and Norma listened for him. Surely, he was dead already. Surely his lungs were full of smoke and his heart still. For Norma, there was only a light-headed feeling, like being hollowed out. She felt incapable of writing anything down, of asking a single question. At the edge of the crowd, a girl of thirteen or fourteen sucked on a lollipop. Her mother rang the tiny bell on her juice cart, and it clinked brightly.

WHEN REY returned from the Moon to live on his father's couch, it was Trini who made certain he didn't give up. It was Trini who told him stories and reminded him of better, happier times. On the evenings Rey's father taught at the institute, Trini would come to look for his nephew, and convince him with persistent good cheer to leave the cluttered apartment, to see what the city had to offer. "The streets are full of beautiful women!" he would say. So they took long evening walks through the district of Idorú, toward Regent Park and through The Aqueduct, often making it as far as the Old Plaza—known simply as the Plaza in those days. Once there, they gave themselves over to the noise of the street musicians and the comedians, to the crowds of people seated around the dry fountain, all smoke and talk and laughter, and Rey, because he loved his uncle, made every attempt to be happy, or more precisely, to appear so.

It's true that his days were oppressively lonely, that he slept poorly, that the same nightmares kept coming back. Rey spent his time pacing his father's apartment, rearranging scattered papers or reading his old man's dictionaries. During the morning hours, he prepared mentally for his midday excursion out to the corner for a bite to eat. It was pure torment. He was afraid that no one would speak to him, and equally terrified that they might. He postponed lunch as long as he could, until three or even four in the afternoon. Once it was taken care of, Rey could sleep, sometimes for as long as an hour.

But on these night strolls beneath the city's yellow streetlights, everything was softer, simpler. The shoeshine boys and pickpockets gathered at one end of the Plaza, counting their day's take. Along the alley on the north side of the cathedral, a half-dozen women set up their stalls, selling fresh bread and old magazines, bottle caps and matchbooks from the city's finer hotels. A crew of jugglers might be preparing for a show, and everywhere, the industrious city seemed poised to relax.

One night in June, Trini and Rey arrived in the Plaza in time to see the flag being lowered. It took fifteen soldiers to fold it. A cornet played a martial melody, and some tourists took photos. Rey kept his hands in his pockets. He felt nothing. In a week, he would start his work in Tamoé, become a representative of that flag. He and his uncle had been talking about it, how strange it was to be tortured by the state and then employed by it, all in a matter of months. The government, after all, was a blind machine: now its soldiers stood at attention, and the flag was folded and passed from one to the next, down the line, until all that remained was a meter square of blood-red fabric and a set of hands at each corner. The cornet blew a last, wailing note. Rey was going to say something, when he turned and noticed that Trini had stopped, was standing still with his back straight and his hands together. Then Trini saluted. He caught Rey looking and smiled sheepishly.

Trini had started a new job a few months before Rey was taken to the Moon, as a prison guard in a district known as Venice because it flooded almost every year. In fact, it was by petitioning Trini's supervisor that Rey had been released. The prison in Venice was dangerous and sprawling, with multiple pavilions for the nation's various undesirables. Six days a week, he was in charge of terror suspects. The war hadn't officially begun yet, and there weren't many of these men, but their numbers were growing, and their demeanor was unlike that of any prisoners Trini had previously encountered. They were not cowed by any show of force, and their swagger was not a put-on: it came from a very honest and confident place. Some had the look of students, others came from the mountains. They felt they owned the prison, and of course, they were right. If it was trouble Trini had wanted, here it was: violent and unremitting. It could boil over at any time.

Rey and Trini walked through the Plaza, past costumed men selling jungle medicine, past hunched-over typists at work on love letters or government forms, to a side street where Trini knew a woman who sold excellent pork kebabs. "Special recipe," he said, "my treat." Sure enough, there were a dozen people waiting. They got in line. Down the street, a city work crew painted over a graffitied wall. "A guard was killed today," Trini said to Rey. "An execution. The IL."

"Did you know him?"

Trini nodded. "We're in for trouble. Lots of it. Those little boy soldiers folding the flag—they have no idea."

The line inched forward. The smoke made Rey's eyes water. He inhaled the scent of charcoal and burning meat. One night at the Moon, he had smelled something like this. It had gutted him: the realization that these soldiers were going to burn him alive, that they were going to eat him. He'd decided very early on that these torturers were capable of anything, and he'd never expected to leave that place alive—why not let himself be eaten?

Of course, they were only celebrating a birthday.

"Are you all right?" Trini said.

Rey nodded. A moment passed. Trini hummed the melancholy tune of an old song.

"How come no one's ever asked me what happened?"

"What?"

Rey looked up and down the line. He felt something sudden and hot within him. "At the Moon," he said, and a few heads turned. "What they did to me. How come no one's ever asked. Don't you want to know?"

Trini gave his nephew a blank stare. He blinked a few times, and the edges of his mouth curled downwards. "I work in a prison." He coughed and waved away the smoke. "I know exactly what they did to you."

A few people fell out of line. Rey stood there, silent and seething. His jaw hurt. He remembered everything, every detail of every moment. At night, he had been surrounded by other broken men whom he could not see. They sobbed alone, and no one comforted anyone else. They were afraid.

"They were going to eat me."

Trini raised an eyebrow. "Keep your voice down."

"Go to hell."

"I do, boy. Six days a week."

Half the line had cleared out by now, abandoned their places. Too much talking, too much indiscretion. A breeze blew, momentarily clearing the smoke from the street. A man in a knit cap sat on the curb, rolling a cigarette. Rey stepped out of line. Trini followed and caught him at the corner. They walked together—or rather, not together at all, but in the same direction. Finally, at a busy intersection, Rey and Trini waited side by side to cross.

"Talking doesn't help," Trini said. "I've learned that. It's why I never ask." The light changed, and they crossed the street toward home.

THE TELECENTER was crowded at this hour. A pale, unhealthy-looking man with greasy hair gave Norma a number: it entitled her to booth number fourteen. Then he gave her a form and motioned for her to sit. "You write the numbers here," he explained, "and I dial them for you."

Norma nodded. "How long is the wait?"

"Thirty minutes. Maybe more," the man said, scanning his list. He looked up with a smile. "But you must have a phone at home, madam. Why are you here with us?"

Norma blushed. She did, of course, have a phone, but what difference did that make? It never rang. Is that what the man wanted to hear?

That she, too, was alone? She ignored his questions and asked him for a directory.

"A local call, madam?" the man said, then shrugged and pulled the tattered book from beneath his desk. Norma thanked him in a whisper.

The end of a working day—all over the city, it was the same. Evening in America, past midnight in Europe, already tomorrow morning in Asia. Time to call and check in, to reassure those who had left that you were on your way, that you were surviving, that you hadn't forgotten them. To reassure yourself that they hadn't forgotten you. Norma sighed. There were twenty-five phones in twenty-five cubicles, each with its overflowing ashtray, and each, she could see, occupied. Men and women hunched over, cradling the receivers tenderly, straining to hear the voices on the other end. Most had their backs to the waiting area, but she knew them even without seeing them: these were the voices she heard every Sunday. She knew them from the needy murmur that rose in the room—always that sound. The phone collapsed distances, just as the radio did, and, like the radio, it relied on the miracle of imagination: one had to concentrate deeply, plunge headlong into it. Where were they calling? That voice, where was it coming from? The whole world had scattered, but there they were, so close you could feel them. So close you could smell them. You had only to close your eyes, to listen, and there they were. They respected the telephone, these people. They handled it as if it were fine china: for special occasions only. The radio was the same. It was even more. Norma hoped no one would recognize her.

She had sent Victor to sit, and she found him now, seated beside a young man with a shaved head and a tattoo that ran diagonally across the side of his neck. Victor had saved her a place, no small accomplishment in this crowded room.

"Manau," she said when she sat down.

Victor nodded.

It was not a common surname; at the very least, Norma could be grateful for that. She had already decided they would not go home that night. Elmer might have sent someone there, to wait for her to arrive, to bring her and the boy in. Elmer was afraid, of course, and this wasn't irrational: ten years on, and still the government took no chances with the war. No, going home wasn't safe. Instead they would find this teacher, this Manau. They would ambush him: squeeze it out of him, whatever he knew. She felt she might strike this man when she saw him. That was the kind of anger she felt: how many times in her life had she hit someone? Once, twice, never? She thumbed through the phone book and found it: twelve different Manau households, in nine different districts. No Elijahs or E. Manaus. He lived with his parents then. Of course. Two could be discarded by the fancy addresses. Rich families don't send their young to places like 1797 to teach.

She carefully wrote the ten numbers on the form the greasy-haired man had given her.

"What will we do when we find him?" Victor asked.

"We'll ask him what he knows," said Norma. "What else can we do?"

"Okay."

Norma closed the phone book. "Why?"

"What if he won't talk to us?"

She hadn't considered that. Not really. By what right would this Manau, this spineless creature, withhold anything from her? Norma was about to answer when her number was called. "Come with me," she said to Victor, and they stepped through the people to the front desk. She gave the greasy-haired man her form, and took Victor by the hand to their booth. "He'll talk," she said to Victor, to herself.

It was hot, and there was barely enough room for the two of them. They pressed in. There was only one chair and a small table with a phone, a timer, and an ashtray. Victor stood. The phone had a green light that blinked when the call was patched through. They waited in the airless booth, and the boy said nothing. The man at the counter dialed their way down the list of numbers. Norma picked up the phone, each time seized by an expectant, implausibly optimistic feeling. Six times she asked for Elijah Manau, and six times she was told there was no such person. She was beginning to suspect he didn't have a phone, that it was all a waste, when on the seventh call, a woman with a tired voice said, "Wait, wait. Yes, he's here." Norma wanted to shout. The woman cleared her throat, then yelled, "Elijah, you have a call!"

Norma could hear a voice, a man's voice, still far away. "Yes, mother," it said, "I'm coming. Tell them to wait." If he was surprised, Norma couldn't hear it. It was as if he'd been expecting their call all along.

• • •

IN THE weeks that followed, whenever Trini came over to visit, he would tell Rey of the latest IL transgression, the latest threat. It was only a matter of time, he said. We're in for trouble. Rey began his own work in Tamoé, and together they shared stories about the teetering ship of the state as seen from the inside: its myopic bureaucracy, its radical incompetence made manifest in Tamoé or in the prison's dark terrors. Rey's father chimed in, that it had always been that way, that everything was always getting worse. He could be counted on for a dose of pessimism. A half a year passed, Rey met Marden, he returned to the university. Trini filed reports and made official complaints, but nothing came of it. Another guard was killed today, he told them one evening, looking distraught, and Rey told his uncle to be careful. Quit, Rey's father said, but there weren't many other jobs available. Bodyguard, security guard—and were either of those really a step up? Safer?

Just before the war was declared, ten months after Rey was released from the Moon, the prison officials made a tactical retreat, ceding an entire pavilion to the IL. It was a truce of sorts, and it held for longer than anyone had expected it to: for a year, and most of another. Trini continued to work at the prison, and no one entered the IL's pavilion. The IL taught classes there, held trainings, and the prison officials preferred not to think of it. Every now and then, an operative was caught and tossed in with his comrades. They clothed and fed him: he had survived the Moon to be nursed to health within the prison's liberated territory.

It was in November, nearing the war's second official anniversary, when the inevitable happened: the prison break that marked one of the IL's first successes in the city. A tunnel the length of four city blocks had been dug beneath the prison walls into an adjacent neighborhood, rising out of the earth in the living room of a rented and then abandoned home. The press went crazy, and a scapegoat was urgently needed. Those in charge wanted a peon, a single man with no family to make a fuss. They found Trini.

When he was arrested, Trini was living with Rey's father. They came on a Sunday afternoon, kicked in the door, and threw everyone against the walls: Rey, his father, Norma, Trini. They would've taken them all if

Norma hadn't threatened them: I work at the radio, she said. I'll make a big fuss. She was only an intern then, but the soldiers weren't going to take any chances. They took Trini. He didn't resist. They took Rey, too, but only as far as the street, and then they let him go. The woman wouldn't stop yelling.

"I warned you!" she screamed. "Murderers! Killers! Thieves!"

The soldiers fired shots in the air to disperse the gathered crowd. Idorú was that kind of neighborhood: where everyone spied on everyone else, where police were not welcome. Because his hands were cuffed, he couldn't wave good-bye, but with great effort, Trini did manage a nod to his family—his brother, his nephew—before he was pushed into the back of an army truck.

WHEN REY disappeared, Norma returned to that night in Tamoé, that night when the war became real. It shook her, it fed her nightmares. She imagined it had been Rey bound to that chair all along; that all the years they had spent together were a lie, that her husband had always been imprisoned by the war. The accusations that he had been IL were, for Norma, irrelevant; the war had long ago ceased to be a conflict between distinct antagonists. The IL blew up a bank or a police station; the army ran its tanks over a dozen homes in the dark of night. In either case, people died. Rey went off to the jungle, the IL made its last stand in Tamoé and lost. Most of the district was razed. Then the killing flared and burned out in the jungle, and then it was over. Just like that, the lights came on. And where was Rey? The war had been for many years a single, implacably violent entity. And it had swallowed him. An engine, a machine, and the men with guns—they were simply its factotums. When enough of them died, it was finished.

That night of the fire, the long bus ride back to the station gave her time to consider her options. Norma felt an animal fear churning in her gut, and suspected she wasn't cut out for journalism. Perhaps she could leave the country, board a plane bound for Europe, and become a nanny, a surrogate mother to a gaggle of wealthy children. She could learn a new language—and seeing the world, wasn't that her right? She was twenty-eight, too old to go back to the university and pursue some other profession. It was too late to do what her father had always asked of her: learn secretarial skills and marry an executive, a man with a driver and a house bunkered somewhere in the hills where problems would not intrude. She had married Rey. He studied plants and was not an executive. He went off into the forest for weeks at a time. They had survived the *tadek* episode, but she knew enough to recognize that with Rey, problems would always intrude.

So lost in thought was Norma that she didn't notice the soldiers lining the sidewalks in front of government buildings, or the driver pushing the bus faster and faster through the streets, or the unusually light traffic. It was late when Norma arrived, nearly ten, but the station was busy. She turned in her unused tape recorder, put her untouched notepad in the file cabinet, and was prepared, had she been asked, to resign. She felt sick with shame, with fear, but no one seemed to notice her. Norma shared a desk with another reporter, a pudgy-faced young man named Elmer. He worked long hours, even sleeping at the station some nights, and so, she wasn't surprised to find him at the desk, rubbing his temples and looking happily beleaguered. A green pen poked out from between his teeth. He gave her a smile and said, "This world is going to shit."

Norma didn't know what to say. Elmer took the green pen from his mouth and twirled it between his fingers. He passed her the text he was working on. "Assassinations," he said. "A half dozen all over the city. All the same, Norma, my dear. Men burned in their own homes."

Norma sank heavily into her chair. "Where?"

"Venice, Monument, The Metropole. A few in Collectors. One in Ciencin and one in Tamoé. Weren't you there?"

A phone rang at the next desk. Norma nodded. "I didn't see anything," she said. "It was already over when I showed up."

"Didn't you get anything?"

"There was a woman. She was selling juice."

The phone kept ringing.

Elmer gave her an incredulous look, but Norma didn't turn away. Something in him alarmed her. He was red-faced and excitable, too young for the deep creases on his forehead. He would be old soon. He was a mama's boy, and he would grow wings before striking another man in anger, but on this night, this splendidly violent city night, he was enjoying himself.

"What?" Elmer asked.

How perverse: this adrenaline, these dead men.

"It's awful."

Elmer nodded and said, "It is," but he couldn't mean it. She was sure of that: he said the words, but they meant something altogether different when he did. He was a voyeur. He wanted to see how bad things could get. If pressed, it was something he might admit. Perhaps he was even proud of it.

"Rey called for you."

Norma looked up. "He's back?"

Elmer handed her a note where he had scrawled the name of a bar not far from the station. "But you should stay, Norma. Tonight, you should stay."

"Tell them I was sick." The phone had stopped ringing. She stood to go. "Please."

It wasn't a long walk to the bar, but the empty streets made it seem so. She saw only one person on her way: a hunchbacked old man pushing a shopping cart piled high with clothes down the middle of an alley. There was scarcely any traffic, and the air was still. Winter had ended, spring hadn't yet come. Norma liked this time of year, this time of night. Why weren't more people out to enjoy it? A streetlight flickered, dimmed, then glowed brightly. She was alone in the city, and she knew, however vaguely, that something terrible had happened. In fact, many terrible things had happened all at once. She heard the clink of the juice-cart bell, still echoing blithely in her mind. She never saw the dead man: how could she be sure he was real? As long as she didn't know, there was an innocence to the evening, and it didn't seem forced to her. It seemed sane.

The bar was quiet. The radio was on, and everyone listened. Norma scanned the room for Rey and found him, sharing a corner table with a few men she didn't recognize. No one seemed to be looking at anyone else; instead, they watched the radio, a dented and scuffed black box sitting atop the refrigerator. A red-haired man chewed his fingernails. An olive-skinned woman with braided hair sat at the bar, tapping her foot nervously. There was an air of worry throughout the bar, and the waiters moved through the crowd with the grace and silence of mimes. The announcer was describing the evening's events: dozens of dead, a shootout in the Monument district, sections of Regent Park on fire. Armed gangs had taken to the streets: there were reports of looting downtown, and burning cars in Collectors. The city was under attack. The president would be speaking soon.

Normally, the people would have jeered at the mention of the man, but on this night, there was no response.

Was it so long ago that the IL had been a joke? A straw man?

"Rey," Norma said across the silent room. He saw her and held his finger to his lips. He got up and wove through the chastened, hushed drinkers to where she stood by the door. He looked tired and sunburned. He took Norma by the arm and pulled her out into the street. There, beneath the washed-out light of a street lamp, Rey kissed her.

"What a way to come home, no?"

"Let me see you," Norma said, but it was dark, and she couldn't make out the details of him.

He'd arrived at the train station just after the first fire, at four in the afternoon, around the time she'd been leaving the station for Tamoé. The buses had stopped running from the station, and so Rey had walked three hours, until he was tired of carrying his bag. He'd been stopped twice at checkpoints. Then, when he felt his legs were about to give out, he found himself in front of this bar, realized he was near the radio, and decided it was best to stay put.

"How will we make it home?" Norma asked.

Rey smiled. "Maybe we'll stay here."

And, in fact, they did. Norma had just asked him about his trip, and Rey was telling her about a town in the eastern forest where the Indians still knew the old language, where he'd met an old man who had walked him deep into the forest and showed him a dozen new medicinal plants. Norma could sense the excitement, the curiosity in her husband's voice. The town sounded like a lovely place. "I'd like to see it myself," she said, then there was a distant rumble. They fell silent. It was somewhere off in the hills, and for a moment, nothing happened. For a moment, they both thought they had imagined this unexplained sound. Then there was another, and then another, a deep shaking, a call and response in the hills. An earthquake? The lights along the street flickered again, and this time, they did not recover. There was a shout from inside the bar. The president had been about to address the nation. He had just cleared his throat when the radio went dead. Inside and outside, the darkness was complete.

LISTEN TO me, youngster. It's how Trini began all his letters. This was his last one, and Rey kept it with him always. By his bedside, in his wallet, in his briefcase—it migrated among his things, but was always near. Sometimes Rey woke in the middle of the night, took it to the kitchen, and read it there. He pulled it out on the bus, or between classes, or as he waited for his contact in some dingy bar in Miamiville. Trini had missed their June wedding. Rey and Norma left an empty chair for him at the table of honor. Rey's father read the toast Trini sent from prison. He had missed the *tadek* mess, though he never would have known who was behind it. He had missed the beginning of Rey's work at his alma mater, the first steps in his career. He'd missed all of this, and the war's rude beginnings as well. Of course, there had been other prison breaks since, and other scapegoats, too.

Trini did not cultivate anger. It never appeared in the letters, and yet, for Rey, it was the essential message of the text. Trini wrote with a single fear: that he had accomplished nothing in his life, that he would never have the chance to make up for the wasted time. Nothing notable, exceptional, or even brave. He tended to list his disappointments, and this last letter was no different: the woman who wouldn't speak to him again, the son who would never visit him. In this last letter, he mentioned the boy by name—something he'd never done before—and wondered if the boy's mother had changed it. It came down to this: everywhere else, he was forgettable—everywhere except here, in this prison full of men he'd mistreated, men he'd arrested, men who never forgot a slight. In his last letter, Trini told stories. About getting drunk with a bicycle thief in Ciencin. About waking up in the arms of a wealthy heiress in La Julieta. He had almost beat a man to death in The Thousands, and claimed not to remember anything about the incident, except that they'd only just met, and that minutes before, they had been laughing together. None of it mattered, Trini wrote. It was a long letter, four pages of cramped handwriting, full of implied good-byes, confessions, and retractions. But Trini had only one thought, repeated on every page: to survive. To live long enough to walk out of the prison. If he were to pull this off, he wrote, it would redeem a life of mediocrity, a life without substance. It would be an accomplishment.

Trini was serving his second year when he was killed in a prison brawl. When Rey's grieving was over, he met his contact. "I'm ready," he said, and took his first trip into the jungle not as a scientist but as a messenger.

IN PREPARATION for his guests, Manau showered and shaved. It was the first time he had done so since his arrival in the capital. He'd spent the previous day and a half shuttling listlessly between his bed and the kitchen table, where his mother sat watch over him, making sure he ate. He did, three times that day with little enthusiasm, then returned to his room, where in his absence, Manau's father had set up an office to organize his extensive stamp collection. The room was crowded with envelopes, laminating books, and tin boxes of small, obscure tools. A magnifying glass hung from a hook on the wall above his bed. There had been no regular mail service in 1797, and his father's obsession now struck Manau as absurd. He had received only two letters during his year in the jungle, neither from his father. The old man wouldn't waste stamps on him. Manau's life scarcely seemed believable to him. He hadn't yet unpacked his bag.

Manau put on a fresh shirt and a pair of pants that he'd left behind when he moved to 1797 a year before. The crease had kept, and he found this admirable. In the jungle, nothing lasted, no condition was permanent: the heat and the soggy air and the light degraded everything. The weather changed a dozen times in a single day. It was the earth in flux, as changeable as the ocean, as terrifying, as beautiful.

Since arriving in the city, he had found that his hours did not need filling. Nearly two days had passed in and of themselves. It was only a matter of time until Victor found him, and Manau neither dreaded nor looked forward to it. Norma would do her job. She would come. And he would tell her what she wanted to know, the secrets Adela had whispered to him on those dark, hot evenings not so long ago. Manau sighed. Or rather, so very long ago. Time had never been his friend. He had awoken one day to learn he was thirty years old, his life half-finished. Now he was thirty-one, and he could sense that the details of this past year wouldn't stay with him very long. Can you remember the forest, the feel of it and smell of it, the people you'd known there—can you really recall any of it without actually being there?

His hair combed, his pants pressed, his body as clean as it had been in twelve months, Manau went to the front room. He was idly rearranging the family pictures when his mother came from the kitchen. Even with his back to her, he could tell she was waiting. She made no sound. Manau let her stand there for a minute. "Who are these people who are coming?" she asked finally.

There were photos here that could not be real. That was not him, and these were not his parents. He squinted at himself. A thin film of dust covered the glass, and with his index finger, he brushed it clean. Still, he couldn't recognize the face in the picture.

"Elijah?"

He turned to his mother and realized, with a shock, that she might cry. Manau frowned; these people and their obscure emotions! She had aged, even in these last two days. He gave her a smile—what question had she asked him? Oh, yes. "They're people I knew from the jungle," he said. "They won't be here long."

"Well then, I'll make tea," she said, and this seemed to satisfy her. But still she wouldn't stop looking at him. Manau held her gaze for as long as he could manage, then turned away.

"Thank you, Mother," he said.

They came within the hour. Manau himself opened the door. "Good evening," he said to the woman he supposed to be Norma. "Victor," he said to the boy, and then another word appeared in his brain and had slipped out before he himself could have known what it meant. It was from the old language: *we* that includes *you*. The boy smiled. They embraced for a moment, long enough for Manau to feel the weight of what he had done when he left the boy at the station. He wanted to say more, but was afraid his voice might break. Instead, Manau invited them both in with the wave of an arm. "Please," he managed, "please, sit."

Norma had not expected to see such an old-looking young man. This Manau was ragged and thin, surprisingly pale for someone who had lived in the tropics for a year. He was dressed neatly, but moved with the

languor of a man who spent the entire day in his pajamas. She felt sorry
for him. Manau's mother, a woman a decade older than Norma, entered
the room with a tray of tea, smiling with the exaggerated glow of a theater marquee. She cast worried glances at her son, she rubbed the boy's
head. Victor's hair had grown just a bit in the previous two days, into a
fine, black stubble. Norma smiled politely when she was introduced,
grateful that Manau didn't explain everything about who she was.

This Manau: he began with apologies that made Norma uncomfortable. She focused on the room to avoid staring as the man began to break
down. It was decorated in pastels, or in once-vivid colors that had been
allowed to fade. She couldn't tell. "I made a mistake," Manau said. He was
hoarse, color bloomed in his cheeks. "I'm sorry," he said, and it seemed
he didn't know whom exactly to apologize to. It seemed, in fact, that he
might choke, that he might expire before them. Norma let him talk. Her
anger had dissipated completely, but she felt he owed this to them, to the
boy. He babbled about promises made and broken, and looked pleadingly
at Norma when he described Victor's mother and her drowning. Before
long, Victor had moved to his teacher's couch, was comforting this grown
man with words that Norma couldn't make out. The old language perhaps, but she doubted that Manau could understand them, either.

She let some time pass, a minute or more, but could hardly contain
the impatience she felt. Her Rey was on this list—alive or dead, here
was someone who might be able to tell her more. It was all she had ever
wanted: more of Rey's time, of his heart, of his body. If she had been
honest, she would have admitted it years before: that she'd always wanted
more from Rey than he was willing to give. The night of the fire in Tamoé,
the night of the first Great Blackout, she and Rey had gone back into the
bar, had huddled inside the tense room full of strangers while someone
went in search of a car battery to power the radio. A few candles were
lit and, as they waited, people began talking. "I live in Tamoé," someone
said. "I knew this was coming. These people have no scruples." Another:
"The police do nothing." Another: "They torture the innocent, they disappeared my brother!" Someone said, "Fuck the IL!" and someone—not
Rey—answered, "Fuck the president!"

And so on it went, a civilized shouting match in the flickering yellow
light. The room had grown unbearably smoky, and someone opened a

window. Norma recalled it now in such fine detail: the way the cool night air filled the room, the yelling that continued, the waves of words, exhortations, of confessions and condemnations. It was impossible to make out who was speaking, only the barest facts that their accents exposed: this one, from the mountains; that one, from the city. This man and that woman, and the varying shades of their anger, spreading, that evening, in all directions. It was a knife edge they walked: they might gather in a giant, tearful embrace; or a dozen weapons might be pulled, and they could kill each other blindly in this suddenly dark, suddenly cold room.

Then someone mentioned the Moon, and Norma felt Rey tense. Whoever the state kills deserved it, someone yelled. Trini had been dead for almost a year, murdered, Rey always said, by the state that had betrayed him. She pushed her body into Rey's, and realized in that moment what she'd been afraid of: that he might say something. That he might say the wrong thing, because how can you read the mood of an anonymous crowd in a poorly lit room? She held him tightly, wrapped her arms around his chest. She ran her hands under his shirt and locked her fingers. There, in his shirt pocket, was Trini's letter. She felt it. He'd read it to her one night, and they had cried together. Trini had been such a nice man. But be quiet now, Rey, she thought, stay quiet, my husband.

"Hush," she whispered.

"Have you seen the list?" Norma asked Manau when he'd finished apologizing. She didn't wait for an answer; after all, she knew that he had. She said slowly, "I need to know about the list." Norma touched her own forehead; she was sweating. Had she begun to lose him that night?

Manau nodded. He knew why they had come. Why she had come. He rose and excused himself. "I have something to show you."

Norma sat with her memories. The boy wandered the room, scrutinizing the photographs in their dusty frames. "It's Manau," he said, pointing, but Norma couldn't do more than smile at him.

Back in his room, Manau opened the bag he'd brought from 1797. He rummaged through it without turning on the light. He didn't need to: there was only one thing he had for Norma, and he found it right away. It was a piece of parchment, rolled up, wrapped in bark, and tied with a string. Adela had given it to him for safekeeping. It smelled of the jungle, and he was seized by the urge to lie down, to sleep and dream until these visitors had gone away, but he didn't. There were murmurs from the front room. They were waiting. Manau shut the bag and then the door behind him.

"I've been to the Moon," Rey said that night the war began, and Norma pinched him, but it came louder the next time: "I've been to the Moon!"

She bit his ear, she put her hand over his mouth: was it too late?

"Fuck you, IL dog!" came the first shout.

"What's this?" Norma said when Manau gave her the parchment.

Then the boy had joined them. "What is it?" he asked. Norma untied the string, unrolled the bark, and spread the parchment on the table. Victor held the edges with his little fingers. Manau helped him. That night fourteen years before, the night the war came to the city, what saved Rey was darkness. Someone yelled, "You IL piece of shit!" and there was a stir, but what more could they or anybody do? It was the first Great Blackout, the war had arrived in the city, and they all were strangers to one another, people stranded on their way to other places, crowded now into this dreary bar. They were squatters. "Quiet!" someone else called, a man's voice, heavy with authority. "The radio!" A crackle from the speaker, a blue spark from the battery. On that night in Tamoé, an angry crowd marched on one of the police stations, carrying torches and throwing stones with the zeal of true believers. The first shots were fired in warning. These were followed by shots fired in anger, and then hundreds of people were running, scattering through the dark night, doubling back to retrieve their wounded, their fallen. The next day, the first funerals were held: slow, dismal processions along Avenue F–10, to the hills where the district ended, where the houses ended. Caskets sized for children were carried to the tops of the low mountains and burned in accordance with the traditions of those who had settled the place. That night in Asylum Downs, many were too afraid to leave their homes, and those who owned radios and batteries listened for news with the volume humming almost inaudibly. Men gathered their guns in case the looters came, and they locked their frightened wives and sleepy children in the most hidden rooms, the ones farthest from the street. Shots were heard into the early morning, the last casualty of that long night coming just after dawn, when an old man, a beggar, was killed next to his shopping cart piled high with clothes, in an alleyway not even ten blocks from the bar where Norma and Rey stayed but did not sleep. All night, the radio spat news that was progressively worse, and sometime after midnight, the decision was made to padlock the door of the bar. The windows were closed as well, and again the room grew thick with smoke. Some people managed to sleep. In the middle of the night, someone called for water, and suddenly everyone was thirsty and hot. Outside, bandits scurried along the streets, but no one paid any attention, because the news held them all rapt: tanks, it was announced, had moved into the Plaza, were patrolling the main arteries of their city. Looting was widespread. A couple had been seen jumping hand in hand from the balcony of their burning apartment building. Inside the bar, a woman fainted and was revived. Two times in the night there was an urgent knocking at the door, followed by a thin, high-pitched plea for help, but the candles had burned out, and inside it was dark, and no one could look anyone in the eye. There was no obligation to do anything except stay quiet and wait. Norma held Rey, and they rested with their backs against the door, and eventually the knocking stopped, and the pleading ended, and the sounds of footsteps could be heard, now fading, as the supplicant moved elsewhere in search of refuge.

"Hush, Rey," Norma said.

It was then that Manau's mother stepped back into the room. She'd been watching through the cracked kitchen door, listening to her son and his visitors for the last half hour, unable to discern who was what to whom in this strange trio. Something was not quite right with the woman named Norma and her own son: what had happened to her Elijah? She carried a tray and a thermos with hot water. "Does anyone want more tea?" she said, with all the innocence she could muster. Her son, the woman, and the boy were looking over the parchment, no one saying a thing. "Oh," Manau's mother said, because silence had always, always troubled her, "what a fine drawing! What a handsome young man!"

"It's Rey," Norma said.

"It's your father," said Manau to the boy.

Understanding neither comment, Manau's mother returned quickly to the kitchen, where she stood by the door and listened for many minutes, but heard nothing.

In the morning, when the door was unbarred and the windows

opened, Norma kissed Rey good-bye and walked back to the radio station. She had washed her face with a splash of water from a communal
basin. "How will you make it home?" she asked her husband. She felt an
acute exhaustion, a soreness that ran the length of her legs. Rey smiled
and said he would walk. The air still smelled of smoke, and the sky was
stained sepia. Many buildings had burned the previous night, and some,
at that hour, were still burning.

PART THREE

ELEVEN

D URING THE summer of the eighth year of the war, a radio
personality at the station where Norma worked disappeared. The
authorities denied any involvement, but the rumors spoke of treason and
collaboration with the IL. His name was Yerevan, and it shook everyone
who knew him. Quiet and unassuming, of slight build and mottled complexion, Yerevan was a confirmed bachelor who lived for his radio show,
a twice-weekly late-night classical music program. He taught a class at
the university as well, specializing in the development of Western music
after the discovery of the New World. He was popular and well liked
among the students.

For a few weeks after his disappearance, there was a clamor. Yerevan
and the station's director had been very close, and so the radio was un-
characteristically bold in his defense, broadcasting hourly proclamations
of Yerevan's innocence and demanding his release. Groups of university
students kept vigil in front of the station. Fans of his show came as well,

and there was a strange feeling to the demonstrations. An unlikely cross-section of the city had been assembled: aficionados of classical music, students of history and art, late-night shift workers, various insomniacs and shut-ins. Most had never seen the accused, but all knew his voice well and admired his keen taste and encyclopedic knowledge of the music. It was, as far as protests go, a joyful gathering. A string quartet, laid off from the recently dissolved City Orchestra, played for the crowd one evening at the hour Yerevan's show would have aired. The radio, in an inspired decision, carried the performance live.

In spite of all this, Yerevan was sent to the Moon where he surely received the kind of welcome that Rey had survived nine years before. Two weeks passed, and Yerevan was not heard from. Everyone expected the worst. It was no secret by now what sorts of things happened to those who disappeared. He had been, in the year or so prior to his disappearance, a friend of Norma's. She had recovered from her fear that night of the first Great Blackout, and proven her mettle on more than a few occasions. She was on the air now with some regularity, though the cult of her voice was not yet what it would become. Norma often stayed late at the station, editing pieces for the following morning's news hour and, when her work was done, she liked to visit Yerevan in the sound booth. The soothing music was a draw, as was his quiet good nature, but mostly, she liked the feel of the room. It was the heart of the radio, and this was before she had become disenchanted with it all. She loved this place, the hum of its machines, its light and music and motion. A few times, she had produced the show, patching through calls from listeners who wanted to request a song or simply speak with Yerevan about music. There was a looseness to it that Norma liked: it was late night, and so there were fewer time constraints. Yerevan was content to let his callers talk, Norma happy to listen, and in these moments, she felt that the radio might actually serve a purpose.

What made the episode so curious was the revelation, a few weeks after Yerevan's sudden disappearance, that there was, in fact, some truth to the rumors. Some of the callers, it was said, had been speaking in code. Norma, after consulting with Rey, went to discuss the situation with Elmer, and he admitted that the station director was afraid. It was, Elmer said, worse than they had previously suspected. The station had indeed been infiltrated. A search had been ordered for tapes of Yerevan's recent shows.

"He was IL, Norma, and no one knew," Elmer said. "What could we do?"

Norma had spent many hours with the accused, had monitored the calls, chatted good-naturedly with people she assumed to be music lovers, but who, in actuality, might have been terrorists. She'd even been on the air a half dozen times, introducing songs, discussing music with Yerevan. Had she implicated herself?

"Should I be afraid?" she asked.

Elmer nodded. He was thoughtful and capable, and it was universally assumed he would one day be director himself. "You can stay at the station for a while. We'll make room for you and you'll be safer here."

That night, her exile began. It would be a month before she would go home again. The next day, the radio abruptly canceled any further protests, and even went so far as to ask the army to disperse those Yerevan supporters who remained. The forces of order complied enthusiastically with the request, and so dozens of students and music lovers and night-shift workers and even a few unfortunate passersby were beaten and then arrested in the lot adjacent to the radio. For an hour or so, there was a pitched battle, with stone-throwing and tear gas spreading in great, sickly clouds across the avenue. Many of the employees of the radio gathered in the conference room to watch the events from the broad windows, and Norma was among them. She had slept there that night, quite uncomfortably, in the same conference room where she would meet Victor eleven years later. Her neck hurt badly. She watched the battle, as they all did, without comment, foreheads pressed against the window, looking down. She was grateful for the tear gas: through its fog, there were intimations of great violence, but she was spared the sight of it. The battle had erupted in the middle of the day, but the station's director decided to omit any mention of it from the news. He felt, quite justly, that his job had become far too dangerous. Within the year, he would authorize a report obliquely critical of the interior minister and pay for this mistake with his life. Elmer would happily replace him.

This was the sort of country it had become.

In 1797, it should be noted, Yerevan was not missed at all. Classical music was thought of as foreign and pretentious. The only fan of his show was the village priest, who had, by this point, been dead four years.

WHEN HIS only son was born, Rey was in the city, only vaguely aware that his mistress was due. These were the days when Norma was a prisoner of the radio station. They spoke on the phone four times a day, and each afternoon, he made a trip to the radio to see her. His life in the city, his life as a husband and scientist, was all-consuming; whatever had or might soon happen in the far-off jungle, Rey couldn't fathom. In the here and now, he was worried about Norma. She wasn't handling the stress well. She was losing weight and, when he saw her, she worried aloud that her hair was falling out. "Stay with me," she asked him one afternoon, a week into her exile. Her eyes were red and puffy. "Stay with me tonight."

They were drinking instant coffee in the conference room: the sun was setting, the mountains and the city below shone orange. Norma had a beleaguered look to her; her day was just beginning. She slept in the mornings now: a few days into her internment, the station director, at Elmer's suggestion, decided to put her on the air overnight. Yerevan's slot had to be filled. "It's not like you're sleeping well," Elmer had said, and it was decided. These were the dead hours of radio, but, to everyone's surprise, Norma had been inundated with calls, requests, advice, gossip. She played mostly romantic songs and, in between, let the people talk freely. The night before, as Rey prepared for bed in the empty apartment, he had listened to his wife's voice and then dreamed of her. It was beautiful, narcotic, lulling, and he wasn't the only one who thought so.

"It's lonely here," Norma said. "The entire place is empty. Just me and the watchman."

"And the callers."

She sighed. "And the callers."

He took her hands in his. "They love you."

"Can you stay?"

Her on-air shift ran from eleven to four in the morning, so Rey had time to go home and change before her show began. He made dinner for both of them, prepared an overnight bag, locked up the apartment, and was back at the radio at ten-thirty. The station was already desolate.

They drank more coffee, strong and sugarless, and Rey could tell she was happy to have him around. A few minutes before eleven, they went to the control room, chatted for a few minutes with the evening host. He was short and thin, an awkward, prematurely white-haired man who had always had a crush on Norma. When he had packed his things and left, and they were alone, Norma threw her arms around Rey's neck. An old ballad played, the record slightly warbled, the guitars falling in and out of tune. She kissed him. By the time the record ended, they were both unclothed and laughing. Norma strode across the studio, picked up the needle, and let the song play two more times before she began her show.

IT WAS a gift to be able to separate so thoroughly the two halves of his life. When he was home in the city, he rarely thought of the jungle, except in an academic sense: the mysteries of plant life, the demands of the climate, human adaptation to its exigencies. Sometimes an image from the cool heart of the forest: the mossy black trunk of an ancient tree, the white stones along the river's edge, water-carved into the most fantastical shapes—and this was all. Not the people he knew there, or the woman who had beguiled him. His trips to the rain forest included a similar kind of disassociation: an hour or two outside the city, when the raw and disordered slums had disappeared and the road wove up into the still-uninhabited hills, Rey felt himself cleansed of worldly responsibilities, going backwards in time, a man returning to a more innocent and purer state. Outside the city, he never went by Rey. So complete was his transformation that the sound of his own name, his city name, had no effect on him beyond the limits of the capital.

He made his first trip to the jungle soon after returning to the university. It was a purely scientific expedition, before Trini's murder changed his mind, a trip made under the guidance of a potbellied old professor who spoke three Indian dialects and walked the halls of the university chewing medicinal roots. The students were charged with writing technical descriptions of plants they found—about the sticky texture of the leaves or their acid smell—and they pressed samples into the pages of heavy books that the professor had brought for this very purpose. The jungle had seemed to Rey, from books, from conversations, from photographs, to be the exact opposite of the city where he had lived since he was fourteen. Uncharted and unknowable, a universe where the rules were still being ironed out and fought over, it was the frontier, and its draw was powerful. This was the first year of the war. Later, when Elijah Manau traveled the same paths, the jungle was already part of the nation—there were schools and roads maintained, at least in theory, by the state—but when Rey went for the first time, travel involved riding atop a truck or bartering with a villager for a canoe ride along the muddy rivers. They encountered natives, who spoke only their own impossible language. They washed in sweet-water rivers, and slept in hammocks, and instead of sleeping, Rey would stay up, eyes closed, listening to the rising and ebbing sounds of the forest, certain it was the most beautiful place he had ever heard.

The land belonged to whoever claimed it, and in those days especially, the dense forest was an ideal place to disappear, to hide from the eyes of the law. As the war progressed, the government would learn to keep an eye on those who came and went from the nation's jungle regions. There were men who moved weapons and men who transported drugs. There were money men who bribed police officers or army captains or village chiefs. There were scouts who cased bridges for bombing, and men who pretended to be loggers or traders or even wandering musicians. And there were men like Rey, who left the city as credentialed students or scholars and who, somewhere along the way, became other people, with other names. These were men who never carried guns, men charged with something much more valuable: information.

He never saw Marden again. But by the time of the Yerevan episode, Rey and the man in the wrinkled suit had been seeing each other, off and on, for almost nine years, like furtive lovers: nine years of meetings at bus stops, of purposefully vague conversations and random duties, enough for Rey to come to know his contact, insofar as one could know a man like that. He came to recognize the man's muted expressions of worry, the way his weight fluctuated with the intensity of the conflict. There were times when Rey's contact looked positively ill, with unshaven, sunken cheeks, slack expressions, and unruly hair. As an agent, he was frighteningly transparent: days later, something, somewhere in the city, exploded, and by the next meeting, Rey's contact had regained some air of calm. Then it began again. In nine years, they had even met socially, at various dinner parties where they had been introduced as strangers and played the part convincingly, exchanging a few polite words before studiously ignoring each other for the rest of the evening. Even Norma had shaken his hand once or twice; had commented, after a party, as she undressed in the blue darkness of their apartment, on the coldness of Rey's contact, his unfriendly, unsmiling greeting. Rey felt compelled to defend him, but of course, he did not: he pretended not to recall—what was his name again? They were even colleagues of a sort: in different fields, at different universities. After the first Great Blackout, which had taken Rey and the entire city by surprise, their meetings were monthly, and the tasks so mundane it was possible for Rey to believe the war had nothing whatsoever to do with him. He left envelopes in trash cans, wore a bright red shirt and sat in a windowed café at an appointed time, or made calls to pay phones, never saying much more than an address to whoever picked up on the other end. His days as a well-known student leader were long past. He was invisible now. After returning from the Moon, he had never again made a speech, or spoken of politics in public, save for his aborted confession in the darkened bar the night of the first Great Blackout. Besides the man in the wrinkled suit, Rey knew nobody in the city who was involved. He had been as surprised as anyone to discover that Yerevan was a sympathizer. For years, Rey had thought of the war and his own involvement in it as an intimate act. Of course, he knew there were other people participating, but he never thought of them, never wondered who they were, felt no kinship with these mysterious and invisible allies. He didn't read the paper much, except for sports, and gleaned what he knew of the war's progress from the increasing militarization of the city streets. And he went home each night to Norma, who had decided to believe her husband kept no secrets.

In the jungle, where his mistress was preparing to give birth, it was the rainy season: the skies alternating between a deep blue and a dark, purplish black. The river had swelled, as it did every year, flooding the fields at the edge of the village. Rey never liked the rainy season: he found the consistent downpour overwhelming, dreary, in sharp contrast to the rest of the year, when the rain came in spurts, brief and violent showers that passed in the course of half an hour, followed by bright and garish sunlight. Travel, never easy, was nearly impossible during the rainy months. The roads were muddy, and the jungle violently overgrown. He had once spent ten days trying to travel a dozen kilometers between a town and a camp hidden in the forest. The jungle was crawling with secretive men. In the rainy months, it was all too gloomy.

In a city hospital, the boy would have been weighed and washed by white-clad nurses, held and inspected by doctors, showed off by a proud father passing out cigars. 1797 was not the city. It was a place with its own rituals, though, at this late date, with the war having bled the town of its men for more than half a decade, one might say the celebration accompanying Victor's birth was half-hearted at best. That year, another eight young men had left to fight. Five would not return—another five names on the list Victor would take to the city eleven years later. The town was in no mood for celebrations. In the old days, a feast would have been prepared and a tree felled for a bonfire, but everything had changed, even the blessings: the standard incantation now asked specifically that the child be protected from bullets. It was common among young mothers to observe that their boys were only on loan to them from the armies.

One tradition had remained, in spite of the war, and it was the only one Adela insisted upon when Rey returned to 1797 six months later. He was sent into the jungle for a night, to ponder his child's future with the aid of a psychoactive root. In its hallucinatory sway, Rey was assured, all kinds of truths would be revealed. He went unwillingly, but felt he owed it to the mother of his child, whom he had mistreated in every other way. He hadn't been present at Victor's birth; but then, no one expected this of him. He hadn't helped choose the boy's name, hadn't been there to hold Adela's hand or take the baby to his chest and feel the infant's warmth. Rey had promised his father a grandson, but when it finally happened, he was unaware that his promise had been fulfilled. Rey's father would never know. When Victor was born, Rey was at the radio station in the distant, gray city, half-clothed and asleep in an armchair in the sound booth.

That night, while Victor slept against his mother's breast, Norma hardly answered the phones. She was content to let the songs do her talking for her, content to watch her husband sleep in the chair across from her. His presence calmed her. Around three in the morning, though, her strength was fading, she'd had her fill of coffee, and she decided to take a few calls, just to help her stay awake. What did she expect? One of the usual suspects: someone lonely or grieving, a man or a woman who found themselves unhappily and unwillingly alone. On a night like this, the radio felt like a public service. She had acquired more than a few admirers in her brief run as Yerevan's replacement, and she was not immune to pride. What harm could come from flirting now and again with a caller? They told her she was beautiful, or that she sounded beautiful, and was there really a difference? It was the middle of the night, the sound booth still smelled of sex, and she was happy. Norma patched through a few calls, listened with some interest as a woman described the confectionery her grandfather had once owned downtown. "It's all gone," the woman said with a sigh. She spoke with unhinged nostalgia, enough for Norma to suspect she'd been drinking. She was afraid to go down there now, the woman told Norma, afraid of what, if anything, had replaced her grandfather's candy store. What if it was boarded up? What if there were squatters living there—a family of those mountain people?

Norma did not judge, she didn't stop her. "Be nice," was all she said. She played a song, then took another call, and was not surprised when a man's voice announced that he'd been trying to get through all night.

"Well, now you've found me," Norma said. "You're live on the air. What can I do for you?" She played a jazz record in the background: something with strings and a bluesy trombone.

"You can't do anything for me," the man on the other end said. "Shouldn't Yerevan's show be on the air now?"

They had all been advised not to say his name on the air. She began to say that Yerevan was away on vacation—this was the line the station was using in emergencies—but something made her stop: the abrupt tone of the caller, perhaps, something in the sound of his voice. She shouldn't have asked, but she did: "Who's this?"

"Never mind who this is. The question is, who was Yerevan? An IL dog. That's why you can find his body in a ditch by the Central Highway. This is what happens to terrorists."

Before Norma could respond, the line was dead. She sat there for a moment, scarcely breathing. The jazz record stopped, and it was ten seconds before she gathered the presence of mind to play another. She grabbed one at random and put it on with trembling hands. It began too fast: she'd set the wrong speed. A horn squealed, a voice crept unpleasantly into the higher register. Meanwhile, the phone lines were lit up, every last one of them. She stared helplessly at the blinking red lights. Rey didn't stir until she had called his name for the third time.

"MUSIC ONLY," Elmer said when Norma called him at home. "Music only until I get there. No phone calls, not on the air or off."

So she sat with Rey, and they played cheerful pop songs and said nothing. Under different circumstances, he might have sung for her, but instead, they put on one side of a Hollywood record, a musical, and went to the conference room. It was a clear night, just past three in the morning, that hour when the sleeping city seemed like the inside of a dimly glowing machine. They could see, from the radio's high, broad windows, the coruscating grid of lights below: the Metropole and its blinking neon sign, the strings of orange streetlamps along the avenues, each pointing toward the center of town. From this vantage point, it did not seem an unpleasant place to live—no fire in the hills, no blackout. The shanties, in this light, might not be shanties at all. Norma and Rey could squint and imagine it to be an orderly city, like any of hundreds that exist in the world. They stood together, holding hands, and there was very little that could be said. The Central Highway ran over the mountains in the east—you couldn't see it from here. Yerevan was somewhere along that road, in a place where he would surely be found.

Elmer arrived within the hour, looking harried and sleepy. "What are you doing here?" he said to Rey, but he didn't wait for an answer. "It doesn't matter," he said and turned to Norma. "Tell me everything."

Everything was very little. In a sentence or two, it was done: Norma sketched the voice, its dark timber, its tone of menace and violence. This was all. Yerevan, dead. Yerevan, IL. "Is it true?" she asked. "Do you think it's real?"

Elmer nodded.

Rey watched and listened without a sound. He didn't like Elmer, this pretend tough guy with a slouch and a paunch. He had the faraway gaze of a gambler who rarely wins, of a man who staggers home to punish his family for his own shortcomings. Rey almost smiled: he was exaggerating. There was no violence in Elmer. Rey could, if he wished, tell this man certain facts. He could tell him about the Moon, for instance, or he could speculate with some accuracy about the nature of Yerevan's final hours. Nine days before, just after the rumor of Yerevan's involvement had first surfaced, Rey had met his contact and asked what was being done for "our friend at the radio."

Rey's contact, the man in the wrinkled suit, had smiled wanly and taken a sip of his coffee before answering. "There's very little to be done once a situation has reached this point."

"Meaning?"

"I don't expect our friend will be on the air again."

Rey nodded, but his contact was not finished. "The same would go for us, should it ever come to that."

Now Rey watched Elmer pace back and forth across the conference room. Norma sat slumped in her chair, frowning. "People heard," she said. "The phone lines lit up."

"It doesn't matter," Elmer said. He rubbed his eyes. "They want us to raise a fuss. That's what they expect. We can't fall into that."

"It's done, though. People know."

Elmer shook his head with a great and exaggerated slowness. "They'll come for you, Norma, if we say anything."

Rey understood then that they weren't going to say anything, that Yerevan was going to disappear completely. Tomorrow, by the light of day, a peasant farmer would come across the corpse somewhere on the Central Highway. The war had been going on long enough for none of this to be a surprise. The farmer would be afraid. He might go to the police—not for answers, just to wash his hands of it—and they would promise to investigate and dispose of the body themselves. They were not paid to ask impertinent questions. Of course, more than likely, it would begin and end with the farmer. If he was a religious man, he might bury the body himself, or see to it that the body was well hidden behind a rock or in a ravine where no one would stumble upon it again. He would be too afraid to speak of it. Not to his wife or his best friend. Not at Mass on Sunday, when he went, head bowed, to confess all his sins of omission and commission. So Yerevan would lie there, for a day or a week or a month. Forever, if Elmer had his way. It would be the easiest and most convenient, to forget.

"Does he have a family?" Rey asked.

Elmer shook his head. "Mercifully, no."

God bless him then. Rey had been saved by his family. By Trini. He would probably be dead otherwise, and no one had ever had to explain this to him. It was clear and frightening. In two weeks, Rey would see his contact again and ask, though he knew the answer, if Yerevan was dead.

His contact gave him a look Rey hadn't seen in many years. It said, Why are you wasting my time?

There was a roundup underway, Rey's contact said after a moment. Yerevan was just the beginning. Already a few operatives had disappeared. Rey listened to the dire speculation, and he meant to shrug; and by shrugging, Rey intended to convey something very specific: that he was tired, that it had gone on very long, this war, that he understood better than most that it couldn't go on forever. Rey meant to imply that he wasn't surprised at all: Yerevan, a sympathizer, had given up perhaps the one name he knew, and this man or woman had been picked up, and then ... Rey had no illusions; he himself would have talked at the Moon, if only he'd had anything to say. The things they must have done to poor Yerevan. The torturers had had nine years to hone their skills.

But Rey did not shrug. Somehow, he felt too tired and defeated in that moment to muster even that simple gesture. Instead, he asked his contact, the man in the wrinkled suit, what it meant. "For us," Rey said.

"We don't know," the man said. "We won't know until it happens."

Then they were silent while a couple walked by, arm in arm: the woman had tilted her head onto her boyfriend's shoulder, and he walked with the regal confidence of a man who knows he is loved. She had a thin waist and long legs, and had maneuvered her right hand into her boyfriend's back pocket. Rey felt intensely jealous, for no reason at all he could think of. His son was fourteen days old.

"We won't see each other for a while," Rey's contact said. He briefly outlined some instructions for the coming months. Rey would be going to the jungle. He would have to be careful, more careful than before. Rey accepted it all with a nod. Then his contact stood and left. He didn't pay the bill, nor did he offer much in the way of good-bye.

SIX MONTHS later, his boy was at that age when children begin to acquire a personality. It was miraculous. The rainy season was over, and Norma was home again. Yerevan had never been found, and the uproar had faded almost completely. Some arrests had been made, but Rey felt certain that most were not IL at all, but those on the periphery: the students and laborers and petty criminals that fit a profile. An unlucky worker caught with a mimeographed flyer, a young woman who asked for an inappropriate book at the central library. They would be tortured, and some would die, but many would be released and swell the ranks of those too angry or too bitter to remain mere spectators of the conflict. In this manner, the war grew.

Now Rey was in the forest again, the city distant and almost unreal. His mistress strode barefoot across the wooden floor, and Rey watched the boy's limpid, gray eyes as they tracked his mother across the hut.

"He can see!" Rey said.

Adela smiled. "Of course he can see."

But Rey hadn't said it correctly, or rather the words were not nearly precise enough: He did not mean to denote any ordinary kind of observation. It was something altogether new—how do you explain it? The boy, with his new eyes and unblemished personhood, was *seeing*. It was discovery, it was revelation. The boy peered into the unknown with the intensity of a scientist, and Rey felt immensely proud. He despaired at his own inability to explain. The boy can see! Rey thought again, and he felt his heart pounding. Maybe Adela had already become accustomed to the miracle: the boy pointing, his first finger, pudgy and minuscule, reaching out into the world; the boy, curious and undaunted by the size of the universe. The startling *perfection* of the child. Rey held his own finger in front of the boy, and Victor took it to his mouth, inspecting its texture with his gums.

They walked through the village that afternoon, for the first time, as a family. It was such a haphazard place: clusters of raised wooden huts, thatched roofs. Rey received the good wishes and hearty congratulations of a dozen men and women with whom he'd never shared so much as a word. He was prepared: a few phrases from the old language were all that was required. They appreciated him for trying. They laughed at his accent. They kissed the baby and moved on.

That evening, his first in 1797 since he had become a father, Adela sent him out into the forest to complete his ritual duty. Rey noted the name of the root in his notebook; he was, after all, still a scientist. The root was mashed into a paste, and Rey spooned it with his finger into his mouth, rubbing the mixture on his gums. It had a bitter, acid taste to it. He interrupted to ask questions, but no one answered him. A few minutes passed, and his face felt numb, and then he couldn't taste anything at all. Adela kissed him on the forehead. The baby's lips were pressed against Rey's. "Now off you go," Adela said. The old women who guided him into the woods were silent. They led him to the bank of the river, where the trees grew thickly, where tendrils of moss hung down over the skin of the water. The women left him, and he sat in the darkness, among the trees, waiting for something to happen. In his mind, he replayed the image of his boy, chasing movement with his little eyes, and the thought alone was enough to make him smile. Through the canopy of the forest, he could see the sky dotted brightly with stars. It was a moonless night. He closed his eyes and felt a throbbing against his lids, an incipient wave, now a shot of color. He thought of the war, his great and unforgiving taskmaster; he thought of its weight and its ubiquity. Everywhere but here, he said to himself. The trip was beginning. It was a hopeful statement and, of course, wholly untrue. The war, in fact, was right there, just over the next ridge, in a camp he would visit in just four days. Rey felt the divide between his lives disintegrating: at home, Norma was, at this hour, missing him with an almost animal intensity. He could guess that and he could, without much effort, reciprocate. For the first time ever in the jungle, he thought of his wife. Maybe it was vanity, to suppose that she needed him. She would never forgive him if she knew. He touched his damp forehead and reasoned it was the root, its dark magic beginning to loosen the tether of reality. Rey took off his shoes and then his socks, and stepped gingerly into the eddies at the river's edge. The water was cool and calming. He stepped out, took off all his clothes now, and waded in again, this time to his chest. The water was all around, doing marvelous and inexplicable things to him: tiny, pleasurable pinpricks of cold all over his body. There were dazzling colors hidden behind his eyelids. My child, Rey thought, what of my child? The boy will grow up in this place, and he will never know me well. He will inherit this war I've made for him. Rey took a deep breath and sank below the water's surface. He held his breath until his mind was blank and everything was still, then he rose and breathed, and then he did it again. He felt colors—to say he saw them would be inexact—he felt them all around, a fantastic brightness bubbling within him: reds and yellows and blues in every shade and intensity. He held his breath and felt he was drowning in a pool of orange. It was thrilling and terrifying and shed no light on his son's future. He exhaled purple into the water: he watched himself blow clouds of it, like smoke. After an hour in the river, he got out, stood naked on the shore, and pondered the stars. He dressed, so that he wouldn't catch cold. Periodically, stars fell from the sky, great waves of them in blinding cascades of light forming shapes: animals, buildings, faces of people he'd known. He tried to recall what he was there to accomplish. He pulled on his silver chain, put it between his teeth, and chewed on it until the metallic taste was too much. He crawled to the river again and rinsed his mouth. And then his face, and then he was in the water again, fully clothed this time, singing, whistling, drenched in electric colors.

A few hours later, he was sifting dirt through his fingers, trying to recall the name of a movie he had seen once as a boy. In his mind's eye, a leggy blonde floated across the screen. An hour after that, he was asleep.

In the morning, the women went for him and brought him back to the village to feed him. He was groggy and sore. All this was duly noted. Already Rey was being followed, his movements, moods, and physical condition recorded by a mole recruited in the village. Three days later, he left for the camp where he was to meet a man he knew only as Alaf. The mole recorded Rey's departure and speculated about which way he was headed. It was a guess, but a good one: that the man from the city was headed down the river and over the ridge. Some days, when the wind was right, the mole had heard shooting. There was, he felt certain, something noteworthy happening in that vicinity.

TWELVE

T HE PORTRAIT was spread on the coffee table, its frayed edges held down by coasters, and Victor could hardly stand to look at it. He didn't feel curiosity at all toward this man, or rather, toward this drawing of a man. A few seconds was enough to decide his father was an unremarkable-looking human being. He had a full head of whitish hair, and eyes and ears and a nose in all the conventional places. Maybe the drawing was no good. It certainly showed little imagination on the part of the artist: just the flat expression of someone caught unawares, looking sleepy. In the drawing, Rey did not smile. Victor squinted at the face. He had no memories with which to compare it. He didn't speculate about any resemblance, and this was just as well: there was none.

Norma asked Manau to repeat what he'd said.

"That's Victor's father," he said again. "I'm sorry."

A dark silence descended on the room. Norma sank back into the couch, and her face turned a watery pink color that Victor had never seen before. She didn't cry, but looked straight ahead, nodding and whispering to herself. Many times, she began to say something but stopped. All the quiet was discomforting. Victor felt the need to be somewhere else. He expected his teacher to say something, but Manau, too, was silent. Norma took another look at the drawing and then at him, until Victor felt the unpleasant heat of being scrutinized. She reached for him, but he was suddenly afraid. These people did not stop disappointing him. "Victor," Norma said, but he backed away from her.

This time, he didn't go to the street, but out of the room, through the only door available, into the kitchen. Norma and Manau let him go. The door swung open, startling the woman Victor supposed to be Manau's mother. He was suddenly in another, warmer world. She dropped the spoon she'd been holding, and it fell into a pot on the stove. She gave Victor a careworn smile, then gingerly fished the spoon out. She held it before her, and it steamed. "Are you all right, child?" she asked.

Victor didn't feel the need to answer the question, nor did Manau's mother seem to expect a response. In fact, she took only a small breath before continuing. Victor pulled a chair from under the table, and before he'd even sat, she was talking, in her aimless way, about Manau and the sort of boy he'd been: ". . . So nice of you to come visit your old teacher because you do seem like such a thoughtful young boy, and I know Elijah had a difficult time there, but he himself was so kind when he was young and that's what must make him a good teacher. I don't care what the exams say. He's such a nice boy, always was, there was a dog he took care of, just a street mutt, but he combed its hair and taught it tricks, and I dare say that people have always liked him, God is merciful. You do like him, don't you?"

"Yes," Victor said.

"Oh, you are a good boy, aren't you?"

A moment later, she had served him more tea and placed a bowl of soup before him. There was a beautiful piece of chicken, a drumstick, poking out from beneath the surface of it. His mouth watered. She wiped a spoon against her apron and laid it beside his bowl. Victor didn't need much more urging, and he didn't need the spoon. He attacked the submerged piece of chicken, wondering briefly if this was bad manners. It didn't matter. Manau's mother had her back to him, rinsing some plates in the sink, prattling on breathlessly about something or other: her husband, she said, was away on business. He drove trucks filled with electronics—had Victor noticed the box of plastic calculators just by the front door? "They come from China," she added with great admiration, and he liked the sound of her voice. "Your mother is very beautiful," she said. He had picked the chicken half-clean.

Victor looked up. It took him a moment to process, to understand. He wondered if it was worth explaining. "Thank you," he said, when he had decided it wasn't.

"WHAT IF," Norma had once asked her husband, "what if something happens to you? Out there, in the jungle?"

It seemed naïve and ridiculous now, but she remembered asking him just such a question, something just as clueless and trusting. Maybe she'd never wanted to know. Rey had smiled and said something to the effect of "always being careful." There were now, of course, multiple and unintended meanings of *being careful*. He had not been careful, she thought. He'd gotten some jungle woman pregnant and then most likely gotten himself killed. Then there was this boy and these ten years she'd spent alone, praying hopefully that her innocent husband would stumble out of the forest, unharmed. Did she even believe that? Had she ever believed it? She was, Norma realized, one of those women she'd always pitied. Worse, she was her own mother: a few details altered to suit different times, and still, an exotically costumed but quite conventionally deceived woman. Old school, uninteresting, common. And as alone as she had ever been. The moment, she felt certain, called for some explosive act of violence: for the rending and tearing of some heirloom or photograph, the destruction of a meaningful item, some article of clothing, but she was in a foreign and unknown house, on the other side of the city from her apartment and all the artifacts of her years with Rey: bizarrely, she was struck by the image of a burning shoe. If she were someone else, Norma might have laughed. She wanted, from somewhere deep inside her, to hate the boy. She closed her eyes; she listened to her own breathing. Manau hadn't stirred; the poor man had no idea what to say besides his repeated apologies. It wasn't clear any longer what he was apologizing for. For this bad news? For this drawing and all its implications? I should ask for details, Norma thought.

I should needle him and see what he knows, but already the moment had begun to pass. The boy was off in another room, and she was alone in a strange house with this stranger and this portrait and this news.

"Is there anything I can do?" Manau asked.

She opened her eyes. "A drink?"

"There's none in the house. My mother won't allow it."

"What a shame," Norma said.

"It's why my father is never here. Should we go somewhere?"

Norma shook her head and managed to ask if he had anything else to tell. "Not that this isn't enough."

"No," he said. The quiet dragged for another moment, then Manau asked if they would stay the night.

Where else would they go? There was nowhere left in the city. She said something vague about being alone, then felt embarrassed as soon as she had said it. This was hardly the time for confessionals. Already this Manau knew things about her life that she herself had not known only minutes before. There were, she imagined, places in the country where no one knew her name or her voice, somewhere in the unsettled wilds of the nation, a place the radio had never arrived, where she could blend into the landscape, embrace spinsterhood, and live quietly with her disappointments.

"We'll stay," she said with a nod. "Did everyone know this but me?"

"In the village? No, only a few."

"But they all knew my husband?"

"Sure," Manau said. "Adela—Victor's mother—she told me he came three times a year."

"Sometimes four. He was working on . . ." Norma trailed off. What a helpless feeling. "Oh, it doesn't matter what he told me, does it?" she said, her voice cracking. What hadn't he lied about? This other woman— Norma very nearly retched at the thought, some jungle tramp fucking her Rey, their bodies pressing together, their sweat, their odors. Their pleasure. She covered her eyes. She couldn't speak.

"I'm not happy," Manau said. "I didn't want to tell you this."

"And I didn't want to hear it." Norma peeked through her fingers.

He nodded, and bowed his head, staring into his lap. "They love you in the village, Miss Norma."

She took his hand and thanked him. "This drawing," she asked. "Where did it come from?"

"There was an artist who came to the village. Years ago."

She looked back at the portrait. "His hair is so white," she said. She couldn't remember if he had looked this old when she last saw him.

Her head hurt. She meant to ask for an explanation, but didn't. Or couldn't. A muffled voice came from the kitchen.

"He didn't make it, did he?" Norma said.

"Madam?"

"He didn't survive. I'm asking."

"You don't know?" Manau said.

"Isn't it obvious by now that I don't know anything?" It took all the calm she could muster not to yell it.

"They took him. It's what Victor's mother told me."

"They?"

"The army."

"Oh," Norma whispered.

WHEN REY returned from the jungle after meeting his newborn son, he had resolved to end his activities. He hadn't seen his contact since Yerevan was disappeared. It was all too exhausting. He felt, for the first time, that he had brought home some of the forest with him, something affecting and real, a germ, a curse. His life—his lives, their carefully maintained boundaries now breached, seemed overwhelmingly complex. He found himself thinking of the child the way a father ought to: with pride, with impressive and unexpected swells of love clouding his thoughts at the most inopportune moments. More than anything, he wanted to share this illicit joy with Norma, and this shamed him. What right did he have to be happy? Still, these things cannot be helped: they are biological, evolutionary. He wished he had a wallet-sized photograph of the boy—to show whom exactly? Strangers, he supposed. On the bus, he could pretend he was a real father, that he'd done nothing wrong. On more than one occasion, after a deep yawn, he explained to a passenger in the seat beside him, always a woman, that he was exhausted because the baby had been up all night. He said it knowingly, nonchalantly, or tried to. He liked the way the women smiled at him, the way they nodded and understood. They spoke of their own young ones, then pictures were shown, and good wishes offered. At home, he and Norma made love every night; at his insistence, they returned to the debauched and beautiful rituals of the first days of their pairing: sex in the morning, before dinner, before sleeping. Norma was happy, they were both happy, until some dark thought intruded and he remembered the kind of man he was, the kind who would lie and make mistakes and one day bring home a child from the jungle to be raised in the city. It was what had to happen: his son would have to be educated. He couldn't very well leave the boy to play in the dirt, could he? But he and Norma would have their own child first, Rey decided optimistically: the two of them, and it would be wonderful, and in this way, she would forgive him.

At the university one day, he decided to take a walk. It was between classes, an hour and a half when he might have stayed in his classroom reading or correcting papers, but it was a nice afternoon, breezy, with skies that could be mistaken for clear. There were students about in packs, and it struck Rey that he could scarcely remember his own days as an undergraduate. It hadn't come easy—he remembered that. He spent a year trying to get in. He did three years, then went to the Moon, returned a year later to resume his studies, and the two parts of his higher education seemed altogether unrelated. He met Norma, he met the man in the wrinkled suit, and this pair had changed everything he thought he knew about his life. Now Rey wandered off campus to the avenue, and then to the corner just past the university gates. There was a newsstand there, and a crowd of young men reading the headlines with hands in their pockets. Rey bought a sports paper, scanned the headlines. A rust-colored car idled at the corner, the radio blaring through the open windows. The driver wore mirrored sunglasses and tapped the steering wheel with his fingers. There was a girlie magazine open on the dashboard. Farther along, beneath a tattered awning, a man in a green vest sold puppies. He had a half-dozen in a single cage atop a slanting wooden table: eyes shut, tiny, the puppies awoke yawning, pawed around, and fell back asleep. The little beasts were putting on a show. A crowd of children had dragged their mothers to see them. A black-haired boy nervously poked his finger through the wire cage; an obliging puppy licked it sleepily, and the boy squealed with pleasure. Rey stood to watch, newspaper under his arm. He was watching the children, he realized, and not the puppies. I'll bring my boy here, Rey thought. Why not? I'll get him a dog. Various images of domesticity played out before him, and he smiled. Just then, a man tapped him on the shoulder. "Uncle," a voice said.

The man had the boyish face of a high school senior, probably didn't even shave yet, but something in his manner of dress was wrong. "What are you reading, Uncle?"

"Excuse me?"

"What've you got there?" the young man asked, pointing to the newspaper.

"Sports. Why?"

The young man frowned. "Let me begin again." He pulled a badge from his pocket and flashed it, just fast enough that Rey could see its glint. "ID, please," he said in a low voice. "Don't make a fuss in front of the kids."

"Oh," Rey said, "is that what this is?" He smiled. These undercovers were getting younger and younger. He'd become accustomed to this, and never again would he make the mistake he'd made the night he met Norma. Just show them something, that was the rule now, show them anything. They weren't looking for you, because if they were, they'd already have you. Rey took his wallet from his back pocket, made a show of taking out his university ID. "No fussing in front of the kids. And how old are you?"

"I'll ignore that." The undercover looked the ID over and nodded. "I thought it was you, professor. Trini was my captain," he said, handing the ID back. "Come with me."

"Trini?"

The undercover nodded.

"Do I have to?"

"You should."

They walked together a ways, down the avenue past the next intersection, where the neighborhood began to change. Rey was determined not to pay attention to the cop. The clouds had thinned, and it was nearly sunny. A child craned his neck out of a second-story window of a dilapidated tenement, gazing wide-eyed at the street. Rey waved, and the boy waved back. The building was in such disrepair, it seemed held together by the clotheslines of its unfortunate residents. The boy ducked behind a curtain, returning a moment later with a stuffed teddy bear. The bear and the boy waved together.

Rey and the officer turned at the corner onto a nearly empty, unpaved street. A woman dunked her clothes into a bucket of water. She didn't look up at them. They were blocks from the university now. "What's this all about?" Rey asked.

The undercover scratched his temple. He pulled out his badge again and handed it to Rey. "It's real, you know. You might show me a little respect."

Rey shrugged and returned the badge.

"I knew your uncle. He trained me and I served under him. Before they turned on him."

"And?"

"And I owe him everything. I loved that man. He was good to me. So I'm doing him a favor."

"By following me?"

"By warning you."

"I live within the law."

The cop was just a kid. "All the good guys do."

"Trini did."

"Are all of you this rude?"

"All of us?"

"You know what I mean."

Rey frowned. "I swear I don't."

"Listen, I'm just telling you what I know. I saw your name on a list. I saw both your names."

Rey looked up. "I haven't used that name in years."

"Good. Don't. Some people on this list are no longer with us."

They had come to the end of the street. They doubled back. The woman was finished washing her clothes. She coughed as they walked by, and approached meekly to ask for money. She followed them for a bit, with an extended hand, but there was no conviction in her voice, and the young detective shooed her away. When they were back to the avenue, the undercover began to turn away from the university. "You were at the Moon, weren't you?" he asked.

Rey nodded. "Years ago."

"It's busy over there these days. You don't want to go back."

There was nothing to say to that.

"Trini deserved better," the cop said.

"We all did," said Rey. "The world owes us." He thanked the young man. "See, we're not all rude."

"It's good to know. Be careful, that's all." The young man held out his hand, and Rey shook it. They turned in opposite directions down the avenue.

"MOTHER," MANAU said, "you're boring him." He stood at the door of the kitchen, arms folded. Victor had the bowl of soup at his lips. A chicken bone lay on the table.

Manau's mother blanched. "Now Elijah, don't be rude."

"The soup is very good, madam," Victor said.

Norma patted him on the head.

"Your boy is so polite," Manau's mother said to Norma. "Not like my son."

"Mother."

"Thank you, madam," said Norma.

Manau's mother smiled sweetly. "Will you be staying then?"

Norma said they would. Manau's mother nodded and went off hurriedly to prepare a bed. They would sleep in Manau's room, of course. Norma didn't even have a moment to answer. Then it was the three of them, in the kitchen. The boy had finished eating. He hadn't touched his spoon. He turned his chair toward Norma and Manau, and the two adults sat. What else was there to do?

"Do you want to know about your father?" Norma asked.

The boy nodded. She couldn't recall with any certainty how much time had passed: had it been a year or a day? Had the boy aged, or had she? There was nothing of her husband in him, or nothing that she could find: he was young still, and perhaps that was it, but his thin face and dark skin didn't seem at all like Rey's. He had small lips and smooth cheeks. Rey's eyes had been hazel green, and this boy's eyes were nearly black. Was it even true? Norma took a deep breath. None of it was the boy's fault. She wanted her voice to come out steady. "The night I met him," she began, "he was taken from me by some bad men. They hurt him and then they gave him back to me. I always knew they could take him again. He was very handsome, I thought so, and very smart, like you. He must have loved you, if he sent you to me."

Manau cleared his throat. "Your mother told me. It was a few months ago. She wanted you to meet Norma one day. She didn't expect that day would come so soon." He looked down at his feet.

Victor rubbed his face. "Okay," he said.

"This is too much right now. Isn't it?"

The boy had nothing to say.

"It is, it is," Norma said. "I left the station this morning, you know. They're looking for us." It wasn't clear whom she was talking to. Norma stood and turned away. She opened the refrigerator, peering inside absentmindedly, inhaling its chemical coolness, and closing it again. I should climb inside, she thought. Shut myself in and die.

Her bones hurt.

"They won't find you here," Manau said. "They won't look for you here."

"Who's looking for you?" Manau's mother said. She had just walked in.

"No one," Manau said.

"It's complicated," added Norma.

Manau's mother looked hurt for a second. "I can see no one is tired here," she said after a pause. She put her hands up. "Won't you three help me with something?"

Norma, Manau, and Victor followed her out of the kitchen and into the dining room. There was a neglected, half-empty cabinet of glassware, and a sliding door with a long, slanting crack across its face. Beyond it was a square patch of grass no more than two meters across. A light was on outside, and Norma could see the small yard was well tended. She gave Manau's mother a smile, this precious woman. She smiled back and pointed at the table, where an unfinished puzzle was spread out on a white piece of cardboard. Dozens and dozens of missing pieces were piled in each corner. Norma leaned over the still-forming picture: there were yellow buildings and a mountain beginning to take shape in the distance. A palm tree or two sprouted in the foreground.

"What's this?" Norma asked.

Manau's mother handed her the box. Of course: it was the Plaza in the Old Quarter. A few shoeshine boys sat on the steps of the cathedral. A woman in a sundress strolled with a parasol, to guard against the bright sunlight, and, in the center, a brass band with trumpets raised high played what was certainly a patriotic song. Norma could have been there the very day this picture was taken. It was easy to forget that the city had been beautiful once, that its elegant plaza had once been the beating heart of a nation's capital.

"I just love puzzles," Manau's mother said.

They all sat down, Victor with his knees on the chair, and each took a handful of puzzle pieces to sift through. It was brilliant, Norma thought. This woman was brilliant. Norma wanted to weep. She stared down at the table. The puzzle suddenly absolved them of the need to speak, and they fell quickly into the rhythm of it: examining a piece, its colors and textures, scanning the box to see where it might fit. Her city as it had been once, the city where she'd fallen in love with Rey.

Manau's mother took the box. "I grew up here," she said to Victor, pointing with her pinky, down a side street that came off the plaza. "Just three blocks away." She smiled and ran her fingers through her white hair. "It was just a village then."

Norma's mother had always called it a village, too, as in, "Your father has slept with every tramp in this village ..." But so much had changed. As a girl, Norma had walked the four sides of this plaza. It didn't exist anymore. For most city residents, its name evoked not this image from the not-so-distant past but something more recent: a great massacre that had occurred in the final year of the war. On Sundays, as a girl, Norma would go there with her father to watch the marching bands. It was a tradition in those days: a casual crash of a cymbal, and the city dwellers looked up from their reverie, and everything was put on hold. A half-dozen musicians and a conductor, quite presentable in a black suit, passing a hat through the crowd. Once, after a particularly rousing number, a conductor had taken the flower from his lapel and placed it delicately behind Norma's ear. With a broad, gap-toothed smile, he announced the next song, and dedicated it to "a princess." He said those exact words! She was nine years old, with pale skin and pretty eyes. She wore a dress with yellow flowers on it, and they were all looking at her. Then her father whispered that she should curtsy, and she did, to the appreciative applause of the gathered crowd. Even now, nearly forty years later, she was nodding to the crowd, thank you, thank you, color gathering in her cheeks.

BACK HOME, they had played games, too. Different kinds: they ran into the forest and hid there. They imitated the frantic music of the jungle animals and frightened the girls. Those were happy memories. The kids took turns reinventing the stories the old people told: about fires and wars, about rivers that changed course in the middle of the night, about Indians who spoke a language even older than their own.

These were strange times. Victor was among strange people. He had never asked his mother about the city, and there was no one else he would have trusted. Plenty of people told stories about it, but they had no way of knowing. Once, Nico returned from a trip to the provincial capital with his father and said he had seen a magazine from the city. Some of the younger kids didn't know what a magazine was; Nico used the word for *book*. "But with more pictures," he explained. "Pictures of the city," he said, and everyone wanted to know pictures of *what exactly*. Describe it. Tell us—they were all dying to know. Nico said little. He was coy, almost smug. It was the way he drew a crowd to him, with a sly smile, always holding back, and he began his list: photos of wide streets, shiny cars. "Asphalt," he said importantly, and the children nodded. Powerful factories, noisy machines, crowded parks—wait.

"Noisy machines?" Victor asked. He couldn't help it. "What does a picture of a noisy machine look like?"

Nico grabbed one of the smaller boys by the shoulders and shook him. "Like this," he said. Everyone laughed, even the boy. He was just happy to be included.

"What else?" Victor asked.

Nico frowned, and continued his list: churches, plazas, trains. These were just words, and they were all impatient for something more, something exactly right, something new. By the time Nico said "tall buildings," the children, Victor first among them, groaned. *Of course* there were tall buildings—wasn't it a city? Everyone had heard of those.

Nico laughed. "Oh, yeah, you know all about the city, don't you?" He looked right at Victor. Nico picked up a stick. "Draw it then."

"Draw what?"

"The city."

Victor smiled. "You can't draw a city." He started laughing and, to his surprise, everyone laughed with him.

"Yeah, Nico. You can't draw a city," they echoed. They stretched the word out, let it linger: *draaaaaaw*.

But what if he had? What if you could? This is not what he imagined: not these people, not this house. Not this puzzle, not the radio, full of light and metal. Not any of it: not Norma and her mystery, not the image of the father he didn't remember, not the list of names, the commercial, or the woman selling bread and cursing them. Draw the city: dark and dense, a knot that can't be untied. Tall buildings, indeed. Shiny cars—he hadn't come across one yet. Victor closed his eyes and yawned. It was the night of the longest day he could remember. He knew enough to know that it was cold outside.

In his life, Victor had told three lies that he considered important. The first, to his teacher, not Manau but a previous one. Victor cheated on a geography test—everyone had looked at the maps his father had left. He had let them; they were the only maps in town. With the passing of time, this transgression seemed less and less significant, but he could, if he tried, still recall the anxiety of that day. The second, to Nico: I don't remember. Victor had said it with his jaw set, stern, so convincing he almost believed it himself. Swear, Nico said. Promise. And Victor did, without hesitation, though the memory of *tadek* never left him alone. The third, to his mother: do you remember your father? she'd asked him once, and there seemed, from the way her voice quavered, from the dull sadness in her eyes, to be only one correct answer. She pulled him to her when he nodded, and began to sob. She couldn't have believed him.

THE WAY Rey figured it, this was the problem: you did not quit the IL— how could you, if you had never joined it? If its existence was not acknowledged, not even between you and your contact? The situation was alluded to, as if it were something that had sprouted, wild and unbidden, from the earth. It was remarked upon, shaped indirectly by your actions, but this fact you could not admit to yourself or to anyone. You read the news and, like all your countrymen, shook your head in dismay at the downward spiral of events. You didn't allow yourself to feel responsibility for any of it.

Even at this late date, some nine years into the war, there were a few adventurous newspapers and radio stations that raised doubts as to whether any organized armed insurgency existed. It might have been shocking to hear if it hadn't been so commonplace. Bogeymen, they said, created by the government with the transparent aim of manipulating a terrified population. Camps in the jungle—the very camps Rey had visited? Hogwash, aerial photographs doctored in a lab. The IL, they said, was shorthand for the many varieties of rage loose within the borders, an unrecognized complaint given voice, lumped together by the powers-that-be beneath one unseemly umbrella. It represented the inability of the governing and literate classes to comprehend the depth of the people's unhappiness. Every angry young man with a rock in his hand—was he a subversive? The learned analysts scoffed at the notion, as if such a thing were unthinkable, but Rey listened and thought to himself: Yes. They are, every last one of them. Whether he knows it or not, that young man is doing our work. Our plan includes him, just as it included me even before the IL had a name.

Over the years, Rey had developed an intuitive understanding of the plan. Coordinated attacks on the more vulnerable symbols of government power: remote police outposts, polling places in distant villages. A campaign of propaganda that included the infiltration of newspapers and radio stations; the maintenance of camps in the jungle for arms training, in preparation for an eventual assault on the capital. Meanwhile, in the city, kidnappings and ransoms, in order to finance the purchase of weapons and explosives facilitated by supporters abroad. Daring prison breaks to impress the average man. No one had ever shown him a manual, nor did Rey know who decided which targets would be destroyed. Communiqués were signed simply THE CENTRAL COMMITTEE and appeared on city streets suddenly, as if dropped from the skies. The violence was ratcheted up: encircle the city, instill terror. The campaign depended upon military escalation from the forces of order, drew strength and purpose from the occasional massacre of innocents, or the disappearance of a prominent and well-liked sympathizer.

What did it all mean?

Consider the improbability of it: that the multiple complaints of a people could somehow coalesce and find expression in an act—in any act—of violence. What does a car bomb say about poverty, or the execution of a rural mayor explain about disenfranchisement? Yet Rey had been a party to this for nine years. The war had become, if it wasn't from the very beginning, an indecipherable text. The country had slipped, fallen into a nightmare, now horrifying, now comic, and in the city, there was only a sense of dismay at the inexplicability of it. Had it begun with a voided election? Or the murder of a popular senator? Who could remember now? They had all been student protesters, had felt the startling power of a mob, shouting as one chorus of voices—but that was years ago, and times had changed. No one still believed all that, did they? The war had bred a general exhaustion. It was a city of sleepwalkers now, a place where another bomb hardly registered, where the Great Blackouts were now monthly occurrences, announced in vitriolic pamphlets slipped beneath windshield wipers like shopping circulars. The government retaliated every fortnight with its army of poorly trained boy-soldiers, one or two died in the crossfire, and partisans took to the streets, filling the long avenues and clashing with riot police, before racing home to listen to descriptions of themselves on the radio news the same evening. Marches became riots of predictable fury, buildings burned while firemen watched, and so on and so on.

"Do you hate them?" his contact had asked early on, and when Rey said he didn't, the man in the wrinkled suit shook his head. "You read too much poetry, young man. Be certain they hate you." This was nine years before. Even then the soldiers fired into unarmed crowds. Even then anyone paying attention should have known what was coming. But they had stepped together into this chaos, the insurgency and the government, arm in arm, and for nine violent years, they'd danced.

The war, Rey hoped, would be finished before his son was as tall as a rifle.

He'd met these boys in the camps. Fourteen, fifteen years old. He met them on the same trip when he met his own son. They came from out-of-the-way places plunged in some craggy forested valley or balanced on a rocky promontory or stranded on a barren patch of desert. Places like 1797. They wore hard, expressionless faces, and were not concerned with what bullets could and could not accomplish. They did not expect to die. They all hoped to see the city one day. They told stories about it, spoke of marching down the wide avenues in formation, of being received as liberators. It was what the commanders had told them to expect. When? they asked. Soon. Next month. Next year. When military equilibrium is achieved. What does *equilibrium* mean? We'll take the capital, the commanders said, and the boys repeated it to Rey, and he could tell they believed it. Meanwhile, they practiced making bombs in the jungle. None had even the cloudiest sense of what the war was about, and none had ever asked. They were happy to be out of their homes. Once a month, they marched into some town to kill a priest or burn a flag fluttering above a police outpost. They ambushed a military convoy on a bridge and shot at boys their own age, boys who came from towns much like theirs. They were paid in cash on good months, but in a pinch, they accepted promissory notes to be redeemed when victory was achieved. And so Rey, the man from the city, heard one question most of all from these eminently practical young men. "Sir," they said. "We are winning, aren't we?"

At first, he didn't understand. Then it was clear they had money on their minds. "Of course," Rey reassured them. "Of course we're winning."

In the city, it was impossible to speak of the war in those terms. Rey thought of it now as a race to stay alive. If he could survive until the weapons were laid down, if he could live to see that day, then his mistakes could be atoned for. When he saw Norma each night, and saw that she loved him, he despaired. He was most afraid of being alone.

There were quiet months when the war went on without him. Rey left on his single trip to the jungle and returned. He met his boy and dreamed of him and sulked guiltily around the apartment. He made love to his wife and bragged of his child to strange women. He was warned to put it all behind him, and this, finally, was what he intended to do when he met with his contact ten months after Yerevan had disappeared.

It had become a year-end tradition in the press to speculate about peace talks. It was all over the radio and the newspapers. Of course, it was impossible: the IL had no visible leaders, so who would represent them? No one expected it to happen, but they spoke of it because it made

them feel better. It was no different when Rey and his contact met at a
bus stop in The Settlement that December, near the hills that rose to the
southeast of the capital. Rey was never afraid to meet his contact: the city
was infinite, designed for hiding in plain sight. They walked to a dingy
little bar that was really a poor family's living room. Christmas lights
were strung along the ceiling, intermittently casting splotches of faint
red and green light. They sat at a wobbly wooden table and drank instant
coffee. The owner stood behind his counter, listening to the radio and
thumbing through an old newspaper. Beyond the bar, from the dimly lit
room that comprised the rest of the house, Rey could hear a baby crying.
He was anxious to say it: I'm out, I'm done, it's finished, let the war go
on without me. It was what he needed to say, but it stuck in his throat.
The air was smoky, and then Rey's contact announced he was going underground. It came as a shock. "And you should too," he said. "From now
until the end."

"The end?"

Rey's contact smiled wanly. "All good things must come to a close
eventually."

THIRTEEN

T HE GOVERNMENT had not survived nearly a decade of
rebellion without learning a few things about defending itself.
Mainly, it had learned how and when and on whom to inflict great pain.
Everyone talked eventually. Suspects were brought to the Moon every
night and submitted to savage and primitive police work: if they were
too strong, or if they had nothing to tell (it was still difficult to know the
difference), they were flown by helicopter to the sea and tossed, flailing,
into the murky waters below. Others were placed in the same tombs Rey
had survived. Some of these suspects were released, and many others
were buried in the dusty hills. By current standards, Rey's stay had been
luxurious.

In addition, and perhaps more important, eyes and ears had been recruited throughout the country—no easy task in a nation as large and
ungovernable as this one. In the city, an army of street persons was paid
to sift through the domestic trash of various suspicious men and women.

This work had yielded a surprising number of arrests. Neighbors were encouraged to turn each other in, with cash rewards distributed discreetly to those who supplied useful information. Outside the city, progress was being made as well. In nearly every regional capital, and even in some remote villages, people were in place; people who, for a relatively small sum, could keep an eye on the strangers who passed through. They traded in gossip and insinuation, but were occasionally quite useful.

In 1797, this man was Zahir. He was typical of these ersatz agents: not naturally suspicious, or particularly inclined to support the government, and as far as the war was concerned, relatively indifferent to its outcome. Like many, he probably believed it would never end, with or without his minor involvement. He was, however, a conscientious father and husband, and therefore happy to accept the small but consistent monies offered, for the good of his family. His simple mandate was to keep an eye on things, and this was something he would have done anyway: as one of only a handful of fighting-age men still left in 1797, Zahir had come to consider himself the man in charge. Unlike the others who had stayed, he was not a drunkard, or dim-witted, and was generally liked by the townspeople. He was a married man with a daughter and a son and a small, unproductive plot of land. Zahir considered his new position—secret though it was—a ratification of his own opinion of himself within the village. Most people in 1797 probably didn't know Zahir could read.

By the time Rey's son was born, Zahir was an expert of sorts on the strange men who passed through the village and into the forest. They stopped to rest for a day or two, usually worn out, and by the way they carried themselves, Zahir could tell they were not from the nation's tropical regions. He took spare notes about their demeanor, wrote down bits of overheard conversation, speculated about the origins of their accents. Their faces betrayed an exhaustion buried deep within, and this was their common trait.

There were few books in 1797 when Zahir was a boy. Once, a traveler passing through left a crime novel with the village as a gift. It caused a sensation. There was an elder who knew how to read, and he took it upon himself to share the novel with the boys. He read it aloud over the course of a month, and Zahir fell in love: there were detectives who wore hats and men who smoked in every scene; there were busty women drinking in out-of-the-way dives, and the odd appearance of a gun waiting to fire. The city it described was full of hoodlums and shiny cars and blind alleys where brave men fought with knives until only one was left standing. Nothing could have been more exciting. Zahir had loved its dark tension, as had all the boys his age, and so the reading of this book became a yearly event until the elder who organized it passed away. The novel itself was lost, or perhaps the village buried the book with him; Zahir couldn't remember. By then, his schooling had already ended.

When he became an informer, Zahir thought of this book for the first time in many years, and was struck, as if by a distant love. His reports, he decided, would be like that novel, but to his dismay, they never came out quite right. The village was full of a darkness, a furtive movement that Zahir found impossible to explain. And the strangers: it was not enough to guess where they came from, where they were going. He wanted to capture the faces of these men, but no matter what words he used, they never seemed quite suspicious enough.

Rey, by virtue of his repeated visits, was the first man Zahir was able to describe reasonably well. He thought little of it, did not at the time consider it to be a betrayal of any sort. It was practice: this stringing together of words, these syllables lining up, and with them, an image taking shape. He wrote and rewrote it, labored until it was perfect, and though he was proud of his writing, Zahir didn't think it was worth showing anyone, at least not yet. Who was this man anyway? Like everyone else in the village, Zahir saw the coquettish way that Adela spoke with the stranger, and neither approved, nor disapproved. It simply was. The man was nice enough, always polite, though not talkative by any stretch. He came three times a year, sometimes more. He spent his time with Adela, and then left for the forest. They said he was a scientist. Of course, no one in 1797 knew him as Rey.

The next month, when Zahir traveled to the provincial capital to turn in his report, he brought with him, in a separate pocket, his description of Rey—three carefully edited pages in which Zahir noted the color of his skin, the shape of his smile, the timbre of his voice, and in which he had invented a story for the stranger to inhabit: the man was IL, a leader, a guerrilla. He had invented tire-burning, he murdered police officers for sport. Zahir transcribed a confession that had never taken place, and these sections of dialogue were, he was certain, the best writing he had ever done. Of course, he wouldn't show it to the government man, but Zahir liked knowing that he could. These meetings always made him nervous.

Zahir arrived in midafternoon, after traveling all day. It had rained throughout the night. The office was off a muddy side street, not far from the center of town, but then nothing was far from the center of town.

"Anything?" the government man asked after they had completed the requisite pleasantries and complaints about the heat. He had never given his name, but the man was nice enough. He was from the city. He leaned back in his chair. His dress shirt was undone and soaked through with sweat.

"It's all there, boss," Zahir said.

The man looked through it—there were only two pages—and frowned.

"Is it all right?"

"I've been meaning to ask you, and please don't take offense. How much schooling do you have?"

"Sir?"

"School. How much did you do?"

Zahir reddened. No one had ever asked him such a thing. With the priest dead and the mayor gone, he might have been the most educated man in the village. "Four years, sir," he said. Then, after a pause, he added, "If you count what the priest taught me, five."

The government man nodded. He was a light-skinned man with a bad complexion, but when he smiled, there was something very gentle about him. He smiled now, and motioned for Zahir to sit. "I like you, you know that. You work hard. I'm embarrassing you. Don't be that way. Listen . . . Well now . . . Out with it: I have a gift."

He opened his desk and retrieved a small book. "I had this sent for you, from the city."

It was red and small enough to fit in Zahir's pocket. He flipped through it quickly and saw that the print was very small, smaller even than the Bible the priest had shown him once. Zahir had never seen a book like this one before. "What is it?"

"It's nothing. It's a dictionary. You're very sharp for a villager," the government man said, "and I thought you might enjoy it. It has words, along with what they mean." He handed Zahir an envelope, then placed his palms flat on the desk and stood up. "I recommend you go to the market now. Prices only go one way around here: up."

"Thank you, sir," Zahir said. He stood and bowed. His heart was pounding in his chest. Had he been made fun of? There was prickly heat on his skin, and he was sweating. With a flourish, Zahir put the dictionary in his breast pocket and smiled. "I have something for you as well."

"Do you?"

The stranger, Zahir thought. Why not? He was suddenly quite hopeful. He pulled the papers from his pocket, unfolded them, and passed them to the government man. "It's about one of the strangers. One of the men who comes to the village."

"Does he have a name?"

Zahir told him Rey's other name. "And he's a scientist."

The government man examined the text. He read it slowly, the edges of his mouth creeping toward a smile, then looked up. "Now this we can use," he said, beaming. "My dear man, you're a poet. I knew you were."

Later, Zahir would look up the word. He knew what it meant, of course, but he wanted to know *exactly* what it meant, and he would memorize the wording of the definition, and repeat it to himself, just for the sheer pleasure of the sound. *A poet.* That night, he would tell his wife, and she would not understand. She would pretend to sleep, but he would not believe her, and though the children would be asleep on the other side of a thin curtain, he would tickle her until she giggled, and then he would make love to her.

"Can I keep this?" the government man asked.

There was no going back. "Of course, sir," Zahir said.

He took his money and left into the relative bustle of the provincial capital. There was a tiny bar at the corner, and he treated himself to a drink. Then another. Zahir drank by himself and looked up words in his new book: *village, city, money, war, love.* He had another drink and then another, and looked through his new book until it was too dark to see. When he left, it was nearly dusk, the clouds beginning to gather for the evening rain. A breeze blew, and the heat had subsided. He felt light-headed.

He found it in the market, on his way to wait for the truck back to 1797. The government man was right: prices only went up. Rice and dried beans and potatoes and yucca brought from the mountains, each month incrementally higher. In the village, there was always silver fish. Salted, boiled, fried. And plantains; and they made do, didn't they? Zahir saw it then: a black and shiny machine worthy of—what was it the man had said?—oh yes, *a poet*. It was a radio, and it played gaudily, loudly from a stall at the edge of the provincial market. It shook him. He went closer. It had been years since he'd heard such an exciting sound.

"All stations," the salesman said, turning the knob lazily—static, music, static, voices, music, static.

Zahir couldn't help but grin.

"First payment today, you take it home in six months."

He gave away his money without hesitation. And it kept him up at night: for half a year, he worried that he'd been swindled, but each month, when he went to collect his money, the salesman was still there, and the radio still played, and it lost none of its power to impress him. Where's the money? his wife asked, but he never told her. I'm investing, he said. He wrote more and more with the help of his new dictionary and eventually got up the courage to ask the government man for a little raise. In six more months, he would own the radio, he would carry it home with him wrapped in a blanket wrapped in a plastic bag to protect the machine from rain. He had just enough money. He made calculations in his head. Six more months until he would shock his wife and his son and his daughter and the entire village. He would take his seat among the bags of rice aboard the back of an open truck, he would carry the apparatus against his chest as one might carry a child. The idea of this moment filled him with hope. I am a man in the employ of the government! I am the mayor of this town! And he was—who else would want such a task? Later, when the IL returned and took his hands, and Zahir could no longer farm or write, the canteen owner extended him a generous line of credit, on which he and his family survived for months. Then the rainy season came, and with it, a sense of despair Zahir had never felt before, and there was no war by then and no money available for faraway spies. The government man would not help him; in fact, he must have returned to the city, because the office was boarded up and inhabited by squatters who spoke an impenetrable dialect. Zahir asked around the provincial capital, but no one seemed to remember the government man at all. Inevitably, Zahir fell behind on his payments, and he canceled his debt to the storekeeper with this same radio, and on that day, he wept. He missed the war, he said to himself, those were the good old days. He gave the dictionary to his boy and told him to study hard, but Nico was never one for school. One day, when his teacher, Elijah Manau, reprimanded him for not completing his homework, Nico dropped the little red book into the river just to watch it sink.

IT WAS the tenth year of the conflict, and Rey's contact had gone underground. Among the literate classes of the city, fear had become recklessness. Those who could flee were already gone. Yerevan had been dead for twelve months, not spoken of for nearly that long.

Rey and Norma were invited one summer evening to a dinner party at the home of a prominent socialite. She was a stylish woman of considerable wealth, who had married a man handsome and vapid enough to be elected senator. They owned a stake in the radio station. It was said that they had secretly pushed for the director to be eliminated after he made some controversial statements, and had handpicked Elmer as his successor. The senator, it was widely assumed, wished to be president. He had survived an assassination attempt four weeks before, in the first week of the new year. The radio had obligingly portrayed him as a hero, and this was his celebration.

They had to pass security twice to enter the party: once at the front gate, where the cab dropped them off, and then again, at the door. There were off-duty policemen in the foyer, one in each corner of the great open room, and one stationed at the foot of the staircase at the far wall. It was a pastel-colored wonderland, this party, full of charming men and well-dressed women. A soft, inoffensive music could be heard just beneath the sibilant chatter. There was something anachronistic about so much wealth: the very place smelled of money, and Rey said as much to Norma.

"Let's be worldly," she whispered. She had spent more than an hour getting ready for this night. Her hair shone, and she was beautiful. "Let's pretend."

The hostess greeted them warmly, apologized for the security. She gave no impression of knowing who they were, nor did she question their presence. She smiled with well-bred elegance and shuffled them off toward the drinks. Norma led Rey through the crowd. They saw Elmer, standing in the center of a tight circle, holding forth on the war and its meaning. As the newly installed director of the radio, his view on the state of the nation was quite sought after. He nodded at them both, but Norma pulled Rey on. A dark-skinned man in a tuxedo poured them drinks.

"At least the drink is strong," Rey said to his wife.

She kissed him, then leaned into him and finished her drink quickly. When she kissed him again, her mouth tasted of liquor. "What's going on?"

"Nothing," she said. "We're celebrating."

"Are we?" He took a sip of his drink. "The senator's brush with death?"

"Not that." She asked the bartender for another drink, then clinked glasses with him. "We should say hello to Elmer."

Rey frowned. "I'll wait here."

It was petulant, and he regretted it immediately. But Norma didn't mind; she pinched him and stuck her tongue out. She went off into the maw of the party. He admired her confidence, and couldn't describe this mood he felt. Fearful? Anxious? It was noisier than he would have expected from a crowd like this. He stood by the table; he saw Elmer's circle raise a glass to his wife. There was a smattering of applause. He should have gone with her. He was remote, and in this crowd, more alone than he had been in many months. When he thought no one was watching, he stirred his drink with his pinkie, then downed it.

"Ah, a connoisseur!" Rey looked up. A red-haired woman was smiling at him. "You're Norma's husband, aren't you?" the woman asked him. When he nodded, she added, "She's going to be a star."

"She is," Rey said, a bit unsure.

"Give me one just like his," the woman said to the bartender. "But I'll stir it myself." She winked at Rey.

The woman was part of a group of people who had come to refresh their drinks. They all knew each other and looked familiar as they jostled good-naturedly for the bartender's attention. It was early still, but already the woman was glassy-eyed and drunk. "Join us," she said to Rey with a languorous wave of her hand. "We're talking about . . . Oh, I don't know. Gentlemen, what are we talking about?"

"The world? The war?"

"Life?"

"Oh, all of it," the redhead said. "Everyone, this is Norma's husband. What was your name?"

"Rey," he said, and they all nodded approvingly, as if his were a special, accomplished name. "What a voice your wife has!" said a fat man. He smiled mischievously. "Does she . . . Pardon me, I've had a few and I shouldn't ask, but I simply must know . . . Does she *talk dirty*?"

Rey was too stunned to answer.

"Gentlemen, I remind you this is mixed company!"

The fat man nodded at the redhead. "My apologies," he said with a slight bow. "You're a tough bitch." Everyone laughed. "But sir, her voice is really quite marvelous."

The rest agreed and offered congratulations, and someone brought him another drink. He drank it quickly. The lights, Rey decided, were too bright in this grand room.

He stood at the edge of the circle, and soon they had forgotten him again. They were indeed meandering from topic to topic: the price of shoes, the strange weather, the awful traffic just before curfew. Occasionally, the name of someone dead or missing surfaced, was lamented briefly, and then dismissed.

At one point, Rey heard his contact mentioned by name.

"What became of that one?" the fat man asked. "I haven't seen him in ages!"

How long has it been? Rey thought to himself.

The redhead said he was on sabbatical. He had gone abroad, she said, to Europe. She was very pale, almost somber as she said it. Rey nodded; was she lying or had she been lied to?

"Who?" Rey asked, pretending.

"Oh, you know him," the woman said. She looked familiar, though Rey was sure they had never been properly introduced. She was a physicist at the Tech, Rey thought, but couldn't be sure. Was she IL?

"I took him to the airport myself," she said.

The fat man shrugged. He took off his jacket and was sweating through his shirt. The flabby skin of his neck hung over his shirt collar. A cigarette dangled from his lips. "Where is that bastard?" he asked behind a curtain of smoke. "Italy? France? That lucky fuck."

Rey smiled with the rest. He breathed deeply. He was, in a sense, free. Was his contact living in a dank basement in The Cantonment, or in a palatial Italian villa? It didn't matter really. Rey scanned the room for Norma. He wanted to get away. The fat man was telling the sad story of how he'd been turned down for a visa.

"Where do you want to go?" someone asked.

"Anywhere."

Rey offered the small group a smile and excused himself. He didn't know anybody, and nobody knew him. The redhead raised her glass to him as he turned away.

A few hours passed quickly. Rey wandered in and out of a few different conversations, each touched by the war. A gaunt, well-dressed man described being kidnapped. He was lucky: he'd been held for only two days and so hadn't been fired from work. Rey met a woman whose maid, it turned out, was IL. "Imagine," she said, appalled, "the nerve of the girl to bring that ideology into my house!" Throughout it all, Rey stayed near the drinks, so much so that the bartender had one ready for him each time he approached. At one point, they struck up a conversation. Rey recognized the accent. He was from the jungle, but no, the bartender told Rey, he didn't miss it. "There was no one left in my town," he said. "Everyone is here now."

Rey sat briefly on the steps. He wandered out onto the patio, where he was offered a cigarette. He smoked without pleasure, his first in many years. He watched the lights of the city bubbling in the distance, and when he came back into the great room, the party had swelled, and he felt, in his drunken state, that he would never find his wife in this multitude. It was nearly midnight by then, and the guests were separating into two groups: those who would leave before the curfew and those who would stay the night. The hostess milled through the crowd, encouraging everyone to stay. "We have a generator!" she proclaimed. She held a glass unsteadily in her right hand, its contents spilling on the hardwood floor. Her husband, the senator, stood by her side, and he, too, was visibly drunk. His face puffy and red, he swayed slowly from right to left. Rey wanted to hug the poor man. He still hadn't recovered; this much was clear. His bodyguard had been killed, his driver wounded, and the senator was lucky to have escaped with his life. It had all happened in broad daylight, on a busy avenue four blocks from a police checkpoint, not far from the radio station. Rey smiled to himself. In a way, it was satisfying to know that the war had gone on without him. The usual spate of bombs and blackouts and extrajudicial disappearances had continued—but Rey felt, for the first time in many years, divorced from it and therefore innocent. He could embrace this stranger, this poor senator. He could appear at the good gentleman's party and bemoan the nastiness of the current situation without feeling responsible for any of it. The senator had unbuttoned his shirt now, and was calling for the music to be turned up, for the lights to be turned down. In an instant, they were, and the grand room was entirely different. He'll be president, Rey thought sadly, and he won't live out his term. Host and hostess smiled. They didn't want anyone to leave. They were afraid of being alone.

"Should we stay?" Norma had appeared at his side, quite suddenly, and her presence made him feel warm. All night he had missed her.

"Do you want to?"

She shrugged, then smiled. She did.

"Are you drunk?" he asked, and she smiled some more.

Many had already left, but now the lights were low, and hours had passed, and among those who stayed, it was as if an animal had been loosed. The scene was unrecognizable. The music was being played at a furious volume, the great room overwhelmed with dancers. It had happened all at once, a lightning strike. The staid function had been replaced with a bacchanal: coats were laid over the banister of the staircase; heeled shoes lined the walls, tossed there by the well-dressed women, who now danced barefoot. There was a faint smell of sweat in the room, and someone was playing with the chandelier, now brightening and now dimming the lights in time with the music. One of the cops leaned against the wall, another sat on the step, eyes closed, tapping his foot to the music.

Then Elmer was beside them, throwing his arm over Rey's shoulder. Was everyone in here drunk? Elmer had a pasted-on grin, and his face shone with sweat. "You've got a hell of a woman," he said.

"Of course I do." Rey smiled at his wife. Elmer had them both now, his arms around them, and Rey felt the weight of the man on him. He was afraid the little guy might fall.

"I never liked you," Elmer said in a low voice.

Rey looked up. Norma hadn't heard. He would have dropped Elmer, except that this fact came as no surprise. "I know," he offered instead.

"I love your wife," Elmer said, again just for Rey. Then he laughed, and so they all did. Elmer planted a kiss on Norma's cheek, and she blushed. He turned back to Rey, who could feel the little man's breath on his ear. "If you hurt her," Elmer whispered, "I'll kill you."

"Why so many secrets?" Norma said.

Elmer ignored her, smiling again at the two of them, as if he'd been commenting on the weather or the theater. "Has she told you yet?" he said.

"I haven't," Norma said, shaking her head.

"Told me what?"

"Can I tell him?" Elmer slurred.

"Tell him."

Elmer turned to Rey. "Norma's going to have her own show," he said. "We just decided today. Every Sunday night. Her very own show. Tell him the name, sweetheart."

"Lost City Radio," Norma said. She reached for Rey's hand. "Do you love it? Tell me you love it."

Rey couldn't stop smiling. He said the three words to himself. He was warm and happy. "I love it," he said. "It's wonderful."

THAT YEAR, a man came to 1797 and announced that he was an artist. He set up shop in front of the village canteen, with only a stool and an easel and sheets of grayish newsprint clipped together, covered in plastic in case of rain. He had the antique look of a wise man, with a dark, wrinkled face and long, thinning hair that tumbled wildly down his back. His name was Blas, and he could draw the town's missing. One had only to describe the person, and he would do the rest. His skill, he told those who asked, was listening.

For two days, Blas sat in front of the canteen door, waiting, and had no work. He seemed patient enough, content to pass the time leaning against the wall, smoking hand-rolled cigarettes of the coarsest tobacco. He ate his meals at the canteen, smiled occasionally, and did not, as many had expected, smell particularly bad. When someone approached, he greeted them politely, offered his services, but wasn't pushy. On the third day, he asked the canteen owner permission to display his work, and when this was granted, he spent one busy morning tacking up pencil drawings along the walls. Then he returned to his post by the door, to wait.

One by one, the villagers came through to see the exhibit. They were skeptical, of course, and none more so than Zahir. He still worked on his writing in secret, usually down by the river, on warm afternoons when it was not raining. He was not above being jealous, and the very presence of this man was somehow an affront: where had this man come from, and what could he offer the villagers that Zahir could not accomplish in words? Still, curiosity took hold, and Zahir strolled into the canteen, determined to be unimpressed. The old man nodded to him as he walked in, but Zahir pretended not to have noticed.

Inside, along the four walls of the canteen, were a dozen faces of men and women and boys that Blas claimed to have re-created from the descriptions of their loved ones. It was, of course, impossible to say if the old man was lying or, if he was not, if the drawings were in any way accurate. Even the loved ones could not say: memory is a great deceiver, grief and longing cloud the past, and recollections, even vivid ones, fade. Still, there was something to these renderings, and Zahir recognized it immediately: they were undeniably human, these faces. These creased women with their sad eyes and dark hair; these prematurely old men with pendulous lips and sagging cheeks; these young warriors, now missing, boys whose very skin shone with an inexplicable bloodlust, an excitement and hunger for life they couldn't help but betray. Together they formed a confused race of men anxiously awaiting some grave disappointment. It wore him down in a manner Zahir hadn't anticipated and could hardly articulate. The village, of course, had been disappearing steadily for years, but it wasn't until he stepped out of the canteen and into the afternoon sun that he felt so acutely the emptiness of the place. He was surrounded by it. There were the sounds of the breathing forest, the cawing of a bird, the distant and susurrant murmuring of water. What else was there?

In fact, most of the village was there. In his grief, Zahir hadn't noticed them. They numbered in the two hundreds, and there were no more than fifty men, one for every three women. Those who had seen the exhibit were, like Zahir, milling about in a daze. They had entered the canteen not quite knowing what to expect, and left despondent. Now only Blas seemed to know what to do. He began taking appointments right then for the following morning: half-hour interviews, he said, and a drawing by the end of the day. "Your name, madam?" he called out. "And the name of your missing?" and it was all carefully listed in a notebook. The women thronged around him, some shook with sobbing. Zahir stepped away from the knot of despairing women and sat on the stump of a fallen tree. It was damp and beginning to rot: a soft, pleasant perch from which to take it all in. The village's women, who had seemed to him, only hours before, to be the very picture of steadfast resolve, had come to this. Even his wife was among them. Her brother had left for the war a few years prior, on an army truck with a captain who had promised every recruit forty acres of land when it was all over.

"But you can have a hundred acres here!" they'd told him. Wasn't the forest infinite?

"Land on the coast," said the captain in his city accent, "is more valuable."

Zahir knew this place and its people: he'd lived his entire life in this forest, kissed a dozen different girls! Fought and beaten twice as many opponents! He had been one of them: one of these bare-chested boys, wrestling in the mud and climbing the trees that hung over the river, all the way to the top, for no reason at all other than to stare at the sky and let the mind go blank. What pleasure! He had followed the river's edge to the cataract a day's hike upstream, and let the water spray cover him, let it bead on his skin like fine drops of sweat. He had let the hugeness of that noise erase him. He had never been alone in his youth—not once in fifteen years. Where were they now? Those boys he'd shared his childhood with, those girls who were now women whom he had kissed and touched beneath the trees?

He looked up. There were hours yet to this day. The children had formed another circle around their mothers, not quite understanding what the fuss was about, and this, too, made Zahir despair—how could they understand? Didn't they want to leave as well? Weren't they just biding their time?

Blas drew more than seventy pictures in the village over the next week. Business, he told the regulars at the canteen, had never been so good. Many drawings, quite surprisingly, were of people who were not yet missing. Women came with their husbands, mothers with their sons. "We're afraid," they said, tears in their eyes. "He's here now, but what about tomorrow?"

"I'M LISTENING, madam," the old artist said. Blas had worked on his voice for years. It was important in his line of work to put women immediately at ease: he very nearly purred. It had rained for two days, and so he had moved into the canteen, at the far end. He pulled the curtain, and they were alone in this makeshift private studio: two stools, an easel, an array of colored pencils. "Tell me."

Adela said nothing for a long moment. Her feet tingled.

"Does the boy look like his father?"

She shook her head. "He looks like me."

"How old is he?"

"Twelve months," she said. "A year."

The artist rubbed his face. He leaned toward her. "The father. How old is the father?"

"Oh," Adela said. "I don't know."

Blas turned the canvas around. It was empty, not a mark on it. "Don't be nervous, dear," he said in a voice just above a whisper. "There's nothing to be afraid of. Close your eyes and talk about him, and we'll do this together."

Adela took a deep breath. "He's not from here. And that's what you notice first. He comes from the city. His smile is like city people smile: halfway. He's careful. His hair flops forward onto his forehead, but he's always brushing it back with his palm. He has dimpled cheeks, and his eyes seem tired all the time. His hair is gray at the temples, with nearly white streaks, but he won't admit it. I think he may dye his hair. He's vain."

"Should I draw it black then? Or white? Which is it?"

"Draw it true. It's white."

"Is he thin?" Blas asked.

Adela nodded.

"His skin tone, madam. Is he dark like coffee, or light like milk?" He still hadn't begun to draw, not really; two very light strokes, vaguely parallel. His eyes were closed, and the point of the pencil just barely touched the paper.

"Like coffee," Adela said, but her mind was wandering. "And he loves the boy, I know that, I can tell." She paused. "But he doesn't love me."

"Madam!"

"A woman knows these things, sir. He has another life. He's told me and I've known from the beginning. I know some other things, some things he hasn't told me. I know that one day he'll come and take my child from me. I swear he will. He'll say it's for the boy's own good, and how can I argue with that? But then what will I do? I'll be like these old women here, who can't remember who used to love them or why they're alive." She took a shallow breath. "He's cruel."

"Madam, pardon me, what does he *look* like?"

"Oh, yes. His hair, for example. It's beginning to fall out. Each time I see him he looks older. His nose is crooked, just a bit, to which side? Well, to the left. His beard doesn't grow in evenly; isn't that the strangest thing?"

"Strange yes, madam, but not the strangest."

"You've seen all kinds of things."

"Of course," Blas said apologetically.

Adela rocked the sleeping child in her arms. "Every time he leaves," she said, "I'm afraid he won't come back."

"Why are you scared?"

"His work is dangerous."

The old artist didn't look up and didn't say anything. Dangerous work was the only kind that existed in those days. The country was at war. He selected another pencil, a lighter color, and his right hand moved feverishly around the paper. He rubbed the page with his thumb, blurring the markings. "Are his eyes far apart?"

"No."

"Are they close together?"

"I'm not sure."

"His hair is curly?"

She thought for a moment. "Wavy."

"His forehead—it's high like this? Or small, like this?"

Adela squinted at the drawing. "In between, I suppose. And more wrinkled. He's getting older, did I tell you that?"

The child twisted in her arms, a tiny hand poking free, a small fist opening, closing, grasping at the air. In an instant, it was over, and the boy was completely asleep once again. Blas and Adela had both stopped to watch him.

"It's a pity for your husband that he doesn't look like this boy of yours. He's a beautiful child."

"Thank you," Adela said. "He's not my husband."

"I'm sorry, madam. God is merciful."

"Are we nearly finished here?"

"Yes, very nearly."

Blas leaned over the page, touching up the drawing. He asked a few more questions: about the shape of the man's jaw, the size and placement of his ears, the style in which he wore his hair, and how gray was it exactly, and how did she know it was grayer than he wished it to be.

"Don't we all want to be young forever?" Adela said.

Rey flashed across her mind, images of him in various stages of undress. He was not a beautiful man and he was not even hers. But the child was. She looked at her boy, asleep: the drawing, she told herself, was for him. When Rey first came to her, he was surprised at how cool the nights were here when the days were so hot. He knew almost nothing about the forest. "What do they teach you at that school?" she'd asked, but it was what she'd loved most about him: he knew nothing, because he was a stranger. His foreignness, his accent, his gestures—they belonged to another place, and just being with him was enough for Adela to imagine another, less claustrophobic existence.

When Blas asked about the lips, Adela licked her own, as if she could still taste him. "They're full," she said. Blas drew, he erased, then he drew some more. When he was satisfied, Blas asked Adela to look very carefully. "Is this him?" he asked. He had a pitch, a tone of voice, prepared just for this question. He had posed it a thousand times since the war began, and the answer was always the same.

• • •

THE DECISION was made for them. By the time they thought to leave, there were no cabs to take them home. Not at that hour, not so close to curfew. The deserted city was a minefield. So they returned to the party, Norma and Rey, Elmer not far behind, and they found themselves once again in the great room, being served drinks by the bartender in a tuxedo. The man had taken his jacket off and was drinking himself now. Elmer spoke, but they couldn't hear him, and they didn't try. There was dancing all around them, and night had fallen heavily on the room. Where there was panic, there was freedom. What a giddy feeling! Rey took his wife by the hand, led her to the middle of the dance floor. He pressed his body against hers. She pressed back, and it was beautiful, and then they were moving, as they had once upon a time: there are things the body won't allow you to forget. It had been too long since they'd danced. "Louder!" someone yelled, and the music rose even more. Her chin rested on his shoulder, and he could smell her. The chandelier shook. The darkness was nearly complete; Rey had to be careful not to lose her to the crowd.

FOURTEEN

T HERE WERE rules, of course, even that first night. The program
would run on a six-second delay. This took some of the pressure off of
Norma. The calls would be screened and everyone warned not to mention
the war. This was good advice, not just for the radio, but for life, because
these days, someone was always listening. *Neutrality* was the word Elmer kept
repeating. Not to be confused with *indifference*, Norma thought. People, she
should keep in mind, went missing for all sorts of reasons, and the show
was not to be a sounding board for conspiracy theories or gripes about this
or that faction, or speculations about a certain prison whose very existence
was a state secret, however poorly kept. The show, Elmer lectured Norma,
was a risk, but a calculated one. There were hundreds of thousands of displaced people who would form the loyal core of her audience. Hope could
be dispensed in small doses to the masses of refugees who now called the
city home. They didn't want to talk about the war, he guessed; they wanted
to talk about their uncles, their cousins, their neighbors from that long-ago-

abandoned village; the way the earth smelled back home, the sound of the rain as it fell in bursts over the treetops, the lurid colors of the countryside in bloom. "You, Norma, just be nice, the way you know how to be, and let them talk. But not too much. Get names and repeat names and the phone calls will come in by the dozens. Ask nice questions. Got it?"

She said she did. The very idea of it gave her chills. Her own show. Of course she got it.

"Need I mention Yerevan?" Elmer said, as a final warning. "Need I mention that he is no longer with us?"

She went on the air that first night with a dry, metallic taste in her mouth. Excitement, fear: things could go wrong, catastrophically, with a single phone call. The minister of state had called the station, to say that someone on his staff would be listening. The theme music, commissioned from an out-of-work violinist, played, and already Norma was sweating. Elmer was sitting in the sound booth with her, taking notes, paying close attention. Three—two—one:

"Welcome," she said. "Welcome to Lost City Radio, to our new show. To all the listeners, a warm greeting this fine evening, my name is Norma, and I should explain a little about the show, since this is our first time." She covered the microphone and took a sip of water. "No one needs to tell you that the city is growing. We don't need sociologists or demographers to tell us what we can see with our own eyes. What we know is that it is happening rapidly, some say too rapidly, and that it has overwhelmed us. Have you come to the city? Are you alone, or more alone, than you expected to be? Have you lost touch with those whom you expected to find here? This show, my friends, is for you. Call us now, and tell us who you're looking for. Who can we help you find? Is it a brother you're missing? A lover? A mother or father, an uncle or a childhood friend? We're listening, I'm listening . . . Call now, tell us your story." She read the number of the radio station, emphasizing that it was a free call. "We'll be right back after a short break."

Cue music. Commercial. Norma could breathe again. No bombs yet. No explosions. "Well done," Elmer said, without looking up. There were a few lines already lit up. They had been building up the show for a few weeks. The people were primed for this. The commercial began to fade. "Nervous?"

Norma shook her head no.

The engineer began his countdown.

"Now the fun starts," said Elmer.

The first caller was a woman, whose thick accent said she was from the mountains. She spoke rather incoherently about a man she had known, whose name she could not recall at first, but who said he came from a fishing village whose number ended in three. "Can I say the old name? I remember the village's old name."

Norma looked up. Elmer was shaking his head.

"I'm sorry. You said the number ended in a three?"

It was all she had—was his name Sebastián? Yes, she was sure now and he came from the north.

"Is there anything more you can remember?" Norma asked.

"Sure," the woman said, but it might get someone in trouble: private things, she said, there were dirty things. She laughed. This would be enough, she added. She would wait on the air for him to call back. She knew he would call. "I'm fifty-two years old," she said slyly, "but I told him I was forty-five. He said he thought I looked even younger." She spoke directly to her lover: "Honey, it's me. It's Rosa."

Norma thanked her. She put the woman on hold, and the light blinked for a few minutes, then disappeared.

Meanwhile, there were others: mothers who called about their sons, young men about girls they had last seen in train stations or standing alone in the maize fields of their native villages. "The love of my life," one man managed, just before breaking down, and in each case, it was Norma counseling, condoling, offering words of hope. "Are they thinking of me?" one woman asked of her missing children, and Norma reassured her they were. Of course they were. It was exhausting. Elmer was gleeful. The calls kept coming: from The Thousands and The Cantonment, from Collectors and Asylum Downs and Tamoé. Husbands confessed to have named their daughters after the mothers they hadn't seen in a decade—but perhaps they were in the city now, perhaps they had found a way to leave that decaying village: *Mother, are you here?*

There were no reunions that day, but the calls never stopped. An hour after they had gone off the air, the phone kept ringing. Elmer twice changed the tape on the answering machine they had set up specially for the new show. He gave the two tapes to Norma the next morning. "For your listening pleasure," he said. "You're a hit."

THE BEDS were prepared, the puzzle left unfinished, the lights turned low. Manau's mother went off to bed, though not before giving kisses all around, and promising to knit the boy a warm hat. She asked what his favorite color might be, and he said it was green. She disappeared into a back room.

Norma still felt a buzzing within her. She wouldn't be able to sleep. Even so, she said good night to Manau, then carried Victor to the sofa and tucked him in beneath a blanket. He didn't resist being held. "What will we do tomorrow?" he asked.

"I'm not sure," she said. It wasn't just tomorrow she was concerned about; it was right now. Still, she told him not to worry. She sat in the armchair by the window. A dim yellow light came from the streetlamp. No cars passed. Curfew had begun.

It wasn't long before Manau came. He said something about not being able to sleep. "Can I sit here?" he asked. She nodded, and he was mercifully silent.

She could guess some things by the boy's age, but without Rey here to answer for himself, Norma was interrogating a ghost. Victor was eleven: where was I eleven years ago? Where was Rey? What were we like, and what wasn't I giving him? She could kill him; if he were here, she would. At what point had their love become counterfeit? When had he begun to lie to her?

The most likely answer, she supposed, was that he had always lied. In one way or another. Hadn't it been that way since the beginning? When they found each other again at the university, after his first disappearance, what was it he did? Remember, Norma, and spare him nothing. *He pretended not to see me.* Then, when you were there before him, unavoidable, human, flesh and blood, what was it he said?

"I'm sorry, do I know you?"

A fragile, tenuous lie; not that it hurt any less. Even now it made her angry, though it hadn't at the time. It had shocked her. Left her speechless. She remembered now that moment of stark humiliation. She had

imagined this meeting for months, had carried the missing man's identification card in her purse at no small risk to herself—what if someone
were to find it? And then to be dismissed so completely?

Later, he apologized; later, he explained: "I was nervous, I was afraid."
Later, he told her what he had lived through, but that day, it was all
opaque, and she had to try very hard not to be disappointed, or not to
let that disappointment show. He was not the man she'd met thirteen
months before, certainly not the one she had recalled so fondly for so
many nights, not the one she had daydreamed of while her parents fought
like animals. He was quieter, thinner, less confident. His wool hat was
pulled down nearly to his eyebrows, and he seemed to be wearing clothes
that were not quite clean. There was nothing at all attractive about him
that day they met again. What if she had walked away then? If she had
handed him his ID and been done with it?

But that's not what happened: instead, he lied, sadly, clumsily, and she
stumbled on with her prepared speech. "I have something of yours."

"Oh."

She fished through her purse for it, and here, the moment she'd envi-
sioned fell apart. The day had grown unexpectedly bright, and they were
surrounded by students, strangers, noise. What was it her mother always
said about Norma's purse? "You could hide a small child in there." It was
less a purse than an overflowing bag. A group of musicians across the way
tuned up their instruments, preparing to play. Already a crowd was forming. Where was the fucking ID? Norma stammered an apology, and Rey
just stood there, a bit uneasy, biting his lip.

"Are you waiting for someone?" she asked.

"No. Why?"

"Because you keep looking over my shoulder."

"Am I?"

She saw him gulp.

"I'm sorry," Rey said.

She laughed nervously. It was March, a week before her birthday, and
maybe she felt entitled to his time. Later, she would wonder, but now
she dragged him by the arm to a bench, away from the crowd, from the
musicians. There she unceremoniously tipped her bag over, spilling its

contents: pens that had run out of ink, scraps of paper, a tiny address book, some tissues, a neglected tube of lipstick she'd used only once—she wasn't that kind of girl—a pair of sunglasses, some coins. "It's in here somewhere, I know it is. You remember me now, don't you?"

She rummaged through the detritus, and he admitted he did.

"Why did you say you didn't?"

But when he began to answer, Norma cut him off. "Oh, here it is," she said. She held it up to his face, squinting against the hard light. She had meant it playfully, but she saw now, as color rushed to his cheeks, how embarrassed he was. There were new lines on his face and dark bags under his eyes. His skin had yellowed, and she could see the sharp outline of his cheekbones. Rey must have lost fifteen pounds.

"I'm not what you expected?" Of course, he knew better than anyone how this last year had aged him.

She pretended not to understand. "What do you mean?"

"Nothing."

She handed him the identification card, and he held it for a moment. He rubbed the picture with his thumb. "Thank you," he said, and started to get up.

"Wait. I'm Norma." She held her hand out. "I wondered what happened to you."

Rey smiled weakly and shook her outstretched hand. He nodded at the ID. "I guess you know who I am."

"Well . . ."

"Right."

"Where did they take you?"

"Nowhere really," he said and, when she frowned, he added, "You don't believe me?"

Norma shook her head. "Sit down. Please. You're running away." He sat, and it made her smile. "Should I call you Rey?"

"Why do you want to know?"

"Because I like you," Norma said, and he didn't answer. But he didn't leave either. The student musicians were playing now, native music with native instruments, appropriately political lyrics. Nothing had yet changed at the university: banners still hung from the lampposts, walls were still adorned with ominous slogans. The war had begun only weeks before, in a faraway corner of the nation, and many of the students still thought of it with excitement, as if it were a party they would soon be invited to attend.

"You should have thrown it away, you know," Rey said. "Or burned it."

"I didn't know. I thought maybe you might need it. I'm sorry."

They were quiet for a spell, watching the students, listening to the band. "I was afraid something was going to happen to you," said Rey.

"I have better luck than that."

"Are you sure?"

"I'm alive, aren't I?" She turned to him. "And you are too. So you must not be as unlucky as you think."

He gave her a weak smile and seemed to hesitate. Then he took off his wool hat. It was too hot for something like that anyway. He had gone white at the temples, shocking streaks of it on otherwise black hair. Or had she not noticed it that night, one year before? How could she not have?

He scratched his head. "Very lucky, I know," he murmured. "It's what everyone says."

THINGS WERE unquestionably bad. The curfew had been tightened, the IL raids on police stations had increased; at the edge of the city, control of the Central Highway was fought over each night after dark. These were days of fear on all sides. For sympathizers, when it was over, it would seem that victory had been tantalizingly close, but this was a misreading of the situation. The IL was desperate for a decisive military victory; recruitment was down, and many thousands had been killed. The apparatus of the state had proved, after a decade of war, to be more resilient than anyone had expected. In this, the final year of the war, the IL had all but lost control of its far-flung fighters. Actions in the provinces were highly decentralized, tactically dubious, and often brazen to the point of being ill-conceived. Heavy losses were inflicted on increasingly isolated bands of fighters. Some platoons responded by retreating deeper into the jungle, no longer warriors and true believers but seminomadic tribes of armed and desperate boys. When the war ended suddenly, they refused to put down their weapons. They continued fighting, because they could think of nothing else to do.

Meanwhile, the IL leadership focused on what it could control directly: the urban war, the central front of which was the embattled district of Tamoé, at the northeastern edge of the city, a slum of one million bordering the Central Highway. The idea was to use Tamoé as staging ground from which to choke off the city: attack food convoys from the fertile Central Valley, starve the city, spark food riots, and then glory in the chaos. They very nearly succeeded. For the six months before the government offensive on Tamoé, the bluffs overlooking the Central Highway were the backdrop for great and violent confrontations. The insurgents laid bombs along the roadside and disappeared into the overcrowded neighborhoods of Tamoé. Truck drivers were kidnapped, their cargo set ablaze. Police checkpoints were attacked with stolen grenades. The army responded by increasing patrols in the area, and were greeted by snipers hidden in the hills or on rooftops.

In May of that year, a girl of five was killed in Tamoé, by a bullet of indeterminate origin. There were soldiers in the area, searching for a sniper. An angry mob gathered around the soldiers. More shots were fired, and the crowd grew. A soldier was killed. The Battle of Tamoé had begun. When this uprising was quelled, the war would be over.

But all of this happened after Rey left the city for the last time. If it weren't for the boy, his son, Rey might not have returned to the jungle at all. His contact had disappeared, left him without any further direction, and it amounted to a welcome vacation. But he went anyway, because he couldn't get the boy out of his mind. When he heard of the battle, he was in the jungle, far enough away to suppose he was safe. He spent an evening with the rest of the village, listening to the radio for news, and was surprised to find that the IL's defeat did not surprise him. It was an all-or-nothing proposition, and it always had been: so now there was nothing. The tanks that ran through the narrow streets, the blocks and blocks burned to the ground, the fighting that raged for four days house to house—in their hearts, hadn't everyone known this was coming? In the aftermath of the battle, while the government proclaimed victory and the rest of the city celebrated, the dry, dusty lots of the district became home to thousands of displaced families, all with sons and fathers missing: a city of women and children. The army kept them corralled together for weeks in a makeshift tent city while the government decided what to do with them. Rey would have recognized many of them, from his work there so many years before.

These are facts: had he postponed his trip by a month, he might have survived the war. If he hadn't returned to see his son, a hundred young men and the handful of women camped a day's travel from 1797 might have lived as well.

Rey arrived in the village only six weeks after Blas had left. 1797 was still abuzz with excitement, and now there were dozens of portraits that no one knew quite what to do with. Many were hidden away, others were displayed prominently in people's homes. He found it strange, as if the village had doubled in size while he was gone. Everyone he spoke to had had a portrait drawn of someone, and all seemed eager to talk about it. The village had collectively decided to address the fact of its own disappearance. He was at the canteen one afternoon when an older woman stormed in, walked directly toward him. Rey was sitting with Adela and their boy. The woman didn't waste time: after apologizing for interrupting their meal, she unrolled her drawings all at once and begged Rey to look at them. They were of her husband and her son, whom she hadn't seen in five years. She spoke so loudly that the baby looked up and began to cry.

"Madam," Adela said sternly.

Again the woman apologized, but she didn't stop. She was pleading now. "Take these. Take them back to the city and show them to the newspapers."

He coughed. "They wouldn't survive the trip," he said. It was the first thing that occurred to him, the first excuse, and it came out all wrong. "The drawings," Rey added, but it was too late: the woman was not quite old, not yet, but in that instant, her face fell, and she aged a decade. She broke into a furious stream of words, berating Rey in the old language for his selfishness before walking off.

Rey and Adela finished their meal in silence. They walked back through the tiny village to Adela's hut. He asked to carry the boy, happily observing that Victor had gained weight and grown in all directions. Adela was pensive, but he chose not to notice, focusing instead on his son, this magical boy who made faces and drooled with beautiful confidence.

"Are you going to take him from me?" Adela asked when they were nearly home.

If you listened carefully, no matter where you stood in the village, you could hear the river. Rey heard it now, a lazy gurgling, not that far off. He remembered the night he had spent, drugged, wading in the cool waters. The rainy season had passed, and now the showers that came were furious but brief. The sun, when it came out, was unforgiving. Adela stared at him. He had a difficult time remembering why he had ever come to this place.

"Why would you say something like that?" Rey said. He passed the boy to one arm and reached out to touch her, but Adela pulled back.

"You'll take the boy one day and you'll never come back."

"I won't."

Adela sat down on the step, and Rey moved in beside her, careful not to sit too close. "Did you have me drawn?"

She nodded. "You're going to leave me."

"You have to destroy it," Rey said. "I'm not joking. You have to."

"I'm not leaving. You're not going to take me to the city and put me in a little house and make me your mistress."

The thought had not occurred to him, but it flashed now, instantaneously, as a way out. He turned to her hopefully, but saw immediately, in the set of her jaw, that she was serious.

"Of course not."

"Play with him now," Adela said, pointing to the boy, "because he's mine." She stood angrily and disappeared into the hut.

He didn't want a mistress. For all her charms, he didn't, in fact, want Adela. He was a bad man, he was sure, a man of convenient morals in inconvenient circumstances. Still, he could be honest with himself, couldn't he? Rey wanted the boy and Norma and his life back in the city, and that was all. He didn't want the jungle or the war or this woman and the combined weight of his many bad decisions.

He wanted to live to be old.

Rey sat the boy up on his knee so that Victor could look out. His eyes were always open, and this was what Rey admired most about his son. He was a hardworking baby: colors and lights and faces, he took them in with deep concentration. Rey tickled his son playfully on the stomach, and noted proudly how quickly Victor reached for his finger, and how strongly he held on to it. Rey pulled, and Victor pulled back.

The following day, Zahir returned from the provincial capital with his radio, telling everyone in town that the war was over.

NORMA HELD Rey's hand when they checked into the hotel. It was a late afternoon of slanting orange light. Night was still an hour away. This was the first time, and they wore wedding bands Rey had borrowed from a friend. They carried dinner in a basket, as if they had come from the provinces. Norma covered her hair with a shawl.

"Yes, sir," Rey said to the receptionist. "We're married."

"Where do you come from?"

"The south." It wasn't a lie, Norma thought, not exactly: it's a direction, not a place.

"Girl, is this your husband?"

"Don't talk to my wife that way," Rey snapped. "You need to show more respect."

"I don't have to let you stay here, you know."

Rey sighed. "We've been traveling all day," he said. "We just want a place to sleep."

Norma took it all in, saying nothing. The receptionist frowned, not believing a word of it. But he took the money Rey handed him, held the bills up to the light, and mumbled something under his breath. He handed Rey a key, and there was a moment of electricity right there, as it dawned on Norma what this meant and where she was headed. Her mother would not approve. Rey never let go of Norma's hand. She was afraid he would.

It was an old building, where even the floorboards of the stairs creaked naughtily. Norma blushed at the sound: maybe she even said something about it—who could remember now?—and Rey laughed slyly and told her not to worry. "We're here now. No one's going to hear us."

And no one did, because they were alone in the hotel that night. It was midweek. They might as well have been alone in the city. They went up early and came out late, when the sun was already up and blazing red in the sky. And it didn't hurt, not the way she had expected it to, the way she had feared it might. And then afterwards, the most wonderful thing was being naked next to him, and the most surprising thing was how easy it was to fall asleep with him by her side. It felt safe.

It was dark, and Norma was drifting toward sleep, when Rey said, "I have nightmares."

"About what?"

"About the Moon." He breathed heavily—she heard it and felt it, because her hand was resting on his chest. "They tell me it's normal. But sometimes I shout in my sleep. Don't be scared if I do."

"What happened?"

He would tell her, Rey said, but not then. He made her promise not to be frightened.

"I won't be," she whispered. She was stroking his face, his eyes were closed, and he was nearly asleep. "I won't. I won't ever be afraid."

"Are you awake?" Manau asked.

Norma opened her eyes. The boy was still there. She was in the same strange house. A light was on by the front door, everything tinged yellow. It had grown cold, and she wondered what time it was. She thought of closing her eyes, of retreating again into dreams. Had she ever been happy? "I'm awake," she said, but even this was a guess. Norma felt he was near—her Rey—she felt traces of him all around, even as her eyes adjusted to this half-light.

She hadn't thought of her husband as alive in many, many years. Not quite dead, either, but certainly not alive. Not part of the world. If he had lived—and Norma had concocted all kinds of scenarios that allowed this—what difference, in the end, had it made to her? He'd never contacted her. He'd wandered the jungle, or escaped the country and fled to a more hospitable place. Perhaps he'd remarried, learned a new language, and forgotten with great effort all that he had previously survived? These were all possibilities, if she accepted that he had made it somehow. But it was unthinkable: how could he have lived without her?

The boy snored lightly.

Rey was gone, of course. And she was alone. The rest of her life spread out before her, vast and blank, without guideposts or markers or the heat of human love to steer her in one direction or another. What remained were flashes, memories, attempts at happiness. For years, she had imagined him as not-quite-dead, and organized her life around this: finding him, waiting for him.

"What are we going to do?" Manau asked.

She had spent all the Great Blackouts with Rey, each and every one, in a room just like this, darker even, telling secrets while the city burned.

"Some people call every Sunday. I've learned to recognize their voices. They're impostors. They pretend to be whoever the previous caller just described: from whatever village in the mountains or the jungle."

"That's cruel," Manau said.

"I thought so too."

"But?"

"But the longer the show has gone on, the more I understand it. There are people out there who think of themselves as belonging to someone. To a person who, for whatever reason, has gone. And they wait years: they don't look for their missing, they *are* the missing."

She looked at Manau, unsure of what she expected from him. In a room just like this one, Rey had told her he loved her. "Is he alive?" she asked Manau suddenly. "Tell me, if you know. If you know, you have to tell me." She didn't want to cry, but she couldn't help it.

"I don't know," Manau said. "No one does."

THE WEEK of the Battle of Tamoé, the show was canceled. It was simply too difficult to screen calls. The answering machine filled up with the voices of worried, anxious mothers: there were tanks in the streets, and their boys had left to fight with ancient rifles that didn't fire straight. Something was happening, and it was out of control. The district was being razed. News reports of the four-day battle were prepared at the Ministry of State, sent to the radio to be read as is, without comment, without any additional reporting. Elmer consulted with the senator, who asked the station to comply. Everyone knew of the little girl who had died, but she was not mentioned. In the official telling of it, the terrorized residents of Tamoé had asked the army to clear out the menacing IL. The Central Highway would be closed for the duration of the military activities, and emergency price controls placed on basic necessities. When this action was concluded, the radio announced, the war would be, for all intents and purposes, over.

Norma's hour that Sunday was replaced by a prerecorded program of indigenous music. She had asked Rey, before he left for the jungle, if he ever came across a radio in the different villages he passed through. He said he never had.

"I would have sent you a message," she said.

"You still can."

So, from her perch above the city, Norma imagined him out there—where exactly?—listening to the radio, surprised to find that her show had been preempted, that the war was ending. Mornings, she read the news from Tamoé: it was spotty and deliberately vague, but someone like Rey would know enough to tell what was really happening. He knew the district, he knew what it meant when she said that the forces of order had advanced past Avenue F–10. He would know the center of the district had fallen, that what fighters were left had been chased into the hills. He would know that the government would not announce victory unless it was in hand. She hoped then that he wasn't listening, that he was in the forest he loved, among the plants and the trees and the birds, that he would miss these unhappy days altogether, and return to the city only when it was finished, when there was nothing left undone.

By the middle of the second day of shooting, Elmer began making small changes to the prepared texts: fighting *raged* instead of *continued*. When these passed by unnoticed, he began culling some safe statements from the Lost City Radio answering machine, to be played on the air as firsthand accounts. In this way, the station was the first to report on the fires. Norma herself took some calls, listened as one or another desperate resident described the inferno that was beginning to remake the landscape of the district. They want our land, the callers said, they want our homes. The fire was still in the lower neighborhoods of Tamoé, and in the slums that bordered the Central Highway, but it was moving up the hill, and north from the highway. One caller after another made the same accusation: it was the army. They were setting fire to everything. They were bulldozing homes and setting fire to the rubble. At night, from the conference room, you could see the eastern district smoldering. By day, the smoke hung over the city, but was not mentioned in the newspapers or on most radio stations.

In 1797, the people gathered in the canteen to listen to Zahir's radio. The reception wasn't bad, and everyone took turns admiring the machine. Zahir, with whom Rey had spoken a handful of times, sat next to it, gracefully accepting congratulations on his purchase. By the third day, they were calling it the Battle of Tamoé on the radio, and the news was exclusively of a great fire. The shooting had stopped. In 1797, the villagers were crowded in—children, too, sitting under the tables, among their parents' feet, or balanced on the windowsills. A soft rain fell, and Zahir turned up the volume of his new machine so they could hear, over the pitter-patter on the metal roof, about the latest block to fall to the army, or the newest official count of dead.

They listened as if it were a sporting match in which they had not taken sides. One woman thought she had a son who lived in this place—Tamoé?—but she couldn't be sure. She sat uncomfortably, pulled a strand of her hair into her mouth and sucked on it nervously. She accepted condolences from the gathered crowd; her worry was authentic and her sadness complete.

Rey sat among them, unnoticed at first, but as the afternoon became evening, something changed. They had in their midst a real expert: the villagers were watching him. Finally, someone addressed Rey directly: an elderly woman whose voice he had never heard before. "Where is this Tamoé?" she asked.

"Yes," the adults echoed. "Where is it?"

Rey blushed. "Tell them," Adela said, and so he had no choice. He stood up, walked to the front of the canteen, and was, quite suddenly, a professor again. He had been a teacher all his adult life. His father was a teacher, and his father's father, too, back when the town Rey had abandoned at age fourteen was a village no larger than 1797. Rey cleared his throat. "It's the edge of the city," he said, "north of the Central Highway, in the foothills of the eastern mountains."

It meant nothing to them. "Is there a map I could use to show you?" he asked.

There was laughter: a map? Of the city—who would have such a thing? Adela had a map of the country, of course; he'd brought it himself.

The questions came furiously. Yes, he knew of it. Yes, he had been there. Was it big? He had to smile: compared with the village where they all sat, how could it be anything but? Hands shot up, and he did his best to keep pace. Who lives there? What kind of people?

"Poor people," Rey said, and the men and women nodded.

"Where are they from?"

"They come from all over the country," he said. The mountains, the jungle, the decaying towns of the north. From the abandoned sierra.

He was very polite, or tried to be, but the questions kept coming. Someone had turned the radio down: Rey could hear his wife's voice, but couldn't concentrate on the words. They wouldn't let him listen. The villagers knew nothing about the war, and here they were, awaiting its end, wanting quite suddenly to know everything about it.

"How did it begin?" a man asked. He wore his black hair in a braid.

"I don't know," Rey said, and there was a clatter of protest. Of course he knew!

Which grievance was it and when? Had it begun that night he spent in jail as a boy? Sleeping next to his father on the damp floor, while an angry mob clamored for his punishment? Before that, long before that: everyone knew it was coming. But it had officially begun ten years ago, he told them. Nearly a decade. How? He forgot now. Someone was angry about something. This someone convinced many hundreds and then many thousands more that their collective anger meant something. That it had to be acted upon. There was an event, wasn't there? Violence to mark a fraudulent election? An explosion timed to commemorate some patriotic anniversary? He thought he remembered an opposition leader, a politician well known and admired for his honesty, being poisoned, dying slowly and very publicly over the course of three weeks. The name escaped him now. Was this how it began? He didn't know what to tell them, this roomful of curious faces; the radio turned down to a low buzzing and the evening having evolved into a disquisition on recent national history by an anonymous city-dweller. It was useless to plead ignorance in this setting. No one would believe him. The war, he decided, would have happened anyway. It was unavoidable. It's a way of life in a country like ours.

The rain let up, and in this new quiet, the evening took on the austerity of a prayer meeting. He answered every question as it came, as well as he could. They had been at it an hour or more when there came the question he would die pondering. Had he ever known the answer? At one time, sure, but that was long ago. The question was posed by the owner of the radio, and there was an innocence to it that Rey appreciated, a genuine need to know, without a hint of malice. "Tell us, sir," Zahir asked, already speaking of the war in the past tense, "who was right in all of this?"

FIFTEEN

I T   W A S   two in the morning when they climbed into Manau's father's car and willed it to start. Manau nearly flooded the engine—it had been over a year since he'd driven—but then the ignition caught, and the engine spat bursts of noise. Manau turned to Norma, flashing a satisfied smile that reminded her how young he was. Victor was half-asleep, resting his head in her lap, and she had laid a blanket on top of him. It was a long way to the radio station. The heater was barely working, and the night was unexpectedly cold. The city was still under curfew. They could make it there and be gone before the morning newscast. Before Elmer arrived.

The car moved slowly through the deserted streets, so slowly Norma imagined they were sightseeing. The headlamps splashed dim yellow splotches on the road ahead, and the engine failed twice before they made it to the first blinking red traffic light. Still, there was an air of leisure to the whole endeavor: the pleasing, throaty rumble of the engine, the city passing by in silence. Even the air had an agreeable crispness to it. Block after empty block; and it didn't seem at this hour to be a city but a museum of a city, a place she was viewing as if from some distant future, an artist's model built to demonstrate how human beings had once lived.

Manau eased the car down to the seaside highway, where they could see the beach dotted with fires. The tide had gone out, and the sand stretched for a quarter-mile, glowing orange and gold. The ocean, mute and black, pushed into the infinite, and the moonless sky was dark enough to be one and the same with the sea. A row of red lights bobbed at the horizon—the fishing trawlers, where at this hour men were sleeping, resting their bodies for the day's work ahead. Norma had one hand over the boy, enough to feel him breathe; in the other, she held the list, which had been touched by a dozen people in the past week, had been creased, folded, nearly destroyed, saved, and stolen. It felt good to have it, but not like a victory so much as a reprieve. Ten years had passed, ten years that comprised a vast, inviolable silence, and then these three days, of which, she suspected, she would remember only noise: the chattering dissonance of many voices, sounds at once indistinct and pressing, calling her urgently in different directions. Wounding her, certainly, but no worse than the silence had.

The road rose back to the city, and there, as they came over the hump, was a police checkpoint, brightly lit with flood lamps, a patch of daylight within the darkness. It was still a half-mile ahead, but there was no way around it. The car chugged forward. The boy was still asleep.

"Do I stop?" Manau asked. She could see in the rearview mirror, even in the dim light, that he was afraid.

She bit her lip. "Of course," Norma said after a moment, and by then, they were there already, there was no choice, and the ordeal was beginning. Or was it simply continuing? In either case, her body tightened, bracing as if for a great impact.

I N   T A M O É , in the last year of the war, there lived a girl, age five. She didn't like the army helicopters that flew over her neighborhood. This is what the war meant to her: helicopters blowing up dust and, with their great noise, keeping her dolls awake when she felt they should be resting. A nuisance. Her father had been in hiding for two years, fighting with the IL. He was an expert explosives man named Alaf. Before he left the family forever, he told his daughter that if soldiers ever came to the house, she should spit on them. He was a true believer. "Say it with me," Alaf whispered. "They're animals."

"They're animals," the little girl repeated. She was three years old then.

"What will you do when they come?"

"Spit on them," she answered and then began to cry. Two years later, she could not remember her father: not what he looked like, not the sound of his voice. Nor would her mother speak of him.

After she was killed by a stray bullet, a battle began in her name. Not spontaneously. The IL had been waiting for a blameless victim. She lived in a corner house without running water or electricity, a house that was always damp and cool and smoky. Its second story had not been completed, and so the roof was sometimes used by neighborhood IL snipers to pick off soldiers who patrolled the area. An army commander made the entirely reasonable decision to put an end to this nonsense. The girl was small for her age, and always had a cough. The day she died, she had not eaten enough and was walking to her friend's house, hoping to be offered a piece of bread. Though she was hungry, she was also proud, and had resolved not to ask for it. But if it were *offered*—this, she had decided, was entirely different. Her mother was at the market, and there were shooters on her roof. Later, men would argue about which way she fell, the possible trajectories of the bullet or bullets that killed her, but the truth is, neither the army nor the IL snipers much noticed her when she first went down. Certainly, no one intended to kill her. The fighting continued for another half-hour. She had hidden behind an oil drum when the shooting began. She would later be described as holding a doll, as flaxen-haired and innocent, and she may have been all these things, but when she died, no one noticed her, just as no one had noticed her when she lived. Later, her face was put on banners that were carried to the edge of the district and then into the heart of the city by hundreds of well-meaning and outraged people who had never known her. They were met with bullets in the plaza that would be razed and renamed Newtown Plaza. There, many more people died, and then the war was over.

Her father never knew that his daughter died in this way, but it would be a mistake to say he was unaffected. The bond between parent and child is chemical, fierce, and inexplicable, even if that parent is a sworn killer. This connection cannot be measured; it is at once more subtle and more powerful than science. In the days before his daughter was murdered, Alaf felt a pain in his chest. For two nights, he couldn't sleep. He ate little, and even went so far as to take his own temperature. He was certain he was dying, and he despaired. In his mind, Alaf began to compose a letter to send to his wife and daughter back in Tamoé, asking for forgiveness. He wondered if his daughter could read by now. How long had it been? How did any of this happen? He promised to learn a useful trade and devote himself to it. He described the exotic charms of a quiet and peaceful life, and it made his heart quicken: late breakfasts on Sundays, afternoons dedicated to home repair or to listening to a soccer match on the radio. He might walk his daughter to school on Monday. He and his wife might have a son. Or, it struck him, they could leave the city altogether and settle here, in the endless jungle where land was plentiful and the soil fertile. A small farm, he thought, and set about imagining a life he would never have. Of course, he did not actually write the letter, and so he did not send it. He died a few days after the Battle of Tamoé, not far from 1797, killed in an ambush before he so much as fired a shot.

THE PERSON Norma missed most of all in Rey's absence was not Rey but the person she had been when she was with him. The roadblock brought it all back: there was a part of her—not a small part—that had been seduced at the exact moment the soldier pulled Rey off the bus so many years ago. She had become in her time with Rey a woman who lived alongside that danger, who, in one way or another, conquered fear in order to be with the man she loved. Because what did she remember from her years with Rey? Not the sword that hung over them, not the tension, the suspicions, but the laughter, the joking, walking down the street hand in hand, the happiness that existed in spite of everything else. The world collapsed around them, and still they stood together, imperturbable, calm; it was the relationship they had made, pliant and modern; the alchemy that happened when they turned out the lights, when they folded their bodies into each other and felt no shame.

She had to remind herself sometimes, because it was easy to forget: Rey had wanted her.

The road up from the beach was lit brightly, the bluffs on either side shining with a white fluorescence. The car rolled slowly to a stop, and there it was again: the point of a rifle insinuating itself into her life. Rey, she thought. She very nearly said it out loud. This was all routine. She looked straight ahead and not at the rifle to her left. There were two staggered rows of stones and razor wire lying across the road. To one side, a soldier, a boy about five years older than Victor, stood warming himself by a fire.

"Out," the rifle ordered. If there was a body attached to the weapon, Norma decided not to notice it.

Already Manau was outside. She roused the boy, and a moment later, she was there, too, with Victor by her side, half-asleep. She held her hands over her head and faced the car the way she'd seen criminals do in movies. The boy-soldier demanded papers, identification, and she felt faint.

The jungle, Rey had told her many times, was a pharmacological paradise. Uncharted and unclaimed, the cures to all the world's diseases were there, hidden, waiting to be found. It would take a generation or more to discover the gifts it held, if they didn't disappear first. One of the war's many unintended consequences—one of its only positive ones—was that it had rendered the jungle relatively inaccessible, therefore slowing the pace of its destruction. People fled the jungle. It was only a matter of time, Rey had said, until they fled *to* it: when the cities became too crowded, too choked with smoke and noise, when peace came and allowed them once again the freedom to roam within the borders of the nation-state.

"Can't I come with you?" she'd asked him once.

"Of course. Once the war is over."

She'd laughed then: "Silly, this war won't ever end."

Rey brought back stories of drugs that cured all kinds of ills, showed her the careful notes he took. The very nation might be saved by the forest: there might be a plant for every kind of miracle. "They have plants for potency," he told her once, as he pulled her into the apartment and onto the couch. "Not that I need them." That day, he still smelled of travel, of buses and smoke and places she had never visited. "Who have you been with while I was gone? Tell me, make me jealous . . ."

"A whole city of men wakes up with me whispering in their ears."

"Stop."

"It's true," she said, biting her lip, and already his hands were under her clothes, her body tingling. She was cold and hot all at once. Looking over Rey's shoulder, she saw the door was open. He had closed it with his foot in his hurry to take her into his arms, and the lock hadn't caught Their neighbor's ten-year-old son stood in the doorway, watching. H‹ was wide-eyed and curious, just a child. "Rey," Norma whispered, bu he wasn't listening. She felt she should shoo the child away, but then she didn't care. They were behind the couch, and he couldn't see anything. So she closed her eyes and imagined they were alone. It wasn't hard to do. The war had always been with them, and she was accustomed to pretending.

"Hands up," the rifle barked. He stepped to Manau and patted him down. He took Manau's wallet out and flipped through it. He seemed disappointed by its contents. He held Manau's ID up to the light. "This is fake."

"It's not fake," Manau said. "Who has fakes?"

"Shut up."

"Norma, tell them."

"I said shut up."

"Norma."

It was cold, and her body stiffened. She turned to Manau and glared. Tell them what? These people didn't want to hear her stories, they didn't want to know of her disappointments.

"Where are you going?"

"The radio," Manau said. "*Norma*."

"Who's Norma? Which Norma?"

"*Norma* Norma."

For a moment, the rifle seemed to consider this possibility. With the end of the weapon pointed downwards, he told Norma to turn around. She did, and he examined her in the harsh, white light. He seemed suddenly nervous. "You're Norma? You don't look like Norma."

"But have you ever seen her?" Manau said.

The rifle was raised suddenly to eye level, Manau pushed roughly against the car, the end of the weapon at his temple: "Are you ever going to shut up?"

crooked, childlike script—"is a pass I wrote. You can show it to anyone else if they stop you." He smiled from ear to ear. She thanked him again. "Miss Norma," he said, bowing. "A pleasure."

They drove on through the sleeping city, through its vacant streets. The boy began to ask a question, but then seemed to think better of it. He was beyond surprise, and too tired to notice anything in the darkened streets. Every now and then, the car hit a pothole, and the windows shook, and the frame rattled, but a moment later, it had passed, and Victor could close his eyes again. Norma held him; the car had warmed, but the boy shivered in his sleep.

The security guard didn't hesitate to let them in. She was Norma, after all, and this was still her radio station. He let the three of them pass with a deferential nod and then led them to the lobby where the boy had first presented his note. The lights were low, and it seemed they had stepped into the crypt of a church. Just as I remember it, Norma thought, as if she were returning to a childhood home. She had been here just the day before, but this is what life does to you: things happen all at once, and your sense of time is exploded. But what exactly had happened, an'

A boy had come. When? It began on Tuesday, she remem⌐   ⌐ now it was . . . She didn't know. Whom could she as⌐⌐   ⌐ng was foggy: there was a list, she'd had a husband. ⌐   ⌐ gone. He was IL, or he was not. The war had e⌐⌐   ⌐ had never begun. Was that it? Was that all? S⌐   ⌐a tightly. Norma felt sure he had grown i⌐   ⌐s, and, at the thought, her heart was off at a ga⌐   ⌐ just to stand. The security guard, she realized with s⌐   ⌐s still talking, had never stopped talking, though his voice   ⌐red at all. She resolved to smile but made no attempt to liste⌐   ⌐an old man with a shiny bald pate and pockmarked skin. He r⌐⌐ed the boy's head and pinched his cheek. He was thanking her effusively, and Norma couldn't help but wonder what she had ever done for him.

With his key, he activated the elevator. The doors closed, and he bade them good-bye with a wave. They were inside.

"I'm tired," Victor said. "I want to sleep."

"I know you do." Norma held him close. She was torturing the boy by keeping him awake, she knew she was—what was it she hoped to accomplish that could not be done tomorrow? "We'll sleep soon," she said, but it sounded less like a promise and more like a wish.

The overnight deejay was easy enough. She couldn't remember his name, but they had met before. Many times. He knew who she was, of course. He had a young face and unnaturally white hair to go along with it. Norma put her hand on his shoulder. He was easy to lie to: the words were coming on their own now. Yes, Elmer had approved it. Yes, it's fine. Yes, a special show. Call him? Of course, if you'd like, but he's probably sleeping. You could use a rest? Couldn't we all. A little laughter—she didn't even have to force it. And have a great night. Yes, a pleasure. With Manau and Victor watching, she had an audience for all this lying, this manipulation of the truth; they were with her. Without even looking behind her, she could feel Manau nodding on her behalf.

But the displaced deejay didn't leave. He shifted his weight from foot to foot.

"Yes?"

"May I sit in?" He smiled meekly. "It would be an honor, Miss Norma."

It felt cruel, but the truth was there would be no room. "You understand," she said.

"Of course," he said, turning red. "Of course." He slinked away, and Norma wanted to embrace him. Her eyes stung, and every part of her was sore. A waltz was playing: it was a woman, of course, and she sang about a man.

WHEN THE IL finally returned three years after the war had ended, it was a surprise to everyone but Zahir. He'd been waiting for them since the day a platoon came and took Adela's man and two others away into the forest. Of course, Zahir knew nothing about the dispersed remnants of a once-mighty insurgency, so he couldn't have *known* they were coming: it's just that he had seen this man pass his son off to Adela and disappear into an army truck, the point of a rifle at his back. He'd seen the desperate way the man had looked at his son, the way the child clutched at his mother, and the way this woman began to sob. Such things do not go unpunished. The two other men said good-byes as well, and Zahir could scarcely remember what he had accused them of in his reports—oh, yes: he had wondered why they spent so much time in the forest. He had reddened at this thought: they were hunters.

It was not the IL Zahir was expecting, not specifically, but some form of castigation, celestial or otherwise, for his role in the war. Before that moment, it had seemed that his monthly reports were filed away and never seen again, that all his effort amounted to a simple exercise with no bearing on the war or on anything else. Then, that day, it became clear: he was not innocent. Three men died. That is, he could guess they had died: three men disappeared because of him. Because he had, on a whim, invented a story about a man he barely knew. Because he had padded his report with musings about what a villager might do in the forest with a gun besides hunt. Something would come to disturb his otherwise comfortable life. In the days after the platoon came, all guns and stern faces, the village continued listening to the radio, now broadcasting reports of victory marches in the city. Celebrations. It rained heavily that week, and they could see helicopters whirring below the purple clouds. They could even hear the rumble of distant explosions. Was the war really over? It was hard to know what to believe.

Then the fighting in the distance flared out, and the placid years began. His own son grew up strong. The school was rebuilt, and a procession of teachers from the city began coming to 1797. They didn't stay long, but they took the place the army had once occupied in the village's collective imagination: the only tangible evidence that somewhere a government existed, and it knew of them. This, too, was a positive development.

The IL arrived on an early October day of limpid sun, firing shots in the air and demanding to be fed. They gathered the village folk together, and one of them, a dark-eyed young woman, spoke shrilly of the victory that awaited them all. Still? Even now? She was thin enough and young enough that Zahir allowed himself to feel pity for her. Her hair was tied back loosely, and when she raised her arms, he could see dark stains. Then she fired a shot in the air, and it was as if a scrim had been lifted.

"But the war is over," Zahir said. Softly at first.

A masked guerrilla walked toward him. Zahir knew what was coming, or thought he did, but when the butt of the rifle struck in his stomach, his vision went gray, and he doubled over, clutching helplessly at his midsection, fully expecting his organs to spill from his body. The guerrilla kicked him, called him a collaborator, and this word struck Zahir as right and just, and so he resolved to take his beating like a man. He heard a child crying out, and imagined it must be Adela's boy. He felt something not unlike pride. He winced, pressing tears from the corners of his eyes, but the boots bruised him like tender caresses.

When he came to, the IL was announcing *tadek*. This he had not expected. His vision was blurry, and a dull pain spread out from his belly to encompass his entire torso, his heart, his neck. He blinked: his brain wasn't right either. They had all been taken to a clearing, and the sun beat down on them with blistering intensity. He was being held up by two women, and everyone was there: an entire village of frightened adults standing shoulder-to-shoulder in a circle. Zahir stood rigidly, only vaguely aware that it had begun, that the boy was loose and drunken among them, ready to accuse somebody. He could barely see the child but could make out his rigid movements, stumbling now to the left, now to the right, hands before him grasping, as if teasing some meaning from the air. Each time he approached the edge of the circle, everyone tensed, and those most in danger backed up ever so slightly. The IL kept a strict watch, firing shots into the air. At one point, Victor sat down in the middle of the circle, balling his fists and pressing them against his temples, until an IL man stepped in, nudging the boy to his feet. "Go on," he said. "Find the thief."

It's coming, it's coming: Zahir could see now, and stand on his own, but the women still held him. One of them whispered in his ear: "Don't be afraid." It was Adela's voice, but he didn't turn or say anything in response. Maybe she was talking to herself, he couldn't be sure. He wasn't scared; three deaths would be atoned for. Wasn't he responsible for this orphan? The boy tumbled and fell; now he stood again. There was dirt on his knee. He was crying, he was looking for her. "Mother," Victor said, and Zahir felt Adela shrink behind him. No one, it seemed, had breathed in many minutes. The shots came every thirty seconds or so, and each time, the boy stopped and looked up, as if searching for the bullet's trajectory in the bright sky. Then Victor found her—find *me*, Zahir thought—and trundled in her direction. It's coming, it's coming: but before he stepped forward to claim his guilt, Zahir was able to see the boy's eyes: glassy with tears, fearful, focused on something distant and invisible, on some dark spot in the forest or a cloud shaped like a beast.

Then the boy touched him, and everything else happened in an instant: with guns at the ready, the IL led the town in baleful chant of "Thief! Collaborator!" The women were crying but they shouted, because they were afraid not to. Zahir caught sight of his wife then, her face red and teary, helpless and shrinking. Another woman held her so she wouldn't collapse. Where was his son? His daughter? He squinted; there was so much light upon him; then he was lashed to a tree stump, and then he was screaming. The IL sang patriotic songs. His new life began with music.

THE SHOW Norma had imagined goes this way: suddenly, there are no restrictions, and all names are fair. The accusations that had been published after the war—that Rey had been an IL assassin, a messenger, or a bomb-thrower—these are rendered moot. There are only missing people, their innocence or complicity unimportant, irrelevant. The show begins: Norma plays a song, the calls come. I knew a professor, a voice says, he was my teacher at the university, and he disappeared.

When?

At the end of the war.

What did he teach?

Botany. He loved the forest, but not the way a scientist would. The way a poet would. He knew the basic stuff, the chemical composition of the soil in different river valleys. The patterns of rainfall and flooding. But that wasn't it. What he most cared about—

And what was his name?

The caller hangs up abruptly. Next.

I knew a man at the Moon who was fascinated by jungle juju. He said everything we were seeing was a hallucination. That in the real world people didn't do things like these to each other.

And what sorts of things were they doing to you?

Dial tone.

Another caller: I had a friend who worked once in Tamoé, gathering information for the census. He said the people had nothing except nearly infinite stores of patience, that they wanted only to keep what little they had and be left alone.

But why wouldn't people leave them alone?

Each time, the callers come closer; it's almost coy, the way they dance around him. After a dozen calls, Rey's life has been described completely: colleagues, acquaintances, friends from every era of his short life. The boys who betrayed him that night of the fire have called to ask about him, and they have even apologized: we were afraid, they said. We were just children and the town wasn't the same after Rey left. Where did he go? A call has come from a man who was with them the night of the first Great Blackout: when you said you'd been to the Moon, I winced. I'd been there too. And there are so many more: a cop who knew Trini. A man with a jungle accent who claimed to be an artist. A woman who was IL: she suspects that they knew the same people. But no one can remember his name. Who is this stranger? Can't anyone remember? It's been so long. Norma is sweating. Even in her imaginary show, she is balanced delicately above a precipice; even here she is afraid. Then it is her own voice she hears: I knew a man, she says, or was he a boy then, this man who took me dancing, who charmed me, who blew smoke into the bus as we rode together across this beautiful city, across the city as it was before the war—does anyone remember what a place this was? And this man, this boy, this lovely and terrifying child, he let me touch him and I loved him until a soldier came and took him away. For my entire life, he has been a great and disappearing angel, a vanishing act, a torturer, and now he's gone and the question is, *for how long*, and the answer I fear most is *forever*.

And here the dream ends, here her grief runs into the reality of it. She can't say his name. She tries, but she can't. Someone else must do it for her.

It is nearly morning in the city and the war has been finished for ten years. Crimes have been forgiven, or at least forgotten, and still her Rey has not returned. She buried his father without him. She placed an obituary in the paper. It read: "Survived by his son . . ." The war had been over for three years then, and it felt like a lie. No one came to the funeral. She hadn't seen the old man in many months. They had nothing to say to each other. Once, her father-in-law had made it past the screeners and onto the air. At first she hadn't recognized him.

"Norma," he'd said, voice breaking. "Where is he?"

"Who?" she asked, because she always asked. It was her job. "Why don't you tell us about him?"

On the other end, there was a long pause. Breathing.

"Sir? Who are we talking about?"

"Your husband," said the old man, now weeping openly. "My son."

Elmer cut to commercial immediately.

And it felt then the way it always had, the way it always would: like someone clutching her throat, trying and very nearly succeeding in squeezing the life from her. The worst of it passed in a matter of seconds, but the recovery took days, even weeks. Or a lifetime. During the long, uncomfortable break, Norma felt no one would look at her. Elmer came in with a cup of tea. "The wrong name, Norma. I'm sorry, but the wrong name and we're dead. You and me both." He said it without looking her in the eye.

She put on a record and let it play through. When she began again, there was a new caller, a new voice that made no mention of Norma's loss, and the show resumed without incident.

Early morning now, ten years without war, and Norma has come to this place again. She is moving without thinking now. Give the boy a microphone. Give Manau a microphone. Headphones all around. There is the couch where Rey and I made love. Close eyes: remember. Not now. Breathe. There are lights blinking, a record playing, and Norma feels as if she is the conductor of an orchestra, that the city just waking or just drifting to sleep is hers to control. Cue music and let it play.

Breathe.

"Ladies and gentlemen," she says when the song has finished. "Welcome to a special edition of Lost City Radio. My name is Norma."

It has begun.

Rey described once the way the world melted in the heat of a psychoactive plant. Why was he so interested in these? The mystery, he said, lay in the discovery: whatever you hallucinated was something that had always been there, waiting to escape. The thrill, the surprise: what is it that you had buried from yourself? What emerged from the shadows, from the cobwebbed corners, from behind locked doors thrown suddenly, ludicrously, open? What did you find, Rey?

You.

Me?

You. Norma. You, in strange shapes and forms. As various animals, as air, as water. As light. As the dense and fertile earth. As a rhymed poem, as a song sung in a high-pitched voice. As a painting. You. As someone I don't deserve.

When was this? Years ago. In the last year of the war. He nestled himself closer to her.

She has been talking now for a few minutes, and the realization scares her: the words are forming in her throat, not in her mind. The words are expelled and thrown into space before she has a moment to reflect on them. Rey. She's said one of his names already, and so there's no going back. *Rey Rey Rey.* There are no calls coming in. It is only her voice, roaming over the city. It might be, she thinks, despairing, that no one is listening. No one at all. Maybe this is the best way. The boy glances at her with tired eyes. "Who are you looking for?" Norma asks.

He shrugs, and she loves him. He looks nothing like Rey. "People from my village," he says.

"Which is?"

"1797."

"You have a list, don't you?"

The boy nods. You can't hear a nod on the radio. She asks him again, until he says yes, he does, and if he should read it.

Of course he must read it. Who else can get away with it? They won't do anything to the boy. He is blameless. But she can't bear it. Not yet. "In a moment," she says.

But why wait? Isn't this what she has always wanted? Isn't this where her perfect show always ended?

"And you?" she says, turning to Manau. She has always loved shows with guests. There have been dozens of reunions in this room, nearly a hundred since the war ended—people have wept joyfully here, have embraced their loved ones, and have received the congratulatory calls of strangers. She has been witness to this, and perhaps if she hadn't seen it, she wouldn't believe it could happen. But now, it is as if she can feel the heat of those many reunions, this room suddenly peopled with ghosts.

"And you, Mr. Manau, who are you looking for?"

He seems surprised by the question. He shakes his head. His expression is glum. "No one," he says.

"You came together. Tell us what that was like."

The boy and his teacher look at each other, each hoping the other will talk. Finally, Manau coughs. "It's a long way to come, Norma, for anybody. Especially for a boy of eleven, but even for me. We came on a truck and then on a boat and then on a bus that drove all night. Where else would we come? In this country, all roads lead to the city."

"Let's return to the list."

"Of course."

The boy says, "They're the missing people from my village," and before she can ask, he adds, "I didn't know many of them. Only a few."

"Do you want to talk about them?"

"Nico," the boy says, "was my best friend. He left."

"Everyone leaves," offers Manau.

Norma smiles. "It's true."

"Aren't you tired, Miss Norma?" the boy asks.

"Oh no," Norma says. "Tired of what?"

"I don't remember him, Miss Norma."

"Nico?"

"Your husband," Victor says. "My father."

Norma blows the boy a kiss. "I know you don't. No one expects you to."

"I told my mother I did."

"You're a good boy."

"I'm tired, Miss Norma, even if you aren't."

"Let's read the list," Manau says. "It's why we're here, isn't it?"

"Sure," Norma says with a nod. She's been stalling, she can't stand it any longer. "It's why we're here. Are you ready? Will you read for us, dear?"

Victor nods. You can't hear a nod on the radio. It is just past three in the morning when he clears his throat and begins.

And now she can't even hear the names. Norma has her eyes closed, and the war has been over for ten years. Let the boy read, let him, they won't do anything to him. They'll send me to prison, they'll reopen the Moon for my benefit, and welcome me as they did my husband. I'm sorry, Elmer. Maybe they'll pretend it never happened. It's the middle of the night, and no one is listening anyway. It's just us. He reads very well, and Manau should be proud of what he has taught the boy. The names mean nothing, not to Manau, not to Victor. One or another is familiar, a surname he has heard before, but most are empty. There is his father's name, and he nearly skips over this one altogether. Norma sits upright at the sound, as if someone has touched her. "Pardon me?" she says. "Could you repeat that last one?"

Victor looks up from his list.

"What a nice name," Norma says. It's all she can do not to scream.

And in an instant, it has passed: here are the names written by the old man with the X-rays, and the ones added by the woman at the beach, and by the soldiers just now. Victor reads these as well, his voice not wavering but gaining strength. Thank God no one is listening. Thank God it's only us in this sleeping city. Close your eyes and imagine we are alone. Nearly three dozen names; what good can come of this?

In two minutes, it is finished.

"The phone lines are open," she manages, as if this were just another show. She looks hopefully at the switchboard, but there is nothing, not yet. There must be a record here somewhere: a song, any song to fill the empty space.

And now, it is time to wait.

I F   R E Y   had no answers about how the war began, it was very clear how it ended: almost ten years after it had started, in a truck, blindfolded, surrounded by soldiers smoking and laughing and poking him again and again with their rifles. He was taken along with two other men from the village, but the soldiers, for some reason, only seemed concerned with him. "Where you from, man?" one of them asked.

Rey strained to see through the black cloth. There was only darkness. "You've never heard of it."

"Junior's read books. You should try him."

"He's from the city," one of the other prisoners said.

"No one's talking to you," a soldier snapped.

They all laughed. They were just kids. Rey pretended he was somewhere else: flying, yachting even. He'd never done either. One of the village men had begun to sob. Rey was seated between the two of them, men about whom he knew very little. Why were they here? The man to

his left was shaking. "Where are we going?" he asked, but the soldiers ignored him. Instead, the one named Junior said, "How'd you end up here,
city boy?"

It took Rey a moment to realize they meant him. He sighed. "I'm not
from the city."

"IL piece of shit."

"There's no such thing," Rey said, and he felt the business end of a rifle
jab his gut. There was laughter.

"Keep talking, funny guy."

"You're famous," another voice said. "You're thinner than I thought
you'd be. They say you plant bombs and kill cops. They say you invented
tire-burning."

Rey blinked against the blindfold.

"I bet you want to go home."

"I bet he does."

"But sometimes we don't get what we want."

The road out of 1797 had been bumpy, but the jeep managed, and
once they were moving, everything changed. The smells changed,
and the quality of the heat that surrounded them. The forest was not
a monolithic entity: it was many places all at once. He'd been down
this road that led away from 1797: grown over with vines, and above, a
thick canopy of trees that broke only rarely. It was cool and damp. He
listened: they had turned and were approaching the water. He'd been
here as well, on one of his trips to the camps. At the riverbank, he was
separated from the two village men. One of them begged: "I'll tell you
everything!" He pleaded with such ferocity that Rey had to wonder what
it was the man knew.

Then they put him on a raft, hands still tied, eyes still blind. By the
sounds of it, Rey felt the platoon had shrunk, or broken into smaller
units. There were three or four soldiers with him. He couldn't tell. It
didn't matter. Yachting, Rey said to himself, for the last time. In the middle of the river, where the trees did not reach, there was golden sunlight,
and for a moment, Rey allowed himself to take in its warmth. He luxuri-
ated in it; he let the light make colors behind his eyelids, let it illumine
scenes and images of people and places he loved and would never see
again. These are the small moments one can appreciate fully only when

death is near. "We're almost there," a voice said after a while, and Rey knew this to be the truth. They hadn't come far, but then the camp had never been that far from 1797. A bend in the river, a hike into the forest from the bank. Two hours downstream at most. The water was calm. Rey was calm. If he hadn't been blindfolded, he might have enjoyed the scenery: his beloved forest, the earth at its most garishly alive. Even from this vantage point, with most of its secrets hidden beyond the banks, it was impossible not to be impressed. These were the dark places that had enchanted him his entire life: he listened for the humming of the jungle, for a bird call or the chirrup of a red monkey. What had he come here for—in the beginning? Norma, he thought and, saying it softly to himself, he felt comforted. What had he come looking for, when he had everything? He'd had her. Norma, he said again, and her name was like the final word of a prayer.

"You're going to kill me, aren't you?" he asked in the dark.

No one answered him, but then, no one had to. The sun warmed his face. A drop of sweat rolled down his forehead, beneath the blindfold and into his right eye. He nodded. "All right," he said, blinking. "All right, okay then." He was still nodding when the soldier everyone called Junior shot him in the chest.

Rey died instantly.

They were all boys, and though the prisoner was a stranger to them, they each mourned him in their private way. The war was ending, and Rey's was one of the last bodies they would see. A battle awaited them at the camp, of course, but that would come tomorrow, and they would not fight it alone. They would come upon a tired band of IL fighters, among them a man named Alaf, who, like many others, would die before firing a shot. But that would be all noise and light, whereas Rey's was a smaller, more intimate death. One of them pulled the silver chain from around the dead man's neck. They checked his pockets, hoping to find money, but there was only a handwritten letter, of no use to anyone. They stared at Rey. From another raft on the river, a grinning soldier gave them a thumbs-up. One of them pulled off the dead man's blindfold and closed his eyelids; another took his shoes. For many minutes, no one spoke. They let the current carry them, and they watched Rey, as if expecting him to speak. Finally, it fell upon Junior, who was the oldest, a three-year veteran, a boy of nineteen, to push the bound man's body off the raft and into the river. It made a small splash, and, for a quarter-mile, it floated alongside them, bobbing and sinking facedown in the river. Still, no one spoke. One of the younger soldiers, of his own initiative, used the oar to push Rey's body toward the shore. With this accomplished, they all felt better.

ACKNOWLEDGMENTS

S INCE 1999, when I began researching this novel, many people
have shared their stories of the war years with me. There is no way
to repay this generosity and trust.

I couldn't do anything without my family—Renato, Graciela, Patricia, Sylvia, Pat, Marcela, and Lucia—and my friends, scattered in two
dozen countries, but always near to my heart.

Vinnie Wilhelm, Mark Lafferty, and Lila Byock provided invaluable feedback on early drafts of this novel, for which I am immensely
grateful.